# THE MAN WHO CRIED I AM

# THE MAN WHO CRIED I AM

*A Novel*

*BY JOHN A. WILLIAMS*

Thunder's Mouth Press • New York • Chicago

Copyright © 1967, 1985 by John A. Williams
All rights reserved
Published in the United States by Thunder's Mouth
Press, Box 780, New York, N.Y. 10025
Design by Juanita Gordon
Grateful acknowledgement to the New York State
Council on the Arts and the National Endowment for
the Arts for financial assistance with the publication
of this work.


Library of Congress Cataloging in Publication Data

Williams, John Alfred, 1925–
    The man who cried I am.


    Reprint. Originally published: Boston: Little,
Brown, 1967.
    I. Title.
PS3573.I4495M3    1985    813'.54    84–24143
ISBN 0–938410–24–5

Distributed by:
PERSEA BOOKS INC.
225 Lafayette
N.Y.C., N.Y. 10012

*To Lori*

# FOREWORD

The publication of John A. Williams' fourth novel, *The Man Who Cried I Am*, in October, 1967, caused critics across the nation to acclaim it as a "seething, angry book," "intensely American," and "in a class with Ellison and Baldwin." *The Man Who Cried I Am* was generally recognized as one of the most important American novels of the tumultuous 1960s and it remained a popular seller in paperback for over ten years. Eventually, it slipped out of print and the occasion of this first reissue by Thunder's Mouth Press allows for a reassessment of Williams' achievement. *The Man Who Cried I Am* is simply the fullest and most panoramic account of Afro-American life between World War II and the 1960s.

John A. Williams is among the best American historical novelists and *The Man Who Cried I Am* offers his unique insights into society. Through the eyes of Max Reddick, journalist, novelist, the reader relives the harsh segregation of the 1940s and the expatriation of a generation of black intellectuals to more accommodating yet more estranged locales of Paris and Amsterdam. Well-told are the initial, brave attempts of the southern Civil Rights movement and the harsh, brutal white reactions. Reddick covers in the north the rise of a new black nationalism. Both Civil Rights and Black Nationalist movements are inspired by the rise of nationalism in Africa and the creation of new African states. Both movements are hampered by deceptive white politicians; in particular, the stark disappointments of the Kennedy years are vividly portrayed. Indeed, the American government is not viewed as the benevolent sponsor of black hopes in this novel, but rather as an insidious, repressive agent of white supremacy. Ubiquitous in the novel are C.I.A. agents; the culmination of the book is the revelation of the totalitarian King Alfred Plan, the "final solution" for Afro-Americans.

Williams describes American society through two devices. First, powerful accounts of actual events and, secondly, by incisive capsule personal portraits. Students of Afro-American history will not only benefit from the penetrating analysis of major events during these two decades but also from Williams' honest appraisals of Richard Wright, Martin Luther King, Malcolm X, John F. Kennedy, James Baldwin, Ralph Ellison, and many others. One of Williams' great virtues as a writer is that, like Theodore Dreiser, he is able to instill a deep sense of humanity and destiny in each of his characters whether they are major or minor.

*The Man Who Cried I Am* is no mere jaunt through the events of the past or through the upper realms of power. It is also a survival manual for Afro-Americans. As Max Reddick spends his hard-earned moments in white institutions such as big-city newsrooms, publishers' offices, liberal penthouses and, perhaps the ultimate example, the White House, he quickly learns of the fragility of his position and the constant, yawning gulfs between his white hosts and himself. Despite the official pronouncements of presidents, corporate leaders and well-meaning intellectuals, American society is not an open-door to opportunity, but rather a cocked bear trap, ready to snap shut at any time and sever his body and his hopes. The novel can be instructive to young Afro-Americans today who are bewildered by the two-faced qualities of corporate life; *The Man Who Cried I Am* is a reminder that despite the pressure from Afro-American movements and from a critical world, white American society only grudgingly gives the Max Reddicks temporary and risk-filled chances.

For inspiration and guidance through this terrible dilemma that is American society, Williams turns to several sources. The book is in part homage to Richard Wright, the most important American writer of the mid-twentieth century. Portrayed in the novel as Harry Ames, the character of Wright is larger-than-life, powerful, a man who could take white society at its own terms and defeat it. Novelist, poet, lover, raconteur, and revolutionary, Harry Ames is the personification of success and personal achievement. Yet even he could taste defeat. Ames is denied an award which had been voted to him (an incident which actually happened to Williams). In Paris, where Wright spent most of his expatriate years, Ames is the central figure of Afro-American exiles. Lionized by the French, Ames is still human enough to help scuffling brothers with loans during hard times. In the novel, Williams describes a searing incident in which Marion Dawes (James Baldwin) acknowledges his huge and unpaid debt to Ames. As white society will only accept one major black writer, Marion Dawes argues that to succeed as a writer he must slay his father-figure, Ames. One great virtue of the novel is that the wisdom and courage of Richard Wright is pronounced throughout.

Even more ominous in this competition is the presence of spies and C.I.A. agents who dog Harry Ames and try constantly to stifle his critical pronouncements about America. Transcriptions of Ames's coffee-house conversations are used to attempt to intimidate the great novelist. Too powerful a figure for such methods, Ames is finally able to offer Reddick, his true heir, information which is the key to understanding and resistance to the overwhelming white society.

Beyond the example of Wright, another area of resistance is Afro-American life in the city. It is in New York that Reddick encounters Minister Q, unyielding leader of a new nationalist movement and the figure with whom Reddick can entrust the terrible secrets bequeathed by Ames. It is in the city that Reddick can experience the blues music pouring out of Harlem bars, hear jazz at Minton's, find solace in late-night parties, and discuss life with the imposing Seargeant Jenkins, the first black policeman in Harlem and without doubt the meanest. It is in New York that Reddick encounters Moses L. Boatwright, black intellectual and cannibal whose ironic example rings through the novel. And it is in the city that Reddick can find love.

*The Man Who Cried I Am* is very much a novel about that most difficult yet highest of human feelings, love. There is the wrenching story of Reddick's love with Lillian Patch, an average, middle-class Afro-American woman, and of their conflicts over the unsure future of a black writer, a theme Williams examined well in *Night Song*. The tragic conclusion of their love sends Reddick through years of searching, through many temporary liaisons, until he finally can learn temporary happiness with Margrit, a Dutch woman. Interracial love has always been among the most sensitive subjects for American novelists. Williams handles it with tenderness and understanding. Although there are many affairs in the novel between blacks and whites which are conducted for satisfaction of the racial guilts or curiosities of the partners, Max's love with Margrit is on a higher plane. They love each other as people, with all the loyalty, understanding and compassion that true lovers can feel. Almost alone among American novelists, Williams' success in comprehending the fullness of this relationship lifts *The Man Who Cried I Am* far above any other work dealing with this fundamental truth: that black and white people can love each other without exploitation.

Finally, *The Man Who Cried I Am* is a major work about survival as an Afro-American writer and, by extension, as a writer in America. A writer in America, for Williams, must stand alone, lose the comforting graces of home life, and learn to confront equitably the hazards of ruthless publishing houses, capricious literary societies, not to mention the more private concerns of having to make a living. Learning how to survive as a writer in America combined with the knowledge of life inherited from Ames compels Reddick into the only possible position true to his life and art: revolution. To be a true Afro-American writer, argues Williams, during the repressive eras described in this book, allows only resistance and revolution as goals. For all of the hopes and dreams of the second American Reconstruction, the snap of the white bear trap in the last decade reaffirms this fundamental truth offered by *The Man Who Cried I Am.*

*GRAHAM HODGES*

# part ONE

part ONE

# 1

IT WAS a late afternoon in the middle of May and Max Reddick was sitting in an outdoor cafe on the Leidseplein toying with a Pernod. The factories and shops were closing and traffic streamed from Leidsestraat onto the Plein. There were many bicycle riders. Through eyes that had been half glazed over for several days with alcohol, Librium and morphine, Max looked appreciatively at the female cyclists. The men were so average. He quickly dismissed them. The girls were something else again, big-legged and big-buttocked. (Very much like African women, Max thought.) They pedaled past, their chins held high, their knees promising for fractions of seconds only, a flash of white above the stockingtops and then, the view imminent, the knees rushed up and obscured all view. Once in a while Max would see a girl pedaling saucily, not caring if her knees blocked out the sights above or not. Max would think: Go, baby!

The cafe was empty. That was a good sign. It meant that the people Max used to know in Amsterdam, the painters, writers and sculptors, the composers and song-and-dance men who were the year-round Black Peters for the Dutch, the jazzmen, were working well. They would be out later and drink Genever or beer until they became high, wanted to talk about their work or go make love. Maybe they would go up to the Kring, if they were members or honored guests, and play four-ball billiards while eating fresh herring. It was time for the fresh herring, the green herring.

Max glanced at the sky. God! he thought. It was like a clear high-noon sky in New York. No night would appear here until nine, but daybreak would come galloping up at close to three in the morning. He finished his Pernod and twisted to find the waiter, raising his hand at the same time. He felt something *squish* as he moved, and the meaning of the feeling caught at his voice. *"Ober,"* he said,

3

then more loudly, *"Ober."* The waiter, clad in a red jacket, black tie and black pants looked up with a smile. This was a new face, a new American. A little older than many others, and a sick look about him at that! Painter, writer, sculptor, jazz musician, dancer . . . ?

"Pernod," Max said. The waiter nodded and retreated to the bar. Max felt a sharp, gouging pain and he gripped his glass tightly. Water came to his eyes and he felt sweat pop out on his forehead. "Goddamn," he whispered. When the pain subsided, he rose and went to the men's room inside the cafe.

When he came out he noticed that the fresh Pernod was already on his table and he said *"Dank U"* to the waiter. That phrase he remembered, as he remembered others in French, German, Spanish, Italian, but he could barely put a sentence together in them. He sat down again, glancing at his watch. Where was she?

She had told him in their exchange of polite letters that she had returned to the gallery. If that was so, she should be passing the cafe at any moment, passing with that long, springy stride, so strange because she was small and not thin, passing with her hair billowing back over her shoulders. He had seen her pass many, many times. Before. Before, when he had sat deep inside the cafe watching, and would only call to her when she was almost out of sight. "Lost your cool then, man," he now whispered to himself. "You ba-lew it!" He always thought of the canals when he thought of her. Now they would be reflecting with aching clarity the marvelous painter's sky. The barges and boats would be on the way in, and soon the ducks and swans would be tucking their necks in to sleep. He had to sleep soon, too; it might prolong his life. A few days more.

*Ah yes,* he thought, *you Dutch motherfuckers. I've returned. "A Dutch man o' warre that sold us twenty negars,"* John Rolfe wrote, *Well, you-all, I bring myself. Free! Three hundred and forty-five years after Jamestown. Now . . . how's that for the circle come full?*

He did not really care about the Dutch except that she was

4

Dutch. She was thirty-five now, fourteen years younger than he. Would she still be as blond? (How he had hated that robust blondness at first after the malnourished black of Africa. The blondness had been so much like that of the Swedish blondes, jazz freaks who lived on jazz concerts, who saw the black musicians in their staged cool postures; but how he had been attracted to it as well!) Did he love her still — billowing blond hair; sturdy swimmer's legs; long, sinewy stride on such a small body and all? (And all? What was all? A memory. Nineteen years old.) He supposed he did love her, transposed, a bit bleached out, in a clinical way, the way you'd discuss it in an analyst's office. *Anal,* he thought, *list.* Shit list. Man, am I on that! But he did want to tell her he was sorry; tell her why it hadn't worked. He was glad he was still on his feet and able to move about. If he had stayed in the hospital in New York, it would have happened, his dying, and somehow she would have learned about it. No. Stand on two feet and tell her you had her mixed up with someone who happened nineteen years ago.

No pity. Didn't want that. Perhaps by that time, back in New York, he would have had it, and taken to the winds to watch her and try to comfort her when she cried. She would cry. He would have — you *are* drunk, he told himself, signaling for another drink.

The first time in his life he had ever had Pernod was in a bedbug-ridden flat in the East Village between Christmas and New Year's. The East Village was just the East Side then. He had drunk it straight and had crossed the street to a party where a painter with a penchant for teen-agers was displaying portraits of rhinoceroses with the words MAU MAU stitched between their legs. As far as Max knew, the painter was still doing rhinoceroses, marrying young girls or knocking them up and leaving them. When last heard from he was doing a trumpet solo in an Athens nightclub — "Saints" — which was the only number he knew, and the Greeks loved him because he was black, because he skipped and danced when he blew, and because he always reminded them of the spring festival when they put on blackface and roamed the streets drunk. There was no more screwing atop the hills in celebration of Oestra. Now

5

the Greeks did it in bed, just like everybody else, nearly. Maybe Max hated that painter so much for so long, not because he was a phony, but because, when he went home that night from the East Village, he felt as though he had a steel-jacketed slug between his eyes. After some time at home, his phone had rung. It was the girl who had sent him fleeing into the streets to get drunk. But everything was all right, after that call. Pernod. What could he associate Scotch with? Bourbon? Gin? Cognac? Beer? There was always something.

Where *is* she? He would hate to go to her house, but he would if he had to. Maybe he shouldn't have come. Maybe he should have gone right back out to Orly and returned to the hospital in New York. Comfort at least. But he *was* here and he hadn't been any drunker than usual when he decided to come by train. There were only three places to go after Harry Ames dropped dead — another section of Paris, New York or Amsterdam. Hell, he planned to go to Amsterdam anyway. Who was he shucking, himself, *now?* It really hurt to think of old Harry going like that. He should have been drunk and stroking and grinding and talking trash in some broad's ear. He always said he wanted to go like that.

Then he thought he saw her and he came half out of his chair, but it was someone else. He sat down slowly. How would it go anyway? She would be walking with that stride that made her seem even smaller, it was so long. He would call out. She would stop, for his voice would be the most familiar of all voices. Unbelievingly she would come near the table. He would not rise, merely sit there and motion to a chair with a smile on his face. (Haw! Haw! Surprise, surprise!) He would have a drink in his hand, perhaps even the one he was holding.

The stride was not the same: he fitted it into the one he remembered watching in Holland, Spain, France, Puerto Rico, St. Thomas, Manhattan, East Hampton, Vermont, Mexico . . . There was something sad about her stride now. The heels of her shoes still rapped sharply on the pavement and the face, that small face with

6

the cheekbones riding high along the sides, was still ready for the smile, the bright, lyrical *"Daaag!"* And that wise body, curving with motion. Her hair was darker, yes, like gold left too long in the open.

"Margrit! [Lillian!] Margrit! [Lillian!] Margrit! [Lillian!]," he shouted, coming out of his chair like a shot, the pain grabbing deeply at his rectum, and he was halfway across the street, all the while fighting the urge to grab himself, tear himself inside out.

And she stopped. Her mouth sprang open. Her dark blue eyes went bulging. With the deepest part of the eye he saw her start impulsively toward him, but she caught herself and stood waving as a leaf in some slight, capricious wind. He stopped too, out of pain and uncertainty; he had blown his lines again. But when he stopped she moved forward. On she came, the bright face ready to brighten even more, the stride now full, heel-rapping, confident. He stood waving, surprised at his own lack of cool, aghast at the waterfall of love he had thought dammed.

"Mox, Mox, it *is* you?" she said.

That goddamn broad A, he thought, but he said, "Yes." His arms trembled at his sides. Should he open them and put them around her? Should he simply stand and wait, then wilt when she placed hers around him? Signals. As she approached, her right hand darted out before her, thumb extended ludicrously in the air. Resigned, he took it, shook it gently and placed his left hand over hers. He led her to the table. "Please sit." It pained him to look at her figure. She wore a blue sweater which, no matter how loose it might have been, would have shown her breasts to tender and exciting advantage; they were always so white and fragile, so vulnerable. Her hips were fuller now. Time does do its work. And her swimmer's legs, big-calved and just short of being too heavily ankled, still made him itch to stroke them from top to —

He looked into Margrit's clear blue eyes. He moved his hand up her arm. Quite suddenly his eyes grew wet with remembering and even as he turned his head to fake a cough, he knew that the Pernod had helped to bring the tears on. "Whiskey," Max said to the waiter, who was watching them. Give her something quick, Max thought, before she starts remembering and runs away. Remembers the bad things.

But she was remembering some things already. She looked at him directly, head on, unblinking, without fear or remorse or pity — without, goddamn it, he thought, *anything*. But hell, he had never been able to decipher her looks, not once except when she cried. God, make me sober — no drunker. ". . . and another Pernod," he called, fingering with surprise the half-full glass already in his hand. He took a deep breath and fought down a rising pain. "How are you?" he said.

"Okay, Mox. You? Hi."

"Fine. Okay. Hi yourself."

"When did you come?"

"Today. About three hours ago."

"Are you well?"

"I — never better." He patted her hand.

"You look sick." She smiled her thanks at the waiter who placed the drinks before them.

"No. Just tired. Took the train from Paris."

"Paris? Harry died, didn't he? It was in *De Arbeiderspers* and *Het Parool* and some other papers. Were you there?"

Max smiled. The Europeans. The goddamn Europeans with their Black Peters and Black Madonnas and blackface celebrations. Five hundred years of guilt transposed into something like vague concern for anyone with a black skin. But Harry was loved more in Europe — and hated too — but not more than back home. There was some kind of balance here that the New York *Times* and the Chicago *Sun-Times* and the "Skibbidum Times" could never have when it came to Harry Ames. He spoke: "I was just a bit too late. We were to have drinks that day —"

"Oh, Mox, it must have been awful for you."

He felt angry. "Hell, it was all right! Harry was my friend, like a brother. But he had to go. We all have to go. He went quick. Didn't hurt at all. I'm all right. You know me."

8

Margrit bent her head and studied her Scotch. It was a very expensive alcohol. Genever would have been all right for her, even though in New York she had come to like Scotch. Yes, she knew. Harry's death had hurt Max. There was a time when he never admitted anything, but then, she thought, there was another time when he did. She stole a look at him. Yes, he was still handsome. He was graying evenly through his hair and moustache, but the lines in his square face had deepened, as if cut by a tired sculptor creating a hardness to offset the wide, soft eyes. But the eyes (how that soft look had deceived her!) were red, the almost amber-colored pupils diffused as though in the process of melting. He *isn't* well! she thought with a shock. "How long are you here?"

Max drank from the unfinished Pernod and then sipped from the other. "Not long. I wanted to tell you something, Margrit. Margrit, baby, I have news for you!"

His voice had risen and gone spinning loudly into space. She looked at him with cautious eyes. She knew the waiter and bartender and the customers who were coming in now were used to *Neger uitbundigheid,* Negro exuberance; they smiled at it. It was the image they had.

"What is your news, Max?" Margrit was suddenly irritated. She and Max had spent so much time talking about images. "Is it good news? You have come all this way to tell me?" She smiled thinly. "Are you to be married?"

He rose and touched her shoulder. Automatically she lent support to his unsteady fingers. "Will you wait until I return? I have to pee." He giggled. She smiled. But as soon as he had left her, she turned to watch him. Something was the matter.

Max wavered to the men's room again. A vicious cycle. If he didn't drink, he wouldn't have to urinate. To urinate was to suffer the most intense pain. But, if he didn't drink he would have to take either the pills or the morphine tucked into the pouch of the jock strap he was wearing. He had thrown the cup away. The morphine got the pain right by the balls he thought, with a weak chuckle, but it didn't let him operate the way he had to during the day. But then the pain was growing every day. It gripped him at the most inopportune moments and left him breathless, weak, and with his eyes watering. *Jesus Christ!* he moaned, leaning against a wall which for a few seconds seemed to have vanished altogether. Did Herod ever have it so bad? He pushed himself away from the wall and went into one of the stalls. Clean. At least the Dutch wouldn't give him as many germs as the French. He took out the cotton and looked at it. It was soaked through with dark red blood. Almost came through that time, he thought, and pulled a roll of fresh cotton from his pocket and tore off a piece. This he pushed gently into place. While sitting, he pulled at the jock strap and looked at the plastic five-cc syringe and at the morphine itself. He felt his breast pocket to see if the needle was still there. Not now, later. The pain subsided.

He returned to the table and without looking at her said, "Margrit, I'm sorry. Easy to say. Said it before, but believe me, I am sorry. Late, I know. Don't want anything. I can't want anything, not even you again. I just wanted to see you and say that."

"Well . . ." She wanted to say that it was all right, but she knew it wasn't and he knew it too. Then she wanted to reach across the table and slap him as hard as she could. *Sorry!* But the black Americans were all the same: they walked away from things mumbling, "Sorry." Sorry! After a moment, the bitterness ebbed. "But you look tired. Maybe you should get some rest. If you like, we can talk later [more sorry!]. Where are you staying?"

Come full circle on the Dutch, he was thinking as she spoke. He knew he was giving her answers. ("Yes, a little tired. Don't know where I'll be staying. Maybe the American. Do it up right. Last trip, Ducks, ho?")

"One more drink," he said aloud. "Then I'll get my bag and go to the hotel. If you have dinner with me. In that corner. You know." He rushed on, not wanting her to decline. "You know where we sat for four hours just watching people pass . . ."

Margrit thought, Yes, I know, I remember, I remember, and the waiters trying to rush us, and it seemed as if the sun would never come down.

". . . and maybe after dinner we can find Roger and some of the other guys. How are they doing? Do you see them often?" He paused. He didn't give a damn about Roger or the others. It was too late. "Will you, will you have dinner?"

"No more drinks then," she said.

"All right." He breathed deeply in relief.

"I will get your bag," she said.

"No you won't," he said. Then with sudden vehemence he said, "Will you *stop* doing things for me!"

Unruffled she said, "Mox, you will walk across the street to the hotel and get your room. I will touch up a bit, call a taxi and get your bag. The driver will help me and the hotel boys will help me. Give me the ticket." She held out her hand for the ticket as his hands went limply into pocket after pocket. Finally he found it. Taking it she said, "You don't look well. I am worried."

"How can you be worried?"

She hunched her shoulders. "I just am. Please go."

"All right, Maggie." He sucked in his breath quickly. The pain. She was right. Let her get the goddamn bag. Get to the hotel. Fast! Get off your feet. Take a pill.

"What is it?" she asked.

"A belch. I had to belch."

"Happy New Year, then."

"Thanks. Shall we go now?"

He paid the waiter and they left. "It will not be long," she said.

"All right. Maggie?"

"What?"

"I am truly sorry."

"Shut up, Mox," she said, not unpleasantly. "I will not be long."

He wondered if her apartment was the same. It overlooked one of the canals, had high ceilings and dark musty hallways. And cats. One was a striped, swollen brown that padded softly about the rooms. The other was a sleek young black with a triangle of white on the face, a female. He had watched them lick each other's backs and play, but there had been no catting between them, only with the other cats that gathered on the rooftops at night. Max wondered if the walls were still thick with the paintings of friends, or if the bedroom was the same, with the windows to the east so that as soon as the sun took a notion to rise, *whop!* daylight in the room. And in that room, he thought, discovering without surprise that he had the key to his hotel room in his hand and that he was following the bellman, she would be touching herself up a bit.

Suddenly he wanted to listen to someone else's rhythms; his own were sonorous, too labored. He paused. There was something he wanted, something . . . Ah, a paper. He had just picked up the *Tribune* when he saw, out of the corner of his eye, another Negro. How the eye catches color in a country where there is so little! Or how that same eye catches no color — an albino in Africa — where color abounds. Kiss my ass, Max thought, drawing back without knowing why, Alfonse Edwards.

# 2

HE SAT waist-deep in the lukewarm water of his bath and watched it turn slowly from a clear to pinkish color. He could hear the trams ringing their bells as they pulled off from the stop in front of the hotel. Why, he wondered, couldn't Alfonse Edwards be in Amsterdam too? What instinct (Negroes not only had that good old natural rhythm, but instinct too) had made him draw back? True, he had *not* liked Edwards from the first, from Nigeria. Even less since he had been with Harry when Harry died.

Edwards had told it like this:

He and Harry were walking out of Rue de Berri and paused at the corner waiting for a traffic light to change. Harry had gone down just like an FFI caught in the crossfire of snipers. Max imagined that crowds gathered and someone finally recognized that dark round face, the bitterness on it suddenly replaced by surprise, and shouted, *"Le M'sieu Ames, le romancier américain."*

"Boom, like that," Edwards had said in Paris, his lean face suggesting rather than actually possessing sorrow. Max remembered that even then he wondered just why Harry would bother with a type like that. He must have been getting senile. Edwards was a black Ivy Leaguer. Close-cropped hair, for he *wanted* Europeans to know that he was American. The other Negroes let their hair grow long and bushy — nappy — in order to be mistaken for Africans. Not Edwards. American all the way. Red white and black.

So, anyway, there was Harry down in the street at the corner where the Rue de Berri runs into the Champs-Elysées, with the Arc de Triomphe humped up through the noon haze. Harry was down and didn't get up and later there was Edwards describing his death: "Boom, like that," and Max also thought then, These hippies, Ivy League or Watermelon League, they never learn. English is limiting but it's all we know well, and there are times and places when it should be used, such as when describing how Harry died. Harry would never die "Boom, like that."

Why not? Because he was too goddamned evil. And why else not? Because.

Max had taken the morphine as much for the shock of Harry's death as for the pain. He stood at the rear of the small, hastily assembled crowd within the walls of Cimetière du Montparnasse. Edwards was there. Charlotte, Harry's wife was there, a few Americans, like Iris Stapleton of the nightclubs, painters and writers. There were some Africans, a few Indians. And it was only twenty hours after Harry had died. Very few of them had been summoned by Charlotte. The papers had announced his death, and they had come unbidden. Max stood there drunk with the drug, sick with pain and shock, and suddenly he noticed that Michelle Bouilloux, even more isolated from the small crowd than himself, was staring at him. He *thought* she was staring. Max turned back to listen once more to the eulogies. When he turned again to Michelle, he let his eyes roam; her husband wasn't there. She seemed to have moved closer to him, and now he knew she was staring from under her veil. And she was doing something with her hands, he couldn't tell what, because she was wearing black gloves and moving her hands against the background of a black suit. Then she took off one glove and one startlingly white hand showed, and one of its fingers curled back and forth at him. Her eyes seemed to come through the veil. Max thought, Ah, Michelle, Michelle, he's dead. The eulogies were over. The crowd started to break up. Michelle threw one glance at Charlotte, who even now was approaching Max, snatched up her veil displaying a glint of red hair, pointed fiercely to herself, then stumbled toward the gate. "Please join us, Max," Charlotte said. Alfonse Edwards was standing at her shoulder.

"No," Max said. He had seen enough men cremated in tanks, the bodies curling and snapping and frying in their own juices. He wasn't going to sit in anybody's anteroom and wait for Harry to be cooked down to ashes. "But why?" he croaked as the others, not invited to wait for the Harry-fry, gathered behind her and Edwards. "Why couldn't you let him lay around a little while so people could come and look at him. He'd like that."

"Oh, Max, shut up," Charlotte said, turning from him. Edwards paused before turning, and there was nothing in his look and yet everything. "To hell with you too," Max said and left, caught a taxi, picked up his bag and took the train to Amsterdam.

Why else not? Michelle Bouilloux. He glanced at his watch. M. Bouilloux would be home now. Maybe not. Maybe he hadn't seen her at the funeral at all. Hell, he wasn't sure of anything anymore except that he had a great, raging pain in the ass. And then, having thought of Charlotte, he admitted to himself for the first time that he had hated the hell out of her ever since he had known her. She had run Harry out of one marriage and into another with her. She understood, she had said. But it faded, of course, that understanding. She demanded more and more time from the great man (and he had had times of greatness, but America pretended not to see them, and Harry *wanted* America to acknowledge his greatness. But America had said in essence: *We may study you in freshman English anthologies, and if we ever arrive at the point where we show our fear or admit that we are guilty and ignore that guilt, we will study you first, Harry Ames!*). Charlotte had been a pain in the ass (Ho! Ho!). Always when things were rough, she made a point of reminding Harry how much she had given up to marry him: family, friends, a whole culture. And Harry had always countered by saying, "Tough titty. You can go. I didn't want you because you're white. Go." But Charlotte never went. She stayed and sulked, and sulked even more when things were going well. She was, after all, a mediocre person when it came to dealing with the things Harry juggled with ease: history, politics, economics, people. Charlotte could only deal with herself. When had sulking turned to hatred?

Michelle. No, long before Michelle. Max looked at his watch again. He would call her. He placed the call and lay back. Great pills, absolutely fantastic pills. Margrit would be coming soon, too. Not too soon. She would give him a chance to rest a little. Damn her anyway. When the phone rang he said, "Max. Michelle?"

"Yes. How is Margrit?"

God*damn* these women, he thought. "All right. We are having dinner in a little while. Listen," he said speaking carefully, "I have not been well. It is nothing serious. But did I imagine that you were signaling me at the funeral?"

"Yes, I would see you. It is most urgent. It is about Harry."

Max mashed out his cigarette.

"It is about Harry," she said again.

"What, what about Harry?" Then he said, "Edwards?"

"Tonight by express, I will come to Rotterdam. From there the other train to Leiden. Will you meet me tomorrow?"

"What address?"

She gave him the address and quickly rang off. Max lay back once more and closed his eyes. What in the hell was going on? Why didn't he leave well enough alone. Harry wasn't going to revert to

15

flesh and blood. Charlotte. I bet she enjoyed thinking about him cooking and curling behind that wall. Got her kicks every stinking minute it took.

Margrit. Even if he wanted Margrit back he couldn't have her. Maybe it was good it went the way it did. He would have hated to have her around now, twenty-four hours a day, shuttling between the house and the hospital, doing with a smile the tasks that every nurse he'd had frowned at.

He had dressed and was dozing on the bed when Margrit called from the lobby. He felt better and smiled as he straightened his tie. The old Margrit would have walked briskly through the lobby, taken the lift and come up to the room and talked while he dressed. And he would not have dressed until afterward.

He took a deep breath, patted his things into place and went downstairs. She had said she would be at the table. "What table?" he had almost asked, but he remembered in time. *The* table, of course.

She smiled up at him. "You got your bag all right, I see."

"Sure," he said, sliding over the seat to the window side. What was she talking about? Of course he had his bag. Then he remembered. When had he slept? When he woke he went directly to his bag, opened it, took out a fresh shirt and underwear. He hadn't even remembered that when he entered the room he had been without his bag. Jesus, he thought, Jesus Christ. "Drink?" he said.

"Yes, of course."

He smiled and looked across the street at the side entrances of the Stadsschouwburg and thought once again that Amsterdam was the one city he could have lived in other than New York. Idly he watched a Surinamer saunter down the street, past their window. Traffic was much thinner now, not so many bicycles, not so many cars; there were many people walking. "It remains constant, doesn't it?"

Margrit turned to the window — she had been looking at him. "The same, you mean? Yes, nearly so."

"Fantastic place." He marveled as they sipped their drinks, how

16

in Amsterdam, except when you headed a little south, all that was new had been built around the old, had not overwhelmed the narrow, steeply gabled houses, nor the canals. Suddenly, he wished he were younger and starting all over again.

"What is the matter, Mox?"

"Nothing, Margrit. Hi. It's good to see you again. Why haven't you married some lucky Dutchman?"

"I haven't been waiting for you," she said.

"I didn't want you to. I didn't think you would."

"And you, Mox, who do you see now?"

"I'm kind of a fugitive."

"Fugi —"

"I'm not seeing anyone."

"Oh. Oh, I don't believe that, Mox."

He laughed. The pill and the liquor were making him high very fast. "I didn't think you would, but it is the truth."

She snorted. "You have had an amputation then."

"Yes." He glanced around the huge dining room. The tables and chairs were a rich, warm brown, the white tablecloths crisp and stiff. An elderly man was sitting at the reading table, poring over the papers from the racks.

"You are with the same magazine, Mox?"

He looked up quickly. He had forgotten that too. "No," he said.

"What are you doing?"

He looked at her with exasperation, then remembered that she wasn't his wife anymore, and that he had no right to be exasperated with her. But she had seen the look. "Or shouldn't I ask?"

"I've taken a leave," he said. "Tired."

"Yes," she said, turning once again to the window, her hair trailing a soft gold, "you were always tired, Mox."

Max signaled the waiter for more drinks. He supposed he was always tired. Bored, that's what brought it on, bored with all of it, the predictability of wars, the behavior of statesmen, cabdrivers, most men, most women. Bored because writing books had become, finally, unexciting; bored because The Magazine too, and all the people connected with it, did their work and lived by formulae. He was bored with New Deals and Square Deals and New Frontiers and Great Societies; suspicious of the future, untrusting of the past. He was sure of one thing: that he was; that he existed. The pain in his ass told him so.

"I guess I was always tired. Tired when I was born, maybe."

"That's what you always said."

"See? Nothing new. How's Roger?"

"Roger? Roger is still Roger, what else?"

"Still macking in his own intellectual way?"

"Still what — ?"

"Macking. Macking. Oh, Margrit, you know what macking is."

"But no, I don't."

"We talked about it," he insisted. Shut your mouth, he told himself.

"No, we didn't."

"Okay, okay. Roger's still the same, that means he's macking."

"Have it your way."

"Thanks."

Roger was not an ordinary macker; he gave a little more than most Negroes in Europe who were thus engaged between books or articles or showings or jazz engagements. Roger gave his women laughs and little peeks at Kafka, Mann, Wright, Jami of Samarkand, the suppressed Books of Enoch; and he talked in ringing poetic tones of Wardell Gray, Bird, Pres; of Fats Navarro and the early Miles, and then, shifting pace, breaking it down into a long, smooth lope, he would go into Kant, Kierkegaard, Spinoza and Walter Van Tilburg Clark's philosophical handling of *The Ox-bow Incident;* he studied Hausa and Swahili and planned to get into Yoruba, Ga and Ibo — oh, Max remembered, Roger macked with finesse. After all this, *then* he would get the money from a Parisienne, a stacked female Swede or Dane or Hollander, and for dessert, he would climb aboard, down periscope and sail that sub. Roger worked at macking. He gave something Mack the Knife never had time for. The others, the pussy carried them away. They could be starving, but the pussy came first. Always the pussy.

They ordered dinner. It was after nine and the night was descending slowly. Midway through, she said, "Do you want to see him?"

"See who?"

"Roger." She hated it when he was this way, his mind slipping from one thing to another so quickly that she could never follow it. She had noticed that he had ordered chopped sirloin well done, the vegetables well cooked and creamed potatoes. Not unusual, only the way he kept jabbing his fork into the food to see just how well done it was.

"Yes. And tell me, do you know a guy, Negro, named Alfonse Edwards?"

"Sure."

Max's gorge rose. What does *that* mean, he asked silently, *Sure*.

"What's his hype now? I mean is he really writing, or has he become a painter or a sculptor or a tourist?"

Margrit was on her third drink and she broke into laughter. "Tourist," she echoed. "Tourist."

"Yeah, so what's he really do?" You can get out of New York, Max thought, but you couldn't get New York out of you; you felt better knowing where a guy's pigeonhole is.

"I tell you they say he is a writer."

Max sagged in his seat then. For the moment he was feeling so good that he wondered if the doctor wasn't wrong. Then he remembered the long session in the doctor's office after the first biopsy. That long session while Margrit was working happily in the gallery in New York. Anyway, he felt good. But they were talking of Edwards. What in the world would he be doing in Holland? Writing? Who, Edwards? He hadn't talked to him about writing in Paris. Why not? When Harry was too busy to talk writing, they turned to him — Max. The younger fellows remembered that once Max had been considered better than Harry, a fact that made Harry sullen for over two years. They turned to Max when Harry was addressing the various Pan-African conferences or busy at something else. *That* was one of the odd things: Edwards had not in any way explained himself lately. A hipster would, somehow, with a casual turn of phrase, a word, a couple of words dropped here or there, let you pick up the pieces and complete your puzzle. A hipster knew how to play the game. No one came up to you and said, My name is Rinky-Dink and I'm a landscape artist. Anybody hip, they dropped signals and you got them. Most of the world went that way.

"What's he written?"

"They say he's working on a couple of novels, and he does articles."

"Yeah?"

"Yes."

Okay, he thought. Edwards a writer? I know what he *was,* but is he now? Max went on thinking. No, with his background he isn't just sitting around Europe starving between books and articles waiting for race riots to break out in the States so he can interpret them for the European press. How long until the next race riot? Edwards in Nigeria, Edwards in Europe.

Dessert, coffee and cognac, and then Margrit asked, pushing back the silence that had fallen, "What is the matter, Mox? Won't you tell me?"

He glanced up, tempted to ask her to go with him tomorrow to meet Michelle in case it became too hard for him. They'd gotten along well, the two of them. But then he thought, To hell with her. I'll go alone. He'd rent a car; it would be better than a train. He could stop and pull over and lie down if he had to. He could change the cotton if it felt too messy. It would be awkward on a train — he remembered the trip from Paris — and worse on a bus. "I told you," he said. "I'm tired."

"There is more than that this time. You won't tell me?"

"No."

"Is it bad?"

"Maggie, it was bad when I was born."

"You mean born black?"

"If you choose."

Margrit said, "Somehow, this conversation sounds like so many we had when we were together."

Max laughed and took her hand. "It does, doesn't it? Ah, Margrit. It's all a bit too much for old Max. Tell me now about Edwards. Does he come up here often? Has Roger cleared him of being a U. S. Government fink? Roger has a nose for that, you know. And Edwards did work for the government in Nigeria."

"They all say he does not work for your government any more, but they don't like him. He starts trouble. He picks fights for nothing. No one likes him. The tables become quiet on the Leidseplein when he is in town. I don't know who his friends are. Roger talks to him sometimes."

"Did he ever talk about Harry Ames?"

"Not to me, and I don't know anyone who ever mentioned his talking about Harry. What is it, Mox? What is going on?"

He said, "I don't know," and looked down at her hand. White, beginning to wrinkle, the wedding band on the right hand. He looked at the hand and pressed it. He too was wondering what was going on. Little pieces sometimes fell into place with a bang. Her voice drifted with a question. He answered it. She spoke again and he answered, but he was back in Paris, his very first time there, on leave from the *Century* and the Korean War was three years old.

He had been working, as usual. (Third novel, fourth novel?) From time to time he paused and looked out on the Paris rooftops, a hodgepodge of color against the blue summer sky. The phone rang. Harry.

"Hey, man, listen. Get right over here, can you? Tell you what's going on: just got a call from Senator Braden's number-one boy. That's right. Is he a faggot, do you know? Anyway, he's coming over to talk about some of my opinions I've put out over coffee at the cafe. He sounded real ominous, you know? After that business with that rotten magazine. I don't want to talk to nobody unless I got a witness. Make a million dollars that way. Come on over and listen to some of this shit. Goddamn Government won't let me alone, I tell you, Max, a man with pen and paper is dangerous, but don't let him be black too — that's a hundred times worse. Make it in fifteen? Go, Max. See you."

When Max arrived, Harry was rubbing his hands in glee. "Those people really think they're pretty sharp. They can scare the pants off the whole of the United States, but they can't scare Harry Ames. Shit, I come from Mississippi; the rest of America can't begin to compare to the crackers they make down there. Where shall I put you? Sure wish that tape recorder was working. All this Philips stuff they got here in Europe, I don't know, man. Don't like General Electric and can't stand Westinghouse, but they gotta have something. Take that Calvados and get behind that closet curtain. That's it. Wait. That Calvados stinks. Oh, hell, take the Scotch, but don't drink too much of it, you bastard. No! Not like that! Max, don't be such a goddamn clown. You drink all that Scotch and Charlotte's going to pitch a bitch . . ."

Sipping the Scotch, Max had peeked out at Michael Sheldon. He was a handsome young man, polite, sure of himself. Max saw Harry's eyes glittering with false cheeriness; Harry behaved just as a shark must behave when it has come across a choice morsel.

"In foreign countries, particularly those with strong attractions to communism," Sheldon began, "we'd like all Americans to be careful in their criticisms. Now, you, Mr. Ames, have been rather harsh on us."

"I have?" Harry asked innocently. "I don't remember. Do you have an example?"

Sheldon pulled some cards from his pocket. "This is one of your quotes: 'Senator Braden's Committee has driven Americans into the far corners of fear.' Another: 'America ought to try communism, just once.' "

Harry said, "On the second one, I thought I said, if everything else fails, America ought to try communism of some kind because capitalism, hand in hand with the American dream, just doesn't work; there are too many people deprived of their rights to vote and to work. That's what I said."

"But there were others," Sheldon said, and he read them back with measured, self-confident cadence. The phrases sounded familiar to Max. Who at the cafe would turn Harry's words over to the U. S. Government?

"What do you want me to do?" Harry was asking.

"We'd appreciate it if you weren't so critical. Publicly. You're only hurting yourself. The alternative is trouble, pure and simple." Sheldon smiled. The Senator's assistant reminded Max of every upper echelon vice-squad cop he'd ever seen. The face was regular, the hair combed just right, the shoes were shined and he wore a dark blue suit, of course.

"No," Harry said. "I plead freedom of speech. I'll speak my mind wherever I am and whenever I choose to. We're in France now, not America."

Sheldon stood up. "Your mouth, Ames, can be made to stay shut."

Harry taunted, "L'il ol' white boy."

"That's your whole problem, this race thing."

"L'il ol' white boy."

"Bolton Warren thought he was pretty tough, too, but we got him down to Washington. He took the stand but he didn't say too much. We adjourned, took him to another room, read him the material in his dossier, and he hasn't stopped talking to us yet."

Max waited while Harry roved through the past with Warren. Warren had gone to Spain to be in the Brigades and had had heavy flirtations with the Party, but who the hell hadn't?

"Are you threatening me, Sheldon?"

"In the name of Senator Braden's Committee, I warn you that your passport may be revoked if you continue the way you are."

"That's what is going to happen if I don't stop my coffeehouse chatterings?"

Sheldon smiled and widened his stance. "Look at it like this,

Ames. My visit can be official or unofficial. I was passing through Paris anyway. It's up to you. But remember your former affiliations with the Party; remember your affairs with several white ladies of some reputation before you left America. Further, don't count on the French so much. They are becoming less and less enchanted with you. A word to the wise should be sufficient. The French, for all their slogans, are becoming modern. Liberty, yes; equality, yes, of a sort; fraternity — with their women — highly questionable."

A cherubic smile spread slowly over Harry's face. "You'd reveal all my sordid affairs, would you?"

"Only if we had to and only to the right people."

"Gee," Harry said, and Max recognized the word as the prelude to the ultimate put-on. "I wonder if you'd do me a favor. You've really got me by the balls, Sheldon. You know Max Reddick, the *other* American Negro writer? Let's face it, Warren's over the hill, so that leaves Max the *other* Negro writer, right? Copacetic as we used to say. Anyway, look there in that closet will you, behind the curtain?" Sheldon did not move. "Max is behind that curtain, you bastard, and he's heard every word you said. In fact, he has taped them and taken them down in shorthand. Didn't know Max knew shorthand, did you? Well, he's one of them bright colored folks. Max!"

Hastily Max had set down the bottle of Scotch and sauntered through the curtain. "Hiya, Sheldon, what's new?"

Sheldon had left quickly and angrily, threatening to destroy them both if ever they stepped foot in the States again. They had laughed for fifteen minutes until Harry remembered to look at the Scotch. When he did, he cried, "Max, you greedy sonofabitch, I'm gonna catch hell! There's nothing left in the budget for Scotch for a whole month! You bastard, oh, you rotten black bastard! Did you see the look on that boy's face? Skin me, man, *skin* me!" And they had smacked palms ringingly.

It wasn't funny later. Later, Max and Harry reasoned that if Michael Sheldon was interested, someone else was too, the fink at the cafe. So, it had all started with a U. S. Government agency and worked its way down to Braden and his committee. And the Spanish Government managed to let Harry know that it wasn't at all happy about the series of articles he had written on the Franco regime. A number of West Africans had started to cut Harry dead because of what he said about them. And generally, the Communists of Europe distrusted him. After all, he had quit the American Communist Party. Harry wrote about all of them; he talked about them. He danced barefoot on a hot stove lid, but no one knew it then.

Max and Margrit were walking now along the Singel. His pace was slow and Margrit had slowed to match it. There were no flowers out that time of night. He was tiring and he had to get up early, but now they were going to see Roger. The pain was coming again in long, stomach-turning spasms.

"We'll take a cab back from Roger's," Max threw in. He watched Margrit nod. "Isn't your boyfriend going to be a little upset with you tonight?"

"Yes," she said, "he is, but he will understand."

"Oh, yeah," he said, thinking to himself with humor, You bitch, Margrit.

# 3

WHEN Roger Wilkinson opened his door, to Max Reddick he was the picture of the writer as a failure. Max pushed Margrit forward into a dingy flat, and he shook hands with Roger who seemed both surprised and embarrassed by the unannounced visit.

But Roger broke into a smile and said, "Sit down, you folks, if you can find a chair. You lookin' pretty tired, Max. You been down to Paris? For the funeral? Yeah?" He was rustling through some bottles. "Ain't got much here. A little beer, some Genever." Roger smiled through his reddish beard. "How'd you find me? You

25

see I've moved." He'd always left his places of residence a mystery. "I'm into my thing," he would explain, and vanish, and in Europe, the black artists went along with your wish to be left alone, most of the time. Until you started to make it, then they came back to bug you back into failure. "You should have let me know you were coming," Roger said.

"Ah, well," Max said, accepting a beer. "What's new?"

Roger cleared his throat loudly and glanced around the room. "You know, man, the same old thing. Trying to make it, you know."

Max nodded. Roger had been in Europe a long time. He had written three novels, which he had been unable to sell. Roger was wound up in himself, Max had concluded. Roger for Roger.

"Articles?" Max asked. Roger was one of those writers who, whenever race riots broke out back home, was summoned hastily by the local magazine or newspaper editors to explain what was going on. *"Le célèbre écrivain noir américain Roger Wilkinson explique pourquoi les noirs des Etats Unis . . ."* With a photo of Roger bearded and pensive, *artistic,* surveying the accompanying three-column picture of rioters.

"Well, they keep me in bread. But here in Holland, man, getting money out of Hans Brinker is like forcing your way into Fort Knox. They tight with the change, man. Tight."

"Yeah-yeah," Max said. He had known Roger back in the States. Then Roger had come to Europe. To be free. He'd returned to New York briefly then back to Europe for good. He knew all the European capitals, having lived in them at one time or another, until he settled in Amsterdam. He would have preferred Scandinavia; the women were the most handsome in Europe. But it was too cold.

"Listen," Max said. "I'm not in town for long. Just came up to see Margrit. Have to get back home."

"You're not going to stay a while, Max? What a drag, man. Really."

"Yeah. Do you know Alfonse Edwards?"

26

Roger feigned drawing away from an unwholesome object. "*That* cat! Well, yes and well, no. I mean I'm not up tight with him; no one is. I see him around when he's in town. That's about all."

"Do you know where he's staying?"

"I hear he's in a hotel. What's happening, Max?"

"I don't know. Margrit tells me he's writing."

Roger drew a dirty fingernail through his beard. His hair was very thick, but no one would mistake him for an African; his complexion was too light. "I *guess* he writes. I've *heard* that he writes. He loads up a car with articles and drives around Europe selling them to papers and magazines. You know, crap all *pre*pared, and about half of it plagiarized. I mean, these people over here just don't know."

"Does he make it, like that?"

"He must. Always wearing some boss shit and got some fine fox on his arm. He *must* be making it."

"Yeah," Max said.

"— and he eats very well," Roger added.

"Is he a fink?"

"A fink. No, man, he's just got his hype going and it's working. If the government planted a fink, wouldn't they make him to be one of the boys, you know, not sharp, an artist, starving, trying to get all the pussy he can. Now, Edwards, he's just a little bit away from everybody. Uncle Sam don't work that way. In the middle, right in the middle."

Margrit was watching Max. What is the matter with him, she wondered. The hand with which he was holding the beer glass trembled suddenly, and Max casually lowered it to the table. But Margrit had seen it. She wished she could be glad he was ill, but she could not; she had got over the past and had even been pleased to see him again. She never thought she would be. She was still attracted to him; the mystery that seemed to be him when they first met to a substantial extent was still there. Perhaps in a way the reason for that *was* because of that big, ponderously walking Negro who led a column of liberating black Americans through the streets

27

of Groningen. Groningen was a city you left just as soon as you realized that the people in it were more German than Dutch. He had walked, Margrit remembered, with a wide step, and there was a grin on his face and chocolate bars were sticking out from his pockets. She had broken loose from her parents and, with a group of other small children who waved the tiny American flags their parents had kept hidden, had raced into the street. The big black man picked her up and laughed, gave her candy and put her down again. Max had said, once when she talked about that day, "Well, the world starts whirling for different people for different reasons and at different times. I'll thank that guy if I ever see him."

"More beer?" Roger asked. "Man, I'm really sorry I didn't know you were coming. We coulda turned one on."

"Your first book, we'll turn one one. You'll be coming home then, I guess?"

"Yeah, I guess it would be time enough then."

Max thought back to when he had ever thought to quit writing. All the time. Roger never thought about it and should have quit a long time ago. After a while, Max thought, all the talk of writing, all the advice, is nothing if you haven't got it yourself. With Harry, they seldom talked about writing or even other writers. That was mostly because they were always talking about women or The Problem at home. It was also because Harry was secretive with his French and British and American writer friends if they were the good ones. Max never knew just who they were; they would show up at a party, and by the way Harry talked with them Max would know that they had been friends for a long time. Harry didn't really like to share things. Like Roger, still looking very young, but starting to age in a strange, distant sort of way, didn't like to share himself either. And chances were, Max mused, that Roger did have a bottle tucked back somewhere, for a very special piece of ass that he had to impress. He didn't bring the bottle out because he had to have his revenge for the invasion of his privacy. In that privacy, Max knew, he was picking dried snot out of his nose, rubbing it into his pants and thinking hard thoughts on a world that refused to read his works. Mostly, he was feeling sorry for himself, whether as a Negro or a writer, Max didn't know. As a Negro, he hadn't suffered, hadn't Armied in the South, hadn't been hungry, and he had never gone south of Manhattan. Roger's Negro anger was ersatz; ersatz, but useful. If he hadn't been Negro, he would have had no reason on earth to raise his voice, or to want to write.

"Listen," Roger was saying. "Shall we look for Edwards' hotel?"

Max spun the glass between his thumb and forefinger. "Maybe tomorrow."

"But I thought you were leaving, like, *zap!*"

"I have to take care of a few things first. Tomorrow morning I've got something to do and then we'll see."

"Where you staying?" Roger asked, sliding his eyes toward Margrit.

"The American," Max said, rising, catching pain midway up, but shuffling in his step so they wouldn't see.

"That's boss," Roger said. His smile was twisted. "One of these days, baby, one of these days."

"Got to stay with it," Max mumbled.

"See you tomorrow? We can have a taste on the Plein. I'll stop by the hotel, okay?"

"Well, yeah, okay, maybe late in the afternoon." Max started through the door after Margrit, then paused. "None of my business. But I talk to your father pretty often. Scribble a note so I can take it back with me. Something?"

Roger's face became blank, then stiff. He shook his head. Max knew that talk of Roger's father, for some reason, was off limits. "No, man, nothing."

"Okay, Roger," Max said. He reached into his wallet. This cat was just too much. Max thought of all the time he'd wasted with Roger. He found the check. "Catch, baby, he sent you a few bills. With love." Max swung his arm in a soft arc and the check tumbled up out of his hand, twisted once or twice and started its green and white descent to the floor. "He's very sick," Max said, watching the check and Roger's face at the same time. "He doesn't think you're a writer at all. He thinks you're pretending; he thinks you're afraid to go home and take your lumps with the rest of the spades." Roger's hand was snapping at the check now. "Don't call me at the hotel, Roger, I'll call *you*."

"Hey, man," Roger was saying as Max closed the door after him; his last view was that of Roger scrambling around on the floor for the check.

"You were hard on him," Margrit said, holding his arm.

"Screw 'im. Christ, why did I have to wait until now to start telling people the way they are? Look, a cab. I don't feel like walking."

"All right."

They passed a herring stand. Max stopped. "Shall we have eel or the green herring?"

"Whichever you want, Mox."

He shook his head. "Neither." They walked to the cabs parked beneath the trees. They were just down the street from the Anna Frank House, and that part of Amsterdam always did strange things to him; it made him sad and it made him angry. It also made him aware of what so easily could be at home.

"Mox, why are you so thin?"

The cab rolled easily over the cobblestones; it passed the couples lingering over the edges of the canals. Max suddenly felt frightened. There would be a billion other nights in Amsterdam as soft as this one, filled with the odor of sea and old bricks and tarred wood pilings; and there would be the smell of food, drifting gently down upon the street from those Vermeer kitchens; there would be young men and young women, unjaded as yet, talking about loving one another.

I don't want to miss it! Max thought, I don't want to miss any of it! I want to live forever and ever and ever and ever . . .

"Mox . . ."

"Oh! That last trip to Africa, I guess. It was kind of rough."

"Thanks for the card." They were at her house now. The cab had stopped. Margrit got out. For a second she waited, then she

30

knew that Max was going on to the hotel. She spoke to the driver in Dutch. "I will see you tomorrow?"

"In the afternoon, Maggie. Shall I meet you in the hotel?"

"What is wrong with the morning?"

"You have to work."

"I would take it off."

"I have something to do. In Leiden."

"Do you want me to go with you?"

She was bending, peering into the cab, and Max could smell her perfume.

"Thanks, no. Business."

"Good night, Mox."

"Good night, Maggie."

She closed the door. "American," Max said, and slumped back in the seat, his eyes half closed. The driver nodded. "She telled," he said.

"Okay," Max said. "Fine."

# 4

MARGRIT REDDICK walked slowly up the carpeted stairs. She should have been tired, but she wasn't. She let herself in and turned on the light. She stood with her finger on the switch and looked around the living room. The same old place. Perhaps it would have been different if Max had come up, but maybe not. She walked heavily to the kitchen. Genever on ice. She wouldn't sleep for a while yet, perhaps not at all. She returned to the living room and sat down. She hated Amsterdam when it was this time of night and she was alone. She hated any place in the world she had ever been when it was quiet and she was alone.

She finished her drink and got another one. She sipped it slowly, thinking. There ought to be someone she could call, slip into an easy conversation, a leading one, and then consent to letting him (it would be a "him" of course, that she would be talking to) come over, spend the night so she wouldn't be alone. And who could tell, perhaps she might even work up a passion, enough to last a few hours. But people were so damned practical during the week. During the weekend it was no problem other than selecting the man with whom she felt most comfortable. Once she started to the phone, but changed her mind. The man she'd thought of, it suddenly occurred to her, smelled bad. Making love was chore enough with its odors and sounds, but at least let them be derived from making love; don't bring them with you. She remembered stories of the people in the Middle East, the well-to-do ones, who made such a great fetish of bathing and perfuming before they made love. It helped. But maybe, she thought as she sipped her third Genever, if she became high enough she wouldn't smell anything. She had done that before. The alcohol froze the sense of smell. Yes, she could do that, and make him understand that he could not stay the night, just until it was over. She could say that she had to get up early . . . Oh, shit! she thought to herself. Max had made her understand the release that came from words like that, the combination of sibilants and stops. She said it aloud and tears welled in her eyes. She quickly swallowed her drink, turned out the living room light and went into her bedroom. She rummaged through her drawers until she found a sleeping pill. She placed it on a dresser and undressed. For a moment in the dim light, she held herself. Then she reached up and gently grasped her breasts, stroked each nipple. The tears came once more. She snatched up the pill, ran to the kitchen and took a glass of water.

Groaning under the lukewarm shower and feeling the sleeping pill going quickly to her head, she spat, *"Zwarte klootzak!"* She dried herself and went to bed. She sighed and closed her eyes and felt for a moment that she was sliding right off to sleep, but then, through a growing warmth, she became aware of her nude body. She pressed her eyes tightly and held herself tense. The warmth continued to grow. She found her hands near her breasts and quickly drew them away. Now they lay pressed tightly against her body. She turned on her back and placed her arms up above her head; the knuckles of her hands rapped softly on the headboard. Her eyes were used to the darkness now, and she could see the outline of her breasts beneath the sheet. She flung herself on her stomach and gripped the top of the headboard with both hands. Sighing, she kicked the sheets from her. She took one breast and began to caress it. The other hand flitted down over her stomach. Slowly, the fingers began parting the pubic hair. She would sleep better, she thought, and she would not have to bother with anyone, whether they smelled good or bad.

But sleep did not come. She lay with her arms thrown out from her body. She felt soiled and young. But most of all she felt alone and fearful of it. She thought, *De zak! Hij had me toch zeker wel een zoen kunnen geven?!* The bastard! He could have kissed me on the cheek.

He had kissed her the first night they met, at the party Roger held for him. He brought her home, up the stairs and to the door. She turned to thank him. He said, *"Een kus?"*

She had smiled. Obviously he had asked somebody to tell him how to ask for a kiss. The dust of Africa hadn't remained on him long; he adjusted very quickly. And she had thought that he might kiss her and had decided that she would let him. "Yes," she said, and she had held up her lips, closed her eyes. But she felt his lips on her forehead, soft and very gentle. He drew away. When she opened her eyes he was looking at her with a little smile and he seemed very tired. Someone at the party had told her that he hadn't slept for two days. What struck her was the innocence of the kiss, innocence, yes, and a kind of gratitude. For what, she had asked herself in the mirror, for what?

The silver light of morning was already coming up and Margrit began to cry again. No sleep. And what had she done to herself? She would be tired and irritable all day. It would serve him right if she snapped at him. Oh, the bastard, the black bastard, she thought, he could have kissed me!

33

When had he said it, how many times and in how many places? But she always forgot.

"Maggie, for Christ's sake, I don't like to be kissed on the street."

"I forgot, Mox."

"Well, try to remember, will you?"

"Why does it make you angry when I kiss you on the street?"

"Never mind, just don't do it."

So, she was always surprised when swimming — Spain, East Hampton, the Virgin Islands — he burst out of the water with a roar, kissed her, dragged her underwater and kissed her again, released her only to grab her again when they came sprinting to the surface to draw breath. Of course, he could have kissed her, if only on the cheek.

She drifted by on a conveyor belt. She looked very much like herself, he noted with a smile. But she had a filter-tip cigarette in her vagina, and it was smoking. She wore no clothes. She came by again, only this time her hair was red. "Great!" he said, "never had a redhead, very good, Maggie!" And there was another filter-tip cigarette in her vagina. He shook his head. She floated by once more and this time her hair was jet-black. "Ah, Maggie," he said. "Italian or Spanish?" Then he said, "Why do you smoke so much?" because there was another filter-tip cigarette right where the others had been. "Maggie, you're a damned showboat," he said, and he moved close to the line and plucked out the cigarettes as she came by on the conveyor belt again and again. He dropped them beneath his feet and crushed them on the floor. "Baby, you don't watch it, you're going to get cancer of the uh-uh."

"You've got it already," she said. He tried to look behind him, but he could not; his neck, hands and ankles were strapped down. The room was different: sterile and white. He was naked now and his buttocks were turned up toward the ceiling. He heard the squeak of the cobalt machine being lowered into position.

"Relax, relax," Margrit said.

"Now, wait a minute, Maggie, that's not the way it works."

34

"I know what I'm doing. Relax. I'll burn it out."

Helpless, he watched the long, slender shadow of the machine descend. He felt the eye of it poking near his anus and he strained at the straps, cursing. "Goddamn it, Margrit, let Dr. Woodson handle it, you dumb bitch!"

*"Zak! Shut up!"*

"Maggie, when I get up from here, it's going to be your ass, really."

"Whose ass, whose?"

"C'mon, now Maggie. I'm through playing with you. Get Dr. Woodson. Get him! Help!" (Maggie, you rotten bitch!) "Help, doctor, help! (Loose me, damn you!) Help!"

"Shut up. Dr. Woodson is in New York."

"Where are we?"

"New York."

"New York?"

"No, Amsterdam."

"Amsterdam?"

"No, Lagos."

"I wouldn't be caught dead in Lagos, Maggie. You know that."

"You're not dead. Yet."

"Maggie, take it away. Listen, sweetheart: New Lucky Strike Filters Put Back the Taste Others Take Away . . . Try New Lucky Strike Filters."

"No, that one's no good. Besides I tried Luckies, in the uh-uh, you remember."

"Yes, darling, but how about this one: Kent Satisfies Best . . ."

"Like hell they do. Something about that filter; kept slipping."

"My love, give me a chance."

"Did you ever give me a chance?"

"Dearest, dearest!" He had felt the eye punching savagely. Quickly he said, "Lark! darling. Richly Rewarding — Uncommonly Smooth; Charcoal Granules, Inner Chamber . . . how about that, baby?"

"No!"

"Help!" he screamed.

"They are much too sweet; no body," Margrit said, busy with the machine.

"Don't be like that, Maggie. How about this: BIG Change! Now Tempo Has *Good* Old-Fashioned Flavor." Max felt the eye of the cobalt machine draw tentatively away. He waited anxiously.

"Didn't I try that one?"

"No, darling. You see, not only is it a brand new filter-tip, but it has already been improved! You know, more charcoal — by the way, Maggie, I don't think you tried the one with the ground coconut in the filter either — white fiber, new rich tobacco . . ."

". . . taste," Margrit said, "it is always the taste that counts."

"Yes, dearest one," Max said, and he kept up a steady stream of endearments while she loosened his straps. Once freed, he grabbed his trousers, pulled them on and raced shoeless past the conveyor belt where Margrit lay trying out the new filter-tip cigarettes.

Trembling, Max reached for a cigarette. He touched his behind and found the cotton wet. He had taken the precaution of sleeping on a towel. He moved and pain lanced through him and it was heavy and dull and he knew it would stay with him this time unless he took the morphine. He rose, changed the cotton and took the drug. It was still dark outside. He looked at the syringe. If he could just avoid steady use of the morphine for the next few days, just a few more. He started to nod. Suddenly there was a sharp pain in his hand and he jerked it up to find that the cigarette had burned down to his fingers. He thought of the dream; if he'd had a filter-tip cigarette, it wouldn't have burned him. He placed the cigarette in the ashtray. He didn't have strength enough to crush it out. Then he went to sleep wrapped in a morphinated stupor.

But by the time his morning call came, he felt better. He couldn't feel the pain anymore and the morphine had not left him too drowsy. He called down for a breakfast he didn't want, then showered. The sun was already bright on the Leidseplein. It made him feel good. He wondered what Margrit was doing, if she were al-

36

ready on her way to work. He should have kissed her last night, on the cheek, the forehead, some damned where. It had been good to see her. It would be good to see her later, when he returned from Leiden. His breakfast of soft foods came, and he picked over it. Then he called to make arrangements for the car. He was shaken by his toilet and he took one of his pills and lay on the bed, a routine prescribed by Dr. Woodson.

He could hear the city waking. The trams rattled around the curve downstairs, bells clanging. The horns of the cars grew in number and volume. He knew the bicycle riders were flowing past too. The hotel was fully awake now; he could hear doors being closed, maids walking heavily up and down the carpeted halls, the harsh sounds of Dutch being spoken in semi-whispers. And there was the rattle of breakfast dishes being removed from the rooms. Soon, Max knew, the chambermaids would be at his door. He dozed again. Another half hour, he told himself.

As he got into the VW (there had been nothing else available) he had another of those periods when he felt good, impossibly good, so much like his old self. Once again he permitted himself to think that the cotton, the pills, the pain, the morphine, Dr. Woodson, were a hideous comedy of errors. Even now, he thought, some obscure lab technician might be on the phone talking to the doctor, saying there had been a mistake. Max shook himself out of the daydream and started the car. Take what you get, man. It's nice, enjoy it. You knew as soon as you could know things that you weren't going to live forever. You got twenty extra years. Remember the war. The tanks. Cinquale Canal. Viareggio. The mountains. The Ghoums. The donkeys. He drove slowly through the streets. They did not look familiar. That is, they did not look *unfamiliar;* they looked, each one, just like one he had passed. He felt his way and was pleased when he arrived at the road south, Europa 10.

A fine silver mist hung low over the level, neat green fields. You could say that for the Netherlands; their neatness was blatant, as blatant as New York's high risers. Going back toward the city were two highway policemen with their helmets and sunglasses and white

37

shoulder belts. They roared along in a Porsche. Max settled back in the seat. It was a nice day. Why was he messing it up with Harry Ames, now dead and gone, sprinkled somewhere over the Seine? Once he and Harry had planned to drive through Holland, but like so many things they'd talked about doing, it hadn't come off. But there had been other things, a hundred thousand other things, he thought, driving along at a steady clip under a rapidly warming sun . . .

# 5

. . . and he started to feel a little too warm. He rolled down the windows of the beetle-backed Ford he had borrowed. He felt good. A part of things. Bigger than the things he was a part of. It was about time. He bounced over the Long Island roads that F. Scott Fitzgerald had made famous, and thought of Tom and Daisy Buchanan, of Gatsby. Hell, he was going to write Fitzgerald out of existence. Most of the reviews of his first book, published only two weeks ago, made him think so, although not one failed to compare him with Harry Ames. He was not going to let that bother him just yet. He would meet Ames that day, at Wading River, at the summer home of Bernard Zutkin, the literary critic. Of course, Max had read Ames, had liked the very hell out of his big book, the one that had made him. He wondered what kind of man Ames was. There were always stories around the newspaper, the *Harlem Democrat,* which, after the acceptance of his novel for publication, had finally moved him from hustling ads from the owners of bars and barbecue joints to editorial. Now Max wrote about shootings and stabbings and cases of discrimination. And the scandals. Especially the ones involving chicken-eating ministers caught with someone else's wife in a fleabag hotel. Ames got a lot of attention in the paper, along with Bolton Warren. So there were always stories. Max knew that Ames was thirty, six years older than he; that Ames had been born in Mississippi, but had traveled around the country, to Baltimore, Chicago, New York, Philadelphia, Washington. Max knew Chicago, had been born there, and he had lived in Cleveland for a while before coming to New York to settle down. New York, the Big Apple.

Max looked forward to the weekend. Perhaps the people at Zutkin's would be groovy. Going in for the beach scenes and all, lots of whiskey and dancing. He wondered if Ames could swim. Yes, it would be an absolute groove, if Harry Ames hadn't sewed it up already. He pictured Ames (on the basis of the love scenes Ames had written) as being pretty great with the chicks. He'd see.

And he'd have to feel his way with Zutkin who'd already asked him to write articles for his magazine. Zutkin, a loner, so the talk went, was a highly regarded critic. His criticism seemed to have roots in the struggles taking place within the society. In Harlem, where no one cared, it was said that Zutkin once had been a big man in the Party. No one knew for sure. He was a small, bald, retiring man with a slow, deep smile. He was the only Jew in Wading River and once the Ku Klux Klan had burned a cross on his lawn. Max had covered the story and it appeared on the front page of the *Democrat*.

Max had met one other critic at a party in Manhattan, Granville Bryant, the "Great White Father." Bryant was a tall and extremely thin, pale man who wore his hair in a long, luxuriant brown mane. He was never seen without a velvet jacket or a silk scarf looped casually around his neck. Bryant singlehandedly had undertaken to open publishing doors for Negro writers and was the inspiration and guide for what was now called the "Black Reawakening." Aspiring young black writers sweated and clamored for an invitation to Bryant's Fifth Avenue duplex, and over the years, just to be invited to one of his affairs came to be a mark of artistic status. Max, however, had kept his distance, for one was either in the Bryant camp or the Zutkin camp and he preferred the latter.

There were a number of cars already parked near Zutkin's large, dark-shingled house. As he was parking, Max heard the slopping beat of boogie-woogie and a number of voices and, punctuating these, the soft, deceptive spit of a .22. Shorts, he guessed, were being fired. As he approached the house, the music and voices began to come low and flat. Zutkin's house was near the ocean. Max circled the house, saw dancers moving to the music, but he wanted to look at the water. He knew people who cared nothing at all for oceans and lakes and streams, and he found that strange. He could not pass a body of water without looking at it and wondering how it was that he and the millions of others had started in places like that. He marveled at it.

A group of people were standing on the sandy ledge overlooking the ocean, clustered around a crouching, broad-shouldered Negro man who was firing a pump rifle. The man lowered the weapon, raised it again and sighted. About seventy-five feet away, down on the shelf of the beach, a can bounded in the air and fell back. The man (Ames! Max had thought) lowered the rifle and looked around triumphantly. His eyes had just locked with Max's when Zutkin approached.

"Hello, Max," Zutkin said, holding out a Scotch highball. "Saw you come in. How've you been? Glad you could come."

"Thanks, Bernard. I'm all right, thanks." His eyes swung back to Ames.

"I'm glad he's not angry with me," Zutkin said loudly.

"Don't count on it, man," Ames said, pulling out of his crouch. The people around him now turned to Zutkin and Max.

"Max Reddick," Zutkin said, and proceeded to introduce Max around. Now Max and Ames stood face to face. They were about the same height, Max noticed with satisfaction. Ames had big hands, but they weren't hard.

"Hello, brother," Ames said. "How's your shooting eye?" He turned back to the beach and fired at the can once more. They could hear sand spray with sharp tinny sounds from the near miss. Ames spun around and thrust the rifle, barrel straight up, to Max.

Max recognized the challenge. The people would be sympathetic if he missed. Even Ames. The comparison would be obvious. It might even carry to the writing of novels. "I'll give it a try," Max said, handing Ames his drink and taking the rifle. It had a bead sight and was light, almost too light, even for a .22.

"I'll bet he's like one of those guys who hang around the poolhalls and pretends he's a sucker can't shoot a lick, but he's really a hustler," Ames said.

"Exactly," Max said, as he aimed, and he knew that Ames had him at both ends; if he missed, well, Ames was a better shot and perhaps all the rest. If he didn't miss, well, he was a hustler, jiving them. Max stood at the lip of the ledge. He moved his elbows and glanced back at Ames. Ames had braced on one of his thighs. Max was showing him that he needed no brace. There was a flicker of Ames's eyes; he understood. A polite silence fell. Max took a breath, let it out part way and held it. He squeezed. The can jumped. He squeezed again. The can bounded in the opposite direction. A murmur ran through the onlookers. Not quite like shooting squirrel or rabbit in Wisconsin, just to show the old man that you could get something, Max thought, but it would do. He pumped and fired again and while the can was still in motion, drilled it twice. He pumped, sighted and the trigger snapped, flatly. Empty. Max was grinning when he turned and handed the gun back to Ames.

"Told you, didn't I?" Ames said, taking the rifle.

"Squirrels and rabbits," Max explained.

"And pigeons," Ames said sarcastically. He smiled. "I don't like nobody who can do things better than me. Ask Bernard. Hey, how's your drinking?"

"Tolerable," Max said, smiling.

"Tolerable? Where the hell you from?"

Max knew then that Ames hadn't read his book and he was disappointed. The dust jacket would have told Ames where he was from.

"Chicago — and Cleveland."

"Ah, now I see. Lots of Mississippi folks in Chicago."

"Yes, over on Indiana, Calumet . . ."

"But you said your drinking is tolerable, that means you got a hollow leg. We'll find out. Got all weekend, hey Bernard?"

"You won't need the whole weekend, Harry."

Right then, Max noticed the edge in Zutkin's voice, although the critic's smile told him that he hadn't meant to let it slip through. A sidelong glance at Ames told Max that he had made a mental note of it.

"Ease up, Bernard, I brought my own hooch."

With an excess of gesture and voice, Zutkin said, "Harry, you know you didn't have to do that."

Max stared out over the water at what he supposed was Connecticut.

Ames laughed. "Sure, I know it, Bernard. Take it easy, greasy, you got a long way to slide."

Zutkin laughed then and gripped Ames's arm. Ames slapped him on the back and snapped a wink at Max.

Oh, oh, Max thought and grinned at both of them.

The afternoon sun began its run toward Manhattan. Record followed record: Tommy Dorsey, Glenn Miller, Benny Goodman, Earl Hines, Jimmy Lunceford, a new group called the Cats 'n the Fiddle. There was talk about the Germans, the Japanese plowing through China, the impending selective service peacetime act. Couples danced on the porch, in the house, in the yard. Some people had slid down to the shelf and were running toward the water, thermos jugs in hand. By now Max had met Charlotte, a rangy woman with long blond hair and full body. But everything she did was precise, and she had had many drinks. They seemed not to affect her at all. It finally dawned on Max that Charlotte was interested only in Ames. Ah, well, what the hell. And later he was still sitting on the ledge, looking at the changing colors of the sea. A redhead was talking to him. She wore a bathing suit. Her legs were very hairy. He could see her breasts bubbling at the top of the suit. "I just love you for that book," she said. "Jesus, it was great."

"Well, thanks," Max said. He turned up his glass, eyes rolling down once more to her legs. The glass was empty. He started to rise to get another drink.

"Let me get it for you." the redhead said, very close to him. "You're a celebrity."

With a show of embarrassed nonchalance, Max gave her the glass. What the hell was her name? Had she told him? He caught Ames's eye. Ames was lying with his head in Charlotte's lap. Ames winked and Max thought: This party is going to be groo–vy! His voice thick with insinuation, Ames drawled, "How are you doing, brother?"

"You tell me," Max said.

"Fine, fine, fine like wine, jack."

"But you the best," Max said.

"Man, I know it, just don't show it," Ames said, laughing.

"Streevus mone on the reevus cone," Max said, enjoying the poolhall, jitterbug, nonsensical word game, a game whose meaning was conveyed not by the words, because they had no meaning, but by the tone of voice, the inflection.

"Until sleptis joon cut out from the moon," Ames countered.

The redhead returned. Ames closed his eyes and said, "Weeby on the streeby and a dit-dit-datty-dit."

"If it's not strong enough, I'll put more in," she said, sitting down on the sand again. "You're not high, are you?"

"High? I'm flying," Max said. What would this night bring, he thought, and really, with so little effort. He was going to like being a novelist; he was going to love the *hell* out of it.

"You don't look high," she said.

"No? Anyway, I got rhythm . . ."

"That's a damned silly thing to say," the redhead cried, getting up.

"Hey," Max called, seeing his night suddenly vanishing, "that was a joke, don't you . . ."

"There are some things," she said, "that you don't joke about."

Max stared at his glass, puzzled. He had the feeling that, although he was lying perfectly still, Ames had heard everything — and was laughing to himself.

The next day, after mumbling his apologies to Zutkin, Max prepared to leave. He was backing out when he heard a voice. He stopped. Harry Ames.

"Heard you were leaving. I think you're smart. Be independent in your own way. They'd love you to stay and pick up another chick, maybe one that hasn't heard that you have a sense of humor. I heard that crack about you got rhythm. I haven't read your book yet, Max. I'm sure it's good. Zutkin's no fool."

The music had started up again. There were voices already raised in tribute to the first round of drinks that day. Ames was leaning in the car window now. "I know there's no future in that paper of yours but you're young. There are in this business," he said, with a heavy air, "people who would like you to be serious, even angry, twenty-four hours a day. If you can't, then you're a renegade Negro, and they won't have too much to do with you. This world is very, very greasy, and it's going to slide a long way. They've been so used to putting it on a certain set of skids that they are quite sure that any way they set it — and at least they're thinking now about where the world should be set — it's the right way. Man, they want you to whip them, whip the shit out of them. But then, will you have energy for anything else? Look, I don't know you very well at all, but we're colored, we write, we talk that streevus mone shit and — thing is — thing is, somewhere in this business we got something together besides being colored and being writers. You're doing all right. Just don't never worry about a little pussy. I tell you this, knowing you can say it fifty billion times. But when you get a chick who can put it on you right with the right combination of other things, that's it, you're locked in and all the talkin' ain't going to help one bit." Ames laughed. "Listen to me. And I ain't even *had* my first one today. I'll call you at the paper, okay?"

"Yes, Harry, and thanks."

Ames started away. He returned as Max started the car. "And

I'll bet you that redhead wishes you two had been alone so no one could have heard, then it wouldn't have mattered."

"Aw," Max said, "now I'll probably never have a redhead."

"But, man, there are blondes, brunettes and blackheads. Or are you color oriented?" Ames walked away laughing. Max decided that he liked him. He pointed the car toward New York.

# 6

PERHAPS the failure of Harry Ames's marriage lay in the fact that so few people knew he had a wife. The women he met especially. Ames did not go out of his way to tell them until it became necessary — when he wanted to be finished with them or if they could not be talked into a quiet arrangement designed not to upset the apple cart.

From where Max sat at the Ames's dinner table many times, he could not see just what in the hell was wrong with Wanda. Graceful, feminine, intelligent, she had been one of the Cotton Club beauties. Perhaps they were just tired of each other and who could argue with that?

Sometimes Max and Harry would appear on panels together; there were not too many Negro writers, and sometimes Bolton Warren would appear with them. It was more fun when they appeared alone; Warren always put a certain kind of chill on things. His mind, his eyes were always somewhere else. Coming up to the war, the scent of death was already in the air, and the saturnalias signaled to begin. Quite suddenly Max found himself escalated from the world of social club formals and jiving nights in barrooms, into mixed functions, teas, cocktails, full-blown parties. Most of the Negroes who attended the affairs were in Negro advancement organizations, the church, or show business. There was a burgeoning of interracial couples, married or simply mating. It was suspected that not a single one of the interested white men,

45

some of them book editors, who regularly attended the functions was without a Negro girl. But no one knew for sure whose wife the girl was. The same was true of Negro men.

At one party, Harry, his face glowing, pulled Max into a corner and said, waving toward the mixed crowd, "Man, more pussy has been got and given in the name of the Negro Cause than can possibly be imagined. You gettin' your share?" And before Max could answer, Harry melted back into the crowd.

One press day afternoon, in the fall, Max lay on his couch reading. Beside him rested a clipboard; sometimes while reading, a passage triggered ideas. The desk light was on and there was paper in the typewriter. His hemorrhoids had been bothering him; it was best to take it easy. But, whenever he glanced at the empty clipboard, the desk, and the typewriter with its surly white paper waiting to be filled, he felt uneasy and guilty about lying down.

He forced himself to read. A little later he felt chills and then was suddenly nervous. He shifted his position. Then he got up and turned off the desk light and returned to the couch. Once more he rose and went to the desk and ripped the paper out of the typewriter. But now his hands were shaking. He was overwhelmed by the idea that he was not a writer, but a pretender, like so many others he had met in Harlem or down on 8th Street. No real writer would be lying on his can when there was work to be done. He had stumbled into a dead-end street, that was all. A writer had to stand the silences that came with being alone, and he hated being lonely and yet it comforted him. You could think when you were alone, and writers needed to think.

He picked up the clipboard and tossed it across the room where it clattered against a wall and fell to the floor. Dilemma. How in the hell did it happen? What had started it? He could get out; he wasn't going to spend the rest of his life like Harry — never knowing what the next phone call or mail delivery would or wouldn't bring; never knowing what life would hold for you at forty-nine or fifty-nine. No. He was going to apply himself; he was going to scheme and jive, dance in the sandbox, Tom, kiss behinds, and

46

wind up managing editor of the *Democrat*. He had a little prestige now. No one else at the office had written a novel and they weren't planning to, either!

His chills and shakes persisted. He thought he would feel better outside. He pulled on a sweater and walked rapidly to the corner and then across the street into the park. There he sat in the sun, but even as he did, his mind floated up words to describe what he was seeing and feeling. A young sharpie in draped coat and pegged pants strolled by, arms held stiffly behind his back. A barge, belly-deep in water, steamed slowly up the Hudson, froth leaping from its bows. Max looked at the Palisades and descriptions came for that sheer mass of stone rising from the west bank of the river. And words came for the color of the sun, for the sounds of the children playing near him, for the arching spiral of a battered football and the taut freckled face that watched its flight. The words kept coming, even when he closed his eyes, words and ways of using them that he knew no newspaper could ever use.

He was twenty-four and he knew he hadn't lived much. He hadn't been anywhere, really, not even to Niagara Falls, the Canadian side. Going to college had only taught him that he would never be able to read all the things he wanted to or should. And if he hadn't read so much or traveled so much, how in hell could he feel so much?

Why me? He asked himself bitterly. He looked at the bouncing back of the sharpie. Why couldn't I have been like him? Anybody who walked like that and dressed like that, well, he seemed to be able to live life as he found it. Why can't *I* wear zoot suits, dance the Lindy better, until my nuts fall, laugh like hell instead of just smiling? Why can't *I* be loud and loose and drunker than I ever let myself get? Why am I the way I am? Mutant, freak, caprice, fluke. Maxwell Reddick.

He thought about his childhood, his parents, and dismissed them. No, it went beyond that, beyond them. He remembered a childhood photo. He still had it, somewhere. It was a photo which, when his parents had passed it around, drew the comment:

"Three? He looks so old and wise." Was there something in that silly photo that could give him answers? So old, so wise, God, about *what?* He would study it once more when he returned to his apartment. What in the world had made him look so old and wise at only three? His family had never starved. His parents had been good to him and perhaps even loved him, coming late in their lives as he had. He didn't know, had never assumed that they had not loved or at least liked him. That had to count for something, although the old man was hell on wheels right up until they laid him out, four years to the exact day and hour after his mother had died. What did that mean? That look he had at three . . . Which spermatozoid, which ovum, preserved for generations in the secret places of bodies, had sensed the presence of each other, finally, and, fiercely subcopulating, created him? Had they come out of the past at all, the future? But why, *why?*

The next time he saw Harry, Max asked, "Do you ever question the way you are, why you're a writer?"

"Every day."

Max waited for him to go on. It was a Saturday afternoon and the uptown bar had not yet filled with dapper Negroes starting the second leg of the weekend; Friday night was the first; Saturday into Sunday was the second, which was brought to an end only by habit of going to church Sunday morning or sleeping into Sunday afternoon.

Harry laughed. "Well, you're colored and you wonder how come you're a writer because there is no tradition of colored writers. Are we related to some ancient Yoruba folklorist, to Phillis Wheatley? I think about that. Then, somehow, it doesn't matter about the tradition; what matters is now. You wrote a book, Max, and published it. As I see it, that makes you, like me, a very special person among all the people who've ever lived. That's cause for some pride, I think; that's cause to produce more books. That also makes you dangerous because they don't burn people anymore, they burn books, and they don't always have bonfires. I love it like this; let there be a little danger to life, otherwise life is a lie.

48

"I'm the way I am, the kind of writer I am, and you may be too, because I'm a black man; therefore, we're in rebellion; we've got to be. We have no other function as valid as that one." Harry grinned. "I've been in rebellion, and a writer, I guess, ever since I discovered that even colored folks wanted to keep me away from books so I could never learn just how bad it all was. Maybe, too, to keep me from laughing at them. For taking it. My folks had a deathly fear of books."

Harry took a deep drink of his beer and gazed moodily around the bar, then he said, "There's something wrong with this ritual these people have here. Oh, hell, I like kicking it around all weekend, too, but that doesn't mean I can't see what's going on. A writer worth his salt is not going to write about how damned lovely it is; it isn't, that's why so many people tell themselves it is. But they don't want to hear what you've got to say if it isn't the same thing they can see or believe, and that's going to make you a target. Talk about sitting ducks! You against them, and all you've got is a beat-up typewriter and some cheap rag bond. And your head.

"If your first book is any indication, you're a rebel, too, just as you should be. Don't be guilty if you make it and Negroes themselves start shooting you down; your subject will always be America or Americans. You didn't make the bed; you just have to lie in it. Even so, when my name is mentioned, I want people to jerk up and look for trouble; I want trouble to be my middle name when I write about America. I wouldn't like it if a single person slept well. We — you, me, Warren and the others — have that function. I'll tell you why.

"In our society which is white — we are intruders they say — there has got to be something inherently horrible about having the sicknesses and weaknesses of that society described by a person who is a victim of them; for if he, the victim, is capable of describing what they have believed nonexistent, then they, the members of the majority, must choose between living the truth, which can be pretty grim, and the lie, which isn't much better. But at least they will then have the choice.

"It must be pretty awful for a white man to learn that one of the things wrong with this society is that it is not based on dollars directly or alone, but dollars denied men who are black so dollars can go into the pockets of men who are white. It must make white men ponder a kind of weakness that will make them deny work to black men so that work can be done by men who are white. How it must anger them to know finally that we know they deny women who are white to black men, while they have taken black women at will for generations.

"And don't they know or want to know that the absence of black voices in the state legislatures and in Congress, unheard since the Reconstruction, wounds them to the death? How painful would it be for them to admit that millions of acres of black men's lands were ripped from them by night riders and county clerks, and are still being held by the descendants of the thieves? Very painful. They'd have to give back those lands, those dollars, that work.

"Ah yeah, there's quite enough to be in rebellion about," Harry said, morosely. "I quit the Party because I became damned sick and tired of white men telling me when I should suffer, where and how and what for. And, Max, I was suffering all the time! And I got tired of writing what I knew was wrong for me, our people, our time, our country. I got tired of seeing young Negroes, *young,* man! beat when they drifted into the Party looking for hope and found nothing but another version of white man's hell. Karl Marx was not thinking about niggers when he engineered *The Communist Manifesto;* if he was, why didn't he *say* so? None of the 'great documents' of the West ever acknowledged a racial problem tied to an economic problem, tied to a social problem, tied to a religious problem, tied to a whole nation's survival. And that's why, man, none of them, unamended, are worth the paper they were written on." Harry jabbed himself in the chest. "Somewhere you know this and you're thinking twice about starting to work. Your job is to tell those people to stop lying, not only to us, but to themselves. You've written and in the process, somewhere in that African body of yours, something said, 'I am — a writer, a man, something, but here for today. Here for right now.' "

Harry waved to the waiter for more beer.

"That could make a man start thinking he's pretty important stuff, couldn't it, Harry?"

"Damn, Max. Don't you understand? If you don't have the perspective of yourself, can you expect other people to have it?"

But during the next weeks no amount of talking seemed to help. Max had a thousand abortive starts on the new novel, but none of them went past page three or four. In despair, he turned to his essays, but finally came to distrust them; he could not begin one with a question and answer it logically. "Does American democracy work?" Logically the essay could be completed by adding two letters: "No."

When he wrote, Max wanted to soar, to sing golden arias. But Zutkin's editor friends wanted emotion: anger, unreasonable black fury; screeching, humiliation, pain, subjects which evaded the essay; articles, yes; the essay, no. Do not sing, Max, the editors seemed to be saying. Instead, tell us, in your own words, in ten thousand words or less, just how much we've hurt you! We will pay handsomely for that revelation.

Until the Moses Boatwright case, few of the Harlem doings had touched Max. There were murders, yes, and reefer raids, the burglaries. There were the big bands at the Savoy and the Apollo; the Garvey diehards, the Ras Tafarian street fights, the dances. After Moses Boatwright Max didn't want to sing at all, ever. Or, he knew it would take him a long time to learn how to sing again and even if he did, he would never sing the way he imagined he could. Maybe he would sing a rumbling, threatening basso like Harry Ames.

# 7

IT HAD been *that* fall, Max remembered, when the Germans had stopped jiving and started working; the next year, August, Trotsky got his, in Mexico. That somehow placed it all in focus: Trotsky and the Germans.

The name Moses Boatwright called up the image of a tall, rangy Negro farmer dressed in faded overalls, in the Deep South, standing astride a cotton patch, a shaggy felt hat pulled low on his head to beat back the sun. But Boatwright's picture, when it was splashed across the front pages of the downtown papers, utterly destroyed that image. Boatwright, despite the blurred and distorted photos — the better to really communicate to the readers of the tabloids that he was a cannibal even though a graduate of Harvard — appeared delicate and small, shy, and even, perhaps, tender.

At first, the managing editor of the *Harlem Democrat,* Dudley Crockett, ignored the downtown papers. After all, Boatwright did not live in Harlem; he had set himself apart from his black fellows. He lived in the Village. And there was something implicitly gleeful about the downtown headlines. You see, they seemed to imply, they *are* nothing but savages. No, Crockett thought, the *Democrat* was pledged from inception to "Negro Uplift." Doing stories on cannibals would not help.

But the Boatwright case had disturbed Max in a nagging, indefinable way ever since it had broken. He had read the papers carefully. He had studied Boatwright's photos, and he had puzzled: How could one man kill and eat another? The more he thought about it, the more it became like a man studying a sore on his own body, a chancre. In the office there were jokes, but there was also an underlying tension, a curiosity, a strange, heady mixture of attraction and revulsion. But no one, maybe because Crockett had given a cue of some kind, brought the case up. Only Max Reddick.

"We ought to do something about this Boatwright guy, Crockett," Max said one day as he handed in some copy, which Crockett promptly dropped as though it had been dipped in acid. He leaned back in his chair and stared at Max. Strange guy. Could be living in the Village — next door to Boatwright. Educated nigger. College even. Crockett didn't trust Negroes who had been to college. *He* had not been and had done all right. But he knew that if, suddenly, all the barriers fell away, he would have to stay where he was and people like Reddick would be the ones to move on ahead. That was the first thing out of white folk's mouths — education. He hated Max for being prepared. But the Boatwright thing: it *would* sell papers in Harlem, but there had to be a hook. Discrimination? Segregation? Cannibalism the result of? Derangement the result of? Crockett knew that the owner of the *Democrat,* a man who owned funeral parlors in four of the five boroughs took great pride in having a novelist on the paper. It was the owner in fact who had suggested that Max be moved from advertising to editorial and given a by-line. At the suggestion, Crockett, sagely nodding his head, said that he was thinking about getting approval for just such a move. What else could he say? He knew that Reddick was the owner's first choice to replace Crockett if he didn't behave. If Max took on the Boatwright case (the owner would be slow to anger if Max were the reporter) and flopped, Crockett got rid of a challenger. If Max succeeded, Crockett got some credit too. For initiative.

Crockett picked up the copy and scanned it. "You know we've got the pride, the racial uplift thing, Reddick. What kind of angle you got?"

"Just the Negro angle. I mean, was there something in his being black that made him do this? He may give us something he hasn't given the white boys downtown."

Crockett tossed the copy in the ready basket. "See how much you can get." Crockett knew he shouldn't have said it. Reddick didn't need to be told how to do his job, and that disturbed Crockett too.

Max entered the jail, leaving a listless Indian summer day flooding the streets; he walked slowly. It was after all ridiculous for a man to be anywhere near a jail if he was not consigned to be in it. And he thought of all the people who had been placed in jail because they were poor and knew no one to help them, of the falsely arrested, the interminable democratic process which frequently placed a man inside with a minimum of effort, but took forever to get him out. This is the place, he thought, walking down the corridors behind a guard, where they locked up black asses and threw away the key. Where they locked up white asses and threw away the key, but not as far. He felt a stab of fear, just as he did whenever he saw a policeman and the cop put that extra something into his casual stare. Perhaps it was that the look carried a threat, a menace. Black boy, I could have you whenever I wanted to, it said, that look. It was not as though Max had not been inside jails and precinct houses before. Maybe it wasn't even the fear of jails and cops as such, but the knowledge that under the existing system they were his natural enemies. And it did not matter that the police blotter could read about a woman who had had love made to her by her dog so that her shoulders, buttocks and back were covered by deep scratches; it was really no concern of his that two men had been hospitalized, under guard, still together like dogs, one imbedded so deeply in the other that one had died and that the live one, still nude, tragedy roughly overriding their perversion, cried and hid his face; could he even bother to finish reading what one lesbian had done to another with her teeth and where? Bother with murders and beatings, why? When it was all said and done, the only clean job a cop could enjoy perhaps was the one where the enemy had but a single perversion — color.

And a cop who labored in the stables of human filth soon lost sight of human values. That was what Max feared. Still following the guard, Max now picked up the smells of the innards of the jail. They were more stark than those in the outer office, the booking desk. They were of urine, clothes worn too long, feces, flat-smelling foods, disinfected floors and walls and rust from exposed pipes. Max thought of the dungeons somewhere beneath him where confessions were beat out of hapless prisoners with rubber truncheons. He thought of the bright lights and circles of detectives, their sadism accepted as normal in that place, their jackets carefully hung, their sleeves rolled, their voices going soft with all the time and patience in the world to make a man scream "YES!"

Max and Boatwright stared at each other through the bars as the guard unlocked the cell. Boatwright held out a slender hand which

54

Max took and moved up and down a couple of times. Boatwright applied no pressure to the handshake; it was almost as if he had no hand at all. "I'm Max Reddick from the *Democrat.*"

"They wanted me to see you in the public room," Boatwright said in a high mournful voice, "but I told them white reporters had been in the cell, why not you, right?" Max tried not to stare at Boatwright's head. It was huge and reminded Max of the people on other worlds in the Buck Rogers and Flash Gordon comic strips. The hairless face narrowed down to a sharply pointed chin. The eyes were large, bulging almost, as if from a thyroid condition, and were thickly lashed, almost girlish.

"Thanks," Max said, noting the position of the guard outside the cell.

They were still standing, looking at one another. "You're the first reporter from a colored paper to come and see me, do you know that?"

"Well . . ."

Boatwright flung himself on one of the unyielding bunks. He got up again. "Cigarette?"

"Yes," Max said, taking one and allowing Boatwright to light it.

Boatwright laughed. "You should be the one to offer the cigarettes, you know. I'm in jail, not you. Like in the movies." He went back to the bunk and laid down. "Are you ready for me to talk?"

"Any time," Max said.

"Any special place?"

"Any place, please."

Boatwright took a deep pull on his cigarette and began talking without looking at Max. "My full name's Moses Lincoln Boatwright. Isn't that classical American Negro — Moses Lincoln — always hated it. And people always called me Moses, never Mo. I'm from Rochester, New York, Kodak city. I went to the public schools there and got a scholarship to Harvard."

"Howard?" Max asked.

"Harvard, Mr. Reddick, HAR-vard."

55

"Umm," Max grunted.

"I have a Master's degree."

"In what?"

Boatwright snickered. "Philosophy. Ever heard of a Negro philosopher?" Max stopped writing and looked across the room at the prisoner. "I wanted so much to be different, special. Philosophy. Oh, I was great in it. Then I woke up one day, not too long ago, and I knew what had happened to me. They didn't want to tell me there was no place for me, but they didn't want to waste me either. Maybe the break might come."

"Negro colleges?"

"Thank you, no."

A snot, Max thought. "Why not?"

"I didn't want to be buried. You must know what those schools are like." Boatwright sighed. "Anyway, they're going to put an end to my misery. I've had all my tests at Bellevue. I'm legally sane. I knew what I was doing." Boatwright kicked himself off the bed. "At twenty-two I've learned many things, Mr. Reddick."

This time Max offered the cigarettes.

"The white newspapermen asked me all kinds of questions. They knew they could never print the answers to them."

"Maybe the questions were for themselves and not their readers. Newsmen are —"

"And that's why you're here!" Boatwright said. "I've been watching you study me. A man has to know evil, look it right in the face, touch it, take its cigarettes before one can really know evil in the flesh. It's always been abstract."

Max shrugged. "I have a job to do. Read into that what you will."

"I know you have a job to do," Boatwright said, "but it took the *Democrat* a long time to get doing it."

"Let's go back to Bellevue," Max said.

"You want to go back to Bellevue, do you?"

Max nodded. Wise little bastard!

"Bellevue was very funny," Boatwright said, laughing a laugh that came out a chill, curlicuing wail. Max felt a coldness at the base of his spine. "That psychiatrist asked me if I liked to eat it."

Max scribbled hastily. Boatwright was looking at him with a sly expression. "Eat what?"

Boatwright shifted his cigarette into his other hand. His eyes lit up, then clouded. "Cunnilingus, fellatio —" He smiled at the floor. "You *do* know what those are don't you?"

"Yes," Max said, "I know. But was the psychiatrist correct, I mean, well . . ."

"Ah, HAH!" Boatwright leaped to his feet in triumph. He reminded Max of a spider trapped suddenly in the middle of the floor. "You see! You can't print that! You can't!"

Max said quietly, "Haven't you ever read the phrase, 'unnatural' acts'?" But Boatwright continued as if he hadn't heard. "And he asked if I'd ever *done* those things and I gave him my answer. I knew where he was going, to Freud, naturally, and he had been reading psychiatric studies of Negro life, he told me. Why was it a white man, not a black man I ate, don't you see?" Boatwright was animated. His eyes were like two searchlights in need of cleaning. Max heard the thrumming of invisible wings in his ears. He changed the position of his head ever so slightly. He did not want to disturb — he didn't know whether it was the tableau: guard, Boatwright and himself — or some delicate balance that could implode in the cell.

"— and we went down to the cellar." Boatwright had been talking rapidly and gesturing sharply with his long hands. "I showed him where I wanted to store the trunk. Then I hit him. He died instantly. I had the tools to take what I needed and got it back upstairs without dropping a spot of blood anywhere. I put it in the top of the ice box. I ate it when I was hungry."

In the corridor the guard shifted. Max wrote with a sense of being far away. He felt lightheaded and he wondered what was the matter with him. Hungry maybe. He looked up at Boatwright who had paused to let him finish. "What parts did you take?"

Boatwright started to talk about something else.

"No, Moses," Max said. "What parts did you take. That was never reported. Genitals? Part of an arm? Part of a leg? Did you cut out a hock for yourself? Did you slice out a steak?" Max felt in some astonishing and circuitous way that he was pleading with Boatwright.

"Do you know what it tasted like?"

"Genitals," Max said, "is that what you got, Moses?"

"He tasted like —" Boatwright's eyes drew down. He pressed his lips together. His small body became one tight knot, frozen motionless, then thawing slowly. The eyes opened, flushed white. The breath was released. The body sagged. Max watched in horror and disgust. "He tasted like," Boatwright continued, panting, "yams with a slab of greasy roast pork, the combination of sweet and heavy richness."

From the pit of his stomach an ugliness gave birth and Max commanded it to die. But it struggled upward. Max struggled with the thing; it was reaching up to his gullet. He choked out one word. "Why?"

"Why? They all ask that."

"And why shouldn't they?" Max said a little too loudly. He closed off his throat. The thing writhed in fury then slid back down where it pulsed hard against Max's belly.

"Look at me," Boatwright said. "Look."

"I am looking."

"But you are not seeing —"

"I'm starting to see, Moses."

"Yes, but you are not seeing *precisely*. I am an abomination. Ugly, black, cutting back on my thoughts so I wouldn't *embarrass* people, being superbly brilliant for the right people. I was born seeing precisely, Mr. Reddick. There *were* times when I chose to. Death, for example. A man would like to pick the way he wants to die. In bed in his sleep, mostly. By my acts I decided how I would die. But those acts had more in them. This world is an illusion, Mr. Reddick, but it can be real. I went prowling on the jungle side of the road where few people ever go because there are things there, crawling, slimy, terrible things that always remind us that down deep we are rotten, stinking beasts. Now, because of what I did, someone will work a little harder to improve the species."

Max remembered the orgasm Boatwright had just had. All of that for just an orgasm? It would be easier to jerk off. But perhaps the orgasm came after the fact of the act. Does he have it every time he relates the story?

"Family?" Max said.

"A mother, father, two sisters and a brother."

"Close?"

"If your father swept the floor at Kodak and you had already done a preliminary dissertation basing a social philosophy on Einstein's theory, what do you think you would have to say to each other?"

"Mother?"

"If you ever want to get rid of all your family, Mr. Reddick, just eat someone."

"I have no family." Max rose and gave Boatwright the rest of his cigarettes. "I'll be coming back," he said, "if it's all right with you."

"Why?"

"It's my job."

"It's not your job," Crockett was saying so loudly that everyone in the converted storefront office immediately became busy, too busy. Mary, the secretary Max had been going with, sat stiff in her red dress glaring at Crockett's back. "You spend too much time with that little cannibal. You gave us the series. You did the man, his family, his education, his crime and why — according to you. What in the hell else do you expect to get from him?"

Max sat down. It was true. He had gone to Rochester, to Boston. He had prowled around the Village and he had visited Boatwright every other day, and had not missed one hour of his four-day trial. Three and a half months had passed and winter was stalking toward New York City. Max's disgust and horror of Boatwright had

59

slowly changed. He did not want to call it pity. Compassion, perhaps. There was nothing else left to get from Boatwright; one week from today he'd be dead. He'd given him books, cigarettes, human company. He was a reporter. He wasn't supposed to feel sorry for anyone, just do his job. "There's just the execution now," Max said to Crockett. "That's all there is."

Crockett glared at him. All right. So Reddick's series had stirred the authorities enough to make them administer a second series of sanity tests to Boatwright — after the tearsheets had been sent to them. Circulation had jumped a few hundred. So? "Are you going?"

"He asked me to come."

Crockett shuffled papers impatiently. "And you're going just because he asked you to?"

Max looked at his cigarette. "Yes."

"Okay, Reddick. That'll wind it up." Crockett watched him rise and walk to Mary's desk. Damn fool, he thought. I don't see no nail holes in his hands or feet.

"Ready?" Max asked Mary. She was a small, brown woman with slight hips but shapely legs. Not much breast.

"In a minute," she said. "I've got to make up. Be right back." She took her purse and walked quickly to the rear of the office. Max felt drained, like a man unable and unwilling to shed an unfaithful wife and who hopes death will resolve the problem, death in sleep, an auto accident, a heart attack. He would feel better next week, after the execution. He wondered what phrases, what look of the eyes, bound him to Boatwright and Boatwright to him.

Mary returned, stuck out her tongue at Crockett's back, put on her coat and they left the office, drifted down Eighth Avenue where they were meeting Harry and Charlotte. Max hadn't spent too much time with Harry in the past weeks. On the way down he debated whether or not they should join them. For one thing, he didn't want to put the damper on what was to be a fun night. Mary wouldn't object. She never objected to anything. That was what was wrong with her. On the other hand, Max wanted desperately to begin living himself again; he wanted to be with people, be smothered by them, people who wanted to live, people who did not seek with uncanny diligence a way to die.

When they were all settled at dinner, Harry said, "I see where your boy gets the chair next week."

"Is it next week?" Charlotte said, tossing her yellow hair with a snap of her sharp chin. "My, how quickly time flies."

"You been invited?" Harry asked, wolfing down some ham hocks and red beans.

"Yes."

"Going?"

"I don't know yet," Max lied. He sensed Mary looking covertly at him.

"Well, there's your next novel," Harry said, nudging Charlotte with his elbow. "The other side of the coin to my last book. Here you have a kid from, for Negroes today, a middle-class family. Good education. Bright. Stinking bright. But black, see. New pressures. New disappointments, frustrations. Hope, but after all, no hope. Right, Max?"

Max gave Harry a wry smile. He thought, Well, listen to old Harry. "You could be right." Inwardly Max drew back, then gave himself to the floor show, the chorus line of fleshy, false-eyelashed brownskins stamping and bucking, shimmying and boogieing to the music, high-kicking. He watched the musicians sitting behind their scarred and battered bandshells in their dark glasses. Most of them had seen better days: some time with Jimmy Lunceford or Duke or Basie; with Andy Kirk and his Clouds of Joy or with Erskine Hawkins. The attraction came on. A man with a phony whip and a sinuous "slave woman" chased each other across the small, dirty floor. They fell panting and slow-moving toward each other. Each time the man, with an excess of facial grimacing lashed forward with the whip, the woman snapped up, rolled her buttocks and moved forward, pelvis in perpetual motion. Finally, to the bray of brass, they collapsed in the center of the floor.

Max looked at Charlotte, then at the couple climbing to their feet for the applause. Charlotte clapped loudly. Harry bent forward toward Charlotte and she stopped. Harry didn't want to be stared at, even in Harlem. The show went on, but Max placed it beyond his thoughts. He would not go to Boatwright's execution. How could Harry have known that he was thinking of writing about Boatwright? Max remembered: they had talked about the relationship between observation and creation. How could he have fooled himself so? He had known enough about the horrors man perpetrated upon his fellows not to be *that* upset about Boatwright. He had been blinded and trapped by his own need to show compassion — which now that Harry had brought it up had been only so deep. He knew enough about Boatwright so that any book about him could almost write itself. Rotten, this business of *seeming* to give of one's self. It was a kind of evil and perhaps Boatwright knew all the time; he was no fool. He could feel pity, play it as a fisherman with a good rod and reel and good wrists, and exact from it precisely what he wanted. One could not only get hung by his own petard, but have it well-knotted in the bargain. Getting under the pretext of giving is as bad as —

Then he had a recognition, that sweet-sharp awareness of having done something before in just the same manner, or having been once again to a place he had visited when . . . ? He turned slowly toward Mary and his thoughts went through her to a day when he had first come to New York and he was driving over the Manhattan Bridge to Brooklyn. In the middle of the bridge a brand-new Hudson Terraplane was stalled. A young man leaned against the opened hood with a book (instructions?) in his hand looking at the motor. Traffic pulled out and went around. Max got lost in Brooklyn, found his way back to Flatbush Avenue, went up to Grand Army Plaza, took the wrong turn to Ocean Avenue. From there he eased his way through heavy traffic back to Eastern Parkway. Driving slowly down the broad Avenue past the library, he saw once more, this time with unbelieving horror, the same young man, the same Hudson Terraplane with the opened hood, the same book. In a fraction of a second, after pulling out to go around, the tableau, immobilized for just another fraction of a second in his rear-view mirror, vanished.

Now Max was looking at Mary. Mary and Moses. Mary, single, middle thirties, always a secretary, always alone, friendless. Which was why, Max knew now, she really enjoyed Charlotte's company, despite the fact that she *talked* about Charlotte. And she liked Harry's company and Max's. Some recognizable part of the world she knew intimately. Mary and Moses. Mary was not pretty nor was she ugly. That uneasy in-between where, with three drinks, one believed her capable of every conceivable act in bed, which she was, Max thought, ordering another round of drinks. Over the rim of his glass, he looked at Mary and she smiled at him, a bit of a pout: Why, darling, did you order another? There's plenty at home. Oh this will be a night, won't it, darling? She stroked him inside one of his thighs and turning directly toward him so she would not be seen by Charlotte or Harry, she flicked the tip of her tongue through slightly parted lips, then smiled once more, and Max let a grin form on his face as he thought, The last time for you too, Mary, with your loneliness, your still, quiet apartment, your Bach and Schoenberg. The last time, Mary with your Shirley Temple theatrics, your Rita Hayworth touches, those yelping little self-created orgasms. Moses, Mary, the Recognition.

"Hey," Harry was saying, "Lunch tomorrow?"

"Lunch," Max said, "sure." Soon after, as the second show was coming on, they left. Harry and Charlotte hailed a cab going one way and Max and Mary another. Max hated the feel of Mary on his arm at times like this. Her body shook, her voice trembled and everything was "Darling." Max hated her because she couldn't wait, and he hated her more because he had pitied her once. He thought of Boatwright when they got in the cab. Ah, man, you saw me coming; it was written all over me, wasn't it? Really, he told himself, I've got to stop this crap.

"Darling?" Mary.

"What?"

She came close. "What are you thinking?"

Goddamn it, they ate you up with their stinking quiet, beaten ways. "Nothing," he said.

Harry's house seemed strangely empty the next day. All the furniture was there, in place. Perhaps it was Harry's demeanor that suggested a change. At first he was hearty and as usual, Harry. He had made the spaghetti and meatballs and bragged about them. But lunchtime was growing to a close; Crockett didn't like for city desk people to be out long if they were not on an assignment. Finally: "Wanda's gone. Been gone four days now."

Max nodded.

"You know why, don't you?"

"Charlotte."

"Yeah, Charlotte. We're getting married."

Max looked up, then speared another meatball and chewed it cautiously.

"Say something," Harry said.

"What do you want me to say?"

"You don't like Charlotte, do you?"

"Jesus, Harry, I don't know her that well. But, are you really getting married?"

"Yeah." Harry looked out the window at the ugly rooftops. "Imagine, me from Mississippi, black, burly, marrying her. For months I've had to examine it alone. Charlotte because she's white? Jesus, Max, in the past five years I've had more fay pussy than black. Once I stumbled on a cute little Negro chick in Chicago and I cried when I held her. I remember (I *was* a little high) watching my tears run down her brown back, a brown back with soft, almost invisible little black hairs."

Max felt the softest of weights descending upon his shoulders; the last part of his meatball went down hard. A phrase from a current song drifted through his mind: *Why are you telling me your secrets . . . ?*

"I want to feel happy, you know, *wild,* but I feel like Sisyphus rolling that goddamn stone." Harry smiled. "I guess I'm worryin' you with my troubles. Okay, you can worry me sometime. Max, do

64

you know the day will come when a black man will not marry a woman he loves *simply* because she's white? Well, not simply, it's not that simple. He'll be afraid to. There'll be too much there, history, all kinds of people, work, play, revenge." Harry threw up his hands. "I'd like you to be the best man."

In that moment when Harry looked at him, Max knew that Harry too was alone and that jolted him. He pictured Harry, when he was not with him, in the center of a crowd at a party talking, gesturing, with every eye following; he pictured Harry practicing lines for Wanda so he could get out to see someone else. He did not picture Harry Ames alone until now.

The weight. It was down now, heavily. The phrase from the song came again: *Why are you telling me your secrets . . . ?*

"Okay," Max said. "Be glad to."

Harry went off to Alabama for his divorce. That was the week Max received the note from Moses Boatwright with a covering letter from the warden at Sing Sing. The note, written the afternoon before the execution said:

Dear Max,
Thanks for coming. There won't be another Negro there. I guess we took advantage of each other, but, they say, all's fair in love and war. To answer your question of some months ago, I took the heart and the genitals, for isn't that what life's all about, clawing the heart and balls out of the other guy? Thanks.

Moses L. Boatwright

Okay, Moses, what was it like to walk out of the corridor and into a room filled with composed white faces? No anger, no revulsion, no hate, Moses, because they *had* you! I see you, Moses, coming out, scanning those rows of faces, scanning again and again because you told yourself there were shadows and maybe you were missing me. Then, Moses, the chair, and you peering out still, growing afraid, the fear gnawing at you like a hundred sewer rats, and the mask, the straps for the legs and wrists, the doohickey for the shaved part of your head. And you knowing now that I wasn't there. Goddamn it, Moses, did you *really* need me then?

The note was burning in his pocket when he met Harry and Charlotte at City Hall where they got their license and were married by a clerk. Max was conscious of people peeking through half-opened doors, of people crowding up to the windows, of a pulsating undercurrent of hatred. Then they walked to the street, released from it, but bearing its stamp as indelibly as the signatures on the license. Behind her veil, Charlotte looked blanched. Harry was somber and then there was a gentleness between them, a sharing of the pain, so keen that Max, then, believed they would last forever, the both of them, together. Harry patted Charlotte's hand which responded by curling around his. Harry looked at Max and shrugged. "Well, the tweeby blee and a ree whee kee . . ."

"Jooby on the sloob pood dooby bloop bah!" Max answered. He turned to watch the streets. Harry and Charlotte were laughing. They drove to their new apartment.

# 8

EN ROUTE TO LEIDEN

MAX let up on the gas and headed the VW toward the side of the road as other cars blasted past him at an ungodly rate of speed. They would be through Leiden and back before he *started* to get there. To hell with them. Where was he now? He felt as though he had been driving all day. *"Sloten,"* a sign read, pointing toward the west. Max pulled up and stopped. His map told him that he was barely outside Amsterdam. He winced; he had not known it would be so uncomfortable. He would have given a fortune for the plush, padded upholstery of an American car. He bumbled around in the tiny car and managed to change the cotton. He took another pill, worked up a glob of saliva and swallowed it. He squeezed outside the car, cracking his knee on the dashboard. He cursed the Germans. Someone had told him that the British had been offered the

66

VW right after the war for British manufacture and consumption, but they, with characteristic arrogance, so different from that of the Germans, more genteel, not quite so personal, less wearing on the nerves, had turned it down, thereby giving the Germans the single springboard they needed to be catapulted back into economic contention.

Max leaned against the car and, sucking deeply of the air, watched the cars rush by. What the British should have done, he mused, was to take the plans for the VW and jam them right up the Germans' asses. Strange, strange about those Germans. Everyone in Europe *said* they hated them. The Germans seemed to feel that hate; they always traveled in groups, as if for protection. Yet, ass-kicked and stomped to death, they had recovered and were far richer already than any three European countries put together. U.S. dollars, baby. Keep that German fox between the Russian wolf and the lambs of Europe and America.

"We cheat them," the European merchants said. "We short-change them or charge them more. We give them the wrong street directions. Oh, yes, we always take advantage of the Germans." But after all these years they hadn't learned, the Europeans, that any kind of exchange, any kind, led one into a subtle kind of obligation; then, inevitably, a deeper, more meaningful one. Now, all over the continent the road signs read, *"Willkommen."*

Max watched a police Porsche blaze up the highway after speeders. He leaned his forehead against the metal of the car. A warm wind played with the tail of his jacket. One could condemn Negroes to dancing and fucking and eternal shiftlessness, he knew, by the same standards he judged the Germans. But the things about Negroes were myths and therefore had resisted proof; they could only be propagandized. But the record of the Germans was clear. Moses, if you had known (you Harvard genius) that the Germans and Turks between them had done in four million Armenians in War I, would you have done what you did? You know, man, the fat was already in the fire, the horror commonplace and no lesson was learned. Naturally with nine million dead (the Jews rarely talked about the three million gypsies and political prisoners) everyone jumped screaming and weeping to their feet. Nine million, n-i-n-e million. Ah, the world got what it deserved. The lessons had been written on the board in big letters thousands of years ago and repeated several times every century since.

*Question:* How many men can I kill if I dig out the Suez Canal?

*Question:* How many men can I kill if I build myself a Great Pyramid?

*Question:* How many men, women and children can we kill if we retake the Holy Land from the heathens? (We'll call it a Crusade.)

*Question:* How many men, women and children can we kill if we establish a slave trade between Africa and the New World?

*Question:* How many men can we kill to make the world safe for democracy?

*Question:* How many men can we kill to make the world safe for communism?

*Answer:* Hundreds, thousands, millions, billions.

And then, we'll start all over again.

No, Moses, your little horror was no match for Hiroshima and history; no match for human lampshades, Zyklon B, cakes of soap made from human fats. (He remembered standing in the Tomb of Destruction in Jerusalem, in the City of David, sandbagged at the top, with Jordanians and Israelis peeking out, with a yarmulke on his head looking at the soap. Yellow it was and big and awkward, like the Octagon soap his mother had used when he was a child; and he had looked at the glass jar with the blue Zyklon B crystals gleaming dully, like wax. Behind him sat the rabbinical students at a little table. They prayed or chanted throughout the days and nights in memory.)

Max opened his eyes and lifted his head from the car. He felt now a strange, steady jubilation. He was going to die. Maybe he would be screaming out of his skin at the end, but he was going to die and he would be out of it; it would touch him no more, none of it, none of the stink, stupidity, hypocrisy. Relief. He placed his

68

back to the car, took out his penis and, gritting his teeth, urinated. His eyes watered. Metastasis. Why couldn't nature in her wisdom have foreseen carcinoma, advanced carcinoma, and put the penis sticking out of the belly button instead of so close to the rectum where those cats sympathized with each other at the slightest provocation? He wiped his eyes and zipped up his pants. He sighed deeply when he was settled in the car.

Further down the road he thought, Jesus! He wished he were well enough to take on Michelle Bouilloux. Just ten minutes! Just one more time! Somebody just once more, Maggie? Tonight? Yeah, sure. He would scream getting it up and just die when all those things inside started winking and blinking and carrying on. Forget it, Max. Close your dirty mind, you've had all the pussy you're going to get. Besides, Michelle was Harry's. But whatever had happened to Charlotte?

# 9

HE HAD come home on leave from Oklahoma, scheduled to report to Fort Huachuca, Arizona, at its conclusion. He was staying with Harry and Charlotte. Harry had not been drafted. His fourth novel was just being published and there was a party. Max had called on people he knew during the day and all had commented on his uniform, how nice he looked in it: Crockett and Mary, who were now lovers, Big Ola Mae who ran the steaming chili house down the street, Sweet Cheeks, the flighty, sassy bartender at the Nearly All Inn. Even Police Sergeant Jenkins, the most evil-looking black man Max had ever met, called to him on 125th Street and, rocking on his heels and looking down at Max, said how nice he looked. Tricky Dick Ricketts, a good friend of Sergeant Jenkins and the policy czar, had even bought Max a drink in the Theresa Bar.

But now Max felt out of place in his uniform. It attracted clichés and platitudes. Except for Zutkin and one or two others, Max knew none of Harry's guests. His circle's gettin' bigger, Max mused, and the contacts better. After the first couple of seemingly unconcerned perusals of the room, Max decided that there was no woman there for him. He hadn't wanted to date someone he knew that first night; that was the Hollywood wartime cliché too. Boy goes home. First night on the town, the old girlfriend or an old girlfriend. Max wanted to enjoy that first night without encumbrances, at least old ones. But he was feeling horny as hell. Zutkin was talking to him, but Max found that he could not keep his mind on what he was saying. Instead, his eyes kept picking up legs, and buttocks and breasts. Finally, he excused himself and went into the kitchen to sneak some of Harry's good whiskey.

Charlotte came in. "So you finally came home. Did you eat out? We saved your dinner."

"I ate, thanks."

She went to the refrigerator for ice. "Does it feel good, Max, to be in the Army?"

"Rotten."

"Are you trying to get out?"

"Too late for that." He shrugged. "What the hell, it may teach me something." Max tried to avoid looking at her. God, she was wholesome! Long legs, hips just right, breasts just large enough to get you on the verge of lockjaw, rosy mouth — damn you, Charlotte! Get the hell out of here. She closed the ice box and bumped him in passing, came back, stood close to him. "Harry's writing well and all? I've been here a whole day almost and haven't said more than three words to him. Out all day, he's been out, and now the party," Max said.

"Harry always writes well. He drives himself, but he thinks he's doing a good job of using the Framework to describe the color conflict instead of the class differences."

Max nodded and sipped his drink. Inevitably Harry would find that the color conflict contained the class conflict too, even among those of the same color. Hell, maybe he knew it already.

"That suit becomes you, Max. I'll bet you're in good shape. Harry's started to get soft around the edges."

"Don't you ride and play tennis anymore?"

"That lasted a month." Charlotte started out of the kitchen. "Got a girl while you're on leave?"

"Not at the moment. Have you any suggestions?"

Charlotte smiled. With deliberate casualness, as though she were measuring, she looked down at Max's pants. "I might."

Max crossed his arms and eased his pelvis forward. "I'm all ears."

"Is that all, Max?" she said and left. Max poured another drink. What was that all about? He returned to the main room; perhaps some additional guests had arrived. He looked around the room. There had to be a chick who wanted to give a little something away, or get something, it didn't matter. Where in the hell was she? Step forward, baby, two paces forward, hut-two! But no one stepped forward, and Max was in a foul mood when Harry came over. Harry looked the same, but his eyes were like hallways with deepening shadows. "You look like hell in that suit, Max. You really didn't try to fight it, did you?"

Knock it, Harry, Max thought, I expected you to. But I'm away from the stink of police blotters and food joints, whores, pimps, the whole ghetto scene; I'm away from the predictable smell, look and acts of people caught in the perpetration of predictable acts, criminal and otherwise. That's good, Harry. In the Army, when they give you your suit, the criminals and faggots, all the bad guys, look just like the good guys, Harry. So far, it's not bad. But Max said aloud, "No, man. I got all my marbles, no syph, and I'm hale and hearty."

"And you can lift ammunition all day. Go, Max."

"Screw you, Harry."

"What do you think you'll be doing, Jack, leading a charge against the Germans? Uh-uh. Don't let that little old suit cloud reality for you; you'll get hurt if you do."

"Listen, Harry, I'm happy for you. New book, so on. I'm jealous and I'm drunk. I don't feel tremendous because I've got this suit on, it's a condition, you see, around the world. But right now, I just want to forget it. I want a girl and that is all. Point me where she is, dear friend, just point me and I'm sure I'll catch the scent and be off and running."

Harry laughed. "You got a filthy mouth when you're drunk, Max. You want a little tonight?"

"Please, ol' Harry. I'm *hurting*." Clowning, Max looked frantically around the room. "I'll take that one and that one and that one and — oh, yes, that one."

"How about a redhead?"

"I looked already, you jive clown. There aren't any."

"When this breaks up, I'm going out to the Island with some of these people. Charlotte's got some business to take care of in the morning, then you can come out with her or stay, as you like. But I'll send a girl to your room, one who thinks you have more talent than me. You got to talk about writing first, you know."

"I don't care as long as she's got 'dat t'ing.' "

"Man, I tell you, she's got 'dat t'ing.' "

"Just like that," Max said, "she'll be there?"

Harry who had started to move away, stopped at Max's touch. "Yes, like that. She likes niggers, Max."

The mock eagerness, the pretended nervousness fled from Max; he felt suddenly drained. "Ah, no, Harry, don't tell me that shit. I don't want to hear it."

Harry took one angry step back toward Max. "You goddamn fool, why do you think she's *here?*"

"No, naw, you're nuts."

"But you haven't even *seen* her yet, Max."

Max was shaking his head.

"Come off it, Max, you want the girl or you want to be righteous?"

"Let's do it like this, Harry, forget it, okay? Let's just forget it, all right?" Max stumbled away to his room. He stripped and piled into bed. You'd like to forget, he thought. Damn them, anyway, the hunted who thought they were the hunters. He thought about the trip to New York.

He was once again on the moving train feeling the sway of the car and, when he stood at the end of the observation car, seeing the twin cold ribbons of steel pouring out swiftly from under his feet, back endlessly back through grades and valleys, around curves. He did not know what time it was when his mind registered too late that someone was in the room. He had a moment of panic, but he remained motionless. There was movement at the foot of the bed, then a weight upon the center of the bed. The fresh sheets slipped and whined. The nude body was cold and hot at the same time. It settled and became motionless also.

"Charlotte, don't be a fool," Max said. "Get out of here." There were no sounds in the house. It seemed that the party had been over a long time.

"Don't be silly, Max."

Without much conviction, Max said, "Suppose Harry came back?"

"Why do you suppose he *went?* To talk literature? To walk along the beach at night listening to the waves crash? To meditate before the fireplace? He's got some woman, some woman who was here tonight. Have you ever had to try to guess which one of your guests is shacking up with your girl? That one who seems so shy? Or that handsome one who carries himself so well? Or that creep over there?"

He felt her turn toward him and he turned away. "But I love him and that's what hurts so. I can't go. Max, I only want to be held, to be loved now. I'm alone. I'm frightened. What happens to us now, Harry and me? We can't quit. It's more than just us, it's the world. They'd think we quit because we are what we are, nothing more. Oh, Max, I'm so miserable. In friendship, do it, in friendship."

Max jerked around. "Look, just lie still. Let's both just lie still and talk and it'll go away. I want to do it. I want badly to make love to you, but I wouldn't be able to look you or Harry in the eye again. Want a cigarette?"

"Yes." Her voice was very small.

He lit a cigarette and passed it to her, then lit one for himself. He visualized his hands touching her. There, there, there, but he remained still. "What happened?"

"I don't know," she said. "At first we just couldn't get enough of each other, couldn't be apart. Then — it didn't take days or weeks or months — just suddenly, he was gone. He was *there,* you know, but he was gone."

"And you?"

"What do you mean?"

"Did you start to go too?"

He turned toward her and saw her cigarette glow brightly, then fade. She exhaled. He took her hand. "You went too, didn't you?"

"Yes, I went."

"And still going?"

"Not as much. There seems to be no point in it."

"Harry know?"

"I don't know. If he does, so what? He's doing the same thing."

"You know it doesn't work that way, Charlotte, not yet."

"Well, I don't suppose he knows. He'd have killed me long ago if he had."

"Feel better now?"

"No, Max, worse. It doesn't go away. Max?"

"Huh?"

"Please."

"Charlotte —"

"Harry wouldn't hesitate one minute if he were in this position with your wife. You know that."

"That's not fair, Charlotte. That's really hitting below the belt."

"Oh, Max, who do you think you are, Joe Louis?"

"Nuts, Charlotte, I'm going to the Y." Max got up and reached for his clothes.

74

"But what would Harry say? He'd think we made love anyway and that you didn't want to look him in the eye as you so poetically put it."

"Tell him anything you want, but you know that when we get through fighting each other, he'll be through with you anyway."

She touched his arm. Max stopped gathering his clothes. "Yes, I know. I'm sorry. Come back to bed, Max. I'll behave. Honest I will."

"But you aren't doing either of us any good by being here, Charlotte."

"One more cigarette, then I'll go."

"You haven't finished that one. Give it to me." Max mashed it out and lit another for her.

"We have to stay together," Charlotte said.

"Aw, hell no, Charlotte, you said after one more —"

She laughed. "I meant Harry and me. We're going to have a child."

"It *is* Harry's?"

"Do you think I'm a fool, Max?"

"Harry know?"

"Strange. I should have had my period two weeks ago. He's been asking me about it. It's too early for a doctor, but I know, and I think Harry knows. I don't think he wanted to be with me because of that. You know, he's a very jealous man, not of me with men, but of my attentions; he wants them, all of them, twenty-four hours a day."

Charlotte had turned on her stomach, propped herself on her elbows. The first suggestion of day touched the window above them. Max could see her profile. Every line in her neck was clean and fast as she looked up at the sky. Her hair was swept long behind her. Good weather for game birds, Max thought. It would be very chilly outside, perhaps a touch of frost, but that would go with the ascent of the sun. And when that sun came fully out, away would go the birds.

She was looking down at him, smiling, he could tell now, and her face and neck and shoulders were all touched with a fuzzy blue-gray tint. "When Harry and I were first married, we would lie awake like this, after making love, and smoke and talk, and agree that we were going down to the Battery and watch the sun come up. We've never done it. All my fault. It always seemed the right thing to do, but somehow, when the alarm went off and Harry jumped up, I'd always tell him that we'd do it the next time. Sometimes he'd go out alone, take a cab somewhere, like 12th Avenue, and walk beneath the highway watching the meat trucks come in and unload. He'd tell me how empty the city was and how the darkness seemed to hang so stubbornly over New Jersey . . ." She stopped. "God, Max, I love that man."

Max had been staring at her face, her shoulders, her breasts. Then he closed his eyes and saw Harry lumbering along 12th Avenue at four in the morning. He felt Charlotte drawing near him, felt first the tantalizing stray hairs on her head as they drifted toward him, then felt the mass of it tumble on his chest, and he lifted his mouth to hers. With one hand he pressed her to him as hard as he could. With the other, he searched for her breasts. She raised herself slightly to give him room. He broke from the kiss whispering desperately, "In friendship, Charlotte." He felt her face melt slowly into a smile and she nodded even as she pressed hard against his mouth.

# 10

BEING in the Army was to be an experience. How much worse could life be? Hadn't you seen it all, all the bad life in Harlem, prowling the alleys and avenues? One must have the confirmation, Max told himself. Armies are like the societies that produce them. Max knew that. But the confrontation with that fact, logically, had to be harsher than the suspicion. The society expected, nay, *de-*

*manded,* that every black soldier within its ranks die as he had lived — segregated, deprived, discriminated against. That is, to die if ever permitted to be in a situation where that was possible. The honor of dying, on the whole, was reserved for white soldiers. And it was clear, as far as Max could see, that the Army was not going to make the mistake it had made during War I: detaching Negro soldiers to fight with the French and accumulate all those *Croix de Guerre.* It had become necessary for the War Department, with help from the French military mission, to issue a paper on 7 August 1918: *Secret Information Concerning Black American Troops.* The usual, official, vicious stuff. Max had seen copies of the report in the homes of Negroes who were veterans of the 369th.

And in one of their homes he had read the history of the division in which he was now a squad leader:

The colors of the regiment first came under fire on August 2, 1867, about 40 miles northeast of Fort Hays, near the Saline River. Company F, patrolling the railroad, was attacked by a band of 300 Indians. The troop comprised two officers and 34 men. The fight lasted six hours. The Troop, badly outnumbered, was in the end forced to retire, after inflicting heavy losses on the hostiles. Captain Armes was wounded, and Sergeant William Christy killed.

The old Tenth Cavalry, the Buffaloes, the 92nd Division. But the echoes of the Indian fighters who never made the history books and were smoothed out in the War Department records, no longer drifted through the hills at Fort Huachuca. While the Division had its beginnings as a Regiment made up of freed slaves docile and fiercely proud of their uniforms, horses and ability to track, it was now composed of bitter, questioning men on the one hand, and on the other, men who never had it so good.

Ten point six percent.

In Army Ground Forces jargon that meant that the number of black men — and officers (how did they handle that in Washington?) — had to reflect the Negro population in America. No more because, after the war, they might disturb the peace (can't let them learn too much about guns) and no less because the Urban League and the National Association wouldn't hear of it.

He was in Louisiana running hot after a Creole redhead when Charlotte and Harry's baby was born, and it was in Louisiana that he chose to write to Harry about Harry's fourth novel, a "Negro novel" the critics had said. Perhaps it was being in the Army, sheltered, that made Max do it. Where else would he have gotten the nerve to discuss Harry Ames's work? The hero of Harry's book was a black Jean Valjean and his loaf of bread which had caused all his troubles was his skin; it was that which would cause him to be hunted down all his life, in the sewers of his existence, and his Javert would be every man who lived within a white skin.

But for all that, the novel wouldn't peel, wouldn't work, and he told Harry so. To his surprise, Harry was not offended and a regular exchange of letters commenced. How did Max like the South? Did being a soldier make the crackers in the nearby towns angrier? Max did not like the South and, yes, the crackers were angry. Beneath all the questions Max suspected that however much he belittled it, Harry envied Max the experience. It was true there was no moral equivalent for war. Max wondered if such an equivalent came to America, would Americans recognize it. At the moment, however, being a man was still tied to being at war.

In the old days you had to walk up to the man you were going to kill, look him in the eye and then spit him upon your sword or spear, if he did not spit you first. Now you took your man out with a call to the Air Force, if the weather was good, or the tanks or Division Artillery. Failing that, you took cover, hoisted your M1 and took your man out at a hundred, a hundred and fifty yards. You only saw his dead face if you were winning and obliged to go forward, past him.

They boarded the transport on a gray, muggy day. They boarded silently, cold eyes mocking the commands of white and Negro officers. And soon the ship, with a gentle rumble, backed from the pier, gulls wheeling and squawking, and the haphazard skyline of

Newport News, Virginia, rose up through the mist. Newport News, which had been as bad as Louisiana, and Louisiana as bad as Arizona, and Arizona as bad as any place in America.

The ship, now in deep waters, began to rumble and wallow, and Max, standing at the fantail, felt the salt water spray blowing in his face. There was not much back there, he thought, and nothing at all where we're going. How in the hell did we get like this? In a time when we fight for the things we can't have. Well, maybe, like Harry said, we'll do the war unloading ships and trucks. That, Max thought, would be survival, but would that be enough?

The 92nd was called a division, but it was not — only elements of a division; thus, from the beginning it was set that its failures would be divisional and its successes regimental. Even as the Buffaloes were making their way inland from the coast of northwest Italy, forcing through the bulwark of the Apennines, word came that the brass were already planning the invasion of France. This war, Max thought when he heard the rumor, was forgotten even before they really got into it. But if the brass had pulled out, the worst was over.

They plodded through the mountains upon which perched sentries of tall black cypress trees, slender, graceful. Then the rains came, drifting steadily down from the gray skies. Mud seemed to grow underfoot. Skirmishes grew in size until they became battles, and ahead, tucked among the mountains and behind the stark, beaten little villages with their somber people, lay the Gustav Line, or what remained of it.

Max did not know the day when his worries, his life, congealed around the ten men in his squad. Beyond that, it was someone else's worry. His ten men were various shades of black or brown, and they were hipsters from Harlem or Southside Chicago, or country boys from the South. The BAR man was from Morehouse College, a dark, thin youngster who had run track there. He reminded Max of Boatwright in many ways. They walked the trails and roads and in their fright and bitterness called out to the staring

79

Italians, "Fuck you, dago," or, "Hello, *paisan;* how does it feel to have niggers save your stinking skin, noble Roman bastard."

They fought those little battles that seemed to have no reason for taking place at all. They just happened. A sniper. That meant his squad was clearing out and he had been left behind to stall the advance. Max calling and pumping his arm hard, "Hurry up, hurry up! We'll kill all those motherfuckers in there!" Slapping the backs of his men as they passed him and deployed. Wondering at how easily the idea of killing came. Or, on other days, the sun breaking through for moments, their breaths steaming up the air, shells bursting about them, Max searching for two of them, the eyes rolling, saying, Please, Sergeant Reddick, don't send me! Max, looking about ever so carefully, and deciding to go around the German position, if they could, and leave the bastards there and let the next guys up take care of themselves. Max wished to God that the next guys up were white.

Man after man was killed and replaced. Another Jones, another Jackson, another George Washington Roosevelt Brown; another Chicago accent, another Alabama accent, and the days humped together. Get up, man, we're movin' out. Overhead, shells flew, sounding like the taffeta skirt of a kootch dancer. And there goes Chicago number three.

By the time they reached the canals, only Barnes, the corporal, remained of the original squad. They followed their tanks. It was quiet then, except for the tanks themselves. Then the air started to convulse. Gigantic clods of dirt V-ed upward before the sound of the guns, the big guns that were supposed to be knocked out, came. Max saw one tank begin to list, and then, with a shudder, it bogged down. He waved his men away from the tank and only saw, fleetingly, the men inside it fighting each other to get out of it. Trapped in the bottom of the bowl through which the canals ran, and confined only to narrow tracks beside them, the tanks took direct hits or, taking evasive action, went into the canals. Steel whistled and whined through the air, punctuating the screams of rage and pain. Another tank hit, and another had its side blown out. Now the tracks were blocked. The infantry raced backward. The tanks tried to back up.

Under the cover of marshbrush, Max waited. Only half obscured by smoke, the massive tanks lay shattered, and those that still moved, moved hopelessly. Nearby a crew sizzled atop a tank like poorly patted hamburger. Look out for your men, he told himself. The men. Then he answered as his knees shook and he could not stop them: Fuck my men, and he cowered against the earth once more. He was bathed in his own sweat and his eyes were blurred. He wanted to move back, but his legs would not support him. The German counterattack began and through the smoke he could see the shape of the helmets; the sight of them had always moved him close to fear, but nothing like now. Small-arms fire wracked across the canals. Finally he stood on shaking legs and ran to the rear with wobbly steps. So many Germans! On they came, deploying around the tanks. But now, in front of Max, the American artillery started up: Ta-wow! Ta-Tawowta-wowtawow! The oncoming Germans hesitated, then began to fade into the distance from which they had come.

There was a court-martial afterward. Who had drawn the maps? Why hadn't the tank captains followed them? Who ordered the tanks to follow so closely behind one another that they could not put up a barrage to protect themselves? The court-martials took place in an old church whose crucifix was bullet-ridden. The ugly word *cowardice* began to seep into the testimony and a chorus was taken up. The Buffaloes were cowards. (Like we said at first, them niggers are cowards, Jude!) A number of Negro officers were broken and stockaded when the verdict, Guilty of Cowardice in the Face of the Enemy, was handed down by the all-white panel of officers.

Shortly after the trial, Max was offered a field commission; there were not so many Negro officers around after that, but he refused it, as did many other soldiers. The white man was determined to undermine the division, but he wasn't going to get too much help from the Negroes in it.

But it was time to move out again. Max gathered Barnes and the new squad around him. He took them away from the other troops; he had made up his mind that he was not talking Army anymore; he was going to talk colored.

He stood in the center of them. The sky had cleared briefly and he could see what they said was Mount Abetone. They were all the same, he mused; you went up and you came down. Even if you were dead and in large pieces, you came down. "All right. You know my name. It's Reddick and I'm the boss. I'm going to tell you like it is." His eyes went over the faces. Young. Hopeful. Afraid. In the background he watched the other squads preparing to move out. "It's like this: the Buffaloes got a bad name. And the white cracker soldiers don't help it none. A lot of our officers been court-martialed. We lost a lot of guys because we weren't trained properly. Now, I've got to tell you that that's because we're colored. No other reason. I want to put it to you straight because if you go out there thinking Uncle Sammy has prepared you as well as he has the white soldiers, you're in trouble; and if you think he cares for you as much as for the white soldiers, you're not in trouble anymore. You're just dead.

"Now it don't matter at all to me how you got here, drafted or volunteered. I'm just trying to tell you how you're going to have to act when the shit sprays the fan. First of all, the Germans think they've got an easy day if they see a black face. I don't know where that started, but you know the white folks back home and maybe even on your flank feel the same goddamn way. You want to live, you shoot first and ask questions later. All you got to tell me is that you saw a white face. Don't tell me what that white face is wearing, because I don't want to know. You get hit and I find you didn't do what I told you, tough titty. You do like I said and I'll break my balls for you." Max shifted his feet. "Now, in case you think that's a little harsh, I might add that we've also lost a few boys in what they'd call little teeny race riots." Max snapped, "If each of you guys looks out for number one — and that means looking out for your buddy — we'll make it all right. What you got to remember is

82

that nobody here likes us; nobody here wanted us. If you've read the papers, you know that our own colonel can't make up his mind about us. And if you haven't read what the General said, I'll tell you: niggers ain't shit. You remember that; otherwise you're going to wind up in some American cemetery laid down in the middle of pretty green hills and your name's going to be in a three-by-five index file — and that place might be segregated. Let's go."

Two days later they approached Castelnuovo. They came down a slight cobbled hill after flushing two snipers and leaving behind one of their nineteen-year-old riflemen. The sniper had been good; he'd drilled the kid right under the nose. There was a house at the bottom of the road. Max sent his men out wide and he came in on it with the BAR man. As they approached the house women ran out, old women and young women who looked old, and all were clad in black. *"Signor, per favore, per favore, bambini . . ."* Some of the women ran into the house and came out with babies, smiling. *"Bambini."*

"Women and kids," Max said.

Barnes said, "Yeah, and the top floor filled with snipers and maybe a machine gun to stitch up our asses when we move on."

Max was finding it harder and harder to work with Barnes. Barnes, if he could help it, never let up the pressure for Max to be as hard and tough as he indicated he was. "All right, search it, but be careful of those people in there."

Barnes moved off without answer, gesturing for the BAR man to join him. This BAR man was short with broad shoulders. Unlike the man from Morehouse who had been killed at Cinquale, this one liked his gun. Max saw Barnes poised at the door. A sudden movement and his foot shot against it. The BAR man was a taut form which seemed to flow and merge with his weapon. It's the helmet that makes him seem so short, Max thought. A few minutes later the BAR man rejoined Max. "Barnes said he'd catch up with us. He thinks he's got him some pussy in there."

I hope the bed's booby-trapped, Max thought, and he led the squad off again, four men on one side of the shattered main street and four on the other. Midway down the street, they heard a double explosion; two grenades, and every man in the column spun, rifles jabbing nervously backward toward the house they'd just left. Smoke gushed from the upper floor. Screaming women raced into the street holding each other or carrying children. Barnes came jogging down the street.

Max did not need to be told what had happened. Pussy no longer meant anything to Barnes. Max did not know how he knew it, but he knew it. Barnes was beyond it. War, inherently bereft of love, breeds hate in its place but even that had a phrase involving love: loving to kill. Max watched the corporal jog up and slow menacingly. He wished he could be as single-minded as Barnes and kill without conscience. He envied Barnes, a product of a deranged society, like Max, like the others, but who had developed his own protection against that society. The corporal slowed about ten paces from Max and panted, "I wasn't takin' no chances. I didn't know what snipers they had hid there. I dumped two grenades upstairs. If there were snipers, they long gone now." Barnes's body was stiff and his arms were stretched out, the one that held his rifle, too, like a gunslinger approaching a deputy in a shoot-out. His face was covered with plaster. His eyes bugged, and when he talked, Max could see the red of his mouth. Behind Barnes Max could see the able-bodied women carrying out the wounded ones; children's cries echoed down the street. Max walked toward Barnes. When he was close, he turned his carbine around and brought the butt down against the corporal's jaw. For just a second Barnes tried to evade the blow, throwing up his arm and backing away. But Max was not to be denied. Barnes went down without a word. He knelt beside the unconscious man and moved him by the jaw. It was broken. "Price," he said, without looking up, "help him along." The column moved forward again.

By the time they arrived at Viareggio, Max was jumpy. They limped into town in the vanguard of the regiment. Max's hemorrhoids had slipped down in the past week and he was shoving them back up with his fingers. When he had done that the pain stopped, until they slipped once more. Two or three times he considered taking himself out and going to the hospital, but each time he did he thought of the squad, still intact save for Barnes and the kid rifleman. This time he was doing a job. As they took the town, fighting from house to house, the Germans started to shell it. The shelling, Max thought, was unusually long. He lay in a hole vomiting and shaking and when the shelling finally lifted and the counterattack failed to materialize, he climbed out of his hole and lay there. No more, he thought. Would to God it had been ammunition-carrying in some safe port, like Salerno, now.

Late in the afternoon Max sat apart from his squad and shivered. He didn't know what was wrong with him. Battle fatigue, maybe, but that only applied to white soldiers. When the Buffaloes complained, they were said to be fucking off. They were at the edge of town awaiting the start north to Massa. From time to time Max could see people moving through the streets huddled over. He watched one fat young woman move slowly back and forth across his vision, a black shawl tied tightly to her head, her black skirts dragging in the dust. An hour passed and the shadows grew longer, but the woman, looking at Max now, still moved back and forth. Maybe, Max thought, what I need is a great big whopping piece of pussy. That might put me back on my feet. He lit a cigarette and extended the pack in the woman's direction. She approached timidly, glancing left and right. Max saw that she was fatter than she had looked in the distance. Everything about her now looked old and worn, except her eyes, which had not dulled, and her kewpie-doll mouth, which had not yet begun to sag.

"*Scusi* . . ."

Roughly Max thrust the cigarettes at her. "*Amore.* Love. We make-a da love, hah, fatso?"

"*Avete da mangiare, signore?*" Her voice was very small and it shook.

Probably, Max thought, the first time she ever looked at a Negro without laughing her fat can off. "Speak English, bitch," Max grumbled. "*Amore, amore!*"

She took two cigarettes and tucked them somewhere in her skirts. *"Amore?"* she said, and her face fell in shame and anxiety. Someone had told her that the *soldati neri americani* were kinder than the *soldati bianchi americani* who were almost as bad as the Germans, but now . . .

*"Amore,* baby. Pussy. Fucka-fuck."

The woman took a deep breath. *"Quanto pagerà?"* She stared at the ground.

"What? Oh, hell," Max said. "Five bucks. Pussy, five bucks."

*"Come?"*

"Five bucks!" Max was close to shouting with frustration. Then he remembered. *"Dollari. Dollari."* He held up five fingers, inspired by her understanding of *"dollari."*

*"Cinque dollari?"* she said, knitting her brows. The people might overlook it now, but later, in her old age, they might point her out as she walked to market.

Max reached into a pocket and showed her the money. The woman nodded. "Okay, Joe. Okay." Max got to his feet and walked beside the woman who now had pulled her shawl far over her face. Max smiled. Let her be ashamed. She needs the money, I need the pussy. Capitalism in action. They went into an abandoned house and Max watched her look carefully around. She gave Max one worried look; she wondered if he would pay after. She spread two of her skirts on the floor then got down heavily on her knees, turned on her back and closed her eyes, and placed one of her arms over her stomach. Max looked from the piles of human feces in the corners to the holes in her black stockings. He approached her and pulled up her skirt. Her eyes shot open in fear and she blinked them and tried to smile. *"Come ti chiami?"* she asked. Perhaps that would make it easier, if she knew his name; there was too much distance, too much coldness like this; she felt like an ordinary *prostitua,* which she wasn't. She was only hungry. Laboriously she moved her heavy body with each tug at her clothes.

"What?" Max was busy at her clothes.

86

*"Tuo nome?"* the woman said. She didn't know whether to keep her eyes open or closed now.

*"Nome?"* Max said. "Name, oh, name. Aw, what the hell do you care," he grunted, unbuttoning his pants and pushing them partway down. "Just call me Joe. JOE!"

Hurt, the woman turned her head and closed her eyes. Why did he have to be so cruel? He didn't look like a cruel man. Wars, what they did to men . . . and to women. She put her hands over her eyes and bit her lower lip as the black American plunged brutally into her.

When he was finished, the woman covered herself hurriedly. With head averted, she waited until Max had pulled up his pants, then took the bills and said quietly, *"Grazie."* she stood to fasten on her skirts.

Max was thinking about his penis. It hurts, he thought. Jesus. Instant clap? Instant syph? Wow, it hurts. He turned to urinate and the woman, about to leave, saw. *"Sangue!"* she hissed and, holding her stomach as if it had been polluted, ran out of the building. Jesus, Max thought, watching the blood come out in a dark ugly stream. Blood, how about that? I've got jaundice. Jaundice? Jaundice!

Joy! He leaped about in the building shouting, YEAH, REET!" Now he was out of it. All the armies in Italy could go on, but he was out of it now, out of the mud and cold, the mountains. He replaced his helmet and snatched his carbine and ran out of the building, pumping his arm up and down in a frenzied "forward" signal. He ran a few steps then bounded into the air shouting, "CALDONIA, CALDONIA, WHAT MAKES YOUR BIG HEAD SO HARD? MOPPPP!" Breathless, he came across his squad and each man in it rose, cautiously thinking, Reddick's had it; he's cracked up. "Look, you bastards," Max cried. He took out his penis and urinated for them. "See that? That's blood. Jaundice. I'm out of this shit, make it on your own." He took off his helmet and spinning around and around like a hammer thrower, sent it whining off the wall of a house. That was the ritual for the man wounded enough to get out of it for good.

I'll have them do the hemorrhoids too, Max thought, bouncing along the road to catch a rearward-going jeep or truck. When one stopped for him, Max turned back to the town. "CIAO MOTHER-FUCKERS, ARRIVEDERCI!" The jeep groaned through the mountains which were now greening with spring and turning purple with the setting sun. Max didn't mind that he had walked through most of them, didn't mind at all. Now the mountains were pretty, even beautiful.

# 11

MAX LED the way and from time to time he paused and looked across the valley at the other mountains. He thought of Italy, spring, before the end, 1945. Now it was autumn, late autumn, 1946, and he and Harry Ames were trudging over a mountain in the Catskills. The deer season had opened only the day before. Max paused and went down on one knee, the 30.30 perpendicular to his body. Harry came up and knelt beside him and started fumbling for cigarettes. "Don't smoke yet," Max said. Harry stopped rustling with the cigarettes, somewhat resentfully. Something had changed between them and Max knew it was the war.

"God," Max said, "smell that air." He lifted his nose and caught the wind bearing the smells of the vast coniferous forests past them, downhill. And the earth had its own scent, rich, sturdy. Max took a pine needle and chewed it. Down in the valley, still covered with the morning frost, they heard shots. They had planned to use the high trails because there were so many hunters down below. Perhaps they'd run the deer back up. For a moment suspended somewhere in time, Max listened for the sound of mortars, for the howl of artillery. None came and he smiled to himself. It was goddamn good to be alive. *Good.* Harry nudged him and pointed off to the left. A buck was shouldering his way through the forest. He stopped and looked around, tested the air and withdrew. Neither Max nor Harry had moved. They would see just what the buck would bring back with him, thinking the coast was clear. Quietly Max and Harry spread out on their stomachs and waited.

Max felt as if he could sleep. He was at peace. In four months he had written a novel complete with rewrites and it had been sold. He had already begun another. And Harry had just published another novel. It seemed to be going well with him and Charlotte now. (Yes, it had seemed so, then.) There was nothing quite like success, American Negro writer Harry Ames, nothing quite like it. It means that you stare at the cops just as long as they stare at you and a host of other things, right, Harry?

For Max, his own novel had begun new seepages in the old well; there was something down there, something after all. His book was about the war, of course, about Negro soldiers in Italy going up the mountains and down the mountains; it was about Cinquale, Grosseto, Viareggio. In the novel the fat woman became a young, almost innocent farm girl with whom the hero of the novel, a corporal, had fallen in love. The novel ended with white MP's catching the corporal and the girl in a barn and killing them and covering them with hay and horse manure.

"Great!" Max's editor had screamed. "Daring. Honest. Dynamic . . ." All the words and phrases that would be sent to echo in his ears for all the years he would be writing. Some of the words would fall into disuse, then be miraculously resurrected, and each time, for a while, they would have not a new, but at least a different meaning until the literary ferris wheel took them underneath again. Max didn't care except that he could repeat them to Lillian Patch, the girl he loved.

It happened in spring, two months after his discharge from Dix, while he was still living at the Y. He would look out the window of his room, straining to see the street below, but he could only see a small line of sidewalk across the street where the Y Annex was.

But looking to the west he could see the white and gray buildings of City College. Then one day, when he was pleased with his work, he hurled a silent challenge at the City College buildings: I will walk to where you are and see if I can see my room from there. He never made it because of Lillian Patch. He followed her from Seventh Avenue, up the sheer rock steps to Morningside Heights to a drugstore on the corner of Broadway and 145th Street. He followed her, marveling; she fit so well with the day. She was young and lithe and she smiled. Mostly it was her posture. Loose it was, as a drifting on the wind, and yet there was a confident control that said, I know my body. In front of the drugstore he pulled abreast of her and found himself strangely tongue-tied. She did not pull away or scowl as Manhattan women usually do. Instead a half-smile came to her face, which was small with the cheekbones riding high along the sides. And when she smiled, the brown of her eyes, a kind of puce, was transformed into brown velvet, the shimmer of them deep. He looked down at her; she was small and that surprised him; she had seemed to have great height. Her skin was as the wet sand, brown, yet suggesting gold.

"I followed you, you see. It was spring — it's spring and it was too lovely to stay in and I came out and saw — you . . ." He told himself, Something is happening, something is *happening*. "Well," he tried to beat himself back, "a fine thing like you walkin' all alone on such a mellow day, and I —" He held up his hands then, and said, "I followed you. I didn't see your face until now. I want to be with you." He flinched from his own words. Seldom had he felt so vulnerable.

"What's your name?" she said.

Hell, he thought, voice too, oh, God, why didn't you let me stay in the Y?

"Max," he said almost too eagerly.

"Max," she said laughing, "are you part Jewish or something?"

"No, all spook, one hundred percent spook. I think."

"I'm Lillian. I have never been followed so far. One or two blocks, you know with the usual — 'shake it but don't break it, baby,' comments. Sometimes they make me feel good. Would you buy me a Coke?"

"Sure," Max said, charging into the drugstore, biting his tongue to keep from saying, I'll buy you *any*thing, any*thing*. He drank three Cokes, she drank one. "You have a last name? Mine's Patch."

"Reddick."

"Are you a veteran?"

"I'm afraid so. Why?"

"I don't know."

"Like veterans?" Some of these broads *still* see a uniform on every vet.

"Not particularly. Don't dislike them either, Max?"

Max almost broke his back turning around; something about her tone of voice. But she said, "Never mind. I don't want to know."

"What?"

"What you do."

"Oh."

"I'm a teacher, you see. Nosey."

"It's all right. Can we walk some more?"

"I live just down the block, but maybe we can sit in the park for a while."

On the way down to the park, Max kept thinking, I ain't never been in love before, if this is what it feels like. Good God! Max, baby! Lookit you! He wanted to touch her arm as they went down the steep hill, but he merely looked and smiled, as she did. She pointed to her home when they passed it; she lived with her parents. They were getting old now and she was the only child and she didn't want to leave them. She had the entire second floor to herself. When, after talking in the park for an hour, she said she had to go home, he said, "But when will I see you again?"

[Now, still waiting for the buck to reappear, he remembered how she had turned ever so slowly to look at the Palisades, then back to him, saying sprightly] "How's about now, for dinner?" They held hands going back to the house, resigned, overwhelmed, aware of all the Hollywood Boy-Meets-Girl movies, American

Love riddled with clichés: eyes, hands, facial expressions, the lot, and after meeting her folks, they went upstairs to her apartment (her mother did the dishes, she was a working girl), talked some more, with long, long pauses in between and many exchanges of the eyes until he simply stood up, gently holding her hand and pulled her to him. There was no resistance, and it rode them down, that thing, swept them up and left them in a silence in which they held each other desperately as if afraid to be blown away. No, Max said to himself. No, no. "What is it?" she asked.

"I am talking to this real dumb guy, Max Reddick," he said.

"About what?"

"I'm telling him, 'No, no, it can't be.' "

Lillian smiled. "And what is that real dumb guy answering?"

"You really want to know?"

"Of course."

"He's answering, crudely because he is crude, 'You're a boom-boom liar, it is *too!*' "

Later Max had run up the hill to Broadway singing at the top of his voice, shimmying when he came to a stop, one of his hands held across his stomach as he shuffled across the sidewalk.

"What in the hell are you laughing about?" Harry asked. "You woke me up. Are you coming loose upstairs?"

Before Max could tell Harry about Lillian, there came a soft, uneven drumming along the forest floor, and even as they turned to watch the buck break out of the brush where it had vanished before, adrenaline pumping suddenly through their bodies, their rifles swinging up, they sighted. Perhaps frightened by someone or something on the lower trails, the deer, his head full of points, bounded clear of the brush.

But Harry Ames, too long away from a rifle and the woods, hesitated for just the small part of a second as he started to lead the deer in his sights. The deer seemed ludicrously slow, but it was in its second bound now, floating lean, long and brown against the backdrop of tree and sky. The instinct of the city man, at once envious and frightened of the abrupt display of animal grace, immeasurably distraught at the sudden gift of power (gun at the shoulder, animal in the sights), made Harry pause a little too long. His resentment of Max was like a spurt of acid. He took in Max leading the deer at the height of its second bound, heard his rifle crack sharply and echo swiftly over the mountain, saw Max's shoulder snap back from the kick of the gun, and saw life go out of the buck as it stretched its legs to land and take off again in another bound. In the middle of these observations, Harry fired too, but he knew he had fired late and had missed.

Some of the buck's antlers had dug into the ground, raking up a line of dead leaves. The shot had been clean. The buck was dead when it came down. They paused a moment and stared at the animal. "Goddamn," Harry found himself whispering. "Man, ain't you a bitch?" Enviously he watched Max pull the buck over to see where the shot had hit. Had to be the heart, had to be. It was.

"Germans must have caught hell," Harry said. "Big one. Meat's going to be a little tough."

"Parboil it first," Max said. "Get some of the taste out, soften it up."

There are some people, Max was thinking, with whom you can share elation because they feel it with you. Harry Ames was not one of those. Max underplayed. "Sure was lucky, Harry. Right in the heart. I thought we'd have to finish it off when we got up close." "We" — wouldn't that help make it all right? The "we" once more. "Now we've got enough venison to last for a little while."

"Yeah, ain't we," Harry said, suddenly mildly disgusted in the presence of death. Max also noticed but said nothing. Death disgusted him too. It was like looking at a snake and being repelled, for it reminded you where you came from and in some electrically quick way, how long it took to come from there and how horrible it had been, evolving.

In silence they secured a sturdy limb and tied the deer's feet to it; they would have to struggle with the 175 pounds of dead weight until they reached a trail. Then, maybe, they could get help from a couple of guys on their way back to the lodge.

93

As they struggled through the brush, Harry began to emerge from his reflections on the kill. "Max, you sure shot the hell outa this cat! Whoooee!" Harry was in front. He turned back. "I guess I knew you would, too. Hey! Do you remember that time you stayed with us on furlough, and I had just published *Though I Be Black?*"

"The party and that color-freak girl?"

"Yeah, that time."

Max stared at the dead deer. "I remember."

"Well, that was the last time I went hunting. I told you I was going to the Island, well, I did, but to hunt bird. Hell, I didn't want you to come because I knew you would show everybody up — mostly me. None of us got anything, Zutkin, me, whoever was with us, so we weren't doing too much talking when you and Charlotte got there, only drinking."

Max gave the pole a little jerk. "Didn't you even see anything?"

Harry was panting now. Just ahead some trails met. They'd wait there and beg a little help; it was a good three-quarters of a mile to the lodge. "That's just it," Harry said. "We did. Birds all over the place and we couldn't hit shit. You would have had the limit in an hour."

"I was tired anyway," Max said, sitting at the edge of one of the trails. "Coming all the way in from Fort Sill. Beat. I couldn't have walked a half-mile without falling on my face."

"I'll bet," Harry said, looking down the trail. Max slid a quick look at him. Max wanted to find out if Charlotte had known Harry was going hunting. Oh, you bitch, Max thought, you rotten stinking bitch. Saw me coming too. *But how?*

"Of course, Charlotte laughed her ass off when you got there. Took me off in a corner and really gave me the old 'I told you so.' " Harry turned toward Max and grinned. "The best I could do was give her hell for making such rotten sandwiches and filling my flask with water instead of brandy. But she knew what she was doing. She hadn't wanted me to go." Max watched Harry stare thoughtfully at the antlers on the deer.

On an impulse, which he understood as soon as he began speak-

94

ing, Max said, "Hey, man, I've got a girl, the most bee-utiful, the most fascinating, the most —"

Harry swung round once more, smiling. "So that's why you're finally moving out of the Y? Hard sneakin' them in there with all those faggots on the desk downstairs. They've got the eyes of eagles. She white or colored?"

"Colored."

"Go, Max!"

"Lillian Patch. Teacher. You'll meet her when we have this venison dinner at your place."

"Are you trying to tell me, Max, that this is the thing?"

Max watched four men coming up the trail, their rifles slung or held in that manner that tells you right away that they were through for the day, and he felt that he was blushing. "You're right!" Max said.

"Well, go, Max go," Harry repeated. Then they both rose to greet the other men. Back at the lodge they would hang the deer by his hind feet and dress it.


"Ga-ood God!" Harry said, pulling Max away from where Lillian and Charlotte were chatting. "Where did you find *that?*" Now, speaking rapidly, Harry said, "I tell you, Max, if she wasn't yours — oh, Lordie Lord — fweepis fwap and ditty-dit-dat!"

Max knew that what Harry was saying was this: I don't give a damn if she's yours or not! Given the chance, baby, given the chance . . .

And Max was suddenly angry, angry at Harry, angry at Charlotte, whose eyes, he could see, were measuring Lillian and doing something else as well. It was the way women were, he guessed, but wasn't she somehow telling Lillian *some*thing? Telling her in that way women have — the eyes (the ever-so-studied, so possessive glance that told the other woman that you *knew,* yes, positively knew what those pants contained, how the arms fit and all), the voice that did things when it should have done nothing or, on the other hand, did nothing when it should have done something. Almost like a double exposure, Max seemed to see Charlotte again holding Harry's head in her lap at Wading River on the day he met Ames. He had seen something then. How much was there to see?

There came a peal of laughter from Lillian and suddenly, as though coming out of a fever, Max dismissed most of his recent thoughts. Lillian was not laughing with Charlotte so much as *at* her. Neither Harry nor Charlotte had seemed to mind Mary from the *Democrat* office, or those others. After all, a man had to get his nuts off. (And after all, in Harlem there was untold prestige in getting as much pussy as possible, in having cats whisper to one another as you passed: That cat is a *Cocksman's* Cocksman!") But now, there was something different with Harry and Charlotte, a kind of hostility Max felt floating around the table. Then he knew what it was, at least on Charlotte's part. The girl he should have fallen in love with should have been white. His loving Lillian was a rejection of their marriage. He was a traitor. Where was his courage to face the world with a white wife and say to it: Screw you, Jack!

("— don't you, Max, don't you?")

("I guess so. Logical.") That bitch, Charlotte, Max was thinking while Harry went on talking after Max had thrown out an answer calculated to show that he was still with him. Harry was talking about Africa, a continent where freedom was going to break out with a bang. The British, French and Portuguese were going to pack up and go home. The United Nations might be a good thing, if it avoided the trap the League of Nations had fallen into. "Africa and Asia," Harry said. "The other side of the globe, that's where things are going to be happening, and I want to be there when they do. Here, it's the same. Look what they did to Robeson in Peekskill; that colored vet whose eyes they gouged out down home. Nothing's changed."

"But we should hope for a change for the better," Lillian said with such confidence that it startled Max.

Harry pushed back his chair. "Why?"

Lillian opened her mouth, pursed it, relaxed. This man would

96

not be argued with. She felt something akin to distaste for Harry and Charlotte. She laughed. Max smiled. Harry chuckled but he was puzzled. Charlotte flashed a look at him, bent her head and played with the silver.

Max and Harry moved into the living room. Max could never help looking at the bookshelves and particularly the one where Harry's books stood. Max always counted them. Charlotte and Lillian were in the kitchen, cleaning up. Max had liked it that Lillian had not volunteered to help, but Charlotte had not been above asking for it. Then Lillian had jumped up brightly. "Oh yes, of course!"

"I was talking with a man from Nigeria," Harry went on, still talking about Africa. "He figures that at the outside, they should be rid of England in ten years. Can you imagine that? A free Africa. Big, rich, three hundred million people, untold wealth. Can't you see what will have to happen to the white man's politics? Africa, Max, I tell you, that's the only frontier left on the globe. Keep it in mind. I know all those stories the white folks have told us for years. But, listen, if white folks took so much time to tell us how bad and silly and heathen it is, then it can't be so bad. What have they ever told us that was of any use?"

Africa. The continent had been like something you knew you had to buy or see or go to, but always forgot. The Black Is Best groups were always talking about it. Then there were the J. A. Rogers books and Max had read them many times, with tremendous doubt and with humor. The Africans had kings and princes and great armies and wealth and culture, Rogers said. Maybe so. The books in the Schomburg Collection up on 135th Street near Lenox also said as much. The Collection was some place. Every Negro feeling the toe of the world halfway up his ass could duck in there and read about how great Africa was and how great black people in general were, but few had done it. The white man's hate-self-serum had created a hard stale rind of disbelief.

But it tantalized, Africa. Which was real, Mungo Park's or René Maran's? Garvey's vision of it or Stanley's dollar-propelled race through it? There were bright spots. The Fuzzy-Wuzzys, the Mahdi kicking the stuff out of the British in the Anglo-Egyptian Sudan, the Ethiopians cutting the balls off the Italians at Adowa, the Zulus cutting up the British.

But why think of it in terms of wars? Why? Because that's just the way the white folks spelled it out. Francis X. Bushman, Glenn Morris, Johnny Weissmuller, Lex Barker, all kicking the natural pure-dee apeshit out of the natives. Go, Tarzan, just don't let them Zulus (Negro actors who ate every time they made a Tarzan movie) catch you with your codpiece down. Or Jane. Maybe you'd better put Boy in a safe place too. You know how them niggers are. Not really like Gunga Din at all.

"Damn it, let's go there some time," Harry said.

"Sure, why not?" They were always planning to do things together, but at the last moment, something happened. Might not be a bad idea, Africa.

But now he was walking through upper Manhattan with Lillian. They came out of the subway at 116th Street, so different from Washington Square Park, the Village. They couldn't even see downtown Manhattan; it was hidden by the trees in Central Park. Up on 145th Street, Max knew, you could stand on a corner and see all the way downtown or, at least, that rigid, square spire, the Empire State Building. One and the same. Uptown where they were, life still flooded the streets. Horse-drawn junk wagons, their drivers asleep, clip-clopped past them. The new sounds drifted out of Minton's, new sounds that no one could dance to anymore. They called the music rebop or bebop and it was played by musicians with crazy names like Monk, Bird, Diz, Fats, Sweets, Little Jazz. These were the streets that belonged to Sugar Ray, the Cutie, The Unscarred, and to a fat, balding Joe Louis and a bullet-headed Jersey Joe Walcott. The streets belonged also to Wynonie Blues Harris whose voice was blasting into the streets from a loudspeaker fastened to the front of a record shop. The double-deck buses, still vibrating the dust of Fifth Avenue, groaned up Seventh Avenue. Hipsters, their legs going loose, their shoulders held stiffly, passed from the shadows to the lights of chili joints, barbecue joints and bars. At the bars they would drink with their left hands, and the other customers would mark them for bad. Max and Lillian sauntered past storefront churches and spired churches, past cops glad that fall had come to cool the blood of the inhabitants. On the corners men stood loudly exchanging jokes and gossip. And the hustlers went by, little ones, big ones, ugly ones, attractive ones, with big tits and little tits, with big butts and no butts at all, and each of them seemed to say with their stride, I got the best that's going. The muscatel smell lingered on corners like a live thing. Ghetto. The people who lived south of Central Park even concealed their lights behind the curtain of trees to avoid exciting the natives. (Watch that codpiece, Tar-zan.) Off in an alley somewhere, Max bet, someone, frustrated and drunk with whiskey and rage at Mister Charlie (although he wouldn't be aware of it; he would lie to himself) was making a pincushion of a man in his own color-image, another Sambo. A man had to strike out. Not many men struck at the right places. Black men at any rate. They moved down the street, past Big Ola Mae's chili house. Max saw Sergeant Jenkins gulping his free bowl of chili. Jenkins liked to work nights; they concealed his sadism. "Nuthin' I like better'n beatin' a bad nigger's head," he often said. They turned off the street at the Nearly All Inn for one for the road they still had to make.

He sat across the table from Lillian and let his eyes tell her that he loved her. Insane when you thought of many animals, their love and hate, the swift couplings and even swifter departures. This thing men have, he thought, this love and loving, how unnatural! What causes it, fear? Possession, like the animals, but bound by men's laws which have also been worse than animal laws. No. Not as good. The laws of man condemned you to repeat over and over the rituals of love and loving to the death. Love. Marriage. A thing for the poor (natives also) to keep them happy, while kings screwed themselves to death or *got* screwed to death, but while all this was going on, there always being more poor than rich people, the attitudes and habits, the arts and language overtook the rich in their clappy beds and shitty castles and made marriage, and love, the human condition. But is the Bible first concerned with man-woman love? No. Stop fighting. Did Rameses ever order a statue of his love? No. Me, me, me. Ever go into a cave and see a prehistoric drawing of a man and woman, boy and girl in the postures of love? No. Animals, yet, eating stuff. Did the White Lady of Brandberg on that cave wall in Southwest Africa allow herself to be discovered in a compromising position? No. She was out hunting, surrounded by hunters and Springbok, looking for that eating stuff again. So what? Lillian, I love you.

They finished the drink and walked once more. Max was still thinking of love when she spoke. The heart, they used it for everything: courage, guts, love. ("Have you ever slept with Charlotte?")

*Floomp,* the heart again. Nothing in the head, just a new set of dials turned on. She knows something, Max thought. No, she's guessed something, and he thought once more of how Charlotte had been at dinner. ("No, why do you ask that?")

"Oh, I just wondered. I'm not jealous."

He heard her clearly now, all thoughts of love whisked away in favor of defending himself. Stoutly. "That's a hell of a thing to be thinking about."

"I'm sorry then."

"What if I'd said yes?"

"I didn't expect you would, Max."

They both sighed with relief when they entered his apartment. It had gotten chilly and too much walking when you are in love can be exhausting. Lillian opened the nightcase she had brought before they had gone to Harry's and pulled out a gown. She was going, she had told her parents, to visit a friend in New Rochelle for the weekend. She looked at the bag and said aloud, "They know. Most people know things. All they want is a lie plausible enough to believe."

"Stop it," Max said. She was, of course, referring to her earlier question about Charlotte. He put his head in her lap. She said, "It was before I met you. I don't care if you did. She is nice and not nice. Harry —"

Max sat up. "What about Harry?"

Lillian put the gown down and got up to make drinks. "Does he really make a living writing?"

"Yes."

"But he's written more books than you."

"Yes, he's also a little older. Lillian, what is it?"

"Nothing, here." She gave him his drink.

"Don't do that."

"What?"

"Start something and not finish it."

"Sorry."

"Go on."

"With what? Really, there's nothing."

"Sure?"

"Yes."

Max gulped his drink. "Okay. One more, then to bed."

Lillian watched him from the chair. She was so quiet that Max turned. "Okay, now what?"

She laughed and went to him, holding him tightly. "Ah, well. Honey?"

"Tell me what."

"I think I love you very much." She didn't look at him.

It was sometime during the far side of the night. Both had heard and seen separately something in black (was it?), prancing at the top of a hill, ready to gallop down. Max turned first. Lillian was there in her sleep, refusing to wake completely, enveloped in that millennia-old dream of women to be taken, to be had; and she was warm when Max slipped the gown from her and the nipples of her breasts grew taut and hard; her skin rippled and her light bones slipped under it. Max came at her and his dream was old too, the dream of men to take (and therefore be free, animal-like, of the consequences), and to match the mock submission he created a mock rage and they stroked and kissed on the knife edge of capture and theft. And they knew each of them, the reality and fantasy of what they were doing and their movements were gentle, as if with great sorrow. Even the bed gave back no sound. After, they held each other; their orgasms had been long and sweet and thorough, as if to signify that that narrow place between what was real and what was not was the best place after all.

Max woke as the first gray sifted through the room. "Lillian," he said, pushing her gently. "Lillian. Let's get married, okay? Okay, Lillian?"

She pushed herself up on her elbows. "Could we live on your writing?" Max recoiled. He had some money in the bank from the folks' house. He hadn't made a dime on his first novel, but had got good money as an advance for his current one, $750. He had socked away his mustering-out pay and was a member in good standing of the 52-20 club, and had disability coming. But. "I don't know. Some of it would be a little rough, but not all of it."

Lillian hated this; she didn't look at him. She remembered the conversation she had had with her parents. "He's a writer," she had told them.

"Yes," her father had said, "but where does he *work?*"

"Couldn't you write nights and work?" Her voice was a little plaintive and she hated it. The stories of writers were romantic and all, but you couldn't eat romance, that kind, sitting around in garrets and drinking Chianti. Besides, who ever heard of a Negro writer making money? The Ames home wasn't so great. The dishes were chipped, the chairs didn't match, the kid was a mess. What happened when people stopped being nice to Harry Ames, where did they go from there? They didn't even teach English very well where Lillian had gone to school, just so some nut wouldn't get the idea that he wanted to be a writer. Now she glanced at Max. "I've gone and spoiled it, haven't I?" She took his hand.

"No," he said. "I'm so damned full now. I'd hate to lose everything working. I feel free for the first time in my life. What would there be besides the *Democrat?* There aren't that many jobs downtown; things haven't changed that much, Lillian."

"You could —" she knew she shouldn't be doing this — "teach, or do casework . . ."

"And if I don't?"

"Then we'll have to work something out."

Max slumped down into the bed. There were always choices. What choice was there to make? He wanted her. Already it hurt to think of not having her. But Jesus, where in the hell was there a job in New York City for him? Madison Avenue? Park Row? Teaching? Social work, who wanted to do that? That got you right next to *them* again, the ones who hurt so damned much that they spilled over on you, like thick sap from a tree in spring. Get a job? Man, wasn't that like the American dream? Boy meets girl, gets good job and everything's all reet. "Wow, honey," he said aloud.

Lillian lay on her side of the bed staring at the wall. The black thing she had seen on the hill just before they made love, moved a little, downhill. Now Lillian knew what Charlotte and Harry had seen: a middle-class Negro girl whose father was a bank janitor and whose mother worked for rich theater people on Central Park West. All right. So what? Did that mean that she could ignore security, the crushing desire to have it? Along with love, and she loved Max. But he was black. Of course he was black, but Negro men, they had a way of starting out with a bang, with the long, long dream, but ending with less than a whisper, so beaten were they simply because they had dared to dream in the first place. Max, her Max, was a man with dreams, but he had to see the hard reality of the present. You couldn't eat dreams; they wouldn't even put cheap, gaudy furniture from the 125th Street stores into your home. If you dreamed too much you got hurt. In her classes she could look out on the children and knew that killers were already stalking their dreams. How had Max managed to elude the killers? Suppose Max said no. He wouldn't say no; he couldn't say no, and she knew it as well as he did. Charlotte had seen all this, the whore, white whore.

Max twisted in the sheets. In the final analysis there is always something someone wants. Lillian was special because she never took from him the way others did when they saw him coming; she had asked for nothing, until now. Now what she was asking for might be the most important thing of all and he had no choice but to give it to her.

# 12

WINTER. Harry Ames stared out the front window at the bleak street. How did he really feel about winter? He tried to bring his thoughts back to work, but he was waiting with foolish anticipation for Max to stop by. He usually did when he was finished with his rounds. Harry looked down at his shoes and they gave him an idea. He'd take all his shoes out of the closet and polish them. Charlotte's too. All the time he'd be thinking about the unfinished paragraph still in the typewriter. Yes, he would polish shoes. Charlotte would be proud of him.

When he had finished the shoes he returned to the typewriter, snappily pulled up his chair, reread the paragraph which paused at a comma. Listlessly his eyes drifted to the pencils on his table. Jesus! They needed sharpening. How come he hadn't seen that before? He took out the five-and-dime sharpener and then, one by one, with the utmost care, he sharpened the pencils. Where the hell was Max?

The *New York Times Book Review* lay under some paper, and Harry picked that up and scanned it again, frowning at the picture of a young Negro novelist whom he had never heard of. It gave him a jolt that the review was what they call "a rave." He looked at the picture of the plump novelist. Fat face, eyes like slits. Hmmm. Have to get the book, see what this young boy is putting down. Could be a challenger to the Ames prestige. Them white folks: divide and conquer or, divide and pay less money for talent because everyone's scufflin' to get there and takin' pennies for the project.

104

Too bad, he continued thinking, that the artists were so terribly distrusted by the Party. The Party people never understood what was what about color in America and never understood painters and writers and musicians, only the workers, and as soon as the workers got theirs, to hell with everything. Labor (workers) was going to be one of the Fattest Cats, Harry guessed, when the smoke of the war finally blew over. It had had the foot way inside the door even when the war broke out. The worst kind of tyrant was the one who once had been a victim.

People Harry had known in the Party were complaining these days about the "Iron Curtain." That Churchill sure had a way of making names stick. Harry's friends complained, but rationalized that the Soviets would soon return to their own borders. They had to stay in those places to help those countries back on their feet, just the way the U. S. was doing. But Harry insisted that the Soviets were there to stay, in Hungary, Poland, Latvia, Estonia and all the other places. He didn't have to rationalize; he wasn't in the Party anymore. To hell with those fools who thought there would be a resurgence of power in America. Nowadays it looked like the Communists were coming back big, riding the coattails of the liberal organizations that were being born with the speed of rabbits fornicating against a stop watch. But there were already blazoning signs that communism was going to catch hell just as after War I when the heady atmosphere of liberalism was becoming just a bit too much to stomach. Americans were afraid to suck every drop of meaning from the words that had given their country birth in the first place.

New liberalism? Look at Max.

Max Reddick was trudging across the street head down.

Max Reddick, a good, competent writer, Harry thought. Ideas to be worked out, a style to be cleaned up and set free. Best reporter the *Democrat* ever had. New liberalism? Look at him. Poor black bastard. All those white boys he knew covering those big stories, that is, the ones who came back in one piece and got their jobs back, were they not liberals? Couldn't they get Max set in a job the way they helped set one another? Uh-uh. No. And Max is still hurting for that girl and a good job. Marriage. By now he may know what kind of marriage it would be. Nothing wrong with the girl, except that she can't do Max no good. All she sees is a house with a white picket fence, a refrigerator and a washing machine. Such a fine-looking broad, too. Jesus! That chick could be so great for Max.

Harry saw Max move out of sight, approaching the house. In a moment he would be ringing the doorbell. Harry was glad Charlotte had a little money. Not a hell of a lot, just enough so they could get by comfortably. And it was getting so that he was commanding larger and larger advances. There had been some talk too about adapting one of his books for the stage. Yeah, it was going all right, so far. But Charlotte. Getting to be a drag, demanding more and more time for other people, places and things. It was as though she wanted to rip him away from the typewriter for good. That was her rival, the machine. But what a rival! It wouldn't scream or fight back. Charlotte hated it all the more. On the spur of the moment, Harry decided to go down and meet Max and pick up the mail. Hastily, he rolled the paper in the typewriter so that only the very top of the page showed. Then he took some blank paper and placed it underneath his unfinished manuscript. With a little skip and a floundering left jab at an unseen enemy, Harry Ames moved to the stairway as the buzzer sounded.

Max Reddick was evil. He wanted to punch out every white face he saw. Evil was beyond anger; it was a constant state, the state of destruction, someone else's. Impatiently he rattled the doorknob. C'mon, Harry, you sonofabitch; let me in from these white folks' streets. He glanced behind him. February. Cold, New York cold where the saline air punched holes in the snow and made it melt faster. Today had been payday for Max. For weeks he had been kept dangling, waiting for the final word to come in on several job applications with newspapers and magazines. He wouldn't have been kept dangling at all had it not been for Kermit Shea.

They had been at Western Reserve at the same time, had met at political meetings often enough to nod to each other, nothing more. Then they had met again while covering the Boatwright case and Max learned that Shea worked for the *Telegram*. They had had coffee and drinks together a few times, again, until Max walked into the *Telegram* office to apply for a job and found Shea in charge of Cityside news. Max knew as he filled out his application that Shea was embarrassed. To hell with him. Shea told him the *Telegram* was full up, but expecting departures momentarily, then steered Max to a number of other editors. The interviews were always the same: colorful newsmen's jabber, changing constantly in order to avoid falling into general use by the public. These were followed by the application-form ritual and, finally (sometimes days later, sometimes at once), the leaning back in the chair, man to man ("You and I are above all this, but the publisher ain't and he's the man who lays out the shekels, right? [The implication being that the Jews were driving the WASPs out of newspaper publishing] but call me next month, right, Max?") And then the handshakes that said that the time wasn't right, but when it is, Max, boy will we call you!

There wasn't a newspaper downtown that Max had missed, armed with Shea's recommendation. (Shea had stopped talking about jobs at the *Telegram*. Now he only talked about when he was in Italy with the *Stars and Stripes* and how he had come close to doing a piece on the Buffaloes. But today had been payday. It had been Shea, that bitterly cold morning, who had turned his chair over to an old criminal courts reporter for an hour so he could spring for drinks. Drinks, that basic American ritual for saying hello, goodbye, it's good to be home unwinding, you're fired, you don't have it. Like that. And yet Max had come to like Shea, a tall gangling man with prematurely graying hair and a face still filled with childish fat. Over drinks Max could tell that Shea was discovering for the first time in his life what kind of world he lived in, what kind of world he had helped to build simply by not building at all. For Max it was the end of the rope as far as downtown was concerned.

If he still wanted Lillian, it would have to be the Harlem *Democrat,* if it would have him. The routine would be galling and regressive. There was no more time to crap around. But what if the crap really had flooped all over the place? Say all the papers had called the *Democrat* for references. Wow! If the people at the *Democrat* even *thought* he had been trying to get a job downtown they'd give him the shaft. Was it human nature or the human nature of blacks bombarded with minuscule hatreds hourly that would make them happy to turn him away just as Mister Charlie downtown had? It would, in fact, give them more pleasure. No, there was no more time. Lillian Patch was pregnant.

Lillian wanted an abortion because, she said, she did not want to push Max into anything he wasn't ready for. Max, on the other hand, was willing to marry and settle for the *Democrat* and write nights. Or was he? Wasn't he going to ask Harry this morning for the name of a doctor who could do the abortion — if they both finally agreed on it? C'mon, Harry, open the goddamn door! Now, he was even getting pissed off at Kermit Shea. Hell, he was white, why not? Aw, crap.

Then Harry was at the door, letters held in his hand. One of the letters had been opened and fleetingly, as Max brushed past, cursing, he noticed an exultant smile on Harry's face.

"How'd it go?" Harry asked. "You going to be city editor for the *Times?*"

"To hell with you, Harry."

"Oh-oh," Harry mocked. "Them white folks been mistreating Max again. Mean to tell me that between Zutkin and Shea, you couldn't get set up? You better see Granville Bryant over in Fag City. He'll get you set up or one of his boys will." Still walking heavily up the carpeted steps. Harry went on, "I got a tremendous morning's work done. It flowed like piss after twenty bottles of beer. Hit it right on the button."

But inside the apartment, Harry took a look at Max's face and stopped the fooling. But he gave it one more try. "Uncle Harry told you how it was, Max. Sit down, I'll give you a drink. Read this."

Max peeled off his coat. It was too much to be faced week after week with the lies, the evasions, even the crudeness, which had been welcome sometimes. He didn't remember when he had felt the first stirrings of undirected anger; now it seemed to have been with him all along and was just finding an avenue of escape. He sat down and read the letter Harry had given him. It said:

Dear Mr. Ames:

I am writing to inform you that the American Lyceum of Letters has chosen you as the recipient of a Fellowship to the American Lykeion in Athens for the year June 1947–June 1948, subject to the approval of the American Lykeion in Athens.

The Fellowship carries a stipend of $1,000 a year, payable in monthly installments, transportation ($450), free residence at the Lykeion, $150 for books and supplies, and an additional allowance of $500 for European travel. All Fellows pay for their food at cost and a study will be provided for your personal use. The $500 balance of the $2,600, which is given to the Lykeion in Athens, is kept by the Lykeion for the various services they render you.

Presentation of this award will be made at our annual ceremonial, to be held on Thursday afternoon, May 24, at three o'clock. We hope so much that you will attend the ceremonial and the luncheon that precedes it at 12:30 P.M.

It would be appreciated if for the time being you would treat this information as confidential since it will not be released to the press until late in April.

May I offer you my warm personal congratulations upon the action of the Lyceum.

Max was showered in his own jealousy, he writhed in it. How in the holy hell could anyone get such great news on a day when he felt so rotten, so up against it, so wickedly caught in the Audacious Stink of Americana? Then, lo and behold, old God lettering the tablet with lightning, miracle of miracles, no Audacious Stink at all! America the beautiful, God shed His Grace on thee! It was too much. One minute they really, *really* got it reamed up your ass, and the next minute Miss Liberty is giving you the most fantastic blow job you ever had. How can you make these bastards out? They keep you off balance. They lift while they depress. They take you apart, then sew you back together again and sometimes you don't even want to be the Frankenstein they have made you. Goddamn them! Max looked up and smiled. "Did you make these drinks triple, man?"

Harry, almost ashamed of his luck and now sharply aware that he must mute his joy because of Max's depression, said, "If you don't have anything to do, we can really celebrate."

"Where's Charlotte?"

"Oh, she's gone to visit her mother. You know, the once-a-month thing, early in the day to keep people from staring when she gets out of the cab with the kid. Her father's not home then, you know."

"Yeah. Look, Harry, that's great, really great. Will you go?"

"That'll put me pretty close to Africa, won't it?" Harry broke into a smile. "Goddamn it, Max, they're beginning to know I'm here, that we're here. Max, this could be a whole new thing. Keep your fingers crossed. We're coming up, Max. Ain't no stopping us. Who's that boy got such a great review in the *Times,* you know him?" Harry retrieved the *Book Review.* "Marion Dawes."

"I don't know him," Max said, amused.

"I'll bet Granville Bryant knows him."

"One of these days," Max said, "them people are going to kick your ass for you. Good."

"Oh, hell. Then I'd be finished in this town, wouldn't I?"

They laughed. "Wait until Charlotte comes home," Harry said, then, "How's Lillian?"

"We need a doctor." Max handed Harry his empty glass. Harry took it, nodding. "How far?"

"Little over two."

"What about the wedding?" Harry was shouting from the kitchen now. Max found it too trying to shout anymore. He waited until Harry returned. "She is not sure."

"You?"

"Yes. I mean, I guess so. There's always the *Democrat*."

"And the new book?"

Max scoffed. "What new book?"

"Man, but I told you," Harry said loudly. "When you have a book ready to come out, as you have in a couple of months, you should always have something in the oven, 'cause they'll forget you in a flash. They wash white writers right down the drain. You *know* what they'll do for us!"

"The doctor, Harry. I just want the name of a doctor. Right now, man, I just can't cut it."

"Okay, Max. Let me make some calls. Want some soup? It's on the stove."

Apparently nearly everyone in New York knew the doctor. There was a little history that went with him. It seemed that his only daughter had "got into trouble" and had an abortion by some hack and died. The good doctor thereafter set himself up for the major purpose of providing abortions for young women who had got into similar "trouble." There was only one hitch, the talk went. The doctor required two visits, one to determine the condition of the patient medically and psychologically, for he would never do an abortion if he felt the couple were good for each other. The doctor was said to have been responsible for more successful marriages than all the marriage counselors, priests, ministers and marriage computers put together. There was a second visit only if the doctor deemed the relationship a detriment.

As it turned out, of course, the doctor was nothing like that at all. He insisted that he did not know the reference Harry had got for them; that he was a legitimate general practitioner operating well within the law and that he felt insulted that they had come to him. Unless, of course, someone in New York City was playing a joke. No, he didn't now anyone who would. Had Max never heard of the Medical Ethic?

Max and Lillian drove back to New York in almost complete silence. The landscape that flashed past them was hard, frozen, as stiff as the black leafless trees. Lillian felt empty. She was almost tempted once or twice to ask Max to stop at the nearest justice of the peace, but she knew that would be no good. He had no job yet, the future wasn't even on the horizon. She had counted on Charlotte's set knowing about these things. After all, *they* were involved in these things more often than Negro girls. But, see? Nothing, not one damned thing. Oh, you just can't trust those people. But it wasn't their fault, really. It was hers. Max felt that it was his too, but it wasn't. She simply had never been much good at counting, that's all there was to it. Well, she'd get back to New York and see about this whole business herself. If you looked hard enough for a thing, you found it. Now Max was saying something about forgetting it and getting married, that things would work out. Good God! Lillian thought. Doesn't he know that those last words are as famous as Lenox Avenue and 125th Street? The cry of Harlem: Things Would Work Out. That was all the white folks ever left, some bedraggled hope. And she answered him with a grunt. What, what was that he was saying, that Negro women had the proud tradition of keeping their children, no matter what? That white people had them cut out of them with no remorse, no nothing. What does this man understand? Doesn't he know that it is all those babies that help create the valley Negroes live in? Doesn't he know that Mister Charlie knew what he was doing when he took away everything except the ability to make love? Max, you are distraught. You aren't thinking. Love? Oh, Max, yes, but love with sense.

She would find a way; someone would know something for sure.

Not in Harlem. There were abortionists there, but the women doubled as hustlers, barmaids, distributors of election campaign material, numbers runners, midwives, boosters and baby-sitters. There had to be something else. The men who were either doctors or orderlies or morticians charged too much and talked too much. "It will be all right," Lillian said when Max let her out at home.

"What do you mean?"

"What I said."

"Come back here," he said. "Come here!" She returned to the car. "I want to know what you meant by that, Lillian. I want to know."

"I meant that I wouldn't let it worry me. We'll come up with something."

"Look, please, let's not do it. Suppose something happens. It will work out. You're tearing me apart. You're making me think I'm not worth anything, that I don't have what it takes to make it. Let's have the kid."

"No, Max, I can't."

Max sighed. "Baby, please don't do anything foolish. I'll call you tomorrow."

It was painful to call two or three times a day now. There was nothing to say and seldom anything to report in the way of finding a doctor. So the calls were now down to once a day and their voices were low, as if barricaded against some evil word slipping out that they could never recapture and hide away. So many times he had wanted to shout out: "Careless bitch, you, Lillian!" And she had wanted to say that he had been inconsiderate, that they *never* saw each other when he hadn't wanted to make love, and that she had told him she wasn't sure and therefore hadn't her thing and he hadn't wanted to use a condom.

Dully, Max watched her enter her house. There was a finality about her movements that made him uneasy. She didn't even turn around to wave goodbye. She was up to something. Fuck around now and get killed, he thought in a grim panic. C'mon, Shea, he thought; c'mon, Zutkin, one of you goodie-goodie bastards. Can't you see I'm hurting, *hurting,* and my girl, my woman is hurting. My whole motherfucking life is a gaping, stinking hurt! *Give me my share! I am a man. Don't make me take it in this anger!* Hot tears poured from his eyes and blinded him along with his anger. He snatched the wheel and the car spun around, skidded across the street on a patch of ice and ran up on the curb. He started the car again and climbed up the hill in first gear.

One week later when her school let out, Lillian went downtown instead of up. She was going to take the bus to Paterson, New Jersey. She had found a doctor. It was all arranged. She would be met outside the terminal by the nurse who would drive her to the office. Afterward, she would be driven back across the George Washington Bridge and placed in a cab. Then she would be on her own. No curettage would be necessary. She would be all right. That was the doctor's personal guarantee. The whole business would cost four hundred dollars.

Lillian felt both relief and dread. Relief that she had found someone to do it, and dread that she had to go through it alone. Just once, while waiting for the bus, she thought to call Max and ask him to be at her house when she returned, although she didn't really know what time that would be. But it would be nice to know that he was there waiting for her. She did not call. She had gone this far without him. She would finish it. Then they'd both be more careful, very careful until things worked out for the future. Going over the Bridge, she saw the sullen clouds break long enough for a smear of bright, golden sun to appear, far, far ahead of her in the west. Then she went to sleep, taking that as a good omen. A relieved half-smile came to her small face marked by the high-riding cheekbones. As she relaxed and became as one with the gently jostling bus, Lillian Patch, in an instant's panic, felt that the thing she had seen in her half-sleep months ago was breaking blackly down that long, eerie hill, coming directly at her.

It was eleven o'clock in the morning. Once again the city was in the grip of a long, bitter freeze. The thick ice and snow in the roads

114

and on the walks showed no sign of thawing. Inside his apartment, Max Reddick, who hated rye, poured himself a half glass of it. Everything else was gone. He took his trousers off the bed and stepped carefully into them. Slowly, he zipped up the fly and fastened the belt, staring at himself all the while in the mirror, which reflected the bed behind him. From the bed they had been able to see themselves in the mirror. Now Max flapped the tie around his neck, paused to drink, then knotted the tie. He pulled the jacket on and, in a sullen daze, patted it down his body. Black suit for dress, black suit for death. Still moving slowly, he went to the bed and snatched off its covers. On his knees now, he looked closely at the blankets and sheets. One by one he plucked up her hairs, the tightly curled, dully glowing pubic hairs, the long, thinner, brighter head hairs. He stood and rubbed them between his thumb and finger. He brought them back to the mirror and laid them on the dresser next to the whiskey. He looked up at his reflection and thought, I am as dead as she. Deader.

He had called her that night, at the time she usually was home. Her mother said that she hadn't come home yet, and somehow, right away, Max had known. He called later and still Lillian had not come home. He did not call again, foreseeing that the conversation would be stiff or angry. It was only later that he learned that:

She had come home very late. Her parents heard her moving softly around her rooms. Then, there had been silence. Later they heard her again; she seemed to be bumping into things. They had heard her in the bathroom, then out on the stairs. Later they figured out that she had been trying to call them. They had not heard. But they did hear the noise of her falling down the stairs; they found her at the foot of them. The trail of blood went back up the carpeted steps into the bathroom where it was a wide splotch, neatly marked with splatters, into her bedroom and in her bed. Her parents had called the police who came with an ambulance. But the hemorrhage had been sudden and deadly. The next afternoon when Max had called, Lillian Patch was dead.

*It will be all right.*

*What do you mean?*

*What I said.*

*Come back here. Come here! I want to know what you meant by that, Lillian. I want to know.*

*I meant that I wouldn't let it worry me. We'll come up with something.*

*Yeah, something like death.*

Max couldn't get their last scene together out of his mind. If only he'd gotten out of the car and walked to the door with her! If he'd gone in and had a cup of coffee with her! If he had given her just one pecking little kiss, maybe . . . !

Max Reddick stared back at himself as he fingered Lillian's hairs with one hand and finished the whiskey with the other. I'll never forgive them. Never. And they don't even know what they did! *They don't even know!* He felt a rage growing within him, small at first, like the cyclone on the horizon, and then it came spinning up, blacker and redder, faster and faster. He could break the mirror, the glass he held in his hand; he could smash the chairs, kick in the bed, tear the books off the shelves, snap records in two, throw shoes through the windows.

But he knew if he had five hundred years in which to smash, it would be as nothing because it wouldn't hurt them at all. He would be just another Negro gone berserk, and they would read about him and think: He should have jumped right up and run after another girl, this one with yellow shoes, maybe. Goddamn them! They could not be accused or convicted of murder or even being near the scene of the crime. What did they have to do with Lillian's death? Everything, and yet, they believed, would continue to believe, nothing. Max wanted to march them into ovens a million at a time; he wanted to see heaps of them dead, mountain-high heaps; he wanted the stink of their decomposing bodies to choke the very atmosphere.

But, *damn them!* They refused to understand why he wanted them dead. This was why: They gave Lillian the photograph, the image of the American Family Group, but when she looked very, very closely, she wasn't in it; she wasn't even the blanked-out one of

116

every ten who would contract polio or clap or pox; nor was she the one who wasn't insured by Metropolitan Life or Allstate. She was nothing and she was not to get that little house surrounded by shrubbery and a white picket fence. But they let her teach about America the Beautiful, and she knew it was not — after all, she saw those kids five days a week and sometimes chased them from the backs of buses on weekends — they let her teach that shit and she knew it was not, but hoped it was and, my darling bitch, Lillian, you got to hoping more than knowing.

Baby, didn't you understand? You over*whelmed* with your blackness, your babies; you choked them with the reek and tremor of the ghettoes they created; you screamed at their injustices which they denied because they must; you stacked up, created a backlog of book-hungry kids before the doors of their quota-oriented colleges, their Wall Streets, communications centers, their theaters; you gave them political hacks, the ones who are worse liars and thieves than they, only to create a wedge through which the uncompromising can later pass; you produced good music for them to copy or steal — and you wrote more; you gave them your sons to help fight their wars (but that must stop — a dead Negro on a German, Japanese, French, American battlefield does very little for a live Negro pinioned to his ghetto). Out of all the garbage they leave for you, you produce, produce, produce, and scare the hell out of them, for if something can be made from garbage, why is it that they have only automobiles, Lillian? See what that desire for old American security got you, baby? Security. You are so goddamn secure now that you don't have to worry about where the next *any*thing is coming from. And God knows, you don't have to worry about me having a decent job so we can live the way you thought we ought to — according to their way, which is, my darling, as pitiable as it is, the only way now. Look what you've gone and done. They have killed both of us. God, Lillian, I'm mad, I am so mad, baby, and sorry for them, for me, for you. How did we get *down here?* We should have been out of here by now. Are we going to have to explode out?

Max moved away from the mirror and all he could do was to shake his head very, very slowly.

Kermit Shea sat at his desk and stared at the gray, sluggish Hudson River. He felt that it was his fault, Max's girl's death. He had failed. Ames had wanted him to feel that way, of course, nothing subtle about it. Shea wondered if he had really tried. Yes. Yes, but in trying to help Max with a job, he had felt himself threatened. Strange, the way you felt it even in the phone calls. Then there were the looks when he had mentioned that Max was Negro. Shea hadn't known Ames except by reputation. "My name is Harry Ames, and I am Max Reddick's friend," he had said over the phone. The only friend? Shea had wondered. "He's had some trouble. I thought you ought to know about it." And Ames had told him and he might just as well have added: Feel guilty, you sonofabitch! Shea hadn't known a thing about the girl, but now he understood Reddick's curious detachment: he didn't want rejection, he needed a job desperately, but he *expected* rejection, which he got. "When's the funeral?" Shea had asked, and Ames had told him and then added, "But you'd better not come."

How many other Max Reddicks and Lillian Patches were out there, Shea wondered, with talents and desires ignored, indeed, unattributed to them? What happened to them and how often? And how thick were those gray ranks who had said to Shea, "How come you know this Negro guy?" All the ramifications of that question, the inherent threat, the contempt and — was it concealed fear? Ames had done his job well. Shea continued to stare at the river. Reddick, what was he doing this day of the funeral? Cursing all white people past hell and into oblivion. Kermit Shea didn't want to be among them on that journey. He wanted to lead them. He felt that guilty.

Bernard Zutkin's office was on the East Side. He sat in it and it was quiet, and that suited him. He had no intention of going to the funeral, although he hadn't been asked. He understood. A man like

Max Reddick knew exactly what had happened to him, to his girl, and why. In trying to help Max get a job, Zutkin had reconfirmed his own position in the literary and communications circles in New York: he was not a well-liked man. He drove hard. His view was uncluttered. He was a critic, not a reviewer. He knew the difference. When he chose to write, he was an author, not a writer. And because he was this precise, his analyses of the communications media had earned him a steady flow of dislike. Zutkin was also a Jew in a shrinking world of Gentiles who did not understand the process of their own abdication of responsibility in both communications and literature (he disliked the term "publishing"). Gentiles had run out of family blood; now they were being beaten out or getting out. When they finally realized what they had done to themselves, they would react just like the Germans. Anti-semitism was always in the American air, Zutkin knew, and to avoid the recurrence of what had happened in Germany, the Jew needed allies. There was the Negro who himself needed allies. But sadly, many of Zutkin's friends who were Jewish and had matched his own climb up the ladder, had taken over Gentile traits. "Look, Bernie, you know and I know that this is not the time for that!"

"Well, when is the right time, do you think?"

"Don't be a *macher,* Bernie. The time will come. Why don't *you* hire Reddick?"

"I'm a critic. I have an office. I teach, I'm a professor. How could I use a man like Reddick? And you know all this. The man needs a job now. You've read his books and pieces."

"So, I'm impressed. Now what?"

"Now? Nothing. Sorry to have been foolish enough to have asked a favor of you, sweetheart."

"Aw, Bernie —"

"The devil take you, *schmuck.*"

Most of Zutkin's calls had been like that or something like that. Stupid people. Time would run out and turn upon itself. One of these days assassins might have to be sent after people like Reddick and Ames because some jerk didn't want to give them a job they could do with one hand because they were black. They would have to be silenced somehow. They were learning too much about America — and telling it. Zutkin always thought of how they had reached out after Trotsky. Lenin didn't get him (didn't want to, really), and if Stalin hadn't ordered him done in, God knows Trotsky would have been around arguing and still making mistakes. And Stalin knew it, Lev Davidovich Bronstein; somebody always knows what you are and how you are, exactly.

Max Reddick fitted no exact pattern yet. The reality of his girl's death might be good for him, Zutkin thought. A hard consideration, but the world was hard. He had a handicap; he was a bit petit bourgeois. Reddick never knew, except in passing through them and reporting on them, the horror of the ghettoes Ames had known. Nor had Reddick, except for his time in the Army, really known the oozing horror of being a Negro in the South. Yes, in the end, the girl's death could rip the last ragged curtain of illusion from Reddick. A lot of white people were going to suffer at Max's hands because of that. That's why Zutkin wasn't going to the funeral; he could wait for his turn. He wasn't jumping in the front of *that* line.

First, Charlotte Ames had called the girl who had given her the name of the doctor in Pennsylvania. She screamed, talked and cursed, then hung up. New York, New York, where everyone wanted to be on the *in* in, and clutched onto the empty in things, like a nonexistent good abortionist in Pennsylvania, even to the extent of making him real enough to have a name, address and telephone number. Now, because of that, Max's girl was dead. Following the telephone conversation, Charlotte had an argument with her husband. She lost. She was not going to help Max with his meals or invite him to stay with them. "Max and I are friends," Harry had explained. "I don't think he wants to be around white people today. We've got to give him time."

Charlotte looked at him in horror. "Do you mean to say that this afternoon, he has to stand out there *alone,* without friends who are white, happen to be white?"

"Yes."

"Is that all I am, Harry, someone white, a white thing, to him?" And she came close, too close to telling him in unrelated screams of anger and sorrow how she had been something else to him one night, how she had tricked him and taken him to soothe her own fears and loneliness and how he had fought her for Harry (*In friendship, Charlotte!*) and how, afterwards, although she knew he hated her, she had become endeared to him in a special kind of way. None of the others gave a damn about Harry. But Charlotte did not become sad enough or angry enough to tell.

"Time," Harry said again, "he's got to have time."

"Then I can't go?"

"I don't think you should."

"All right. Harry?"

"What, dear?"

"When, *when* will it ever be better?"

Charlotte had not been a member of the Party. She had been amused when her friends who were members had discussed the Party line: maximum integration — marry a Negro. And she had observed that nothing wonderful or special had resulted. They were such fools, the Communists, sometimes, but they were the most interesting people she had ever known. At least they were *doing* something. She was glad Harry was no longer in the Party; it was too restricting for him. There had been times when, waking in Harry's bed or entering a room where he was, she had drawn up short, wondering what she was doing there. Then one day she had walked into the corner of the room where he was working. There had been a slight film of sweat on his face and he hadn't combed his hair. He still had on his pajama bottoms. She had paused and watched him and thought, Yes, yes, I do love this man, what he is, where he came from, how he survived. Like Desdemona, thriving, loving, finally, on Othello's talks of his deeds. But Desdemona too had defied custom. (Brabantio: *Fathers, from hence trust not your daughters' minds / By what you see them act.*)

Or your wives. Or your husbands. Charlotte knew that she had not always been fair to Harry, nor he to her. But, more times than not, those affairs, both hers and his, were unimportant, birthed in ennui. They had never brought them home; that had helped.

She wondered if Lillian had had affairs while going with Max, if Max had had any. In a kind of warm amazement, Charlotte could not conceive of either of them being unfaithful. They had been in love! God, she thought, good God, and now the girl's dead. No, she hadn't liked Lillian. Negro women — and it was not their fault — took their men very lightly after the first blush of love. They wanted them to be just like white men in terms of success, which meant, of course, the gracious acceptance of responsibility, the desk job where you bossed instead of being bossed, the lawn you mowed reluctantly when the leaves you raked half-heartedly were not on it. Charlotte had spotted it in a second. One day that would change; the men would stop deceiving themselves and the women would be proud of them. The Lillian Patches would become, with reality, extinct.

"He's all by himself, Harry," Charlotte said.

"No. I'll be with him."

# 13

MAX REDDICK was not sure if he was all wound up or all run down. He drank alone nights, sitting in a chair, thinking of nothing at all, it seemed, then suddenly becoming aware that he was thinking of it all, the whole brief life with Lillian Patch. Mornings, like a madman, he rushed from the house, fleeing before some prickling obligation to get for himself the kind of job Lillian had wished for him. The day came when, after stopping by the office of the NAACP, he was advised to register at the Urban League. When that was done, he drifted home, slipped the new bottle of whiskey from its brown bag and sat down in his chair. Now he had done all he could do, except report back to the *Democrat,* and what was the sense of that — now? This night Max sat on a pillow, for his rectum had started to throb with, he thought, all the drinking. But he was damned if he'd stop. He sat and waited for Harry's call, Harry's nightly call, the single touch of balance, the remembered thing, an origin, a point of departure or return. It came.

"You working, man?"

"No. Just sitting around," Max said, suddenly aware that he had been saying the same thing for a month and a half now.

"Did you eat?" Why the hell did Harry think eating cured everything? "I had a bite," Max answered, although he had eaten nothing since lunch when he'd got a Nedick's frank and coffee.

"Are you drinking?"

"Sure, I'm drinking. What did you think I was doing, jerking off?"

"Bad day, huh? Listen, did you work at all today?"

"No. I registered with the Urban League."

"Whatever in the hell for?"

Wearily, Max said, "A job, Harry, a job."

Harry said, "Oh, shit — listen, uh, goddamn it, Max, how long's it going to take for me to educate you to the way things are? Wake up. You're not their kind of Negro. That's an enclave, man, a niche. If they've got a spot, they're going to slip it to some cousin or brother or some guy like *them*. You sure got a nerve, dragging your raggedy ass into the Urban League. This is 1947, Max, time for you to be alert! Tell you what: if them niggers come up with a job for you, I'll buy you a whole case of whiskey myself, but hell, don't you worry about that; my money's safe."

Max was trembling. He shouted into the phone, "Harry don't try to fuck up my mind like that, Harry, don't! What's the matter with you?"

A shocked silence of a long moment's duration hung like lead between them, then Harry said, "Max, I'm not trying to fuck up your mind. I'm trying to straighten it *out,* man, let you know where it *is.* I've known those fellows for years. I know what goes on, Max. Listen, I'm sorry, really sorry, but Max, you got to let this go. Get

123

out of it. Write, Max, don't let them get to you. There's more than what shows and everybody's looking at the top. Get your crumbs together and meet us in Europe. I go to see the man tomorrow, the interview for the Lykeion. After that, it'll be getting near cut-out time. C'mon, Max. What do you say?"

Max stiffened against his trembling. "Europe. Harry you're trying to straighten out my mind, but I don't understand yours. Why run to Europe? There are more white people there than here. They haven't built any ovens here *yet;* I keep hearing about concentration camps, but *I've* never seen one here. What is this, with all you niggers running off to Europe? Man, don't you know *they started this shit that we're stuck in? Don't you know that, Harry?*"

"Okay, Max. The thing is, Europe is closer to Africa. Africa is where I'm aiming, Max. I know what's happened, and why. You got to cool it, man. Sounds to me like you're a little shaky. Want to come down?"

"No."

"I'll grab a train and come up."

"No, I'm all right."

"Can I say something to you without you blowing your top?"

"You've said everything else. Go on."

"You'd better knock off drinking alone. Get a broad, get that pussy, lots of it and maybe it'll pass. You got to try to help it. Max? Max, you listening to me?"

"I hear you, Harry."

"Do it, Max, go ahead."

"Goddamn it, Harry, I don't think I could even get it up. The blues got me and turning me every way but loose. I can't do anything. I don't want to do anything."

"You sound just like a white man, Max."

"Get up off me, Harry. I'm going to be all right. I'm going to be just fine. I'm going to be whole again. One day, you'll see."

"That's a deal?"

"Man, that's for real."

"Okay. And eat once in a while too, will you?"

"Yeah."

"You sure you're okay?"

"Yeah. Thanks."

Harry Ames hung up, stretched and walked into the room where Charlotte was listing items they would have to take with them to Europe. "How is he?" she asked.

Harry sat on the arm of the chair. He liked Charlotte in horn-rimmed glasses; they gave her a settled look. "I guess he'll make it."

"You were shouting."

"So was he."

"Bad boys, both of you. I suppose you suggested that he get himself a girl or two?"

"Nah. Just told him to stop drinking so much and eat a little bit."

"Of course."

Harry bent forward to look at the list and Charlotte said, "I guess we'll have to get little Max's clothes a couple sizes too large. He can grow into them."

"Hell no. Buy things that fit." Harry was thinking of all the too-large clothes he had ever worn: socks pulled back under the foot half a length; pants rolled up two or three times, the tops pinned together to fit at the waist; the shoes packed in the toe with cotton or toilet paper . . . "Charlotte, you don't know what it does to a kid to have his clothes not fit properly."

"Insecure?"

"Yes."

"Then you'll have to make more money and we can buy brand new, two complete outfits each year. How about it?"

Harry rose. "Don't get smart. Just don't buy them so big that he gets lost in them."

"What's the interview to be like, dear?"

"I don't know. Didn't even know that there was to be one until I got the note. Kierzek said it was just routine."

"I like him."

"Who, Kierzek? He's all right, for an editor."

"You've had much worse."

"It'll be good for us, Charlotte."

"What?"

"Europe."

Charlotte lowered her pencil and said softly, "Yes, it will. The big break. But I do wish you'd mute some of this talk about Africa. You're not African, Harry." She bent back to her pad.

"But I'm black."

"Really. I always thought you were brown. You've deceived me, dear."

"You know what I mean." Harry had retreated to the kitchen. "Want one of these?"

"No, just water. You're not going to get me high tonight and take advantage of me." She smiled to herself.

"Why would a man have to get his own wife high?"

She laughed aloud. "Because it's fun sometimes." She paused. "Darling?"

"I'm getting the water."

"Yes, but put a little Scotch in it, will you, like a good seducer?"

Harry Ames sat down across from the man. "Tell me about yourself, Mr. Ames." The handshakes were over; it was time to get down to business. "I started your last book, but haven't finished it. I'm about halfway through."

Harry stared across at the man, Mr. Kittings, director of the Lykeion in Athens. *Tell me about yourself.* Something's wrong, Harry thought, but he talked carefully, watching Kittings' eyes. "I've not been a member of the Communist Party for almost ten years," Harry said.

"We're interested in your art, Mr. Ames, not your politics." Kittings nodded affably and Harry continued, uneasily. Perhaps it was a look in Kittings' eyes, perhaps in his tone of voice as he broke in to cover more fully some point in Harry's monologue. Whatever it

126

was, Harry felt suddenly and shockingly that he was in hostile territory. He stumbled for a moment, trying to find some reason for this judgment, but he could not. He went on until he had nothing more to say. Then he asked questions about Athens which Kittings answered with a reserve that was not communicated to his secretary. She said, "Oh, you'll have a fine time there. We'll make the best possible accommodations aboard ship for you and your family." Why, Harry wondered, did he shoot his secretary such a sharp look?

The handshakes once more. "You'll hear from us," Kittings said.

"Hear from you?" Harry said in sudden alarm. "About what?"

"It is usually the practice for us to stay in touch with — people who — er — ah — come in for interviews."

Outside, on the way home, Harry thought it all very strange. Kierzek had said that the interview was routine. No one selected by the panel of judges had ever been refused admission to the Lykeion. Well, then, who was this prick, Kittings, to tell him he would hear from him? The decision was made! Seven of the best writers in America (Harry considered himself the eighth, now) had chosen him, Harry Ames, to receive the Lykeion Fellowship for the year. What in the hell had Kittings to do with it?

I'm cracking up. Just routine, like Kierzek said. Maybe Max is right. I'm into this thing too goddamn far. What did he say, Kittings? Nothing really. Maybe it was what he didn't say. But his eyes, his eyes? So? Maybe the bastard's just got naturally shifty eyes. Harry, man, ease up, eeease on up. By the time he arrived home, most of the feeling of foreboding had gone. It was going to be all right. The thing was, you couldn't distrust them *all* the time.

The sap of the earth began to run beneath the ground that Friday; spring teased the air. Windows that had been bolted against the winter were opened briefly. A few elderly people bundled themselves up and sat on the park benches, their pale faces lifted to the sun. Now the scarves of the students hung about the necks and coats and jackets were left unbuttoned. Charlotte went out and was a long time shopping, but Harry understood; it was the kind of day he would have liked to go walking in, but he couldn't. There was too much to do: the inventory of the things in the apartment, finding a broker to handle the sublet, plus the writing. There had to be time for that.

When Charlotte came in, she handed Harry the square envelope marked, *The American Lyceum of Letters*. Harry took the letter without comment; he had not said anything to Charlotte about the interview except that it had gone all right. Charlotte went to the kitchen with the groceries. Little Max paused, wondering if he was going back out or was in to stay.

"Don't open it until I come back," Charlotte said. "Help him with his clothes. It's pretty nice out, but too much of this uncertain weather isn't good for him."

"C'mere, Max. Let Dad help you out. Attaway." Harry felt sad as he helped him out of his outer garments. He looked at the café-au-lait face and smiled. "Now come up here and kiss your old Dad. Big ones, now, Pow! How to go. Another. Pow! Pow!"

Charlotte was back, smiling expectantly. "All right, go into your room. Play. But go. Kiss first. Smack, smack. Bye-bye. Peanut butter and jam sandwiches coming up." She watched him go. "Open it, open it," she said, feigning extreme anxiety.

Harry passed a hand over his forehead and carefully broke open the flap of the envelope. His eyes raced down the short paragraph.

"We regret to inform you that another candidate, also recommended by the American Lyceum of Letters, was awarded the Fellowship in creative writing . . ."

There was more, but Harry's eyes swept back to:

"We regret to inform you that . . ."

"We regret to . . ."

Charlotte had moved to him, was crouching, one hand on his knee, ready to sit on the floor, but seeing his face, she paused,

128

became motionless, awkward, half down and half up, and read his face once more, suddenly gone lifeless, suddenly fulfilled, invertedly, and she struggled upward, taking the letter from his dead hands and screaming before she started to read it, "My God, Harry, they did it, didn't they, they *did* it!"

Harry rolled his eyes up at her. How painful it was to move them; he hadn't noticed that before. Charlotte's eyes raced along the letter. They were cold, her eyes, and a blue growing darker. There was a vast silence between them. It took a couple of minutes before Harry could begin to think. Another candidate? How could that be? The first letter said he had been *chosen,* selected, preferred; there had been congratulations. He, Harry Ames had been *the best.* Now he was nothing. There was someone else. What a fool he had been! Of course, he had seen it in Kittings' eyes as he had seen it in white eyes all his life. But *why?* They had had former Communists at the Lykeion. Clifford Jacobs, the composer, was Negro and had won a Fellowship in music there. Bolton Warren had been there as a Fellow in creative writing. Why? Charlotte, or rather, Charlotte and *himself?* Why? Did he have to be a faggot? Why, why, why? Would they ever tell him why? Could he find out why?

"Why?" his wife said.

Very carefully he said, "Charlotte, I don't know why."

"The Party?"

"I don't know."

"Us, you and I?"

"I don't know."

"But they said you'd been *chosen!*"

Harry didn't want to look at her face. "I know, dear. That's what they said."

"Well what do they mean, 'another candidate'?"

"Darling, really, I don't know."

Charlotte folded the letter along its original creases. "You said it wouldn't be easy."

"I guess I did. It's the kind of thing you'd say in our situation.

The important thing — look, Charlotte — let's not hate each other . . ."

"But, Harry, I don't," she said with her eyes wide, her mouth held open. "Darling, I don't."

Harry nodded, but he didn't believe her. Even he, thinking for her in times of crisis, thought how nice it would be to have married a white man. And why hadn't he, Harry Ames, married a Negro woman?

"I don't want you to hate either, Harry," Charlotte said, for she knew that he too could think how much easier it would have been if he had married a Negro woman.

"No," Harry said, reaching for the letter. "They offer some consolation money. Let's take it and run."

"Whatever you say."

"It's not much."

"It would be hard, Harry. The baby."

Harry sighed. "I have to think about it. Hard. The motherfuckers, the lousy, rotten cocksuckers, the bastards, the sonsofbitches, the faggots, the —"

"Harry," Charlotte said, thinking of the child, for although he was not shouting, he was speaking slowly, distinctly and clearly and without anger, with rather a kind of helplessness, a resignation.

"— the shiteaters, cornholers, hermaphrodites, pricks, assholes, cunts and cunteaters —"

"The boy, Harry."

"Let him learn it from me. He should learn it from me. Why can't he learn *some*thing from me, like *pain*, Charlotte, *pain!*"

"Harry," she said, "Harry!"

"What!" he flung at her.

"It hurts us, too. It hurts like hell, you can't imagine."

Harry went to her and rubbed her shoulder. Goddamn it! They were almost out of it, almost. "Let me think about the other money. As soon as I can." He smiled. "They kinda took old Harry by surprise."

John Kierzek had had it, really had had it. Everyone in the office knew by now that Harry Ames had gotten *the* barbed shaft from the Lyceum, but all they said was, "How strange!" or "Gee, what happened?" or grimly said, "Those dirty bastards, how could they?" But no one came up with an answer. Now, Kierzek pounded down the carpeted floor to Donald Kenyon's office. Kenyon was the president of the company.

"Isn't that a goddamn shame about poor old Harry Ames?" Don Kenyon asked. He was blond, in his forties and liked being a publisher. Kierzek was fifty, bent, with a pot and too many jobs in too many New York publishing houses under his belt. Kierzek closed the door behind him and pulled up a chair.

"Don, we have to do something. We really can't let that man go up there at that ceremonial or whatever the hell they call it, and take a thousand dollars when we know he should have been a Lykeion Fellow, we can't let him do it!"

Don Kenyon blinked and pushed at his thick, waved hair. "You're fuckin' A right, John, but what the hell do we do? What *can* we do?"

"I'd like to suggest a few things. Okay?"

"Sure, John, anything we can do to help Harry out of this mess, goddamn it, we'll do it!"

Kierzek waited until Kenyon finished cursing the Lyceum. He liked Kenyon all right, but the trouble with the business was that there were too many people in it who should have been elsewhere. Wall Street, for example. And Kenyon liked him or needed him. Well, that was all right. It kept Kierzek in books, and he liked books. He couldn't be glib about them. His rejections were very readable; no fog, none of that overstocked or untimely business for him. That was really creeping into publishing these days. Snotnosed editors, still jerking off on the sly, or half or whole faggots. Jesus! For two days Kierzek had watched and listened to them in the halls and at the conference tables before the conferences began. No guts in the business anymore. Everyone broke their balls looking for talent, but when they had it right in their semeny hands, it scared the crap out of them. Kierzek couldn't understand it. During the war he had been an overaged navigator on first the B-24's and then the B-29's. He had made many a flight from Tinian to Japan and back. It was strange that in this world of desks and manuscripts, of spry, sexy little girls and homosexuals, of long lunch hours — a world so free of the direct approach of death stalking down the sky — fear ran rampant.

"First," Kierzek said, "we'll give him a three-thousand-dollar advance on his new book. His plans to go to Europe are made; he's been set to go for months. It'll kill him if he doesn't go. If we can help him, it'll be great for his ego —"

"Yeah, yeah, fuckin' A," Kenyon said, tapping at his hair.

"It won't hurt us to help him," Kierzek said. "We back up our authors."

"Of course, we do," Kenyon said.

"We'll give him that much of an advance on one condition —"

"— that he won't accept that fuckin' Lyceum money, right, John?"

"Right."

"Have you see the new book?"

"No."

"No?"

"No."

Kenyon waved his hand. "Doesn't matter. If it's Harry Ames, it'll be good, right, John?"

"It should sell. Now, Don. It's really very important that you write to the Lyceum and on Harry's behalf, demand an explanation. I mean, the poor bastard's wondering if he's diseased, nuts or a few thousand other things."

"John, do you think it's because of his wife?"

"Who knows and so what, Don?"

"No, no, you know what I mean. You know how people are. Doesn't make any difference to me — gee, she's a nice-looking doll, isn't she?"

"Yes. No, I don't know why. His Party connections, being

132

Negro, his marriage, I just don't know. It could be just one of those things or all of them, but he should know what he's being charged with or penalized for. Can you get the letter off today, Don?"

"You're fuckin' A. Mabel, baby," he called to his secretary in an outside office. "C'mon, you gotta go to work, sweetie. Let's hit it. Anything else, John?"

"Yes, we ought to get the publicity department in on this. Let Chris work full time on it. Maybe we can embarrass those bastards half to death; this is 1947, they can't get away with things like this."

Kenyon's secretary had come in. "Make a note, sweetie. Call Anthony, and tell him I'll be over at three for a haircut, will you? John, you fill Chris in and when she's got things organized, we'll get together. Four-thirty all right?"

Kierzek rose. "All right, Don. Just one more thing. Why don't you give Harry a call? He'd appreciate it."

"Have you called him?"

"Yes. Yesterday."

"Yeah, okay. Mabel, after this letter, get me Harry Ames on the phone. Thanks, John. Great thinking. We'll give those bastards hell. C'mon, Mabel."

Kierzek left and returned to his office. Why in the hell did people have to be told to do the right thing, he wondered. It was all so simple.

Harry wrote to the Lyceum, refusing to accept the consolation award. He turned in his novel, as far as he had gone, when he received the advance from Kenyon; a deal was a deal, and it was an all right deal as far as he was concerned. The publicity director, Chris Lumpkin, had worked overtime preparing a dossier on the case, for letters continued to flow. One judge on the panel who had selected Ames now wrote and asked him to accept the consolation money. Another judge who had been out of town wrote asking Ames to forgive them all. For the rest, there was silence. If ever in his weakest moments Harry had thought artists to be a tightly knit group, ever ready to back each other up in times of trouble, he

133

knew now that it was a dream. Why in the hell did he keep giving people credit for things that never even crossed their minds. *That* kind of shit was for someone else, not Harry Ames.

When Chris Lumpkin's fact sheet on the Lyceum case turned up on Kermit Shea's desk, he put his head in his hands, smoked two cigarettes and wished to hell that the paper had a book section. Then he called over a reporter and turned the sheet over to him. At his favorite bar he ordered a hot roast beef sandwich, his usual double of bourbon and two glasses of beer. He was worried. Suppose this sort of thing happened to every black man, woman and child in America every day? Suppose it had been happening, suppose it would continue to happen? There would be a reckoning; there always was, as history proved. That awful balancing out of things. Nature. *But what did one do?* Kermit Shea ordered another double of bourbon, drank it neat and caught a taxi. When he got out he hunted up a telephone book. Clutching the address in his hand, he walked swiftly until he came to the house, Harry Ames' house. He rang the bell. When the door opened he took off his hat and moved slowly up the stairs. "My name's Kermit Shea," he said to the man at the head of the stairs he took to be Ames. Photographs were funny. "You're Mr. Ames? We've spoken on the phone."

"Yes, you're from the *Telegram?*"

"Yes." Shea had gained the top of the stairs. He stood puffing and he didn't know whether it was from walking so fast, climbing the steps, emotion, or all three. They shook hands. Ames showed him in and offered him a drink which Shea refused. "I just came to say something, Mr. Ames. This morning we got some news from your publisher — about the Lyceum. I came to say that I'm sorry. I'm sorry for myself, I'm sorry for white people, I'm sorry for black people. I don't want to be your enemy, and I sure don't want you to be mine. I want peace for us, Mr. Ames, I want peace. I want to help make that peace, but I'll be goddamned if I know how. I don't know what to do or say, except what I've just done and said." Shea put his hat back on. "I guess there are a lot of people like me. They just haven't had four bourbons." Shea turned. "Give Max Reddick my regards, will you?" He started out of the room and down the stairs. Harry rocked back on his heels and came forward. He watched Shea go down the stairs. "Mr. Shea," he called softly. Shea turned around without stopping. "Thanks," Harry said.

Harry returned to his dressing; he was going to lunch with Zutkin. He thought of Shea. What a strange, exhilarating and at the same time depressing land, he thought. Only in America. C'mon, Harry, he told himself. Put the Stars and Stripes back in the locker; you can always count on some of the bourgeoisie to join you, always.

Harry Ames and Bernard Zutkin were lunching on the East Side, of course. What they should have planned was lunch at the Algonquin in the center of the front dining room. The lunch was to be nothing special. Zutkin had already called the five judges who had not broken silence, since he knew each one personally, and asked if they were aware of what had happened to Ames. Yes, they had heard something. Didn't it make them angry that Kittings had overridden their choice? Well, of course. What were they going to do? Nothing. Zutkin had suggested that the panel be reconvened and that the judges demand that Ames be sent to Athens, or resign. The suggestion fell on deaf ears. Now Ames was going to Paris instead of Athens and Zutkin was going to give him some names. And during lunch Zutkin would pick up some quotes to use in an article he was doing. It was, really, an observation of how an author's private life seemed more important to the world at large than his craft. Ames fit very well into that observation. Zutkin did not think the piece would attract a great amount of attention, but he wanted to do it anyway.

A couple of days later badly written stories on the rejection began to appear in the New York papers. Three reporters from the *Criterion* called Ames at different times for his side of the contretemps, but no copy ever appeared. Well, the Russians had their iron curtain, the Americans had one that was velvet; you couldn't hear it when it came down and you didn't believe it was there when you brushed up against it. The outlandish stories began to filter through to him.

He was a pimp for his wife.

He was drug addict.

He was a pusher.

He was a cockhound, and all his bitches were white.

He was part of a Communist-inspired plot to create a web of interracial affairs and marriages along the Eastern seaboard.

And they grew progressively sillier, the stories. To hell with them. All he wanted now was out, to Paris, France, for who with good sense would go to Paris, Texas? The time was coming. Ten days after what the Lyceum called its ceremonial, and they'd be gone, gone, man. One incident occurred that seemed to offer a restoration back into the good graces of whatever person or persons had first cast him into the shadows. It began with a phone call as Ames was packing the trunks, following a lunch in Harlem at Big Ola Mae's with Max.

"Me, Chris."

"Oh, hello, baby." He liked Chris, her husband Jerry. They didn't sweat over anything. A life was a life and they lived it the best way they knew how.

"News." Chris could be so goddamn businesslike.

"You've noticed that the *Criterion* hasn't run anything?"

"Yes, after talking to all those reporters."

"The gal at the Lyceum said not to wait, because they wouldn't print anything whatsoever about the Lykeion."

"I'm not surprised."

"Something else. Arthur Lawrence called." Lawrence was a books columnist for the *Criterion*. "He wanted to know if you were homosexual."

"I see," Ames said. How could a man feel sad and angry at the same time?

"What did you tell him, Chris?"

136

"I told him I didn't know, because I hadn't slept with you. It's still wide open, you see."

"Chris, you're precious. What am I supposed to do, call him and lisp that I am *one,* and he'll pass the word along and I'll have it made, Athens and all the rest?"

"Is that what it smells like to you?"

"You're goddamn right, that's what it smells like. What right does that dried-up old sonofabitch have to ask about my personal life?"

"Down, boy, just laying out the terrain for you. Bumpy, isn't it?"

"Thanks, Chris. We're ready to go. This can go to hell."

"Y'know, Harry, they really are rotten people. When I think of them sitting in their cold clubs or at their teas or cocktail parties, I get so goddamn mad. That bastard Kittings has gone back to Athens so nobody can get close to him."

"What could he say?"

"I goofed. How's Charlotte? The kid?"

"They're holding up."

"Great. Gotta go, sweetie. See yuh. Lunch one day? Call? Love to the gang," and she was gone. Harry Ames hung up slowly. Is Harry Ames a faggot? Is Harry Ames a faggot? He sat down. He felt as though a great many people had defecated on him. He wanted to strike out, but he knew if he did, he would not stop until he had killed. God, let us get out of here before it's too late. I don't want to have to kill someone. I don't want to kill. Well, Paris would be different. Paris and, if everything went all right, Africa. His friend Jaja Enzkwu from Nigeria had sent him a note of consolation on the Lykeion incident. "In our new, bright world, Africa, brother, we will have to ask them for nothing. It is a prospect that pleases me immensely. The Black Mother will forever beckon to her sons in the West. It is good that you plan to come home."

It was good to know that there was, after all, somewhere to go if times got that hard. For Harry, times were pressingly hard. He would admit it to no one, but he hated to leave America, he hated being driven out. No, they would never admit that they did that. *But Harry Ames no longer believed, as they had taught him and his father and his father's father, that he was a nigger.* Once he had believed that he was everything the books had said; worse even than what they said with their mouths, with their magazines and newspapers, with their radios, and he assumed that with this new thing, television, they'd continue. For example, Amos 'n Andy would go over big. And Negroes themselves would laugh and fall out in the confines of their homes, but get extremely angry about it (Amos 'n Andy) in public. Because they were still niggers.

The worst stories about Harry and the Lykeion were written by the Negro press. The *Democrat,* for example, had not bothered to check out other Negroes who had been at the Lykeion. Sloppy, all of them, as if, that being the way the white man saw them, they would then be that way. But in the process, Harry knew, and he and Max had talked about it often, the Negro press deprived the Negro community of worthwhile newspapers. At least the Negroes were getting smart enough to buy the downtown papers; they merely lied, they weren't just plain slovenly. Perhaps by the time he returned from Europe and Africa (he didn't know when that would be), things would be different. He knew that Charlotte also felt ambivalent about going. A kind of surcease, yes, but at such a cost in money, energy and emotion. How did one go about learning quickly to speak French, for example? They'd just have to do it, a few necessary phrases first, and then others. Harry was confident that it would come; they'd be talking that shit up a breeze.

The spring days whisked by. The American Lyceum of Letters ceremonial was approaching. Harry and Charlotte spent a great deal of time looking out of the window as if trying to memorize every shadow and the position of every light pole, the colors of the houses and doors on the other side of the street. At those times, Harry would study his wife's face. Such a flitting sadness. She looked with such longing at the Italian ice vendors. But then she'd lift her head and stare across the street. Envisioning, Harry imagined, Paris. Paris in the spring. (Hell, she was a woman, wasn't she?) Bittersweet the going, bittersweet the leaving. Harry turned from the windows. The good thing (and he knew it was a desperate rationalization) was that what they did to you kept you on your goddamn toes. Made you think a little faster. Or else it was your ass. You lived once, but damned if they didn't make it seem like forever. Prometheus Black. Only they don't know it's fire they got, these American eagles.

The night before the day of the ceremonial, Daniel O'Brien called. O'Brien was a poet and Harry had heard that O'Brien was the man who had been given his Lykeion Fellowship in creative writing.

"Harry Ames? I'm Daniel O'Brien."

"Hello, Daniel O'Brien."

"Hi. About tomorrow. I'm going to take that Fellowship. I did a lot of thinking about it, and I'm going to take it."

"You're a writer, I think you ought to take it."

"Yeah, well this is why I called: I'm going to say a few words tomorrow. Can I say something for you?"

Harry heard the poet breathing regularly into the mouthpiece.

"Well, I am going to say that I was the second choice and that you were the unanimous first choice. Maybe a couple of other things. Is that all right with you?"

"It's all right," Harry said. Why didn't they just leave him alone? Why piss on him too?

"I'm sorry," O'Brien said, "but I want to go, I couldn't turn it down."

"Sure, I understand," Harry said. "Well, go ahead, say what you will. Good luck."

"Yeah, sure. S'long, Harry Ames."

The ceremonial was an especial one. Burke McGalpin had been dredged out of the Okefenokee Swamp and urged to set his bourbon aside. He was getting a special medal. It was somehow ironic that the Master of Southern Literature was to be at the ceremonial; it was almost as if the Northern Literary Masters were saying to him: "This is how we handle our niggers. Give a little, take much more."

Max joined Harry the afternoon of the ceremonial so they could listen to the broadcast together. Charlotte would listen to it at her mother's house. Max was looking better, Harry thought, as they settled in the living room. He wished Max were going with them. Maybe later. Max had promised.

Now, over the radio there came the blabbing of many voices which were faded under an announcer. Max glanced at Harry. The entire business had cut his ego to ribbons, but perhaps this was the end of it. There had been petitions, phone calls, conferences. Harry had stood firm in refusing the consolation prize — which was easy enough to do if you got a three-thousand-dollar advance. Well, Don Kenyon was no fool. All the copy would be good for his house and he'd get a good book besides. He'd always wanted to be a fighting publisher.

Names were called off in monotone. Over the radio they heard the shuffle of feet, the scuffle of chairs, the sound of the mike being adjusted and readjusted. Then, finally, Daniel O'Brien was on the air. "Harry Ames declined the Lyceum Grant because he was refused the Lykeion Fellowship in Athens after having been the unanimous choice of the Lyceum judges. I was runner-up in the competition and therefore won it."

The voices babbled and bubbled again. Max was grinning when he looked at Ames. "That's a gutsy cat," he said.

Harry looked out the window. "Max, don't you know that guy's dead? He's blabbed, he's taken their money and he's called them names. Yes, he'll go on off to Athens for his year, and he'll write poetry and maybe he'll publish some of it. But that man is dead. They'll get to him. They'll make that poor sonofabitch sorry for trying to do the right thing."

Max said, "He should have kept his mouth shut. He didn't have to say a damned thing."

"Yes, *he* did, Max. He had to say it."

Max turned off the radio. Neither of them moved for a long time.

140

# part TWO

# 14

Now, seventeen years later, Max remembered that afternoon, perhaps because it had been a spring afternoon. And Max remembered the kind of dazed look of Harry and Charlotte and the kid in their room on the *Flandre*. It's not for real, the look seemed to say; it can't be. Yet there they were, the odor of the North River full in the room, that room crowded with well-wishers, flowers, champagne, muted voices that ship departures always bring.

Once Max had looked into a corner. He saw Harry and Daniel O'Brien raising their glasses. A toast, Max thought. To what?

One year later Max knew. It had been a toast to America. O'Brien had written a poem hinting at it, a poem that said if we must sacrifice some to get where we must go, then count me first. Harry had been right about O'Brien; that was the last published poem of his Max had ever seen or heard about.

"LEIDEN" the sign said. Another half mile and Max peeled off the main road, shifted into third and moved slowly through the streets. Once he stopped to look at his directions, then drove on to the train station; the street he was looking for was near it. Twice he missed it and had to double back on one-way streets. The third time he hit it just right, drove past a weatherbeaten wooden windmill (left up for the tourists) and went down the street until he came to the number Michelle Bouilloux had given him. There was a wall around the house. Max got out of the car and stretched. The first thing he'd do was go to the bathroom; the cotton felt wet. He glanced at the sun; it was directly overhead. Noon, or just about; it shouldn't have taken him that long to drive down here. He'd do better going back, he thought.

Max rang the bell. He breathed the scents of spring, the water in the canals, the fresh blooming trees, the noontime cooking and, faintly, the exhaust fumes of cars. He heard the lock on the garden door snap open and he pushed at the ancient, browned slab of wood. In the garden, color rose layer above layer. First was the thick carpet of grass divided by a walk, then fern bushes and daffodils, then red and pink roses, all dwarfed by giant spreading oaks on either side. He almost missed seeing the house behind the flowers and plants, but he started down the walk, closing the door behind him. Up ahead, at the other end of the walk, the door of the old stone house opened, and Michelle Bouilloux rushed out, her red hair glinting copper as she ran toward him through the different levels of color. Max perceived her dimly, rushing out of the past as it were, and heard her shoes slapping ever so gently upon the old slate walk, and for the first time he smelled the flowers themselves.

The black she wore this time was not so formal; it allowed her form to show and beneath her simply cut dress her breasts heaved up and down with each crimping little stride she took toward him. He thought with surprise, She's a redhead! Of course, she was a redhead. He'd known that once. Why had he forgotten? It was just the day, the time of day, that hour in life through which all past thoughts and desires filtered once more. As she came closer to him, her ripe, reluctantly aging body still — (how would he say it?) *succulent; un repas succulent* — he noticed that she fixed his face with her eyes in such a searchingly bright manner that he inwardly recoiled, not from her, but from what it was she saw. "Hey, Michelle, *ça va, chéri, umm, très chic toujours, ah?*" Only by bracing himself was he able to take her crashing embrace without falling. It was his own fault. He had thrown open his arms and thrust himself forward in a feeble attempt to recapture the greetings of old. They kissed and hugged and kissed again, until she drew back and let her eyes go over his face again. "Max, *es-tu malade?*"

"What?"

"I'm sorry. Are you sick, Max? I noticed in Paris that you did not look well. Now you are here — Max — you look worse. Come, I will fix you a coffee." She took his arm and they walked to the house.

As soon as they entered Max said, "Michelle, I must use your bath."

"But of course, Max."

When he came out the coffee was ready along with neat little open-faced sandwiches. "You are hungry, Max?" Michelle asked.

He nodded. As she poured the coffee, he leaned to look out the window. A canal flowed right next to the house. He guessed it was a pretty cold place during the winter. The house was very old and extremely Dutch in style. "Is this your house, Michelle?"

"Yes." She passed him his coffee. "Way in the back," she said, "in history, one of my relatives was a soldier with Napoleon. Coming back from Waterloo, he simply stayed and took a Dutch wife. They built this and used it from time to time when they were not in France. But," she added hastily, "we are far more French than Dutch."

As he was sipping his coffee, Max felt an urge to turn; it was as if someone was looking at him. He looked up at a photograph of Harry Ames standing in a far corner on the mantel of the fireplace. Max turned and looked at Michelle, then back at the photo. It was Harry's devilish photo. His eyes danced and his brows were arched like mountain peaks.

"My husband never knew of this house," Michelle said with a little smile. "It belongs after all to *my* family."

"So this is where you and Harry used to vanish to."

"Yes." She sat back in her chair and crossed one leg with a flash of white. "But, how have you been, Max? Are you still with the magazine? No more novels, Max? What happened? And Margrit, you saw her in Amsterdam. Is she well? Is there any hope for you two or is there someone else?"

Max shrugged. "There's no one else. Margrit? She's fine. The magazine? [What had he told Margrit? That he had quit three months ago or — No] I took a leave for a little while. I was getting tired, Michelle. Too much traveling, too many different countries and people and things in too short a time. Not like the old days, they say, before the jets. Just tired, honey."

"We always hoped you would come back to Paris and settle down to live, Max. So much was missing when you decided to return to America. Harry felt badly about it. You made him feel that he might be wrong. It was not a good feeling for him to have. Harry was not a good man to know when he was uncertain about things; he thrashed about and he hurt people. And your swift passings-through were never enough."

"Well . . ." Max let his voice fall off. Tired, he thought, damned tired.

"I often had the feeling," Michelle was saying, "that there were certain important things America could do or say in some fashion, and they would have been enough to send Harry rushing back to New York. America never said or did them. All day I've been thinking: maybe he wasn't happy in France after the first few years. Maybe he wasn't."

Max said, "He never wrote about the French; he never wrote about France, nothing in love, hate, anger or even indifference. Maybe he was wrong."

"His heart did lay in America, and one could always find time to reflect on that and be sorry —"

"Michelle," Max said, breaking in more sharply than he intended, because he was feeling a sudden lurch of pain even through the morphine. Anticipating it after the morning's drive, he had increased his dosage in her bathroom. "Why are we here?" Michelle closed her mouth slowly and firmly. Ah, he is not well, she thought; that explains it. That must explain it. She glanced out the window. Max saw her in full profile. His eyes went down to her chest where her breasts swelled to bursting against her dress, then mercifully sloped back to her stomach. He was now conscious of her perfume, a faint something. Violet? Michelle uncrossed her leg and crossed the other. She leaned forward and took a sandwich and glanced at the window again as she took a bite. Max waited, staring at the dark waters of the canal. Why didn't she get on with it?

"I have something to give to you." She took another bite of her sandwich. Max, warm in the stupor he felt himself tumbling into, watched her open her small, rounded mouth. No lipstick. Fluttering like a newborn snake, his penis strained toward an erection. Max groaned and clutched his coffee, wincing. Michelle frowned. Her pout vanished and she came forward, setting her cup on the small table that stood between them. She touched his knee. He placed a hand over her hand and with the other wiped the stinging tears from his eyes. She looked up at him quizzically. "What, dear Max? Tell me. You are ill. O! Max!" Her own eyes filled suddenly with tears. "We are *all* getting old and sick and dropping dead, with everything still a mess."

"Michelle," Max said, trying to laugh lightly. "I never made love to a woman with red hair. Never in my entire life."

Michelle laughed a little through her tears. "Why, what an extraordinary thing to say!" She giggled. "Max, why do you say that?"

Max leaned forward now, spinning rapidly somewhere between a wild high and stupor. "Would you let me make love to you if I were going to die and could complete that act just once before I did?" Max smiled at her.

Michelle smiled back. "But we are both so old — I would not like the responsibility of having your death on my hands, dear Max —"

"I would do it for you, Michelle."

"You would?" Michelle frowned and smiled by turn. What a strange conversation. How odd, how odd! She stood and retrieved her coffee and then coquettishly said, "I might consider it. But enough of this game, Max. It frightens me." She wiped the edges of her eyes with a tiny lace handkerchief.

"Michelle," Max said, feeling some of the tension ease from his body, "the mess was a long time in the making; it'll take a long time in the cleaning. Harry thought he could do it all. Now tell me what Harry left."

She went to a nearby cabinet and opened it and pulled out a worn leather briefcase. From her purse she took a key. She laid these on a sideboard. "I will have a whiskey," she said. "This is all too depressing, to talk of love and death in the same breath. You, a whiskey?"

Max felt his head going forward and in a panic he jerked it back up. It took him the greater part of a second to focus and see if Michelle had been watching him. No. "Yes, I'll have one," he said. How many times had he seen junkies and cops standing within three feet of each other on Eighth Avenue and 125th Street, the junkies nodding just as he'd started to, and the cops pretending not to see.

"Water," she said, "or soda?"

"Plain."

First she brought the whiskey and then the briefcase. She lay the key gently in his hand. "You rather than Charlotte, Michelle?"

"Yes, of course. Yes."

"Almost from the first, wasn't it?" Max remembered the letters: *. . . and man, there is this French chick, with red hair! (You had one yet?) I've never known a woman like her . . .*

Michelle smiled shyly. "Yes, almost from the start." She looked into her whiskey glass. "You should have seen him *then!*" she cried fiercely, and Max saw that she was sobbing once more. Her voice began to wash back and forth over Max. Her gestures with her hands (whiskey splashing in light brown arcs) were like frightened little birds springing in a hundred different directions. Her face lighted up. She tossed her head. "He was like a breath of fresh air when he came, like the first strong smell of spring skipping along the Boulevard St-Michel. His eyes were big with seeing, and his heart, oh, Max his heart! it was big enough to catapult this world to the moon and farther! We thought him the first true American existentialist, and I will never forget what he said at a party: 'Existentialist? what is that?' Of course, he was kidding. But two of his books, I forget which ones, made us see America through eyes we'd not used before.

"He was very much in demand. He went to many parties and came to know Jean-Paul — he had just published the second book of his *Le Chemin de la Liberté* — Simone, Albert, Jean Françoise,

148

André." Michelle laughed, throwing up her feet. "And at one party he met your American star, the eh, eh, the bullfight man? Yes, of course you know who I mean, but Harry would not talk to him, said, 'No American writer can be called great unless he deals with American themes, problems and aspirations. That man could write about losers so well and not even really know any; he went here and there to find them and all the time they were right beneath his feet. Millions of them.' We needed that then, with the war not long over and Dienbienphu still before us. We needed the confidence of someone who had taken more of a beating than we, generations and generations of beatings, and who could still see *le chemin de la liberté*. So Harry was not a good existentialist and sometimes we think Jean-Paul, beneath it all, is not either. Yes, France rolled out the red carpet as you Americans say, and I met Harry at one of those parties. My husband, you remember, was quite close to the Ministry of Culture. I saw Harry's wife then and many times after. She seemed — petulant, that so many people were concerned for her husband's work and concerned for *him*. I could tell right away she was not very good for him. What do you do to writers in America?"

Michelle had had two more drinks by now, Max noticed through the soft, cottony gray cloud that waited to envelop him. Concentrate, he told himself, but he also told himself that perhaps a nap would do him good. It was still early; he would get back to Amsterdam in good time. Perhaps Michelle would even drive him there and take the train back. *Do something!* Open the case. Pandora's box, maybe. He thought he was laughing. Pandora's *box*. Were those Greeks clever! Talking all that hip Harlem trash for centuries. Pandora's *box*. Yes, indeed. How did it go: "For Pandora carried a box which she was forbidden to open; it would bring misfortune to man." Wow, Michelle, let me open your box.

". . . Max! You're not drinking!" Michelle reached for his glass and he slipped his hand over her wrist. Brown and white, he thought. Nice. She took the glass. "I'll get you another and together we'll drink one to Harry."

"No, Michelle," he said. He tried to rise, but gave it up and crashed softly back in his chair. The cottony gray fog now swept over him in thick, choking gusts. "No more Michelle." He fingered the key to the case. It slid through his fingers as though it had been coated with graphite. He wanted to get a firm grip on it and he wanted to scratch himself at the same time. The nodding and the scratching — well, he knew what that was.

Hours passed, it seemed, time telescoping as if it had resigned itself to the play of mirrors. Michelle was still standing motionless, the glasses of whiskey in her hands. Max blinked. The attaché case on his legs suddenly became unbearably heavy and his knees began to quiver. The cold sweat was back, popping out on his forehead. He thought he smiled at Michelle. Finally, he thought he was putting the key in his pocket. "Michelle," he seemed to be saying from some distance away. He cleared his throat and spoke louder. "Michelle, I must lie down for a little while."

"Max, what is it?" She did things before she came to him. Putting the glasses down? "What is wrong? Of course you can lie down. I did not notice until now, I was so busy thinking of myself with Harry. But come."

Max leaned on her when he finally got to his feet. He leaned on her and felt her breasts pressing into his chest. With an unsteady hand he touched one, slipped his hand around on it until he felt the nipple.

"Stop. Be a good boy, Max. Give me the case to carry."

"I can carry it."

They struggled up the stairs. "I hope this doesn't disturb any plans you might have made."

"No, no, it is quite all right. Shall I get a doctor?"

"No, Michelle. I know what is wrong."

They were near the top of the stairs now. "What?" Michelle asked, gently pushing aside the hand that sought her breasts in slow motion. They paused, breathing heavily. Max took his hand from her breast and tilted her chin to his mouth and clumsily kissed her.

"What is wrong with me is what is wrong with all of us. I'm simply dying. Like you. Like everyone."

"Shhh," she said, helping him into the bedroom, to the bed and then removing his shoes. "Why do you make such jokes, Max? You do worry me. Another kiss, Max? Oh, Max, should we get so? A little one, Max, no more."

Max was being washed up in it, the unzipping of her blouse, the mute struggle to unclasp the brassiere, the wide, heavy-tongued kisses and finally, the stark, white, fat breasts tumbled out and hung formlessly before him. Michelle had remained motionless, as if sensing that this was something he must do, and he sensed that and stopped. Yes, he had wanted a redhead. Tenderly, he placed her breasts back inside her blouse. He heard a long dry stroking somewhere. He listened very carefully and heard sparrows in the yard downstairs. Then he knew what the sound was, the rubbing of a giant limb against the house. Breathing deeply and not looking at him, Michelle raised herself from the bed. "It is not much good without the love, Max, is it? After a while, the clichés have meaning once again."

"Yes, Michelle." Pain had been riding hard between Max's buttocks, now it was subsiding. Max started to fall between the gray clouds as Michelle's voice came distantly to him. "There is an awful smell, Max. Do you smell it? Could a small animal from the garden be caught in the eaves and rotting? Max, do you think so?" She snapped her brassiere and zipped up her blouse.

"I don't know," Max whispered.

She leaned over and kissed his cheek. "Sleep, Max." Then she went out, closing the door behind her softly. He heard her going slowly down the stairs. The smell, the cancer smell of rot and death. Sort of sweet, sort of heavy, sort of like being near a corpse on a battlefield and not even seeing it. The senses, like those of a beast, remember the smell of death. Max winced in pain and fear. Now he was just like anyone else. Mortal. Stinkingly mortal. Until Michelle had spoken he had pretended that the smell was not his.

His falling was slow and he did not know whether it was from the morphine and whiskey or the inevitable cachexia or all three. Why couldn't he have died on one of those wet, naked Italian mountains? There were so many *decent* ways to die, so many *acceptable* ways to die. It would have been romantic to die of drink after Lillian. Or pills. A hunting accident. ("I thought he was a deer, Mr. Coroner.") Starvation in the richest city of the world in the year of our Lord, 1947, the same year Harry Ames arrived in Paris like a breath of spring.

# 15

MAX had read Harry's letter in the Pork Store while he was waiting for the man to wrap up the ham hocks. Harry was having a ball in Paris. That redhead he always wrote about. And all the famous French writers he'd met. Goddamn, Max thought, I'd like to talk to that Camus. That's a tough cat. That Harry. Luck. Now Max was walking back home, through a late September sun. Pretty soon ol' Hawk would be on the scene and all these cats standing on these corners lying and crying would have their asses cut a duster. The corners would be clean. Yes, sir. You could always tell when winter came to Harlem. No*body* on the street.

Max clutched his bag containing two smoked ham hocks. His mouth watered. It was his day to eat and waiting at home was half a pot of navy beans soaking in water. He had moved to a smaller apartment. It was really a room with a small closet and even smaller bathroom. There was a sagging, high-rise bed, a battered table and two chairs and a dresser whose veneer peeled every time someone in the building slammed a door. Max's savings were gone. Whiskey, he guessed, and flowers for Lillian's grave. There was the 52-20 club money and the ten percent disability. At home Max moved to the table where his manuscript lay very near completion. He hummed. If he had found a job, he wouldn't have finished the book so quickly; the book had kept him sane. Outside, downtown, they had rejected him completely and he had crawled back into his hole. Not to die, but to begin to live any way he could. Survival, Harlem style: when the wagon comes, every swinging goes. Morals in an immoral society? Later for them. One way or the other Max Reddick was going to make do, and further, make it. Hell, he had him some beans and hocks and was going to get him some money *and* some trim later.

Max washed off the hocks and placed one in the freezer compartment. The other he placed in the pot of navy beans after he had drained the water and replaced it. He put a pack of cigarettes on the table and sat down to work. He worked until the smell of the beans and hocks came from the pot, then he rose, tasted them, added seasoning and sliced an onion into the pot. The beans were getting soft and the hock was still in one piece, although its flavor had gone through the beans and colored them a light brown. Close to an hour later when he left the typewriter again, Max removed the ham hock, rinsed it off and placed it in a saucer to cool. Later he would wrap it in aluminum foil and place it in the refrigerator to be used the next day when he made kidney beans. And when he finished the kidney beans, he would use what was left of the hock for a pot of lima beans. That single hock would keep his beans seasoned for about six days. Then he would start on the other hock, using it just as judiciously with cabbage, string beans and collard greens. Two ham hocks and less than two dollars' worth of dried and fresh groceries kept Max going for half a month.

Luxuriously, he gorged himself on the beans and bread with thick slabs of butter. He wondered if he had not been Negro if he could have survived so well in a place like New York. He lit a cigarette and lay down. It was Saturday. From somewhere in the building he could hear a ball game in progress. Soon football would take over. Max liked it when it was quiet like this. He knew people were out, walking or sitting in the parks. Weekends made him feel better because hardly anyone worked. During the week he had to fight being embarrassed because everyone else in the city, it seemed, was hustling toward work while he dragged around at home. He had got over that. Those people out there, they had their thing and he had his. That's all there was to it.

The girl came later that afternoon. Her name was Regina. Max had met her on the ship the day Harry and Charlotte left. He had gone drinking with her and her date, Bob, until Bob had to catch a train home. To his wife and children. Max and Regina had had more drinks and he took her home, made love to her and a thing of sorts was begun. Max knew that she still saw Bob. That was all right because she knew he saw other girls. When she was troubled about Bob, she came to him. He would punish her for being involved with a married man. What greater punishment could there be than to be involved with a Negro man and giving him money?

Max had already given himself a name; he was a pimp without briefcase. When you pimped without briefcase, you borrowed money from the girl and the girl knew you'd never pay it back, and chances were, every time you met you'd borrow more money. Sometimes you apologized for not being able to pay the money back and if you did this right, not only would the girl not become middle class and bitchy and dun you for the money, she might even lend you more. Later, in Europe, they would call it macking.

Regina (Max remembered) had been in a quietly belligerent mood. "Beans and hocks again," she said. Then she sighed. "If I were coming again I'd bring you a steak."

"You're not coming again, Regina?"

"No, not anymore. I'm not even staying over tonight."

"I see." Max wondered what had brought it on. He had counted on the ten bucks. "Do you want to tell me why?"

"I don't mind, Max." She touched his hand. "You don't think I know what I'm doing, do you?"

"I'm sure somewhere you do."

"I'll tell you anyway, all right?"

"Sure."

"Well, it's not any good without love, Max, and I don't love you and you don't love me. We just — well, we *just!*"

154

"Everybody just justs, Regina."

"Well, I don't want to just just! I want something more."

"Like Bob?"

"Just like Bob."

"Can you have him?"

"No. I mean, sometimes I think no, and he says no, but when we're together it's yes. But when he hurts me I —"

"You come to me."

"Yes."

"I understand. It's part of the game."

"Max, I know it's part of your game, our game. But no more. Listen, can't we somehow be friends? I know it sounds like nonsense, but I mean it."

These girls who work in publishing houses, Max thought. They read too many novels. "You just can't shake hands, Regina, and say, 'Okay, we're friends now,' you know."

"Oh, I know it," she said, placing her face in her hands. She got up and took her bag. "If it's to come, it'll come, but let's shake anyway."

"I'd rather kiss you."

"No. A shake, Max. Don't be like everyone else. Please shake. I'm tired of passion."

Regina and the other girls made him feel a part of things. Now, for this weekend at least, loneliness. No, he tried to tell himself, the book, the book. He'd be working, working like hell. He reached out and took her hand. She stood in the door and said, "Think of how you'd be if you had your Lillian; I know how I'd be if I had Bob."

Max closed the door and walked back to the table. He laid out the manuscript and inserted paper into the typewriter. He worked easily and steadily, pausing from time to time to listen to the news or to light a cigarette. He thought of the city, monstrous and writhing beneath the weight of people running pell-mell in search of pleasure. No one looked for pain or, if they did, they were careful first to drape it in pleasure. Finally, a gray sheen fell across his window; morning had come. The phone had not rung once. Eight million people in the city and not one of them had thought to call. Not a single one. He bounced up from the table. What the hell was he thinking like that for? Everybody else had been balling — all eight million of them — but *he* had been working. I'm nuts, he told himself. Or going nuts. He fixed a cup of instant coffee and carefully stacked his sheets. Work, Max! he told himself, Go, baby!

While he sipped the coffee, he pulled out Harry's letter and re-read it. Maybe that was the answer, Paris, Europe. White people, sure, but maybe a different kind of white people. Good enough for Harry. No, don't believe it. Dump five hundred thousand niggers on Paris streets and it'd become just like New York. But, maybe, Max thought, if I ever get in any kind of shape . . . Maybe *this* book will take off. Max shook his head. The goddamn city was so filled with clichés that you started thinking they were your own golden words. Some agent had used that phrase, "take off." Max knew that no book took off unless it was first catapulted by the publisher. The gray sheen outside was taking on a slight orange hue. How nice it would be in the country now, breaking through the brush and surprising the pheasant, the big game, as they broke their sleep for water and food. Got to get in the country soon. This city is killing me. Then he wished for Regina. There were others he could have wished for, but Regina had been there, could have been there if he had talked her into staying, but she had been right. Games, there had to be something else. He lowered his window shade and got into bed.

It seemed that he had slept only five minutes when the phone woke him up.

"This is Granville Bryant. Max Reddick?"

Bryant, Max thought.

"Did I wake you?"

"Well . . ."

"I hear you're looking for a job, Max. How've you been?"

"All right, except for the job."

"You need a good publisher too."

"Yeah," Max said, laughing.

156

"Did I say something funny?"

"Oh, no. I've only been looking for a job since last winter. As for the publisher, ha-ha."

"I know. It's terrible."

"You have a job, Granville?" Ah, well, it had to come to this, the fags. They had their games too.

"Well, yes, Max, but I wondered if you should take something that'll keep you from your work."

Their solicitousness kills me, Max thought. They could starve you and later say they were doing it so you could become proficient in your art. They've got all the answers, white folks. Well, Max, welcome to the round-eye set, the shitpacker crowd; maybe I can't get out of this hole (ha-ha) until I make that route. "Granville, I need a job. Besides, the novel's just about finished."

"Oh! is it really? Splendid, Max! Are you pleased with it?"

No, Granville, it's a rotten novel. I helped kill my girl because I wanted to write a rotten novel. I like ham hocks and beans and cabbage and collards for a daily diet, Granville, so I can write rotten books. But Max said, "Yes."

"Well, then, a friend of mine is starting a new daily. He's gathering staff now. It will be somewhat left, but you don't mind that, do you? [And Max was thinking: How can a broke nigger mind anything?] He's not interested in what a man's color is. He's read your work and the pieces you did for that Harlem paper and he'd like to see you, if you're interested."

"I'm interested."

"I'll give you his number then. And say, you know Marion Dawes, don't you?"

Dawes was the young Negro writer who'd gotten such a rave review in the *Times*. "I don't *know* him," Max said. "I know *of* him." It was important to make the distinction.

"I see. I wondered if you'd be good enough to give me Harry's address in Paris so I can give it to Marion — he was shy about calling you. Marion is planning to move to Paris before long and he'd like to get in touch with Harry."

Max kept thinking, Harry ain't gonna like this, ol' Harry ain't gonna like it at all.

"You know," Bryant was saying, "Marion has gotten a fellowship, so he'll be able to skimp through in Paris. But perhaps Harry will be able to help him with some contacts."

"Sure," Max said. Those bastards. They really looked after their own. "What kind of fellowship?"

"A Laurentian."

"Nice," Max said. "I wonder what I have to do to get one. They seem pretty hard for some people to come by."

Bryant laughed. "It does take a little luck."

And a little suck, Max thought. "That's all, huh?"

Bryant laughed again. "As far as I know, Max. My! You do seem out of sorts. Really, I didn't mean to wake you."

"It's all right," Max said. "I've never been out of work nine months before. It upsets me a little."

"Yes," Bryant said. "I'm sorry for that. Max, I'd like to have lunch with you sometime. I know you don't like me, but for a couple of hours — it won't hurt will it?"

Max beat a retreat. "What do you mean, I don't like you?"

"Come now. Both you and Harry. I know that."

"It's not *that*, Granville," Max said weakly.

"Well, let's talk about it another time. After you've spoken to Julian Berg. Remember," Bryant said mockingly, "the lunch won't hurt."

"So all those liberal bastards couldn't between them find a job for you, huh?" Julian Berg spoke as if he were musing to himself. He was a round little man with graying hair and light blue eyes. His nose was fiercely hooked as if to exaggerate his Jewishness. "I suppose this paper will be called liberal. That's a pity, because from the position of the others, we have to be. Everybody on his dot, like dancers. Okay. We'll take the label." Berg grimaced. "So you won't misunderstand. I want you on this paper because, number one, I want a Negro, as many as I can get. This is not pure altruism, Max.

There're whole segments of this town that have no voice. I'm concerned with Jews and Negroes. You can help me with Negroes and Jews and readers in general. Some Jews are reading the *Times,* the well-to-do. Too many Jews and Negroes are reading the reactionary press because they don't know the difference in papers. There's another view of things yet to be presented. That's our job, that's the *New York Century.* If you want the job, Cityside and specials, it's yours."

"I want it."

It felt better, after all, having a job. Max resigned himself to it; he was pretty much like everyone else. No job, panic or depression or both swiftly followed. Truly middle class, he thought. I *need* to work. Perhaps with the publication of the next book he could stop working. In the pig's rump.

He liked the way Berg was handling him. Max covered all kinds of human interest stories. The City Hall beat followed and, briefly, theater and books. Mostly it was Cityside, where he became familiar with the reporters of the other papers, the neat, young *Times*men, always dark-suited and soft-spoken, cerebral. The *Trib*men were cerebral without the dark suits and better drinkers. The reporters from the *Mirror* and the *News* seemed ashamed of themselves, while the men from the *Journal* and *World-Telegram & Sun,* constant, not quite plodders, drinkers in the old tradition, like French cabdrivers right after lunch with the hooch still curling around their mouths, were solid, underrated newsmen. *Criterion* reporters were not cerebral or good drinkers but pretended to be both. Max never was late and never missed an important news conference. The others, on a first-name basis with the whole range of public figures, were always late. But no matter, they could debrief Max Reddick of the *Century,* who was always on time. Handouts, follow-up calls and Max Reddick, and the story was covered, then written mentally in the nearest bar and given ten minutes on the typewriter at the office. Max didn't quite know how to handle the situation. There were two alternatives, of course. He could refuse to float any more of his material (the juicy color and meat no reporter gave away anyhow) or he could continue as he was, hoping that, if ever he became bored or lazy or ill, then he might be able to debrief other reporters. Max chose the latter alternative through the months, picking up in the meantime plaques from the NAACP and the National Urban League and B'nai B'rith for "superior reporting," but really for being a Negro reporter on a white Manhattan daily. They did not know how it had been the first few months, being stopped by guards and police and doormen, being refused entrance to press conferences until the *Century* office was called and his connection with it verified. Winter hit hard and was followed by a sullen spring, during which he thought of Lillian. He wondered now how it would have been with the writing. (He was riding the crest of anticipation. The new book would be out in early fall.) Would he have accomplished so much? On the other hand, wasn't this job for her, for her memory? He had done it; he had secured the kind of job she believed he deserved. Aha, baby! I didn't get it by deserving; I got it by knowing! Fags! (God, I must call Granville.)

If this book makes a nickel (he was still thinking) instead of buying a new car — zap! in the bank. Think France. Yes, think France. Six months, a year, it won't hurt. See Harry, move around a little, see just what it is all these niggers are raving about.

The city seemed to give a heavy, concrete sigh of relief with the coming of September. Labor Day had passed. The department stores were filled with parents readying their broods for school and children bent on spending every penny their parents had not already spent on camp and trips to Grandma's during the summer. The accidents on the road seemed to have been particularly gruesome over the Labor Day weekend; Max had covered three. But now the dead were buried, the injured attached to splints, blood, dextrose and in hospital beds. Football was poised to replace baseball, and quite suddenly, Max thought of Regina. He had spoken to her last Christmas and had decided then that perhaps it would be better if he didn't call her and if she didn't call him. But Max was feeling gracious and expansive. Maybe he was ready to be friends with her now; ready to suffer lunches and dinners and long talks and going to movies and theater together — with nothing afterward. Max had never known a woman with whom he wanted that kind of relationship. Regina was different. He called her.

"I've been waiting for you to call," she said. "I wondered how long it would take. Almost a year exactly, right?" What about last Christmas, Max wondered? He said nothing about it. "I've been reading you, of course," she went on, "and I read your new book in galleys. I have a friend at your publisher." It pleased Max to know that she had been thinking about him; he was glad he had called. "That's your best book so far, Max. You should be proud of it, I am. But most important. Did you call because you're feeling horny or are we friends? We are, aren't we?"

"Honest Reg, this was just a friendly call. How are you? How's Bob? Is it any better for you?"

"No, just the same. I think I'm getting used to it. Couldn't we have dinner tonight? I'd like to see you and talk to you. It's been a long time."

"That's just why I called," Max lied, although he would not mind the dinner or seeing her again. He felt proud of himself. He hadn't called because he wanted to get into her drawers (although he knew and she knew it too, that if she felt inclined to take them off for him he wouldn't have said no). He couldn't explain to himself his feeling for Regina. When she wanted to be friends why hadn't he said, "It's been nice, later?" Maybe she saw him coming, too. Regina Galbraith (formerly Goldberg) had been the sole member of her family spirited out of Nazi Germany. The rest were dead. Gassed and cooked, most likely. From what she'd told him, they were nice people, willing to please everyone, more German than Jewish. They would not have died in isolation, say, in an escape or during the murder of a prison guard. Those acts were in quarantine; they were not for those who needed the safety of a group. Regina went first to England and spent a few months in the London home of a mammoth, brusque woman. From there to Scotland. (Max had often pictured her, a small, puzzled child, still

161

speaking High German, her head swiveling from side to side in order to see it all, her face a blank as her mind interpreted what the adults around her were saying by placing their words in a context with time of day, expressions on their faces, how loudly or softly they spoke.) She spent many years in Scotland and then was sent off to Australia. Years later, a young woman in her twenties, she arrived in the United States via San Francisco and thence to New York where she charmed everyone with her Scottish accent.

"How was the year for you, Regina?" he asked.

"I was tempted to call you Christmas. It was too much for me again."

You did call, Max thought, sadly, and it would have been too much. Christmas, Chanukah, Bob in the bosom of his family (yours dead), Bob in someone else's pants besides hers and his wife's. Well, it was all a part of Regina's thing, apologizing to hell and back for being alive with the rest of her family dead. The holidays were bad. Then (she had told him) she usually checked into a mental clinic, or friends did it for her, afraid of what she might do to herself after her ten-times-a-night calls.

"Hi, there! This is Regina Goldberg Galbraith. Oh, you know who this is. Well! Merry Christmas! Happy Chanukah! God, I feel so lonely. What are you doing tonight? I thought you might take a few moments out to talk to me. It's good I have a friend like you to talk to when I feel this way. Where will you go Christmas? What will you do? Max [it was the call last Christmas] we are friends, right? You'd let me talk to you anytime if I needed someone to talk to, wouldn't you? I'd let you talk to me anytime if you were a little ill. I mean, if we were very good friends, true friends. Last night, Max, I called a man, just to talk to. I was *very* ill." (Max had not asked if it was Bob.) "He said he would come over and stay with me for a while. I said not to sleep with, I didn't want to sleep with him, and he said yes, he understood and he came over and after a while we were on the rug, the red rug on my floor, and he made me go put in my diaphragm and we both got naked and he made love to me on the rug, oh, he fucked me and he fucked me in dirty places and I felt very dirty, dirty, Max, ohhhh, so dirty, and I thought he would stay with me after that, but he got up and left and I cried and cried, then I got up to look for my pills, but I must have hidden them from myself or — maybe he took them! Yes! He took them from the medicine chest! [Max listened and felt a chill creeping upward from the middle of his spine until it fuzzed somewhere in the front of his head.] Now I have no more pills!" She said the last, Max remembered, with a scream.

She had continued to scream and moan and Max had tried to calm her down. "Max! I need someone *now!* Come over, Max. I've no pills, what'll I do, what'll I do?"

"Whiskey," Max had suggested. She dropped the phone. He could hear her drinking from a bottle. "Come talk to me, Max. I know you won't do what he did."

He couldn't call Bob. Stay out of that mess. Besides, he would start wondering. She couldn't either. Max had sat and listened, inserting a word here and there when he could. He knew he should have gone to be with her through the night. How well he knew that. But, suppose she continued screaming and moaning even if he were there, and finally the neighbors called the police. Sure, try and get out of that one. A half-naked girl (he assumed), out of her mind, her gray eyes bulging with fear and incomprehension, and a spade cat sitting there. Shit, he'd be in more trouble than she. No, he didn't need that. He listened to her a long time, then he hung up without a goodbye.

It was after the New Year before he could think of her without a great deal of remorse. He had told himself over and over again that he hadn't made the world; he just lived in it. He could have shown the cops his press card, but, so what? He was still a spade who was driving a nice young white girl to madness, they would think. And there was no certainty that Regina would not have led them on with her rantings.

But she had forgotten, or rather, she had not remembered the

Christmas call. Max said, "I was away anyhow, Christmas. I was hoping it would be better for you. What about the Christmas coming?"

"Oh, don't. I don't want to think about it."

"Okay, then, let's arrange to meet for dinner," he said, but he was thinking, A black man sorry for a white woman. A sucker for the people who hurt. Who's a sucker for me? But then the world was gleefully crashing its way toward a kind of Jewishness. The war, the horrors of that war, had done it. Jewish comics were stomping out of the Catskills and clustering around the coaxial cables; they shot their biting, mother-geared humor across the land. Yiddish phrases were becoming national catchwords. The nation (and the world) was guilty about what had happened to the Jews in Germany. Therefore, we will take this Jewish thing and, finally, make it American. Forgive us for the delay, Sholem Asch and Henry Roth. Better late than never. And there was Regina. Who did what about her, bubi? The day after dinner with Regina (she told him that Bob was doing so well with his painting — he'd had two successful shows in two months — that he was thinking of buying a house in Manhattan, to her delight), Berg summoned Max to his office.

The *Century* (quite naturally, Max reflected now) was for Wallace. The defection of Southerners from the Democratic Party to form the Dixiecrats made the question of Truman's election more than unlikely. Dewey looked like a shoo-in for the Presidency.

"We're giving you Wallace headquarters in town," Berg said. He seemed to be looking for a paper on his desk; he didn't look at Max. He kept looking for the paper, but really, he was waiting. Max knew he was waiting. It was an important assignment. There were more experienced political writers on the paper. And Max also knew the assignment would entail the digging out of Jews and Negroes high up in the Wallace hierarchy. Portraits, color. He said aloud, "Jews and Negroes, portraits, color."

Berg stopped looking for his paper. He turned a dour eye on Max. "Oh, Max. Oh, Max. Say it with *sincerity*." Berg broke into a sheepish grin. "Guess you know the paper pretty well by now." He broke off the smile. "That's exactly what we want, Jews, Negroes, portraits, color. If you can catch Wallace, we want to know about the abolition of the poll tax, enforcement of the statutes calling for the end of Jim Crow in interstate travel, the continuing apprehension and conviction of Nazi war criminals. We want to know if he's going to expand the Marshall Plan or drop it as soon as he gets a chance. Okay?"

"Okay. And thanks."

The Wallace people relied heavily on dramatics. Theirs was an uphill campaign. From the first it was not directed against Truman; Dewey was the target. Wallace, the thin man with the long face, the stiff, sweeping mop of hair, the toothy, embarrassed, adolescent grin, attracted young people — and, Max noted at the time, the younger veterans of the war. There was a certain vibrancy to the campaign, the kind only underdogs wage. Pete Seeger, Paul Robeson, blacks and whites. There were spotlights in a thousand high school auditoriums that cut through the darkness with the speed and force of a knife wounding the eye to disclose Henry Agard Wallace.

The volunteers and staff people worked around the clock. Many nights Max left headquarters, leaving Regina behind with other volunteers who had come in from full-time jobs to ink the mimeograph machines and cut the stencils and run them off for the next day. But dramatics, spotlights, guitars and folk songs were not enough; nor were crowds of young people dancing in blue jeans. That was when blue jeans came to have their first bad connotation, because the people wearing them, the folk singers, brethren of the people and prebeatniks, were for Wallace. Long, long before Election Day the outcome was foreseen through that mysterious American device, the poll, the polls and talk; talk and the lack of money in the Progressive camp; the lack of money and the snowballing whisper campaign about the Communists flying high on the Wallace coattails. Tom Dewey's star rose higher and higher. The Dixiecrats were going to hurt Truman, wound him mortally. Dewey all the way. The Gangbuster, the Governor. Truman? President by accident. Wallace? Even Roosevelt had kicked him out. Dewey all the way.

It seemed to Max that Wallace started to quit in October; the fire was cooling. Papers like the *Century* were few and damned far between. The rumors started whipping the man. Who would Wallace be able to trust if he got in? There was all of that and more. It was the black and the white. The sudden equality in 1948 (much too early for America). It was the deep fear of that as well as anything else. Henry A. Wallace went quietly that November Tuesday, quietly and early. Harry Truman retired in the Muehlebach Hotel in Kansas City and everybody felt sorry for him, thinking that when he woke the next morning, he would have two and a half months left in the White House. Max Reddick felt sorry for him, crusty little bastard, haberdasher, symbol of the American dream, little guy gone big. Max preferred Truman to Wallace. Wallace had too much to think about; Truman took a step at a time and took it decisively and later for the rest of you cats. Who really could like Tom Dewey? The polls told the story on Wednesday morning, the same day Truman woke and fired his Secret Service chief who had stayed in New York to guard Tom Dewey, who lost the Election.

Max had laughed his ass off; it was just like Truman. Then it was all over.

In Leiden, high on the morphine, Max laughed softly and clutched his paining rectum. How naive he had been then. It had not been over with Wallace, it had just begun, that pulsating, murderous desire to be near or in politics, for that was where power was. Politics was some American game; it had its pauses, but never an end. It was the Ultimate Game, while you lived. It had sent people back to where they came from; it killed others and drove still others to the psychiatric wards or alcoholic clinics. It was where one learned the sorry truth about his countrymen.

For example, Stevenson's great losses to Ike brought forth the terrifying realization that unless the people could have a rich Presi-

166

dent who had had the leisure to study their problems and learn the right phrases and how to utter them (the European heritage — a good King Wenceslaus) like Roosevelt or Kennedy, they'd make do generally with someone pretty much like themselves. A five-star hero, perhaps, who, from the age of eighteen or nineteen had only to answer the call of a bugle to be fed, clothed and provided water for washing for most of his life, with time out for other jobs which were equally unfamiliar, until they made him their President. A man in their image.

There was no faking that image, as Humphrey could tell anybody; it was no good rambling about the old days as a druggist. Kennedy had put the spurs to that concept of the good old guy next door.

Max had been an incurious Democrat, but had never thought of himself as a politician, in fact, not even a good, Northeast variety Democrat. But the co-speechwriting, the tremor of Washington, the cold, steely scent of power had touched him. The social crisis that loomed black over the land had attracted him, but now Max wished that it hadn't turned out the way it had.

Max's third novel came out during the end of the Wallace campaign. ". . . now bests his master, Harry Ames . . ."

"The *Tribune* here [Harry wrote] says you're better than me. Do you believe it . . . ?"

Letters from Harry were few after that. When they came they were unexpected, and therefore they threatened. They contained no warmth. It was just as well, for Max, in a manner he never would have admitted, was weary of being compared to Ames, to Bolton Warren, and now, to Marion Dawes, who was in Paris. The critics and reviewers were unrelenting because, Max concluded, they did not know what they were doing; and because they were supposed to be knowledgeable people, they'd never admit to an ignorance of discrimination. The effect was the same. White writers were compared only to other white writers; black writers were compared only to other black writers.

Max was deep in bitterness when he received a call from Kermit Shea, who was now a senior editor at *Pace*. Shea had changed, Max noticed. He was no longer a hot roast beef sandwich and two double-bourbon man. Now he ate two-hour lunches at the best French and Italian restaurants in midtown. His suits were pressed, his shoes polished, his hair neatly combed. Now he wore glasses with complexion-tone frames. He was a different kind of newsman.

"I'm glad you got the break with *Century*," he said. "And of course, I've read your book. We gave it a good review."

Max remembered the lead. It had been about Harry Ames. "Who were you writing about, me or Harry Ames?"

"Yeah, yeah, I noticed that too," Shea said. "Well, a review in *Pace*, good or bad, doesn't hurt sales, you know."

And Max knew it.

Shea chewed his food slowly; he had expected some bitterness. "You know, we've already had some discussion at the magazine about opening up, the way the *Century* has. Nothing's come of it yet, but I'd like to be able to throw your name in the hopper when the time comes."

Max made him work. He listened and nodded or said nothing. He spoke only enough to keep the conversation from dying. He kept thinking: Kermit Shea, white, senior editor, *Pace*. Western Reserve, class of '37. Italian campaign, *Stars and Stripes*. Age, thirty-four. Future, a snap. Why? White. Max Reddick, black, city reporter, the *Century*. Western Reserve, class of '37. Italian campaign, infantryman. Age, thirty-four. Future, doubtful. Why? Black.

"You mentioned Ames. What do you hear from him?"

"He's all right."

"Is he coming back?"

"I don't know. Why?"

"Well, I mean, things are . . . you know what I mean."

"Yes, I know." Max lit a cigarette. Seeing Shea again combined with the hurting business of the book brought on all the old pains.

"Do you think he should come back? Would you, if you were him?"

"I don't know what I'd do if I were him," Shea said. "But he was born here. It's his country. You care for it —"

"*I* care for it? Kermit, this is my day for not giving one good fuck where or how this country goes. I couldn't care less."

"You can't mean that."

"Am I really permitted to be as conscientious about these things as you? C'mon, Kermit. Since when?"

Shea waited before answering. "I should think you'd be even more concerned. What if you inherit ignorance and indecision, as I have?"

"Well then, whose fault is that?" Then Max saw him climbing Harry's steps once more and remembered Harry telling him about what Shea had said then. "My mood is foul today," Max said. "Let's not talk about these things. Tell me about the job. And tell me, does *Pace* pay more than the *Century?*" He saw Shea start to relax. At one point he thought, He would be good for Regina. Never seen him with a woman. What's his bag? Max's publisher was giving a party for the publication of his book. He would invite Shea and Regina. And Granville. That would take care of that obligation. As the lunch was breaking up, Shea said, "Army-Notre Dame. Saturday at the Stadium. I've got two tickets I lifted from the Sports people. What do you say?"

The man won't let go, Max thought. What's the matter with him he won't let go? But he said, "Sure. Pick you up?"

"Twelve-thirty."

It had been a different kind of meeting. Max had not been broke, distressed with a girl, or in the pit of a depression still finding its bottom. His bitterness had not, for a time, been muted. He had called a halt to the conversation about "conditions." Once, he would have allowed Shea to continue talking about them. No more. He knew about the conditions. They had cut him to ribbons, but he had not died. Instead (thanks to Granville) he now stood heavily on his own two feet. The book helped too; a book always did. Well, then. If Shea wanted to unburden his soul, let him find someone else; if he wanted to hang around, goddamnit, he was going to hang around like a man, not a creep!

At the party for the publication of his book, Shea turned out to be a very shy man, which amused Max. It was Regina who did the wooing, hurtling into this new thing with the force of a bird trying to escape captivity. When last he looked, it seemed to be going okay. He talked for a long time with Zutkin, whom he had not seen in over a year. Granville Bryant was there with a young man who stood silently at his side and listened to his conversation without expression.

It was Bryant who, midway through the party, said, "Is he your only Negro friend, Max?" Bryant gestured toward Roger Wilkinson, who was indeed the only other Negro beside Max present. Max laughed briefly. "They were invited, Granville, they were invited."

"Why didn't they come?"

Annoyed, Max shrugged and moved away. How in the hell did he know why they hadn't come? He had worked hard on the invitation list to bring about a balancing of white and Negro friends. He hated to do that. To secure the right balance he had set down the names of Negroes he didn't really like. Like Harry, he thought, I've become the marginal man. Where were they? Had he alienated every single one of them at precisely the *same* time? How? Glumly he watched Regina and Shea, then Roger Wilkinson talking with Bryant. That was good. Roger was a young writer; perhaps Bryant could be of use to him. Of course, Roger knew what he was doing. Max had had that feeling ever since his first meeting with Roger, who had thrust himself on Max, asking him to read manuscripts, discussing this writer and that one, eagerly writing down the advice Max half-heartedly gave him. What was wrong with Wilkinson, Max suddenly realized as he took another Scotch from the tray, was that he liked *names*. He thought they gave medals for reading

Stendahl and Giraudoux and Auden and Henry Adams. He was a walking encyclopedia of famous and obscure writers, the good ones. ("Honest, Max, that Andreyev is something *else!*")

Goddamn it, why hadn't they come? Now he knew. He had been lucky. He had made it, they thought, and that made him less Negro; that made him no longer one of them. Dick Ricketts, the policy man in Harlem, greeted him in the uptown bars with, "Hey, Money!" Dick had sense and Max had told him more than once that writers made money if they were lucky, or said what other people wanted them to say. Ricketts, sharp yellow face taut, lidless reptile eyes cold so that you couldn't tell if they were comprehending or not, listened carefully, then said, "Okay, baby, you tell it your way. I *know* them white folks don't publish your books because they *like* you!" Max had told him he had it all wrong. "But dig, man," Ricketts had gone on, his handmade suit falling about him like gray velvet, his shirt open at the neck, a little gesture to establish and maintain rapport with the nickel-and-dimers, his Aston-Martin double-parked outside, unticketed on 125th Street, for every cop knew it. "And you writin' for Mister Charlie's paper too. Don't I see your name in the paper? How you sound? C'mon here and let me buy you a taste even though I know you can't get into your house for all the hundred-dollar bills you got jammed up in it."

Damn them, Max thought. When you're down, scraping through on ham hocks and beans, they don't want to be bothered with you. But when they think you've made it, they're either afraid of you or put you down for being a Tom. What's worse than being black? Being black *and* lucky. Max took a final look around at his party, then slipped out. Harlem wouldn't come to him; he would go to it.

"Every time I see you up here, you're runnin' through. Them white folks run you out from downtown?" Sergeant Jenkins. He seemed bigger, blacker, badder. Drugs were starting their poisonous flow through Harlem and, rumor had it, Jenkins was hell on pushers and junkies. Max nodded briefly. Black sonofabitch, he thought. Like I don't have any business up here. Like they were all *waiting* for me to leave Harlem for good.

"I spend a lot of time around here, Jenks," Max finally said, wearily. "Right now," he lied, "I'm doing a story on police brutality. Can you help?"

Jenkins grinned his big bad grin. "Police brutality, eh. What's that, son? I don't know nothin' about that. Sounds like Communist talk to me. You know the friendly, neighborhood cop is a public servant. That's right, son."

"Yeah, sure."

"What happened to your ace-boon-coon, that other writer fella?"

"He's in France."

"France, huh? Hell, he married a white girl, didn't he? What the hell's he in France for? Did he divorce her or something, or just can't get enough of that white nooky? Is he coming back?"

"I don't know."

Jenkins laughed. "You got your back up, son. Don't shit me. I know your type. Police brutality, huh, you goddamn nigger intellectuals and them nigger leaders, soon's you get two quarters to rub together you got your ass on a ship for Europe. You don't even know what's going on here."

"We try, Jenks, we try."

"That Boatwright boy, he was an intellectual too, wasn't he, son? Look what happened to him. Look what he did. You cats is as queer as three dollar bills. If it ain't sex, it's in the fuckin' head. I seen all kinds, son, and all the noise you make don't help a junkie or a cat done messed over his wife good, one bit. Cats say I'm hard. Sure, and I like to beat a bad nigger's head. Know why? Because when he sees me coming the next time he's gonna get the hell outa my way. I'm hard because I got to be. These niggers up here are harder on my ass than a hundred paddy cats. And I got to live, son. I got a family. Wife and kids. And I mean to come home in one piece when my day's hitch is done. And every single day, *every* day, there's some motherfucker up here sayin' I ain't gonna make it. What you damned intellectuals still got to learn is that this ain't no classroom, son, it's a jungle." Jenkins hitched up his pants, those heavy dark blue pants with the flashlight in one pocket, .38 revolver low over one cheek of the ass, the row of cartridges, the blackjack and nightstick, the notebook, all attached. The paraphernalia made a jangling noise. "Cool it, son. I got to go. Keep your nose clean."

Sweet Cheeks, the bartender at the Nearly All Inn greeted him as soon as he entered. "Here he is, ladies and gentlemen, the prodigal. The black Ernest Hemingway, Rudyard Kipling, Honoré de Balzac all rolled into one. Furthermore, he is the black Richard Harding Davis, Edward R. Murrow and Walter Winchell also all rolled into one. Hey, baby! Where you been? Have you come over to our side yet? Gay is best, baby, I shit thee not. Have a taste!"

He fled as soon as he could to Big Ola Mae's. He should have known what to expect from Sweet Cheeks; his was the most vicious tongue in Harlem. He loud-talked you, if he didn't think his tip was large enough. Now, Max sat down and Ola Mae waddled over. "Maxwell? It is you. Child, where you been? Is you hungry? You lookin' a little bit peaked, there. I know, you done got married and your wife's a little too fast for you. Right? No. Well you eat somethin' anyhow. Did you know your boss at the *Democrat* —" she bent close to Max, "that raggedy-assed nigger paper — married your girlfriend, that cute little thing, Mary. Sure enough did."

Mary. In restrospect, nice, they all were then, softened by time and other women still. They spoiled a guy though, the women. Maybe it had to do with the male–female ratio he had heard about so much. He never thought about it the way he had thought of some European villages where whole male populations had gone off to war and been killed. What happened to the women? They must have become ravenous. New York women were a very special breed. Just as most knowledgeable American women hesitate to compete with European women, so most American women pause before climbing into the same arena with New York women. Special. Tough, lovely, knowing, playing the cards the way they were dealt, most of the time. Maybe the war had done that, set women free. But Big Ola Mae was still leaning on the table, her fat, deep chocolate brown face benignly creased, motherly behind the out-of-place gold-rimmed glasses, talking. "I bet you got one of them little white girls now, ain't you, Maxwell? You're a big man now, and every big nigger gets him a white girl." She leaned back, brown flab encased in whalebone and elastic, laughed and slapped Max on the shoulder with a heavy hand. "I sure am sick of you colored men. Runnin' just as fast as you can after them. Whoo! Why don't you menfolks wake up? It ain't nuthin', now, is it?"

She had killed his appetite. But he ordered coffee and sweet potato pie. When he finished, he left, walking home. At some point, going south on Broadway, past Juilliard, Barnard and Columbia, his pace slow with heavy thought, November's cold slashing softly through the Heights, he decided that, with the first break, he'd get out of it for a while. His piles were kicking up more. The Army operation seemed to have done no good. Nerves, one doctor told him; too much sedentary work, another had said. He found himself bored with people, tired of them, and that seemed to gather in his rectum. There was pain, but that seemed easy, compared to the rest.

# 16

TO HELL with the rest.

In successive days, Zutkin asked him to do some articles. (All right, going-away money.)

Berg was getting him set to do a series on Jackie Robinson, how he spent his time off-season.

Shea was giving him almost daily unsolicited reports on his burgeoning romance with Regina.

Still there was no mail from Harry. (Well, if that's the way he feels, later.)

Both doctors were agreed that what Max needed was another hemorrhoidectomy.

What I need, Max told himself, is a little orgy. For Thanksgiving maybe. Mildred.

After the long depression following Lillian's death, there had come the women. He met them at parties, conferences, through intermediaries — in all the ways there are to meet women. He overdid his first affair, put too much into it, made it meaningful when he really hadn't wanted to. He had to back out of it, and in order to do that well, he had simply begun another, then another. One of his early girls (Betsy!) had been very young, in her twenties, a graduate student at New York University. She wore T-shirts under her blouse ("I sweat a lot."). The way she liked to make love, it could be done with all her clothes on. She went for nothing else. *That* had been a mistake. A man likes to grab hold of more than just a head of hair. Most times. The ingenue he had met while writing theater copy liked to drink sherry. She had to have at least one entire bottle before she even *thought* about making love. During which time she whined about her career. Irene. The Swedish stringer at the UN, Frederika, was all right, except she never came. She liked jazz, but couldn't shake her head to the music to save her life. There were a few tough hairs on her breasts that made lovemaking somewhat uneasy. And that *thing,* that ugly, dangling, crippled labia; it felt like taking hold of a piece of warm chitlin. And she was forever shoving it up out of the way. Regina was another who never came except when she masturbated. She guessed that was why she couldn't have an orgasm when lovemaking. Sometimes she had seemed quite close. Her eyes would narrow, her movements grow short and choppy, as if she were nearing the crest of a hill, running. Then with a long, sorrowful gasp of resignation, she would quit. There was the model, Hélène, who made love with quicksilver passion because she didn't have to, the way she had to with photographers, agents and others who made it possible for

175

models to get to the top. A telephone call to a woman, or receiving one from a woman late at night, the work lying limp on the desk, meant one thing: the business of pursuing pleasure. Sometimes when one left his apartment and he was still keening his condition which was the murder of loneliness, he would call another and go to her, or she would come to him, giving him just time enough to change the sheets. Once when he had carried five changes of sheets to the laundry several times in a row, the laundryman asked, "Are you from the hotel down the street? Tell me, because we can give you a discount." Max left hastily, mumbling, No.

Manhattan became a city filled with lonely women frowning at their telephones, anxious to make love, desperate to be with some-one, and they would speed to him after a brief call, or he would dress hurriedly for the next day's work, toothbrush and comb jammed into a pocket, and hail a cab to go speeding through a stroboscopic city to the Village, the East Side, Harlem, Chelsea. It was always the same during the first moments. A kiss, an embrace, small conversation, unwrapping the bottle, or, briefly, watching the Late Show, delaying deliciously that moment made possible by the New York Telephone Company and UTOG, the United Taxi Own-ers' Guild. Sometimes, darting unbidden into the night there would come a phone call. Max would sit or, if they were already in bed, lie and listen. He liked it when the phone was near the bed. There is no better way to learn a woman than to listen to her talking on the phone to her lover, husband, lover-to-be, while you are fondling her breasts and making a soft, flanking foray. How calm they were, the women. Like electricity, always there awaiting a finger to push the right button. Max marveled at it; he accepted it. They were the winners, the women, and the man who thought not was the fool. Sometimes, high, Max would hold the woman he was with and let the words spill, cascade, knowing full well somewhere behind the drinks that this was not part of the deal, and whenever he was like that, he noticed in retrospect the next day — in the middle of an assignment having nothing whatsoever to do with women — that tiny, pitying smiles had played around her mouth. He would shrug, as if to her, and continue working.

Then came Mildred.

One night, soon after he began with the *Century,* he had some people to his apartment for drinks before going out to dinner. He did not really know his date; he had only met her the week before. Mildred — he had glanced at her twice, pleasantly surprised that he would not be the only Negro in the dinner party. She came with a natty young man who said he was in television. During dinner Max's date said she was coming down with a cold and Max sent her home in a cab. The signals had not been coming right, anyway. The party returned to his apartment where Max noticed Mildred (and Charley, he thought) in a corner. A few minutes later Charley (?) rose and, making his words and attitude nonchalant, bid everyone good night. When the people who'd brought Mildred and — *was* his name Charley? — rose with those familiar overtures to departure and saw Mildred still sitting, they asked Max to see that she got home all right. Max put on a somber, responsible face as he assured them he would. When he had closed the door after them, he turned to Mildred. "Drink?"

"Yes, of course." She was tall. She had "blow" hair, processed hair. Her eyes were a deep brown and her skin was the color of loam freshly turned in spring. She went to the kitchen with him and for lack of anything else to say (Mildred sent and received signals), Max said, "Can I kiss you?"

She had been leaning on the refrigerator, fingers in her hair. "Sure," she said, "if I can kiss you too."

He stroked her face after the kiss. Then they returned to the living room and played a record, "Night in Tunisia." They drank in silence listening to it. (That had been the hard bop period.) Then he had said, "Stay." In their situation the word had but one meaning. There was a whole list of words, a complete dictionary, for making love, or wanting to.

"No, you come home with me," she countered. He had not

known then that Mildred was strict with herself about making love with her diaphragm; that was why she left it at home. Conditioned. Determined. No one was knocking her up. Quickly, Max changed shirts, seized his toothbrush, and they left, arm in arm at three in the morning.

There was a cat in her apartment and also many paintings of Greek male nudes. Mildred had put on *Wozzeck* while she made drinks. After, without a word, she pulled down the sheets on the bed and slipped into the bathroom. Max undressed slowly. God was good to him. Thank you, God, for seeing that I don't go without when I need it. Thank you, Man. Mildred came slowly through the bedroom door, her hair down, her diaphanous gown drifting about her. She sat at the side of the bed. "In the morning," she said, "we must be very quiet. [Charley?] will be ringing downstairs." Laughing softly she moved the telephone from the side of the bed and, unwinding the extension cord, took it to the outer room. "He'll call if I don't answer the door. I put the phone out there because if I don't answer that he'll kick the door in. I don't want you to hear me lie to him. I may have to lie to you one day."

She had been confident that there would be more than one night. At the foot of the bed that night the cat had yawned, blinked and snuggled close to Max's feet. "Daisy likes you," Mildred said. "That's a good sign. She doesn't like just anybody."

Mildred was a poet and worked as a salesgirl at Lord & Taylor's in Junior Misses. So she left in the morning, chic, neat, appearing unviolated, unloved, and ready for more. Only her eyes were somewhat streaked with red. She wore a burnt orange coat and scarf (Max remembered) and had pleaded with Max not to forget to feed Daisy before he left. Please.

There had been one bad moment between them. Mildred had slipped from the game. "Why don't we get married?" she asked one night after they had been seeing each other for several months.

A good thing at an end, or was it? Before he could answer she said, "I'm sorry. It's just tonight. It's my birthday. I'm twenty-nine years old. I want to be married and have children. This being a swinging chick and all is birdturd. Tonight, just now, it bothered me, this thing we have, Max."

Max grabbed the straw. "Why didn't you tell me it was your birthday? We could have —"

"I know, I know, one of those special screwing parties with great martinis and champagne at dinner. I don't want anything special. Unless you're it." In the background was *Wozzeck* again; it was her favorite record, that and *Madame Butterfly*. Mildred continued. "Lillian died and you're not going to have anyone die on you again, not anyone you're in love with, so you're not going to fall in love, right?" She knocked her ice cubes together in the glass and stared out over the rim at Max.

"So I'll give you a quarter for your two-bit analysis, okay, Mil?"

The climax of *Wozzeck,* the child's scream, came between them.

"I'm sorry. I shouldn't have said that," she said.

"I'm sorry too."

Yes, to hell with all of it except Mildred.

Max borrowed Ricketts' Coupe de Ville and Mildred brought a turkey just in case and even though, which meant, she translated as they rushed northward on the Taconic Parkway en route to the Catskills, that if he didn't get anything hunting, they'd have the turkey. And if he did, it being Thanksgiving, they'd still have it because she wasn't going to clean and cook anything he might be lucky enough to shoot. He hadn't told her that Ricketts' cabin had food in the freezer and on the shelves and that Ricketts had called his caretaker and told him to get the house in shape for company. Ricketts used the place for relaxation and business too, the latter being meetings with precinct captains of New York's Finest, and current bosses of the Cosa Nostra.

In the mountains the skies became clear; far-off stars and planets gleamed sharply in a sky lighted by cold moonlight. "This car is too much," Mildred murmured about the Cadillac. Max grunted. He tried to match the tone of her voice to something she'd said to him — "You're too much," or "It's too much" — he forgot. Something as sensual. Americans made their cars like women, for luxury, and sleek and powerful, with points all over and long buttock-smooth lines. Think of America and you think of cars and Hollywood; one in charge of the national debt, the other overseeing the national libido. They turned off the main road and onto a smaller one topped with macadam; a dirt road followed, then an access road. Max pulled up before a low, wide cabin. White smoke curled slowly from the chimney and sought the stars. It looked cozy. "Here's where we have our orgy, Mil."

She said nothing getting out of the car, but at the door she paused, pecked him on the lips and answered, "Yes, the first one in eight weeks." He had not thought her words ominous then nor of the kiss as the kiss of farewell. The look she had given him after their first kiss, just inside the door, still clutching bags, also had no meaning. Then.

He rose just before dawn, drank the leftover coffee with a sandwich, slipped a couple of shells into the double-barreled shotgun and stepped out on the porch. He felt deliciously tired, sated. Mildred slept, curled softly on her side of the bed. Max pulled hard on his first cigarette then closed the gun with a dull, steely snap. Putting the safety on, he stepped to the ground and mashed the cigarette underfoot. He walked slowly down the road, now pushing the safety off; he might catch a bird at the edge of the road. The gray mist of day was giving way to the lightening morning. Birds whickered through the air, sparrows. A steady, biting wind snaked around the mountains and stalked stiffly up the road. Max pulled up his coat collar and blinked his eyes to clear them of the water brought to them by the wind. He thought he saw something down the road, a brown blur, a rough triangular shape. He hoisted the gun almost chest high and moved off the road, through a slight path; he would come from the wood onto the road at the spot where he thought he had seen the pheasant. He walked swiftly, the dried twigs clutching at his clothing. He approached the road fast, crashing through the brush, his finger curled around the outside trigger. When he had gained the road he found nothing. He lowered the gun and stood motionless, watching the vapor of his breath rise from his mouth and evaporate. Bastard, he thought, and everybody felt sorry for the birds.

I ought to marry Mildred, he thought, proceeding down the road. I ought to. He glanced about him. The sunshine was climbing through the mountain valleys now, laying down straight golden fingers, reflecting light from the brooding, dark-green acres of spruce and pine, warming the naked maples, teasing the great, twisted oaks. Come out, come out wherever you are . . . Max thought. She was all for him, Mildred. Whatever he did was all right, whenever he wanted to. That was important to a man. She understood. The cliché again. Well, all right. Let it be. Max held his face to the sun and glinted against its brassy glare. Good, feels good. Thanksgiving Day. Alone in the woods. Fine babe waiting in bed. Nice.

He had spent two hours more in the field, he remembered, and then, returning to the cabin through the brush, just beneath him, suddenly, twisting and running like the head of a gigantic serpent, the designs on its back like those on a reptile, the hen burst cover with a dangerous sound of her wings. Max, still recoiling from the snake image, hesitated a moment, but then as the pheasant fled through a break in the brush and flew up against a small patch of open sky, Max fired, and before the echo of the first shot caught the hillsides, he let loose the other, tracking the bird down its sudden plummet to the ground, and he heard the pellets hit — thrrepp! — and saw feathers burst clear in the sky. The bird's falling was now straight down. The hen was still warm when Max picked it up. He broke open the gun and plucked the shells from the hot, smoking barrels. He lit a cigarette, then stood dry-plucking the hen. When that was finished, he took out his skinning knife and cut its throat to let the blood drain. Then, slipping the point of his knife just beneath the breastbone, he sliced open the stomach and shook out the contents. He'd give the bird to Ricketts, a thank-you gift.

Mildred was waiting for him, backing away from the pheasant. He laughed at her and went to get drinks while she fixed the turkey. There had been two days more of the orgy, but they would have others, he thought, driving back to the city. He really had thought that. But over coffee she had told him. Charley (?) was back in the picture. Eight weeks between dates and no phone calls, what did Max expect? And she knew Max well enough, she had said, to know that even if he promised to do better, to consider, even, the ultimate in the American affair, marriage, she didn't know; he had demonstrated a fierce selfishness and it left nothing for her. Charley (?) would marry her, give her all the things she'd never even think about if she were Max's wife. She'd accept. That's all there was to it; she'd made up her mind. She had not wanted to ruin the weekend by saying anything before now. It had been her turn to be selfish. And during this, Max sipped his coffee and thought foolishly of the bird downstairs in the car. Then, blinking, he glanced around the room, at Daisy, the paintings of the Greek nudes, the shelf of records with *Wozzeck* and *Madame Butterfly* set apart, and knew he was going to miss Mildred. This was what the look and kiss in the cabin was all about; this was what the complaint about the eight weeks was about. It was all about Goodbye, Max. He said the proper things when he rose to go, and kissed her and stroked her behind. She walked him to the door. And closed it softly behind him.

He had not known what he felt then. His tongue had lain silently in his mouth, a little dry perhaps, but it had not been stuck. He whistled tunelessly driving to Ricketts' home. The Cadillac purred beneath him, prowling its way uptown. Who else had gone like that? They all went differently. Some drifted, some fled, or he drifted or fled. It was all motion, these affairs, energy, and the ones he enjoyed most were those that took the least mental toll. Goodbye, Mildred. Do you ever laugh when you call out, "Charley"?

Or *was* it Charley?

A soft rain was falling, months later. He was walking with Kermit Shea to Shea's midtown apartment. They had had dinner and Shea had drunk a lot and become glum. The wet streets reflected store lights and the headlights of the slowly moving traffic. At Lexington Avenue they paused on the curb, waiting for the light to change. When it did, it caught a small, white sports car. Laughter trickled out of the car and Max, standing on the curb, just about to step down and proceed across the street, looked down into the car and saw Mildred, a filmy kerchief bound to her head, her white teeth flashing in the darkness, the whites of her eyes rolling up and widening. For just a moment. Max nodded and his mouth formed up to a smile and he stepped down, passed in front of the car and gained the opposite curb. A few paces down the walk he heard the traffic move, heard the sharp deep roar of the sports car, then he turned around. Old Mildred. Go, baby.

"How's Regina?" Max asked. He could ask that now. Max and Shea had already gone through a scene when Shea, laughing of course, had wanted to know how Max had come to know her and Max lied because he knew Shea wanted him to, to make it all right for him to be involved with Regina, to even be in love with her.

"She's all right," Shea said quietly, handing out drinks. But when he sat down, he said, "Max, I haven't seen her in a while."

Regina's pulled her number on him, Max thought. That Christmas bit. "Oh," Max said. "I didn't know. I haven't spoken to her."

Max stared into his drink. When he looked up, he saw Shea dabbing at his eyes. Was the bastard *crying?* "Well," Max said, cheerfully, "you're holding up all right?"

Shea nodded, gulped his drink and poured another. He took out his handkerchief and blew onto it. "I was having some problems," he said.

Max nodded. Don't go on, man. I don't want to hear it. Yet he knew that was precisely why Shea had asked him to have dinner with him.

"An old problem, really. I couldn't, I couldn't —" and Shea's voice rose in muted anguish above the sound of the steadily falling rain. "Goddamn*it!*" he said, stomping his foot on the rug. "I couldn't get it up, Max. We'd be there and, I'll be a sonofabitch, I'd want to so much it was killing me, and I couldn't get it up until I told her I couldn't get it up and then it was all right. For months, it was the same, and with every girl I've ever known. Once I tell

183

them, it's all right, but it's like I have to tell them every time I see them."

Max looked at the floor. Goddamn. He's going to hate me tomorrow. Maybe he hates me *now*. It won't ever be the same. There'll be nothing at *Pace* now. No man should make a revelation like that to another man, *especially* if they are supposed to be friends. "Maybe you were trying too hard," Max said. "That can be murder. Too much hooch is bad, too."

"It wasn't either one," Shea said sadly. "I just couldn't get it up."

Max thought, Didn't he have anyone else to tell this to? Is he so bankrupt of friends that I'm his best friend? Maybe because he knows I don't move in his circle; I'm certainly not going to tell his friends, because I don't know them. He did not look at Shea. He thought of Mildred, her laughter, the white sports car. What had she thought the instant her eyes widened in recognition? Gone now, tearing through the middle of Manhattan. She had been sitting on the rider's side. Who was the driver?

"You ever had any trouble like that?" Shea asked.

Kill him, Max thought, *kill* 'im. Tell him *never*, not once in your life. Max studied his man, measured him. Should he decline the role of God or accept it? Shea worked hard to be honest and to do that you had to ask shallow questions, not questions at all, but make statements about yourself. If he suspected that Max and Regina had been lovers and Max had not had the problem getting it up, then Shea was going to hate him not only for hearing the confession but for having a harder cock. Harder and up longer. "Doesn't everybody?" Max said, tossing down his drink.

"Really?"

"Come on. You know it."

Shea brightened a bit. "I thought that might be the case . . . ah, Max, I'm screwed up and you know it and I know it."

Max shrugged. He felt bone weary now. Something very old was starting all over again. After the operation he was staying out of

184

complications, and he wasn't going to make any. Jesus, two operations on a man's ass. "Look, man," he said to Shea, "You're going to be all right. Talk to a headshrinker, maybe. But I'll lay ten to one that you're going to wind up with one of the stiffest pricks in the city, maybe the whole Eastern seaboard. You won't be able to get enough pussy; your reputation will spread from here south to Washington and from here north to Boston. You are going to wear chicks out. You are going to tear trim up. When you walk down Madison Avenue, the guys in the Look Building are going to say, "There's goes a *cock*sman's cocksman!"

The series on Jackie Robinson completed, Zutkin's articles finished, Max checked into the hospital so he could be out in time for Christmas, give in to the season, the celebration of the impossible occasion, the rich man's chance to dissipate the image of Scrooge; celebrate the lie and in consequence celebrate the massacre of the babes (while one escaped, that one — with his mother, Miriamne, made Mary by the *goyim,* secret bride to Antipater — victim of his father's wrath for striving for his father's throne through Herodian power and the Hebrew law of succession through Mother; and Joseph and an ass. Lies again.) Celebrate the named and unnamed wars, the heroes and cowards in them, the cruelties of them, drink to the civilizations brought crashing together in hate and being civilized no more, toast the miseries of the naked, starving, illiterate poor; pay homage to the squadrons of cherubic young faces wrapped in swaddling collars, loosing soprano Christmas chords upon the world; celebrate the millions upon millions of acres of trees ripped screaming from the skin of the earth to molder in corners under costumes of glass and metal junk; and, sadly, celebrate Handel and Bach, the sopranos, tenors and *basso profundos* who sing the lie as though they believed it, and in fact, make it believable; celebrate the unsmiling jingle of hard coins and the surreptitious rustle of dollar notes; celebrate the choruses of the Reginas shrieking in depthless anguish; drink to the unloved who haunt the high places and galloping winds with only water or asphalt below, or drink to the pill-takers who leave electric lights and radios and television sets on to ease their going. Yes, all of that, but he wanted to be home for Christmas.

In the hospital, smelling of wax and starched sheets and rubbing alcohol, they took his temperature, pulse and blood pressure. Up from the lab a cutie with pipette and tube for the complete blood count. The intern asked him questions in his most bored bedside manner. They did not feed him. The next day they gave him pills and shaved his buttocks. And after, through the swinging door, they rolled a stretcher. For him. Then he was on an elevator filled with sweet-smelling nurses, young, and even the starched rustle of their uniforms made them somehow more alluring. The whiteness, the purity of white did it. It made him want to scatter some dirty old semen all over it, the whiteness, make it more human. OR. Lights overhead, faces darting in over him. I am not going to die from shock or some jerk's stupidity, he told himself. Gently they held his arm, pushed the needle into the big vein and slipped in the sodium pentothal. Max went over the precipice.

He was depressed. People whittling gleefully away at your flesh. Did they flush it away to join the shit and cloudy condoms floating in the rivers? Did fish nibble at it, a delicacy? *Look, man, here's a piece of Max Reddick! Have a taste!* Just what did they do with the flesh? It was a little bit of dying, already, *faster*. Even with their clean sheets, drugs, voluptuous nurses, flowers, diets, stainless steel tools, you were dying. But you knew that — piece of flesh, massed calcium, hunk of gristle, haphazard bit of matter, product of warm, ancient seas, still steaming lands wracked by unimaginable diastrophisms; the dark, dark memories of that time (and the puzzle — reptile and fowl related — love them birds, have snake fever????) contained where, in the blood, the very atoms of the bone? Why remember more than most the vast laboring distance so filled with internecine horror and commonplace death, the gift of that raving bitch, evolution, nature, now made gentle with the title, Mother, and keep crying I Am?

186

*You am whut, Max Reddick, you piece of crap? Turd. Lost a small hunk of asshole. Big deal. You am whut?*

*The end of the line, as far as it's come.*

*Whut fuckin' line?*

*Man.*

*Man? You tougher than rats, bedbugs, roaches; angleworms, bluebottles, houseflies?*

*Yes. I kill them all.*

*Tee, hee, yeah, but you don't breed as fast, and whut you breed, man, sometimes, I just don't know.*

*That is not the same and you know it; an insect or a rodent can never be a king. I am. I am a man. I am a king.*

*A whut?!*

*A king.*

*You am a fool. Look around you. You ain't related to these other fools?*

*Yes, and we are kings.*

*O, Max, whut a king look like with maggots crawling out his eye sockets?*

*I don't mean then. I mean now. Nobody counts then. It's all over.*

*It's all over now. It was over when you were born. Youse a fool. Got chick nor child. Whut you king of or over or under?*

*I told you. The line as far as it's come.*

*Youse ain't no king. Know whut youse is? Wanna know? Youse a stone blackass nigger. Hee, hee, hee. Say sumpin'. I'm right, ain't I? Tongue fell off, nigger?*

*Your momma's a nigger.*

*Oops! The dozens, is it? I made you salty, eh? Now you slip me in the dozens, just like that. I told you, you was a nigger.*

*Your mother's a nigger.*

*Hee, hee, well, your mother don't wear no drawers.*

*How could she, when she was giving birth to you — my son.*

*Ha! So you know your mother don't wear no drawers. How's*

*that? Youse a motherfuckin' motherfucker, Oedipus Rex. Thass how come you knows so much.*

*I know so much because I'm your daddy.*

*Lissen to old king crap.*

*I am. I am a king.*

*Youse an ass. This ain't nuthin'; this ain't shit and needer is you.*

*I Am, I told you, damn it, I Am.*

Fresh flowers surrounded him and their scent filled the room. Granville Bryant, sitting in a chair, smiled at him. Beside him was another boy, a very pretty one, with violet eyes and flaxen hair and the tan of a youth always in the sun.

Granville said, "Well now, Max, how are you feeling?"

Max nodded his head slowly.

"Now you can't get away, can you? You can't avoid lunches or slip away from parties, can you, Max?"

"Cigarette," Max said.

Bryant made a slight, almost unseen gesture and the youth glided forward, a glittering, golden cigarette case opening in his hand. In the other there appeared, magically, a lighter. After Max had taken a pull on the cigarette, Bryant said, "They tell me that's just like having a baby." He laughed softly and smiled at his boy. "Never had one of those. One of my friends did though. He was very careful after that. Sailors and writers — oh, they can be so sadistic!" Bryant crossed a leg — elegantly — and leaned back as if preparing to tell Max something important. Or a story.

Once upon a time, and it seemed to Max that just recently he had been having silly dialogues with someone, an object was seen hurtling down from an Eastern sky. When the nearest townspeople arrived, they found the object, curiously, large enough to have contained people, but no one was in it. First, it was thought that Buddha had cast sinners from the heavens and the sinners had evaporated in transit. Many, many years later, centuries, it was thought that the object was a part of the original Black Stone hidden away by the evil Qarmata in the Far East. Then the object was forgotten altogether; it was covered by swells of the earth, the dirt and rock. The truth, however, was that the object was a craft from another planet and the creatures in it, who looked very much like humans, their planet having the same makeup as ours, were stranded here. Looking very much like humans, they mixed with the populace without attracting attention to themselves. Being of superior natures, they soon mastered the skills of the earthmen, then went on to become their betters. These were men who did not know women. By our standards the first group were extraordinarily handsome. On their planet females were used only to keep the population constant. These men knew each other. But, in order to appear as genuine earthmen, they came to know earthwomen, and their handsomeness was altered in their offspring, some of which were like them and some just like other earthmen. They traveled across the earth and across the five seas, the succeeding generations of these men from space, and in due course they became stevedores and bankers, philosophers and hoodlums, musicians and clerks, writers and actors, unskilled laborers and atomic scientists; they became soldiers and sailors, warriors and generals. They were of all conditions, high, low and in between, and they were all colors; no discrimination existed between them. They could tell their own from an arch of the brow, a vocal inflection, a bend of the wrist, the pelvic walk. Slowly, over the centuries, they came to control many of man's efforts on earth, but they did it secretly. They were laughed at, hated, legislated against, harrassed, made vulnerable, all of which made them band together more quickly for protection. They were always aided by the ability of the earth people to rationalize them as persons with an inherently ill nature; earth men traced that nature through legend, literature, art, business and rumor. During this time, the most brilliant made their way into the offices of ministers, kings and presidents with the purpose of serving whatever nation they found themselves in loyally and to the full. Some were found out and dismissed. Others continued on, trying to improve the earth. Slowly, ever so slowly, with the power well within their grasp, they will improve the earth. Women will be defeminized by them, made nude, and the mystery of their bodies will exist no more. Or, if they are clothed, their breasts will be flattened, their hips squared, their mouths and hair painted in outlandish colors. They will, these men from out there and their descendants, design men's clothes, make them more feminine. There will be no other styles available. They will continue to work with the languages. In polite company, few people will say aloud, "gay," "queer," "faggot," "fruit," "queen" — they will say homosexual or nothing at all and they will make works by homosexuals more and more acceptable. They will seek in the legislatures of the world surcease from police and other social harrassment. However, with all these things against them, they have taken on the burdens of the races of which they are now a part. There are small problems: some who do not belong try to in the most ostentatious fashion. And some who do are always fighting it. Max, I know that secretly I am called the Great White Father because I help young Negro writers get started. I did not help you, Max, so you have no cause to be grateful to me on that score. I don't even want your gratitude for the job; you deserved it. I have told you our story. Be tolerant. We too are outcasts. We have a natural empathy for your people. How well we understand your impatience!

You don't understand *nuthin'!* Max was thinking. He saw that the chair beside his bed was empty. Where the hell is he? Where's that kid? That cigarette! Max floundered in bed looking for it, until he thought to look in the ashtray. There was one cigarette butt in it. Max rang for the nurse.

"Yes, Mr. Reddick?" Her voice came out through a loudspeaker.

"What time did Mr. Bryant leave?"

"Mr. Bryant? There was no Mr. Bryant here to —"

"An old man and a young fellow."

"There was a Mr. Wilkinson here."

There was a Mr. Wilkinson here.

There was a Mr. Wilkinson here.

190

The voice was no longer female, nor was it really male either. A voice without body. The words spiraled down Max's consciousness and he remembered that as a child he had had to make spirals between the two blue ruled lines on his paper during the penmanship lessons; the white circles where he started and ended the exercise looked like the entrance and exit of a tunnel. Max's eyes shot open in fear and his heart raced like a slipped clutch of a car. He remembered the words, the last line of the last of a series of crazy dreams, dreams which slipped with envious ease back and forth in time: *There was a Mr. Wilkinson here.*

Max stared at the beams in the ceiling of Michelle's house in Leiden. Why ever in the hell was his heart racing because of a dream about Roger? Did it know something? Was it recalling the pieces? Was it blackjack now? Gin? Where else had he been? At the table in Paris where Max, Harry and a few others had had their morning coffees, listening mostly to Harry talk against the roar of traffic rushing down Boulevard Raspail. Roger again, saying that he had gone to one of those Catholic colleges that specializes in prelaw courses and which was always being visited by people from the FBI and the CIA to recruit personnel from among the student body. ("Man, they talked to me, once.") There had been laughter, stomach-bursting laughter. Talk to a clown like Roger? Desperate, those CIA cats; had to be desperate. Max saw images of Roger: Paris, laughing over coffee, talking his French jam up, beret hung down over one eye. Roger in Rome: standing on the Via Veneto talking Italian to the Italian hippies with their shades, thick heels and eight inches of shirt collar open at the neck. Roger: sauntering down Leidsestraat shouting hip phrases in Dutch to the Dutch hippies cooling past in shades with sticks of pot in their mouths. Roger everywhere. Smiling, laughing loudly, mimicking. Roger: enough to crack your ribs with laughter. Clown. But why, Max wondered, am I thinking of him now? Guilt, maybe. Bad scene last night with that check. Very bad. The only other time he had been sharp with Roger was when he was stalking Regina; Regina now married, kids, their friendship over because she knew as Max knew that there were not too many white American husbands who would not lose sleep if their wives took from the attic a sambo toy from the past. It was, as far as Max knew, a good marriage.

After Shea, Regina had floundered a little through the spring, giving off strong scents of her weakness, which was to be loved, wanted, forgiven for surviving, and Roger, like a dog sniffing the crotch of a woman during her menses, was there. There had been something wrong with it — what, exactly, Max hadn't known — but he made it clear to Roger that he was to stay away from her. Roger had smiled, of course, wisely, *Like, okay, man,* the smile seemed to have said, *I dig she's yours no matter how much you say she's not. If she's yours, well, boss. You the best, baby.*

After that summer, in a way, maybe she had been his, but not in the way Roger meant. In a different way, a bigger way Roger could never understand. Max felt himself relaxing when he thought of Regina, and going back to that summer . . .

". . . and get the hell out of Korea," Arthur Godfrey had said. His radio audience had applauded.

Had it been hotter than usual that summer, Max wondered, or had it just been Korea? He had had the postoperative itch bad and the heat had sent him running back to the doctor for a soothing massage and a careful look-see. He had climbed on the table, lowered his chest and raised his rear, waiting for the rubber-coated finger. The doctor had been good; his single failing was that he liked to listen to Arthur Godfrey. But Max had depended on the doctor's finger, the expert massage it gave, the immediate relief from inner torment. "Steady," the doctor always said. "Relax. Make like you're making a stool."

Max went to an air-conditioned movie when he left the doctor's office. The movie would cool him off, make the afternoon's work at the paper a little more bearable. The movie was about Paris, and some wrinkled little old guy with the hots for a skinny little librarian. In a way the movie was about incest too. These old guys, Max thought, loving it up, taking on generation after generation of broads. Gable, Grant, Cooper and the rest. What the hell was going on? There was a new crop coming up: "The Toothies," the film critic on the *Century* called them, and many were Jewish guys who had changed their names. More freedom to be any kind of racial member now, yes, but, Jeez, Mac, don't bring me the Abie Finklestein bit, okay, baby? Soon "The Toothies" would be the old guys, and they'd take on the chippies for another three generations. No wonder everyone was so screwed up.

But Paris was some place. It made Max think of Harry. New York hadn't been the same since he had left. Max had learned that Harry had been to Africa to see Jaja Enzkwu, then to China, then back to Africa. He was resting in Paris now, awaiting the publication of his collection of articles on Franco Spain, two of which Max had read. It seemed that Harry was spreading out, taking on the world instead of just white America. Oppression was oppression, Max and Harry had once agreed, and there was a relationship between the oppressed Negroes of America, the oppressed Spaniards, the oppressed brown peoples of Asia and the oppressed black peoples of Africa. But Harry's books, which did not deal specifically in fiction or nonfiction form with Negroes, were not well received in the United States. Yet, old Harry had been around the world and was now telling of the Spanish mystique, the extent of police power, the lack of religious freedom, the toppling of the Spanish people from the peak of pride down into doltish stupidity. The Republic had been their last chance and they had blown it. Now there was little else except to trap as much foreign currency as one could and to become, whenever possible, as corrupt as the next *caballero*.

Going back to the office, Max decided that he would write to Harry that afternoon. Enough, this being salty over what white folks said. Harry should have been bigger than that. Max walked into the office and pulled off his jacket. The windows were open and the heavy smell of the river came in. He sat down and loosened his tie and rolled up his sleeves. In the aisle behind him the copy boys and reporters brushed past with coffee and sandwiches. "Hey, Max," some of them said, "going to Korea?" They had asked with laughter and Max laughed back. Then he sat down to write to Harry.

It was no secret that Berg desperately wanted Max to go to Korea and see Harry Truman's integrated Armed Forces take the field against the North Koreans. Berg had broached the idea in a roundabout way and Max had beat a rapid retreat. The joke in the office was, who in the hell was foolish enough to want to go out and possibly die for the *Century?* That was the way the white reporters put it in their discussions. Max could see a white reporter doing it, but not himself. It made no difference that Berg had said he could see a Pulitzer for Max; that the Negro fighting man for the first time in American journalism would be given credit at the moment he deserved it; Berg could see that too. But, Max thought, he could see Berg being beside himself with joy if circulation tripled in Harlem, Bedford Stuyvesant and Astoria as a result of the articles. Max used his operation as an out, but he knew that if the pot bubbled over in Korea, he'd have to tell Berg, no. Max assumed he would not have to do that. Berg had sense enough to know that any Negro really aware of his position in American society in the year 1950, if given the chance to refuse to go to a real fighting war and still remain economically and socially solvent, would refuse. Berg should know that, Max thought, Berg the cynical liberal (his own words). Besides, when the white Americans called out, "Gook!" it sounded awfully like nigger. Max had heard about that kind of war in the Pacific; he wanted none of it. But there was no reason why Korea would not turn into that kind of racial war. Instead of the British and French kicking the Orientals in the ass, now it was steady Uncle Sam. Ultimately there would be China to face. Racial wars called something else. The Russians understood the hell out of that. They carried the blood of the Khans and the Timurids. Thus tinged they were the least white of all the major Allies in War II — and suffered most. Could they forget Stalingrad, for example, where they lost more men than were lost by the Americans throughout the entire war? And the Japanese. If ever there came a chance to kick Sam's ass, they wouldn't pass it up. Sure, they were coming along fine, the Japanese, becoming Americanized and all that. But who could forget Little Boy peeled down the sky upon Hiroshima and Nagasaki? Military humiliations could be forgiven under a military code, but racial humiliations dealt under a military code never could be forgiven. Crazy, these wars.

But there remained something haunting and curious about the chance to go to a war in which you yourself did not have to carry a gun or suffer in the foxholes; a war in which you were not the primary target counting off with every fearful stride the seven seconds it takes the enemy to get you in his sights and kill you. Given the chance, most men preferred war that way. It was true that correspondents were killed during wars, but those often were the ones who forgot, after all, that wars were only current news, that they were simply reporting the extensions of national policies foisted upon the shoulders of a poor pfc eating regularly for the first time in his life, or a second looey trying to wrest command from his sergeant. War II wasn't quite five years dead and they were at it again, the French, the poor, stupid, losing French. *Now* they were in Vietnam, and losing their shirts. And Israel, surrounded by Arabs and the Mediterranean. How long would *that* last?

The thought of Israel made him think of Bob Loewenstein; he had interviewed Bob the day before for a "Portrait" because he was donating the proceeds from his current show to Israel. There were some loose ends Max had to tie up. He ripped the letter to Harry from the typewriter, reread it and put it into an envelope which he addressed by hand. Wars, he thought, as he picked up the phone to call Bob, I want no part of wars. How can one write intelligently of an act that is basically stupid? Somebody would; lots of somebodies would, but I'm not going to be one of them.

Then, he had believed that.

Max glanced over his notes as he dialed. Bob was doing great. Making all the money and still had his art and it was not commercial. Bob hadn't spoken about Regina, but Max knew that he (Max) wasn't supposed to know about her. The meeting aboard the ship when Harry and Charlotte were leaving had been by chance, Bob would have him believe. Max hadn't mentioned Regina either, of course. After, he had marveled at how easily one passes through the cuckoldry circus of Manhattan. If you choose to become involved in the games, you must honor the rules. Bob had had a hacking cough yesterday and had taken many cough drops along with a few martinis to ease a sore throat, but nothing seemed to help. When Bob got on the line Max would inquire about his cold, of course.

"Hello." Letitia, Max thought, Bob's wife. The voice sounded hollow, as if she were speaking in a great cathedral to no one in particular.

"Max Reddick," Max said, "How are you, Mrs. Loewenstein?" He'd never met her. He went on. "I've got a couple of questions to finish up with Bob. Is he there or at the gallery?"

"Mr. Reddick? From the *Century?* Yes he told me. Mr. Reddick, Bob's in the hospital." Her voice now sounded very small and very hurt.

"What's happened?"

There was a pause, then she said, "He came home late last night, went to sleep, but didn't wake up this morning. He was in a coma. He's still in a coma."

"What hospital?"

She gave him the name of the hospital, but added, "You can't see him. Just the family."

"Can I call you to find out what's going on?"

"Yes, yes, of course, Mr. Reddick."

"Do they know what it is?"

"They think it's an aneurysm."

"Oh, Jesus."

"I've got to go now."

"Yeah, sure. I'll call later."

Max pressed a button on the phone and got the "Portraits" editor. "Loewenstein is in the hospital with an aneurysm. Coma. Want to switch it to city desk?"

"No. Not a big enough name. If he dies we'll run the portrait with the copy we have. Hold it for now."

Max hung up. Should he call Regina or let her find out? If Bob had seen her, he probably told her about the "Portrait" and she would have asked which reporter on the *Century* was doing it. Max called her. She sounded very cheerful, having just come in from work and having seen Bob the night before, she told Max. And he thought, Oh, God. He imagined Regina, calmed and sated, perhaps combing her hair while she talked. Then he thought of Bob, lean and spare, as still as the death he was moving toward under an oxygen tent. For Regina, it had always been Bob, even when she was seeing him, Shea and the others. Always Bob with the blue eyes, the head that looked sort of squeezed in from the sides, the thin broken nose, the sandy hair. Bob with the hip phrases. "Yass, baby, how you doin'?"

"How's Bob's portrait going?" Regina asked, slyly.

Max had guessed right. "Baby, I got to talk to you," he blurted. "Can I come over?"

" 'Baby, I got to talk to you,' " she mocked him. "What's the matter, horny?"

"Naw, hell no," Max said, suddenly wishing he were and that was all he had to see her about.

Suddenly the cheerfulness was gone and in its place was a urgency. "What is it, Max?"

"I'll tell you when I see you."

"No! What is it?" Regina's voice was instantly demanding, startlingly harsh, as if some instinct had signaled her that a diaster had occurred.

"When I see you," Max said tensely.

"Goddamn it, you're not going to see me, Max! Now what is it? Is it about Bob?"

Max was stung. "Later, Regina."

She crashed on, "What's happened? Where's Bob? What's this all about? Max, *tell me!*" Her voice was now a scream so loud that Max moved the phone away from his ear.

"Bob's in the hospital. In a coma, honey —"

"Aw, *no!*"

"Reg —"

*"When?"*

"Reg —"

*"When? Where?"*

"Reg, it was sudden. His wife couldn't wake him this morning. She called the doctor and they took him to the hospital. He's been there ever since. He'll be all right."

"He's not! He's going to die!"

Then Max saw it. She *wanted* him to die for the torment he had caused her, and this realization was tearing at her as brutally as the fact that he *was* dying.

"He was *with* me last night," Regina said. "We made love! He had a sore throat . . ." She wanted him to die and now he was dying. She had put that pussy on him and it killed him, finally. That weapon they have, the women. There was nothing else to do at the paper. Max left Regina's number at the desk and took a taxi to her house.

Regina cried at his side while he called the hospital and got a report. "Condition serious." Well, it wasn't critical yet, Max thought. But they lied to you. Nobody's going to lie to me when my time comes, if I know it's coming.

[Now that I know, Max thought to himself in Leiden, I try lying to myself.]

He held Regina in this arms. It was kind of stupid, that, but it was Man perhaps a million and three quarters of a thousand years old since Zinjanthropus sat around with his bereaved while they cried. Some people laughed and danced to keep from crying. Max remembered some of the wakes he had gone to as a very young man, when everyone came in with cake or potato salad or hams or fried chicken, barbecued spare ribs or cole slaw or macaroni salad, and whiskey. Then came the music and the slow drags and the Lindy Hops, the boogie woogies. The older people, they'd sing,

"Didn't He Ramble," but maybe in the next room that corpse wasn't going to ramble anymore.

"It just can't *be!*" Regina kept saying. Her love for Bob should have kept him strong and incapable of dying? Regina, he thought, we should be wise now. This is a time for setting precedents, you and I. We should be making love, stone screwing and drinking and playing records and screwing some more, and eating; it is a time for letting those who are going to die, die. But there is that weakness bred up in us. We must pause to mourn, reflect on dying. Except in war. Then you want to get away fast from the place where the dying is done.

"No, no, *no.*" Regina sobbed, smashing her foot against the floor. Mad at God, Max thought. Mad at Jews who get themselves gassed and mad at the ones who escaped. Mad at Bob for not wanting her badly enough to throw out his wife and four kids, and now mad at him because he is dying and she had told him to his face (she was saying now, mucus and tears strewn through her hair) that she wished he were dead. Max led her to the bathroom and washed her face, dug the cloth into those deep, grief-carved creases that had suddenly lined her face. He opened her medicine cabinet and asked what pills she wanted to take. She gestured toward the blue-capsuled sodium amytal. "How many do you usually take?"

"Two," she said in her shattered voice.

Max gave her three, then sat in her room while she undressed in the bathroom and readied for bed. Once he had known what it felt like to lie in her bed, to pad barefoot from the bathroom to the kitchen to put up coffee or to make a sandwich. She came out of the bathroom, her face bare of makeup, as if she had gone into mourning. She got into bed and let Max pull the covers up. "Call me if you need to," Max said.

"Thanks. Thank you, Max," she said drowsily. He closed the door to the apartment and heard the lock snap behind him. He hoped she wouldn't call in the middle of the night, but who else was she going to call? Could she say she was crying over a guy who was dying when he left her in bed? Could she tell anyone who the guy was? No. She would have to go back to the beginning, the way she had with Max. That would mean telling of trips when Bob, using business as an excuse, met her in the Catskills where they fished in a small lake at night and Bob tried to imitate the whippoorwill's cry, or met her in the little hotel in Taxco where, with the sun setting, all the mountains of Mexico, harsh and grim during the day, turned soft, and the vultures on their last flights through the valleys had not seemed repulsive at all? Could she tell about meetings and bag lunches and long, arm-in-arm walks along the promenade of Carl Schurz Park? Could she tell of begging Bob to impregnate her and how, untrusting of her then, he had not seen her for three months?

What Max hadn't heard before, he heard that night and there had been so many times when, in genuine anger, he wanted to ask: Why, why, do you hurt yourself so? But he knew the answer and that made the question invalid. He called her the next morning, then called the hospital for another report. Condition: "Serious." Still under oxygen, of course. Bob needed the oxygen to retard further damage to the brain. The sore throat he had complained of had been a broken vessel in his head, spurting a steady stream of blood against the back of his throat. Max reported to Regina, then dressed and took a taxi to her apartment and made her eat. The tears had not stopped and she had not slept. Twenty-four hours ago, Max thought, she had been her usual lovely self. Today, she looks ugly and a thousand years old. Could I have ever broken my neck to get into bed with this? Regina wanted to go to the hospital and Max became angry.

"Don't be a stupid broad all your life, Reg. What about his wife and kids? His sisters and brothers and his parents? What have you to do with any of that? All they need right now is you running in there screaming all over the place."

The tears, the body-shaking sobs, the forlorn body, sexless now, the gray eyes transformed into two wild, red balls, the brown hair like damp, stained straw. Max, watching her, thought, Those rotten little truths. He could almost hear them strike her, see her body recoil from them. He reached across to her and held her. "I'm sorry," he said at last, thinking, World, look at this tableau. Look, world. We suckle your babies, clean your kitchens and shithouses, gave you all the blackertheberry your men ever wanted, take all the jobs you don't want, fight in your wars and now you want us to stop short of loving and consoling your women too? "Try to call your office, Reg. Come on, now. When this is all over you won't want to have lost your job. If it happens bad —" He paused. But some preparation was necessary. "— the job'll be good to have. You'll appreciate having something to do, some place to go." He listened while she talked on the telephone. When she returned she said, "I suppose you have to go?"

"Yes."

She started crying again, then silently, mouth pursed into a pout, until the scream burst from her trembling, tightened lips. "Oh, Max, what in the hell am I going to *do?*"

Max remembered the endlessly long days after Lillian's death; he remembered watching the sun come up and its light fill the room in which he slept, and he remembered the way it had eased down at the end of the day when the radios and voices, the slamming doors of the other apartments, jarred his being, made him think for the first time of the living. How had the fat couple on the second floor made love to each other? Was the tall, skinny, light-skinned woman on the first floor a good lover? Why did the guy beneath him laugh so much and so loudly? Much of the emptiness had remained, sometimes it hurt, at other times it merely ached. Remembering, Max took Regina in his arms and tucked her head onto his shoulder. His own eyes began to water and he held her tightly to him so that she might not spring free before he had a chance to blink the tears away.

He left soon afterward and went wearily to the *Century* office where he spent the balance of the day plodding through work. He paused only to call the hospital and to call Regina, who now demanded that Max call Bob's doctor and get an up-to-date prognosis. Max did not pass that along to Regina. The doctor did not hold out any hope whatsoever for Bob's recovery. Just as well, Max thought. The brain's going to jelly now, or parts of it. Better off dead. When Max was about to leave the office in the early evening, he called Regina to tell her to dress so they could go out and eat. He called the hospital once again. Now it was, "Condition critical."

Max rang Regina's doorbell and heard her inside running to open the door. "He's dead!" she screamed into the empty hall.

Max pushed her inside. "No, he's not. I just called the hospital before I left the office. His condition's critical, but he's still alive."

"No, goddamn it, no. He is dead, I tell you, dead, dead, dead!"

It was no good trying to reason with her. Max called the hospital and asked for Bob's doctor again. He hung up slowly. Puzzled, he said aloud, "'Why would they say 'critical' when he's already dead?" Reg must have felt it and called. Max took her arm. "C'mon, we're going to get something to eat."

"I don't want to eat!" She tore away from him.

Max sighed. "Reg, I'm very tired and you look pretty bad. Let's eat; this'll all wear a little better. After all, what can you do now?"

She wiped her eyes. "All right, Max. I appreciate all this. I'll try to be good, honest. But it's so hard . . ." The tears again, then down the elevator, the hot night greeting them as they stepped into the street. She held him tightly as if she might lose him. She staggered against him sometimes and he would mutter, "Straighten up, baby, straighten up, Reg. That's better."

He did not remember where they ate, but he remembered the walk back to her home. She held him tightly, as before, and bumped against him again. Her face chased grief and anger, anger and grief. Max heard her grinding her teeth; he caught the saw's-teeth sound of the sobs she could not suppress, but she did not give way altogether until they were in the elevator. Upstairs he placed her on her bed and called her doctor, as she had asked. He handed her the phone and listened to her talking. She was asking the doctor to call the place where she usually went. "Will you help me pack a few things, Max? I know you're tired, but I would appreciate it if you just dropped me off at the little hospital. I feel so tired, I'd be afraid to try, myself."

"Sure," Max said. He got down a bag for her and watched her comb her hair and put makeup on. Looking in the mirror she said, "Shea. He was the only person I ever met who was weaker than me, and I was happy. I could see Bob, fading into just a memory. I could have helped Shea — Kermit, but he broke it off. Didn't want to be weaker than me. He could have helped me too, because I need to be able to help someone, not always be helped. That's important —" She glanced at him in the mirror and spun around. "Oh, Max! Don't look so sad." She kissed him on the cheek. "Do you know something? Whenever I fall sick, I feel dirty. This time, Max, I just feel tired, not dirty at all, just so tired I could sleep for a thousand years." She drew back as if a thought had just occurred to her. "Before we go, should we make love, just once more, to say goodbye to the old Regina? I really feel something else, Max. I mean it. Would you?"

And Max looked at her carefully. No hysteria, no blankness. An earnestness, an innocence even. "I am very tired, baby."

"Yes. I'm sorry. Not about the offer, but because I made you tired. Max?"

"Yeah?"

"I don't really know anyone else who would have done for me what you've done."

"Forget it."

At the small, East Side hospital, Max walked her to the door, carrying her bag. He rang the bell and a nurse answered. "Hello, Regina." The nurse was silhouetted in the door in her white uniform.

"Hello, Collins," Regina answered. "In for the last time, sweetie, so don't fuss over me." Max kissed her on the cheek, then on the mouth and returned to the waiting taxi. The door to the little hospital closed with a *bam!*

# 17

*BAM!* MAX jumped in the bed, his mouth agape, his hands held protectively in front of him. Slowly, the bedroom in Leiden came back into focus. Max lowered his hands. *What in the hell is scaring me besides the cancer? That I know about. It's something I don't know.* He looked at the floor where Harry's briefcase had fallen and its brass fittings had clattered on the oaken floor.

"Max! Max!"

He heard Michelle racing up the steps. She burst through the door, her eyes sweeping the room in fright. "Are you all right? I heard something fall."

Max pointed to the briefcase. She said, "Oh, I was frightened. Haven't you started on the papers yet?"

"No, I've been drowsing. I'll get to them in a minute."

"If you need me," Michelle said, "just call." There was something in her eyes Max saw, something familiar, knowing, like Mildred's eyes had been when she knew she was going to leave him. Like Regina's eyes when she knew even their friendship was over. "Max," Michelle said. She had been about to close the door.

"Yes."

She simply stared at him, pityingly.

"Yes," he repeated.

"It is nothing." She closed the door gently, almost reverently, as if someone were dead in the room. *She knows,* Max thought. *She's thought about the smell.* Max retrieved the briefcase from the floor and unlocked it. He took out a yellowing envelope addressed to Harry in Paris. He took the letter from the envelope and scanned it, then paused at the signature. Theodore Dallas. Max knew Dallas; he had been with the U. S. Mission to the United Nations. A blond Negro with blue eyes, a Democrat who managed to secure some important positions. The letter was dated two years ago. Max read

204

and reread the letter. It seemed friendly. He set the letter aside, then removed the contents from the case and saw that the packets were numbered. He removed the packet numbered "1." In the distance he heard a train rushing toward the station he had passed trying to find Michelle's house. Max placed a pillow beneath his buttocks to ease the throbbing pain and opened the packet.

Dear Max:
You are there, Max? It is you reading this, right? I mean, even dead, which I must be for you to have these papers *and* be alone in the company of Michelle, I'd feel like a damned fool if someone else was reading them. I hope these lines find you in good shape and with a full life behind you, because, chances are, now that you've started reading, all that is way, way behind you, baby.

Max blinked and reread the lines. What was this? It was like listening to Harry talk once more, perhaps in Paris in the cafe, or in his house, in his study, with Charlotte and Little Max in the other room, and he, Max, tingling from feeling good, just being in Europe, and grateful that Zutkin had taken him to task for not writing novels.

# 18

GRATEFUL later, but resentful then. Max's plans had been sketched out and the talk with Zutkin had stung enough so that he moved up his timetable.

They had been lunching at the Algonquin — Zutkin liked the Algonquin — and Zutkin was being the old writing master, táking Max to task: "It's spring, Max, 1953, and you haven't published a book except those essays in over three years. They'll forget you. Is the *Century* taking it all out of you? Don't squeeze your talent out on Berg's paper. In another ten, fifteen years the best writing has to come from Negroes simply because whatever transition comes will be because of them. Things are moving fast —" Zutkin raised his hand placatingly. "I know. A cliché, but that doesn't mean it's untrue. There is a task force of sociologists, psychologists, attorneys and educators, and people of good will —" that was the first time Max had ever heard the phrase, "People of good will" — "are working now on papers that will shake this nation from top to bottom. School segregation has an excellent chance of being outlawed by the Supreme Court. The speed of the change will tell us what kind of country we're living in and about the people. No issue so reveals what people are or will do as this one of race. This is going to be an exciting and terrible place until that problem gets settled or, at least, people decide that it must be settled. Take your break now, Max, so you can be back when it all starts. For a couple of years now you've been talking about going to Europe to write. You've made your peace with Harry. You made it in a very sly way; you simply stopped writing books; you stayed out of competition with him. We know what the critics do to Negro writers — hurl them into the pit and let them kill each other off — that's going to change, too."

"Don't hold your breath," Max had said. He had glanced around the room. There was a female novelist he had met. She had a long, racehorse neck and was eating very daintily. At another table sat a male novelist with heavy brows who, it was said, drank a fifth and a half of bourbon every day and liked his women under nineteen years of age. Zutkin was right, of course, it was time to get out; get out before you got used to the weekly paycheck, the travel, meeting the famous people; get out before death and corruption, the seedy side of life, became a fatal attraction. Max had been planning to ask Berg for a leave starting in the fall.

"All this is none of my business, Max," Zutkin said.

Max smiled. But, Zutkin had noticed, it was a smile without mirth. "No, it isn't," Max said. "But you've got all the answers anyway, haven't you?"

Zutkin lowered his head as if expecting a charge. He had always done that, even as a child. People had thought that because he was

206

involved with books and writing he was a punk who couldn't take care of himself. But Max had said nothing else and Zutkin had raised his head, noticing with some distress that Max now seemed bored by his presence. Strange, Zutkin thought, how for a time you think you know someone and then — you just don't, not at all. A word, a look and there's the end of something. "Except that you're a good writer. I care. In a way I suppose that makes it my business." Zutkin shrugged. He had had his say and he had meant it; Max could do with it as he liked. Max had changed. Maybe it had started with his girl's death. One could not any longer call Max petit bourgeois. The change was good to see, but what did it portend?

Against the background of writer's talk and the clattering of china and silver, Max felt momentary regret. It was hard, damned hard to dislike people who liked you. Here Zutkin was talking about great changes coming over the land, this great, vital American land and he didn't know shit about what great changes, at least, not American ones. Wise, yes, he was wise, but the wisest men looked stupid when it came to exercising that wisdom about America. What about now, right *now,* never mind the big picture. Max swung his head around the room. How foreign it seemed after small dark kitchens in the South where the meals had consisted of grits, grits, always grits and greens cooked too soft, fried chicken or pork, and the people in those kitchens with their dark, impassive faces coming out of clothes that always smelled of cooking. The Algonquin dining room smelled good and the faces in it were so goddamned innocent, even those etched with some genteel kind of evil. God, these people don't *know,* Max thought.

Sure, he had avoided going to Korea, using his operation as an excuse. He hadn't gone to witness and report on the military industry and how it was brought to bear upon and obliterate humanity. Instead, he seemed to have become the *Century*'s ace reporter on lynchings in the South and the subsequent trials for murder, if the murderers insisted on being apprehended. He had made many trips to the South, to the small, still belligerent towns in Mississippi, Alabama, South Carolina — towns with their Civil War monuments surrounded by neat lawns of St. Augustine grass upon which sat old Negro men, as watchful as tomcats, wearing sweat-stained felt hats, wrinkled khaki shirts and faded overalls; and he had been into too many courtrooms down there, in the colored gallery sections, of course, and smelled the sheepshitty, acrid odors and seen the Confederate flag stretched open behind the judges' benches; he had seen too many dead, mutilated Negroes and tough, alive, giggling crackers.

There was your war; there really was no other.

Max had looked at the white defendants, at their relatives in both the jury box and audience, and had come to know, *really* know that to be oppressed was not enough to win ultimately; that to be in the right was not enough. You had to win the way they had won — with blood. Words, petitions, laws, ideas, were not going to be enough. The common denominator was blood, white blood as much as black blood. The politicians he had met, the personalities, black and white, their publicized indignation, were as nothing. They made no waves. How could they, when Negroes themselves were a part of the very system that ground them under? The teachers, the schools, the minute grants of status within the segregated communities, the security derived therefrom. You talk about change, man? You'd better talk about an explosion.

There had been one man who might have started the change, averted the explosion. Max had taken a short leave, with Berg's blessing, to work for that man, because the *Century*, after all, was coming out for him. The man had not won. Damn, he had sounded right; he had seemed like the kind of guy willing to start things. People with sense, unafraid for the first time in a long while, had popped up from behind every bush, as though at the bidding of a master gardener, to lend support. Max had worked on speeches and organization and at the convention. No good, all of it. There were many little things that had killed the man, but none were as effective as the intellectual label. Intelligence is the enemy of the

American people; too much of it and they would come to know that it could happen here and that it would be as nothing that had happened anywhere, anytime before. Maybe the answer was that they were intelligent enough, the American people, to not want to know. The old-line people in the man's own party had helped to cut him down. Deals, they wanted deals and could not understand why the man was not dealing. They had helped him on the way down. The man had been capable; he might have heralded the end to the hundred years stench of Negro deaths. The other man: a nation did not move well in the shadow of a man who had performed other tasks with a Jim Crow command.

It was all eating at Max now. Even before he had the lunch with Zutkin. He found himself wanting to get away and write. He wanted to do with the novel what Charlie Parker was doing to music — tearing it up and remaking it; basing it on nasty, nasty blues and overlaying it with the deep overriding tragedy not of Dostoevsky, but an American who knew of consequences to come: Herman Melville, a super Confidence Man, a Benito Cereno saddened beyond death. He wanted to blow the white boys off the stand — those who couldn't blow like niggers — before they took the whole thing and made an intellectual exercise out of it. Goddamn it, yes! He was going to get out. Pitch camp elsewhere and get sharpened up and rested for the battle that was coming: the battle in black and white.

Max took the ship with the summer equinox. At Le Havre where cranes stud the docks as gigantic, long-limbed insects, Max looked down from the main deck and saw Harry waving; he saw no other black faces. Max waved back. He was glad he had written that first letter; it had led to a resumption of a regular exchange with Harry once again. Max had known when he wrote the letter, that it was a matter of pride with Harry. Who would write the first letter after that long period when Max's letters had gone unanswered? Max did, and it was all right. Pride, one of Harry's weaknesses; pride over terribly small things.

Max said goodbye to the people he had come to know aboard the ship; they rushed through the exit for the boat train to Paris. Standing beside his luggage in customs, Max could see Harry waiting for him at the exit. Through wide grins they studied each other carefully, and when Max was through, Harry embraced him. They placed the baggage in Harry's car and Max was glad Charlotte was not there; he'd wanted the first few moments alone with Harry. Their conversation was swift and jovial, but the studies of each other persisted. Harry had put on some weight; that was an ordinary observation. But Harry's face — it seemed to encapsule some grim wisdom, some sad affirmation.

"How's Zutkin? Shea? Granville? Chris? Kenyon? Kierzek?" Harry asked, and without waiting for Max to reply went on. "Fill me in; what's *really* happening back there?"

It is a four-hour drive from Le Havre to the Left Bank if you stop for a late lunch and get caught in Montmartre traffic, if you detour, but by the time they had reached St. Clair, Max was almost talked out. Harry, pausing from time to time to curse French drivers ("These bastards over here don't seem to realize that cars can kill you. Just like Africans."), went back to the time of his departure and told Max all the things he hadn't known then about the American Lyceum of Letters, the deal with Don Kenyon (the book hadn't done well), and all the little hurts; the sudden flare-ups between Charlotte and himself. "That incident changed my life," Harry said, driving crisply through the swollen green Norman countryside. "They made me mad. They made me a writer." South of St. Clair, the traffic heavier, the gray, ugly factories more frequent, Harry turned to Max and said with sudden and curious warmth, slapping him on the knee, "You're in France now, man. Vive la France. You're going to work here. You're going to sit down and write. Paris is the place for it. It's going to be a special thing because they don't shit on you here if you say you're a writer. You can say it and not feel ashamed. Every writer ought to do it, come to Paris, if only for once in his life. Goddamn, Max, you look good. A little tired. Them crackers been running the shit out of you, huh?"

They both sat in warmth for several miles, not talking. Max leaned his head back on the seat.

"Dawes is over here, you know," Harry said.

"I gave your address to Granville and he gave it to Dawes."

"Yeah, I know. Don't see too much of him. Travels in another kind of crowd. And there's another cat here. Three weeks ago, I think he said. Roger Wilkinson."

"I know him. We were as tight as I'd let him get, which wasn't very much. Young cat. Says he's writing, but I've never seen any of it. Haven't seen him in a few months. Had to set him straight."

"Woman?"

"Just a friend."

"How can a man have a woman for just a friend. Baby, you're slipping!"

"Long story. Tell you about it sometime. Funny. Wilkinson never said anything to me about coming over here. I thought he loved the civil service."

"What, was he a social worker?"

"Yeah."

Harry laughed. "Boy, I tell you, those white folks back there got the best of everything. Now they got so many Negro social workers listening to Negro problems they don't have to be bothered with them anymore."

"I guess that's what he did. I never asked."

"Well, I hope he produces. Paris is full of jive cats. Just hustling the best they can. However hard or evil the hustle, they still think it's better than putting up with that nonsense back home. By the way. That Dawes has been on my ass like white on rice. Essays. He's really been stomping me."

"Why?"

"How in the hell would I know? I suppose it's easier for spades to run each other down than paddys. You know."

"I'm really in France. *Really* in France."

"Damned if you aren't." After a while, quietly, Harry asked, "How's Mississippi? Just as bad?"

"It'll get worse. All of it. The whole goddamn place."

"That's too bad. You keep hoping."

"It'll get better."

"But you just said —"

"After it gets worse."

"Yeah. I got you. How's the hunting?"

Max said, "Falling off. The weather. I don't know. You don't see too much out there anymore." He was remembering the last time he'd gone hunting with Harry and shot the deer. The day he discovered that Charlotte had lied to him. Well, then, they had known each other fourteen years. Where had the years gone? "Got one bird last fall. I was out all morning. Ricketts' place."

"He still in business?"

"Yeah. I think he's even printing dream books now."

They laughed.

"Women?" Harry asked with a smile.

"Catch as catch can," Max replied. He had gone through a very dry spell in the weeks before he left. Ending everything. He hadn't wanted to borrow any trim and he wasn't going to lend any joint. Clean slate. Ledgers balanced.

"It took you a long time, it seems," Harry said.

"Catch as catch can?"

Harry's laughter, booming, filled the car. "No, hell, that's everybody's bag. Don't worry about that in Paris. I mean getting back to writing."

"Yeah," Max said. "Well, I had to learn the other world. I mean, sleeping with white women isn't the whole thing. You can learn the men from them, though, but you've got to see them in action, the white boys. These guys run the world and when I stop and think about *that* I either get scared or mad."

"Some world, man."

"Hip."

"Tough, your man losing the election. They liked him here. Good tongue; good head. The other cat — well, it's a good time to be away."

The sun had been bright that day and there were many cars on the road, the sun's rays glinting from their tops. Before taking Max home, Harry swung up the Champs toward the Arc de Triomphe. "Look at that motherfucker, Max, look at it!" Then they went back to Notre Dame, to Sacré-Coeur, the Sorbonne, pausing for a drink here, a drink there; they became high, not merely from the liquor, but from each other, and being in Paris in summer; and that night in his room in Harry's house, where he was staying until his own flat a few blocks away was ready, Max looked out the window. Paris. *Paris!* And Harry burst into the room with another bottle, just as though he knew Max would be at the window looking out . . .

I'm sorry [the letter went on] to get you into this mess, but in your hands right now is the biggest story you'll ever have. Big and dangerous. Unbelievable. Wow. But it's a story with consequences the editors of *Pace* may be unwilling to pay. And you, Max, baby, come to think of it, may not even get the chance to cable the story. Knowing may kill you, just as knowing killed me and a few other people you'll meet in this letter. Uh-uh! Can't quit now! It was too late when you opened the case. This is a rotten way to treat a friend. Yes, friend. We've had good and bad times together; we've both come far. I remember that first day we met at Zutkin's. We both saw something we liked in each other. What? I don't know, but it never mattered to me. Our friendship worked; it had value; it lasted. I've run out of acquaintances and other friends who never were the friend you were. So, even if this is dangerous for you — and it is — I turn to you in friendship and in the hope that you can do with this information what I could not. Quite frankly, I don't know how I got into this thing. It just happened, I guess, and like any contemporary Negro, like a ghetto Jew of the 1930's in Europe, I couldn't believe it was happening, even when the pieces fell suddenly into place. Africa . . .

"Jaja Enzkwu'll be here next week," Harry was saying. Max had been in Paris a month. They were the first at the cafe where they took midmorning coffee.

"How is he?" Max asked.

"A prick," Harry answered. "I'm going to tell you before Wilkinson and the other cats get here. Africa is in for trouble. If the white man knew what's going to happen to that continent when he leaves it, he'd change his mind, but he knows what he's doing, and them dumb niggers are falling flat on their faces. I wouldn't tell anyone else this, but that place crushed me. Enzkwu. In Africa and out of Africa, he's always talking about how much he hates whites. Told me the only reason why he puts up with me and Charlotte is because he likes me; we're 'brothers' says he. But that man goes stone out of his mind, *stone,* when he's with white women. Never saw anything like it. If I didn't keep a close eye on him, he'd have his hand up to his wrist in Charlotte's crotch. That's just the reason he gets out of Africa so often."

Max, bent double laughing, did not see Wilkinson's approach, but Harry did. "Cool it."

Max, who found himself laughing more and more at Harry's secrecy, as much as his comments, was still laughing when Roger arrived, pulled out a chair and sat down. Harry flashed a quick, amused glance at Max — the kind of glance exchanged when you've allowed an outsider (who almost too quickly takes advantage of it) to thrust his way into your group. Wilkinson ordered coffee and croissants and joked with the waiter. "Where you learn all that French, boy?" Harry asked, mocking paternal gruffness. Roger smiled shyly. (He *always* did the right thing, said the right thing at the right time, Max recalled.)

"In school. I was pretty good at languages." Roger laughed. "You know what they say — psychopaths usually *are* good at languages." He laughed again; broke himself up.

Generally, the passing of a beautiful woman sparked part of the daily ritual, the "lying and crying." Harry: in Spain; a girl who had an apartment in Gaudi's La Pedrera on Paseo de Gracia in Barce-

214

lona. Roger: *two* girls in a tourist-class cabin aboard the *Flandre,* hopping from upper to lower berths. Max: a church-going land-lady in a Tunica, Mississippi, boarding house. Harry: a girl in Peking who was lean and soft. Roger: A geisha in Tokyo while he was in the Army. And on, until the others — a couple of musicians, an actor and an opera singer — joined them. Then politics, mostly concerned with U. S. racial problems, replaced the girls. But not until Roger, seeing a tall, firm blonde pass by, announced that next he was going to Scandinavia, where the pussy was said to be climbing out of the walls, out of every open bottle of Aquavit.

If they stayed at the cafe long enough, soon, it seemed, every American Negro who was in Paris passed by or joined them, like the nightclub singer, Iris Stapleton, and the drummer she went with, Time Curry. Marion Dawes never stopped. He passed at a distance, usually, waved at no one in particular and continued on, his regular entourage of at least two companions at his side. "The only time he ever really talks to me," Harry mused one day, "is at those Franco-African meetings."

And yet, one night when Max had had dinner with Harry, Charlotte and the kid, the phone rang. "Dawes," Harry ducked back into the room to announce. While he talked, Max and Charlotte edged into a conversation. Charlotte's alert, disdainful New York look was gone. Her face was beginning to assume a slight, perpetual frown, as someone with constant migraines. She seemed in a hurry to end each topic of conversation she became involved in. On the whole, she looked fine. She too had put on weight, but carried it well for a big woman.

Harry returned. "He wants to borrow some money. We'll meet him at the cafe, okay, Max?"

"Sure. It's on the way home and I'd like to meet him."

"He's got his goddamn nerve," Charlotte said. "After all the rotten things he's written about you —"

Harry pulled on a jacket and said, "Can't let a brother starve, baby. Says he hasn't eaten in three days."

"How much?" Charlotte said. "We're running through money like water. The family fortune isn't unlimited, you know."

In the middle of buttoning his jacket Harry stopped and dropped both hands. Then he said very quietly and wearily, "Baby, it's all right." But Max had heard distinctly the warning in his voice. Charlotte cleaned the table silently, but with an abundance of ferocity that she obviously wished to direct at Harry.

Little Max walked Max to the door. He needed his own child. How did that saying go? "Ain't got chick nor child."

Max and Harry walked quickly to the cafe, Harry frowning all the way. They never went to the cafe at night; now it was a strange, dingy place with weak lights and faded tablecloths. Marion Dawes sat huddled at a table in a corner. He was very dirty and he looked tired and bloated, like an exhausted beetle trapped. His round dark face was slack, but he managed to stand and give a weak smile when Max and Harry approached.

Harry said first thing, "Hungry?"

Dawes smiled again and nodded. "But I can manage if you let me have the francs."

"The meal won't be deducted from the loan," Harry said, just short of being curt. They sat down.

Max said to Dawes, "I'm Max Reddick. Good to see you."

"Yes," Dawes said. His hand went briefly into Max's and was withdrawn.

Harry signaled the waiter and ordered, without consulting Dawes, soup, a steak with fries.

"You don't have to —" Dawes was trying to say.

"You'd better eat, Dawes," Harry said gently. "I've been hungry. Nothing looks right, feels right or sounds right. Nothing *is* right. Go ahead and eat. We'll get a drink."

"Thank you," Dawes said, taking the francs Harry passed to him. "I'll pay you back as soon as I can."

"Sure."

Max sat back and studied both of them as Harry looked at Dawes who was bent over his plate. He was hungry, but he ate neatly, pausing to smile and say, "Sure is good."

When Dawes was drinking his coffee, Harry said to him, "How come you've been attacking me, Dawes?"

Dawes's head fell slightly and his thick, unkempt mop of hair glowed dully in the cafe lights. "Well —" he began.

"You make it sound as though we *know* each other. You know that's untrue. We've spoken to each other exactly five times and I spoke more than you. You've never been to my house, and I've not been to yours. What is this? What are you running me down for? And now — I'm not putting you down because anybody can have bad luck — you call me to borrow five hundred francs. I got a family and I'm a long way from home, too. All right. I understand you're having bad luck. But why call me to help you after you've been running me into the ground? *That's* what I can't understand."

Dawes's voice broke from him high-pitched and sharp. "It's the *duty* of a son to destroy his father." Max watched Harry recoil. Harry then looked Max full in the face; his face, Max observed, was at once a puzzle, flooded with understanding and rejection of that understanding.

Gruffly Harry said, "What in the hell are you talking about? I'm not *your* father."

Dawes loosed an exasperated gasp that sounded like a hiss. "Harry, well, if you don't *know* — you're the father of all contemporary Negro writers. We can't go beyond you until you're destroyed."

Cautiously Harry said, "You're crazy, man. You've been hungry too long." But Max noticed a sudden gleam rise in his eyes and then slowly fall. Dawes finished his coffee in Harry's lingering silence. "Really," Dawes said. "As soon as I can, I'll pay you back. I've got a couple of pieces on desks in the States right now."

"I hope they're accepted," Harry said. "But aren't you working on a novel?"

"I've just finished it."

"Good," Harry said simply. Then he stood. "We've got to go."
He shook hands with Dawes and then Dawes, turning crisply, took
Max's hand. "Mr. Reddick, I'm sure we'll meet again." Whistling,
Dawes merged quickly and plausibly with the shadows that lay
close to the cafe.

Max and Harry stood watching and listening. "That motherfucker's got some nerve," Harry said with a suggestion of admiration in
his voice. "Let's go. I have to think about this one." After walking
some distance, Harry stopped and said: "Do they really think that,
these young guys, of me being the father of Negro writers?"

"Yes," Max answered, remembering how eager he had been to
meet and talk to Harry ten years ago at Wading River. "We've
been thinking it a long time."

" 'We'?" Harry laughed. "You trying to destroy me, too?"

Max laughed.

"No shuck?"

"No shuck," Max said. "You've been away too long or you'd
know you're the father."

"Too long?" Harry scoffed. "Do you think they'd let me back in
without hounding me to death after that visit from Michael Sheldon
last week? I got news for you: no. I'm also getting a little tired of
France. Not enough brothers here for me. But where else can I go?
I tried to get a permanent visa to live in England — no dice. They
won't let me live in Spain. All I have to do is to show up at the
frontier once more and you can forget about old Harry, writing
about Franco Spain like that. Africa? I've got nothing in common
with Africa." Harry laughed and the sound was rich and full.
"Man, I'm dangerous!"

Dangerous or not, Max observed, Harry was the darling of the
French intellectuals. Several times it happened that they met at parties to which Harry thought Max had not been invited. Harry never
said, "I'm going to Jean's, did he ask you over?" But when Max
was invited, he would ask if Harry were going and Harry would
grumble and run the host down. But he would show up at the party
and seldom, it seemed, was able to break away and exchange a few

words with Max. By the middle of that fall, Max had come to understand. Harry's friends were very much like his books: they were not for lending; they were his. He had bought or written them, and he wasn't going to let them get out of his sight — or be shared. But Max enjoyed the gatherings because most of the people who went to them spoke English. There were times when he hungered for the sound of it; sometimes the cafe didn't count because the talk was often about race or women and sometimes politics. He longed for talk of people and doings and he didn't mind if the English was badly pronounced. At other times, Max preferred knowing just enough French to ask for directions, prices, buy food and carry on a light conversation with his concierge or a woman.

Michelle Bouilloux, who usually attended the affairs with her husband, a short, plump poet from Avignon, made Max speak in French. She waited while he searched for words or stumbled over them. Sometimes she supplied him with the word he was seeking and then laughed, heartily, showing her white teeth and letting the ceiling lights play on her red hair. Max liked her and envied Harry. Had Max not known of her affair with Harry he would not have conceived it; Michelle seemed unattainable. A souring Charlotte helped.

A souring Charlotte whose brief moments of hilarity now came because of the attention paid to her by Jaja Enzkwu. Knowing Harry as he did, Max was not prepared to dislike Enzkwu. On the other hand, he was not going to like him on sight, either. The Africans Max had met at the Franco-African meetings had made him cautious. But his first meeting with Enzkwu did turn Max violently against him.

The party was held at André's and when Enzkwu came in, his silken agbada swirling about him, he paused and glanced about the room, then came swiftly toward Max and his date, a tiny, small-boned but tough magazine reporter named Janine; she spoke British English. Enzkwu, a Nigerian, had met her before. He much preferred the French to the British and wished he had been born in Senegal, first; the Ivory Coast, second; or Dahomey, third. Most people, Max thought as Enzkwu swarmed around Janine, for the sake of courtesy at least, tend to guide their meaningful remarks through innocuous ones; or they work with the eyes. There is, after all, some *guideline* for these sorties and it was usually observed between a man and a woman trying to come together, particularly in the company of others.

There were no guidelines for Enzkwu. He simply ignored Max and gave his full attention to Janine, pausing to adjust his sleeves and to puff rapidly on his Gauloise bleu. His eyes were as uncontrolled as his rather suggestive conversation. Janine was laughing. Max was embarrassed for Enzkwu. He knew the laugh. *Pig*. That was what Janine was thinking. But one must be nice, musn't one? And not offend our black brethren. Max knew that when Enzkwu got the message that he was being put down (and he would believe Janine was putting him off simply because Max had got there first), the message would be garbled. For Enzkwu (and Max knew the type), every white woman who was courteous to him was really offering to share her bed with him.

"So, you will not go dancing with me tonight," Enzkwu said, scowling at Max. But his eyes were already searching the room. "I will call you tomorrow, then . . ."

"No, Jaja, not tonight. Thank you, you are a dear. Tomorrow I have an interview. Adenauer is in town, you know. Yes. Ta-ta." Enzkwu rustled away, heading for, Max could see, Michelle. Enzkwu's stock with Harry was submarining with every rustle of his agbada.

A momentary, floundering silence came between Max and Janine. "Say it, it's all right," Max counseled.

"Oh, Max," she said, tiredly. "What does one do? I find him loathsome. To think that he may even become a First Cabinet member — and I didn't want to offend you."

"What's he got to do with me?"

"You're right, of course. Nothing. Well —"

"You people have got to stop being so foolish." Max was both sad and irritated. "Do you like the Germans? They are white."

"No. You know I don't."

"Well, then, isn't it the same?"

"I'm sorry. I knew we'd have words about it. It's the reaction, you see, bending over backwards."

"Stand straight up for me."

Janine smiled. "Always?"

Max grinned. "No," he said, and then, watching Enzkwu swirl away from Michelle and veer toward Charlotte, he had promptly dismissed him.

God, Max, what doesn't start with Africa? What a history still to be told! The scientists are starting to say life began there. I'm no scientist. I don't know. But I do know that this letter you're reading had its origins with what happened there. Let me go back to the beginning. I doubt if you've heard of Alliance Blanc. In 1958 Guinea voted to leave the French Family of Nations, and at once formed a federation with Kwame Nkrumah, or Ghana, whichever you prefer. The British and French were shaken. How could countries only two minutes ago colonies spring to such political maturity? Would the new federation use pounds or francs? The national banks of both countries were heavily underwriting the banking systems of the two countries. There would be a temporary devaluation of both pounds and francs, whether the new federation minted new money or not. More important — and this is what really rocked Europe — if the federation worked, how many new, independent African states would follow suit? *Then*, what would happen to European interests in Africa after independence and federation? Was it *really* conceivable that all of Africa might one day unite, Cape to Cairo, Abidjan to Addis? Alliance Blanc said *Yes!* If there were a United States of Africa, a cohesiveness among the people — 300,-000,000 of them — should not Europeans anticipate the possibility of trouble, sometime when the population had tripled, for example? Couldn't Africa become another giant, like China, with even more hatred for the white West? It was pure guilt over what Europeans had done to Africa and the Africans that made them react in such a violent fashion to African independence.

The white man, as we well know, has never been of so single an accord as when maltreating black men. And he has had an amazing historical rapport in Africa, dividing it up arbitrarily across tribal and language boundaries. That rapport in plundering Africa never existed and never will when it requires the same passion for getting along with each other in Europe. But you know all this. All I'm trying to say is that, where the black man is concerned, the white man will bury differences that have existed between them since the beginning of time, and come together. How goddamn different this would have been if there had been no Charles Martel at Tours in 732!

# 19

TOURS. Except for a few phrases found in the encyclopedias, its meaning had been lost in history, perhaps intentionally, Max remembered thinking when he and Harry had stopped there on the way south to Carcassonne to buy smuggled Spanish shotguns. Somewhere between Tours and Poitiers, Charles Martel had halted the Moors driving up from Spain in, the encyclopedias said, "one of the decisive battles in history."

There was a stinging clue, Max thought, as they were taking lunch in a cafe along the Loire. Otherwise how white would Europe be? Or America, for that matter? They misled you, the historians, balladeers, the monks. Like ancient Egyptians, they destroyed the histories of the vanquished carved on stone stelae and wrote their own. Was Alexander's chief captain, Clitus the Black, black after all, or only by nature, like Nero? How could Balthazar of the Three Kings be black when historians wrote that black people came out of the ass-end of history? How then could Balthazar be king of anything? But at Christmas who questioned? You got your gift and you got drunk. Go, Balthazar. Why couldn't they tell you straight out who was a Moor? They told you a Moor was a Berber, a Saracen, an Arab, anything to keep you from knowing that Berbers, Saracens and Arabs were often black. But the Spanish knew; how well they knew. (Max had gone on a brief trip to Madrid and had been there only long enough to know that Spanish women didn't like to remove their brassieres when making love [saving the contents for the kiddies] and to hear the Spanish whisper ioudly to each other when he walked along the Plaza de España, *"Mira! Mira! Un moro!"* Max had heard the history resounding in their voices.) So great a conspiracy, Max thought; the extent of that conspiracy which, conscious or unconscious, had the same effect. It really was too much. What they wouldn't do, the white folks, to keep you from having a history, the better, after all, to protect theirs.

Max had felt empty walking beside the Loire after lunch; he even felt stupid. There was so much he wanted to know, but never would know. How wonderful it would be to be able to read Arabic; what answers would come from that! Or classic Chinese to understand what had happened to the great Chinese navies and find a clue, perhaps, to the presence of black people in the Melanesian islands of the Pacific. How did they get there? What immense traffic in goods and people took place between China and Africa, and in which dawn of which history? Caught up in the spin of history, Max tried to imagine the battlefield upon which he walked, the snorts and neighs of horses, great, ungainly Percherons against small, fast, surefooted Arabian steeds, the jangle of armor, the shouts in Old French and Arabic, the lung-bursting cries for god and country, as usual.

Harry broke into his thoughts. "Goddamn." Max glanced at him, then followed the direction of his eyes. Coming toward them, motionless above the knees, was a small, wrinkled Negro. He was wearing a beret faded to an ugly purple; a white shirt out of which sprang in every direction a huge, red, polka-dotted tie, the kind which had not been seen since the days of Bop City in New York in the midforties. He also wore a zoot suit and highly polished black knob shoes. The man, as black as his shoes, his lips as red as the inside of a watermelon (he would have gone well in a 1930's Hearst caricature of a Negro), moved steadily across the green, stone-dotted lawns as if someone had wound a crank in his back and pushed him forward.

"Professor Bazzam," Harry said hurriedly.

"Hello, hello," the man called Professor Bazzam said. "I saw you people cooling it along the river here. Haven't seen you in a couple of years, Harry." He took Harry's hand and shook it, while studying Harry keenly with myopic eyes. "Came down here for a bit because Paris was getting too crowded, know what I mean?" Turning to Max, he said, "You from the Apple? How's the Apple? You like this side of the ocean, man? Nice, isn't it? Everything's cool here."

Max hadn't heard New York City referred to as "The Apple" in fifteen years. The Professor, Max estimated, was at least sixty years old and he was, in the flesh, the kind of Negro every white man laughed at and pointed to. Yet there was about Professor Bazzam (which of course wasn't his right name) the uncompromising self-possession one sees in clowns performing before thousands in Madison Square Garden. What great penance was the man paying to degrade himself so? Looking at him closely, Max could see that the Professor hadn't combed his hair; it stood balled and napped on the sides of his head as berries left for the birds after the passing of the berry picker; his suit hadn't had a cleaning or pressing in months; the white shirt collar was ringed with dirt. Of all the black American characters Max had met so far, Professor Bazzam was the oddest. Even standing still his forearms were held forward, his hands bent toward the ground, like a bird's legs seeking to come to roost. Harry and the Professor finished their brief conversation and Bazzam stuck his gnarled hand into Max's, pivoted and marched off, nothing about him moving save his legs. "See you in Paree." His knob shoes sliced neatly through the grass and expertly topped the small stones.

Harry shrugged, and anticipating Max's questions, said, "I don't know who he is. He pops up in the strangest places: Paris, where I first met him; London, Amsterdam, Munich, Berlin, Stockholm, Copenhagen, Barcelona. Nobody knows who the hell he is. When he shows up, he reminds all the Negroes, who'd like to forget it, that they are; they don't like to be reminded. I wish to hell he'd get a new suit and throw away that tie." Harry shook himself with irritation. "He's like a bad penny or a conscience."

The next day they continued south to Carcassonne and purchased the Spanish guns. Then they returned to Paris along the Rhône via Mâcon, roaring down the highways bordered with ancient plane trees that had white rings painted on them; passing the ugly French farms, the farmers and their families with centuries' old dulled looks ground deeply into their faces; passing giant wine tank trucks and Max thought, How different after Paris, just as all America is different after New York. The long ride made him think of the day, months from now, when he'd have to take that four-hour drive to Le Havre again to the ship that would carry him back to New York, the *Century* and the future. It would be time then, for the book would be finished and perhaps he would be tired of Paris. But there was plenty of time yet. Time for hunting in the fall; he would be disappointed if French pheasant and duck were as similar to American pheasant and duck as French women were to American women. A change in locale did not make Max lose perspective; a woman was not better in bed simply because she was French. The same did not apply to French wines, however; they were better.

"How goes the book?" Harry asked.

"Good." Max struggled from the grip of his own thoughts, suddenly aware of the long silences they had had on the trip north. Well, he assumed that Harry, like himself, didn't like long, drawn-out conversations on the road all the time. Max said, "It's going to be all right."

Harry glanced at him. "Sure would like to take a look at it. But I'll wait until it comes out."

*That* tone of voice, Max thought, knowing what the tone and the words meant. Most rigidly observed by writers who are friends is the rule that one never reads (or asks to read) the work of another while that work is in progress. Harry was aware of that rule, yet, however you cut it, Max thought, Harry *had* asked. Did Harry think he was in it? Did Harry *want* to be in it? Max knew that a lot

225

of people thought they were in novels or wanted to be in novels, but he'd never thought Harry was like that. Then watching the suburbs of Paris, Moret and Fontainebleau rush up and slide behind them, Max knew what it was. The old jealous bit; Harry thought he would have reason to be jealous of the novel. Goddamnit, Harry, Max thought in the silence, it's *not* me against you; it's you against them working out of your bag and me against them working out of my bag; us against the bad guys. Harry's unanswered question hung heavily in the car until he started to whistle tunelessly. Then Max hummed a tune and finally they came to Place d'Italie and Harry became involved with the heavy traffic. Max breathed a little easier, but he knew Harry would never forgive his unspoken refusal to let him read his manuscript.

By autumn Max was feeling like an old Parisian. The steady flow of Negroes from America, he noticed, was on the increase. During their first few weeks they savored Paris to the full, then a few of them drifted off to be seen occasionally selling the *Herald Tribune* in front of the American Express office or sitting glumly in the cafes in the Quartier, speaking their high school or college French which of necessity was becoming sharpened with the flavor of Paris. It was one thing to quit New York or Chicago or San Francisco because of discrimination, but the youngsters hadn't learned yet that Paris wasn't going to welcome them with open arms because they were discriminated against in the States: if you had no money, the world discriminated against you. Generally, the newcomers were young. Their hatred for the United States was loudly and volubly voiced. Still, it seemed to Max that what they had suffered was, after all, negligible. Perhaps America's blacks were getting soft.

Max seldom saw the older Negroes, the ones who'd come after World War I, except in passing through Neuilly or San Gervaise or other sections that did not throb and seethe as the Left Bank. Sometimes he saw middle-aged mixed couples, expatriates, walking arm in arm, speaking English. They were unnoticed except by other

Negroes. Max wondered how life was for the mixed couples, how it had been, what had caused them to come to Paris. He would watch them walk out of sight along the quays or in the Tuileries. O, beautiful for spacious skies and amber waves of grain . . . If Janine were with him, she would give him a look of triumph, as if to say, You see, we French *are* different! That difference, of course, making them better. That implication was always there.

It was in the hundred little clubs that Max saw other American Negroes with their French men or French women listening to bop, France's latest American import. And he saw them when the great musicians from the States came through on tour, Ellington, Parker, Davis, Mingus, Roach, Mulligan.

Most of all, Max noticed the white Americans in Paris in their often inadvertent contacts with Negroes. Gone now was their self-assurance that an entire nation was behind whatever they chose to do or say to a Negro. If a Negro was with a French woman, the white Americans might glare or ignore them altogether; some rankling embarrassment kept them from seeking any middle ground. White Americans who at home would not be caught dead trying to smile at a Negro, did so in Paris when recognizing a Negro as an American by his dress, and often, very often, they were cut dead. Smile at me at home, the sullen Negroes seemed to be saying, not in Paris. In Paris I don't have to give a good goddamn about you.

Early in September, after having Paris largely to themselves during August, the tourists went home. The new Negro expatriates cast about with increasing desperation. Summer was over and so was the first flush of Paris; they had to be set for winter, somewhere, somehow. Requests for loans of francs came more frequently now. The one restaurant in Paris that served food home-style was crowded with Negroes waiting to meet other Negroes who might be able to put them onto something. Others resigned themselves to the mean hustles that would carry them through their first Paris winter. Max watched all this grimly. He recalled the nine months he was out of work. Would Paris have been better than New York? He admired the youngsters. Starve in Paris first, rather than in New York where you'd starve and get your ass kicked too. He hoped Paris changed very slowly, so the kids wouldn't see that it was becoming in many ways very much like home. Then they'd do all right, those kids. But none of them would be Josephine Bakers or Redtops; the French were over their black exoticism. The kids would be just people, which would be all right for a change, if things just held steady.

When the first autumn chill hit Paris, Max and Harry took Little Max with them on a hunting trip to Viviers to try out the Spanish guns. Harry, Max remembered, had driven the entire distance with a furrowed brow, and Max knew that the reason they had driven so far and fast was to put as much distance between Charlotte and Harry as humanly possible in three days. Little Max was along not so much to be introduced to the sport (Harry was often both sharp and short with him) as to deprive Charlotte of his presence.

Once, when they had paused at the end of the shooting for cigarettes and cognac and were watching Little Max handle the unloaded guns, Harry asked, "How's Janine?"

Max was surprised. That was another rule he'd broken. You didn't talk about each other's girlfriends until you had brought her name up. "Okay," Max answered. Had he and Janine been seeing *that* much of each other? Harry snorted. "I'm glad she's French. If she were American I'd have to kick your ass!" He shouted to Little Max: "Hold it higher, boy, *higher!*" Harry sat down upon a hummock of grass. The late afternoon sky was tinged with greens and reds. "Sometimes I wish I hadn't left the States, goddamn it!"

"Getting to you?" Max asked.

"To me? You mean *through* me." Harry sighed and watched his son. "I sleep badly. My work isn't going well. I wake up in the morning sometimes and wonder who in the hell is this broad next to me. Charlotte." He sucked wetly on his cigarette. "Tell me the truth. If I could get back into the States without being hounded to death, what would it be like for me — hell, forget it. I feel this way every fall when the tourists have gone. I miss the accents from

228

Nebraska and even Mississippi. When we first got here, I used to sit in the lobbies of hotels where Americans would be, just to hear their voices. I miss Harlem too. The summer. The first warm day when everybody gets down in the streets, lying and crying, and it's hot and muggy, the niggers are evil and the jukeboxes are blaring and you can smell fried chicken and barbecued ribs in the air on any corner; I even miss the cops holding up the corners in threes and fours when the summer comes. And the watermelon cats, hollering and jiving and getting rid of those melons as quickly as you'd spit out a watermelon seed. How I miss it."

"Yeah," Max said with a slow smile.

Harry said, "Being here, I feel like I'm not doing enough to make things better. Here I am writing about Spain and China and Africa. If we solve the problem at home we solve it around the world."

"What's solved around the world could also solve it at home," Max countered. "Yeh, I feel that way too, sometimes, like there's more I can do."

Harry grinned cruelly. "I'll bet. All summer I've been watching you while *you* were noticing the happenings. I'd say to myself, Look at old Max. Digging it all. What does he think about it? Me, I talk too fucking much to notice anything." Then Harry laughed and it was kind of a release. "That's what you are, Max, a noticer, a digger of scenes. Max the Digger; Max the man."

"Get off me, Harry."

"Man, I ain't never been *on* you." Harry eased his bulk down between his legs, coming off the hummock, as if about to diagram a football play on the ground. "You're anal, man. I mean tight. Like you're determined to be the only cat surviving this whole mess. It's hard to get to you, Max. You never got over that girl, Lillian. You write good. You knock me out, but open it up a little. For myself, I wonder where it went. I don't *feel* it anymore. Maybe being away. I don't know how a guy keeps the feel of it."

"You haven't lost anything," Max said. "I worry about losing it.

It's tough enough worrying what the faggots will make *in* in any year. That's what kills you, Harry. It's all like women's fashions, that's the way it is now."

"There's Zutkin," Harry said.

"So what else is new?"

"Like that, huh?"

"The man's getting tired. You *get* to be tired, doing what he does. They stymie him, too."

"Then, there's the being black."

"There's that too, yes."

Harry said, "That's insurmountable."

"That's exciting," Max said. "Never a dull moment."

"Ain't it the truth?" Harry crushed out his cigarette. Together they turned to watch Little Max hold his father's gun and say, "Boom! Boom!"

"We ought to clean these birds and get them on ice," Max said.

"Yep, guess so," Harry said. "I don't feel mad at Charlotte anymore. Y'know, sometimes all this gets to her. She loved her old man, and was sure he wouldn't mind. She'd never liked her mother, but it was the mother who came through. You remember how Charlotte used to take Little Max to the house when the old man wasn't there, in a taxi, at some ridiculous hour so the neighbors wouldn't tell the old man. The old man died since we've been here. Her mother came once to visit us. She's getting on; they always get on when you're away from them. Charlotte won't come out and say she wants to go home. In a way she doesn't. Here, no one stares at her when she's got the boy; no one curses under his breath — that she knows of — when she passes. It's all right. I think she feels that she owes her mother her presence. All this has been bugging her and making her impossible to live with. That and the good fortune I've had. If it had been otherwise, we'd have no choice but to go home. Then, there's always Michelle for her to find out about. Aw, hell. She gives herself to the kid now. Maybe you've noticed; you notice everything else, you bastard."

Max laughed and gathered up his birds.

230

Winter came and Paris was naked of charm except under a fresh snowfall. What was the big deal about Paris, Max wondered, glumly, staring through his steamed window. This you could get in New York with better central heating. The novel rolled slowly ahead. On the days when nothing came or he was just too lazy to work, he fled to the museums or to the streets or spent an afternoon and evening at Janine's, a woman who was all for the lending and borrowing of those bits of human flesh and company without ever asking for an accounting. They were good for and with each other. When he left Paris she'd find someone like him; chances were that before him there had been some guy he had resembled in the ways that mattered to her. If he could, Max would find someone like her in New York, but they didn't grow that type as thickly in the States as they did in France. If he did not see Janine or go to the museums, he walked the sodden streets, peering into cafe windows to see if he knew anyone. Sometimes he found some of the new expatriates and treated them to drinks or meals in the restaurants that lace the tiny streets in the Quartier. Whatever he did, his single concern was with his novel. New York, his job and all the people he knew there seemed from another time when he had met them only in passing. There were times when he thought of a person in New York, pictured that person, but could not call up the name. Except Regina. He thought of her with pale, swift concern. He had received two notes from her. The first asked, when he had been in Paris two weeks, if he had caught the clap yet. In the second note she said she'd never had a desire to return to Europe, and felt that those who had earlier escaped it were foolish to go back to the slaughterhouse just because slaughtering had stopped for a season or two.

Not once did Max think of Shea until a letter came from him, asking if Max would consider working for *Pace* when he returned. When was he going to return?

Roger Wilkinson reappeared, claiming that the Swedish broads were great, but he could do without the winters. The group still took coffee in the mornings, but they'd have to brush the steam off the windows so they could see who, head bent against rain, snow or wind, was passing. As usual, rumors filled the cafe: Dawes was going home soon. His book was finished, sold, and he had got a nice piece of change. He would be missed at Les Halles where, when he had money, he and his streetboys would sit in one of the cafes extolling the virtues of a rotten onion soup. An expatriate Negro, caught stealing sheets he had hoped to pawn from a little hotel on Rue Jacob, had been arrested. One of his buddies was taking up a collection from among the Negroes to pay his bail. Time Curry and his group (he was having trouble with his old lady, Iris) had gotten some bookings on the Riviera. Another policy battle had exploded between the Afro-Americans and the Franco-Africans. Harry Ames (who was not at the cafe that morning) had insisted that true independence, when it came, meant working outside the French Family of Nations, not within it. The Africans had answered that the French, responsible for curtailing their development in the first place, should be willing to contribute economically and socially to the Africans and the easiest way for them to do that was for the African countries to stay in the Family. Harry then told them that what they would get would not be independence; that the single difference with the coming of what the Africans chose to call independence would be black people instead of white people stealing and taking from black people, with the French seeing that their boys got the most. He had left the meeting in an uproar. "Slave!" the Africans had sneered at Harry. *"Negro!"*

It was also in the cafe that, when winter began to loose its grip on the city, the plans for spring dominated the talk, while everyone looked around the table, as if surprised that they were still there, had survived still another winter.

"Holland at tulip time," Harry said. "They still love me in Holland."

"No, man, Scotland."

"Portugal."

"Are you crazy!"

"I heard of a place tourists ain't been to yet — Ibiza. Next year

232

this time you won't be able to get on the island. Tourists; they're just like flies gatherin' over a horseball."

"Tangier, that's the place they tell me."

"Yeah, sure," Harry said. "Every place under the sun but black Africa."

Everyone laughed. "We'll take you at your word about Africa, Harry."

One of the musicians said, "We ought to take up a collection and send Professor Bazaam down there. Wouldn't he be a smash with his Apple shit, them knobs and that four hundred-year-old suit?"

"We know where Max is going to be come summer," Harry said. "Back home."

They looked at Max, smiled and said nothing, each with his private thoughts of home, the good thoughts of home which, seconds later, were ambushed and wiped out by the bad ones.

"Back to the paper?" Roger asked.

"I don't know. I've got an offer from *Pace*." As soon as he said it, he wished he hadn't. The eyes swung toward him again and fell away. Max could almost hear their thoughts: Here they were, by the dozens, wondering where their next meal was coming from, not all of them, but a great many of them, and there he was, Max, just like them, spade, boot, nigger, with a job waiting at *Pace* — everybody knew *Pace* — and another book almost ready and advances were going out of sight these days. Whose ass was he kissing, this Max Reddick? Had to be kissing somebody's ass. Otherwise a spade just don't make it in the States. Hard to believe old Max is a Tom.

Max cleared his throat and asked Roger, "When are you going home?" They always needed social workers in the States. Things were getting rough for ditch diggers, but they were clamoring for social workers. Progress.

"Sometime in the summer," Roger said. "But I tell you, man, it's mighty appealing over here if your bread doesn't run out."

"Maybe I'll go back one of these days," Harry said absently. "For a visit."

"With your luck," one of the group said, "you'll probably wind up back in Africa and Dawes will wind up the greatest Negro writer ever."

Harry nodded wryly. "Strange, Africa. Really. You're glad to get away from it, yet something keeps pulling you back to it."

"Oh, man," someone said.

Harry smiled. "Go. Just once and you'll see what I mean. It's like the very touch of the sun, in some insidious way, planted a seed deep inside you. You may hate Africa with all your heart, the way it is now, and the way the white folks like it; you may rant and rave about how bad it is, but you seldom turn down a chance to go there." Harry laughed somewhat self-consciously. "It's in your skin, you see." Everyone at the table laughed again, heartily.

Max couldn't concentrate; his thoughts kept flying off. He put Harry's letter on the bed and lit a cigarette. He glanced at the window. About one o'clock. He wondered what Michelle was doing downstairs. It seemed quiet. They shouldn't have had those drinks. In the old days, yes. Lunches in New York, seeming to fly down Madison Avenue after three martinis and two stingers. The old days when no one was ill, and liquor and cigarettes put a fine edge on any part of the day, even in the morning, if you found yourself with nothing to do. He remembered drinking warm beer at eight in the morning in Kano in northern Nigeria, when the temperature was already over 100°. Max frowned. He was drifting again. He brought Harry's letter back before him. Was it true? Had he never heard of Alliance Blanc? The letter continued:

The Alliance first joined together not in the Hague, not in Geneva, not in London, Versailles or Washington, but in Munich, a city top-heavy with monuments and warped history. Present were representatives from France, Great Britain, Belgium, Portugal, Australia, Spain, Brazil, South Africa. The United States of America was also present. There were white observers from most of the African countries that appeared to be on their way to independence. The representation at first, with a few exceptions, was quasi-official. But you know very

234

well that a quasi-official body can be just as effective as an official one; in fact, it is often better to use the former.

I don't have to tell you that the meetings, then and subsequently, were held in absolute secrecy. They were moved from place to place — Spain, Portugal, France, Brazil and in the United States, up around Saranac Lake — Dreiser's setting for *An American Tragedy*, that neck of the woods, remember? America, with the largest black population outside Africa, had the most need of mandatory secrecy. Things were getting damned tense following the Supreme Court decision to desegregate schools in 1954.

# 20

PARIS — NEW YORK

1954 May 17! How they celebrated that day! They gathered at the cafe the morning of the 18th more briskly than usual, glancing searchingly at each other, the Paris, London and New York papers clutched nervously in their hands.

"Don't mean a thing."

"Looks like some very powerful shit to me, man. That 'with all deliberate speed' means just that."

"But you know Charlie and Miss Ann ain't going to sit still for that — their kids in the same classroom with black kids."

"Charlie ain't got no choice. The *Court* says YEAH!"

"No, man; it's got to be a fake-out."

"Wonder how they're taking the news back home. Max, write to us when you get back, hear? Goddamn these papers; I want to know what our people are saying about it."

"Those peckerwoods — there'll be another Civil War."

"Or a stateside Mau-Mau uprising."

"All right, let it come then."

"Yeah, with you three thousand miles away."

Laughter.

"Suppose it turned out to *really* be something?"

"And we didn't celebrate. Let's celebrate, because it might *start* a whole new bag back there. A whole new day."

"That makes sense. Sure, let's order a little taste."

"If it's the real thing, I might have to pack up and go home."

"Time enough for that. Time enough."

At the end of the celebration, which lasted two days, in and out of bars and cafes and restaurants, Harry had driven Max back to Le Havre. Max's leave was up; his book was finished. "When are you coming back, Max?"

Max countered with, "When are you coming home, Harry?"

"Never mind. Just put the blocks to them, man."

"You too, Harry."

Passengers pushed and shoved against them. "I probably won't be coming home at all. This is home now, for better or worse."

"Not ever? Not even now?"

"A man could raise hell there now, yes," Harry said. Then proudly, "But you'll all have to look back to me."

"Dawes too?" Max asked.

"Him most of all."

"Give Charlotte my blessing, the kid too. And Michelle."

"Yes, of course. You'll come back, won't you?"

"Maybe. How can you tell?" Max walked Harry to the gangplank; the ship's signal had blown.

"Back to work," Harry said with a sigh. "Keep your head low and your chin covered."

New York remained unchanged, a testimony to its strength against the minds of millions of people who leave it every year and expect that with their departure, something about it will change. When the ship had come into the harbor, he thought of the people he wanted to call right away. But once unpacked and having checked to see that his subtenant hadn't ruined the place, Max decided there was no one he wished to call that day, and he dug out the liquor he had hidden and fixed himself a drink.

He expected and received no trouble from Michael Sheldon.

Senator Braden's Un-American Affairs Committee had been washed away by the eloquence of a lawyer from the Midwest. His third day back, Max called Shea. He had to talk about the *Pace* job before reporting to the *Century*. Shea invited him to dinner at his apartment that night. The apartment was in the upper floors of a new building on lower Fifth Avenue, and Max arrived in a belligerent mood. He had had a shoving match with the doorman who had blocked his passage and asked in a nasty tone who Max wanted to see; finally backed off and allowed him to get on the elevator. As soon as he'd shaken hands with Shea, he started to complain. Shea listened, his face flushing. He called downstairs and ordered the doorman to come up. And apologize. "I don't give a damn what the house rules are," Shea said loudly. "When you see Mr. Reddick, you let him in without a word. You tell the other doormen too. If I have any more trouble like this, I'll have your head." The doorman flushed. He didn't know if this was one of the elaborate games the liberal tenants sometimes played or not. If it was, Mr. Shea played rough. If it wasn't, what the hell was he going to do if some nigger waltzed through the door and cleaned out the whole place? This one looks like every other one. The doorman apologized; he'd take the matter to the agent.

"Welcome back to New York," Shea said dryly. "You can see that things haven't changed that much."

"No," Max said. He sighed with relief. He had been so close to corking that sonofabitch right in the mouth, so close. Max looked around. Shea had a view of the Avenue down to the Washington Arch. He's done well, Max thought, very well. And here I thought *I* was raising hell in a couple of shabby rooms in Paris. Hell, I *was* doing better. Max had forgotten about the opulence one can find inside even an ordinary building in New York. If I had been white, he thought . . . Shea fixed him a drink. "Look, Max, we can talk about Paris and Harry after you tell me your decision about *Pace*. We're most anxious to know. We expect things to start popping around here with the Supreme Court's ruling on desegregation. I'll

237

be candid with you: We want Negroes on the *Pace* staff. Sooner more than later, everyone's going to look around and find that they aren't clean; they won't be able to point to the South. We want to start with someone who knows the South, who knows something about the Negro mood, generally. I'm telling you this. At the office someone else would tell you something a little different, but it would amount to the same thing. Also in the future is a desk in Africa — maybe. This Mau-Mau business has us half expecting the whole continent to go. You'd get first crack at this if it came about. Now, you'd work out of New York, in National Affairs, but when you're on assignment, you'd work with bureau people in that area. You'll have to learn our systems, but that's a small problem. What do you say, Max? You can name your price."

Max named it. It came spinning off the top of his head, nudged by the doorman and Shea's current luxury; it had no basis in reality. Max looked boldly at Shea. His hair was the same gray; yet he seemed to be growing younger instead of older. The white boys get all the breaks, Max thought, knowing it was a thought to be laughed at. Max wondered how it was with women for Shea these days. He hoped he would have the good taste not to go into it, even if he got high. Shea nodded. "That's in the ball park," he said.

Max swallowed his drink. In the ball park? In the *white folks'* ball park! His father had had to work over five years to make what he was going to make in one. What was this, a welcome to the white folks' ball park? Max wondered suspiciously, What if I had asked for more. Would I still be in the ball park?

Shea went to the telephone and when he came back he said to Max, "Congratulations. You're on the *Pace* staff now. I only wish I could have done the same thing a few years ago when I was on the paper. Now, I guess, you'll have to talk with Berg over at the *Century*."

"Christ knows we can't pay that kind of money," Berg said. "Well, I knew it; it was inevitable. They all sit back and wait and then they buy out the poor bastard who made it possible. What am I to do, stand in your way? How? It's a free country, more or less,

238

and maybe now we start on the more part. Tell you what, though. If you get tired of that East Side crowd, come back. I'll give you a little raise, but it won't be *Pace* money. Is that a deal?"

They shook on it.

(Lillian, look. Look at it, Lillian, the money. Look! Goddamn it!)

Max felt like an object rather than a new employee when he reported to Shea his first day. Max shook hands with at least fifty people, but remembered none of their names, only their titles: " 'Back of the Book' editor"; "books editor, you'll want to remember him."

Sure, Max had thought.

"National Affairs editor, Mannie Devoe. You'll be working under him." "Photo editor; he'll assign photographers to you when you need them." "News editor."

Six floors, Max thought, as he and Shea wound through offices and back to elevators and through offices again. Six floors and one black face. That wasn't true. Here and there, emerging suddenly from around doors and desks, he'd seen Negro women. They were researchers or research assistants. Max had seen three, but he had seen no black faces at the news desks. Oscar Dempsey, the editor, who wore colored shirts with bold stripes and white collars and neatly knotted ties, assured Max, however, that "with your reputation, you can count on a by-line occasionally. We know that it's one thing to have a college kid come in who isn't used to having his name stamped on what he's written, and another thing to have a novelist and newspaperman who's used to having what's his labeled. We can run boxes, can't we, Kermit, with say, three hundred lines and Max's name?"

"Sure, no problem."

"Yes, there is," Dempsey said. "He's got to have news." He laughed and his huge yellow teeth bucked out.

"That goes without saying, Osk."

Dempsey offered Max a cigarette. "Seriously though, I'm glad you joined us. This is more than an experiment, you know. It's what *Pace* believes. We want qualified people of any kind here; the pace of the world demands it."

Dempsey did not like air-conditioning. His window was open and the street noises raced up the walls of the buildings and rasped into the office. Shea sat idly, toying with a cigarette. For Shea, Max thought, the fat was in the fire. The great democratic experiment had begun. If it flopped, *Pace* would turn the hose on him. Max only half heard Dempsey tell his secretary to reserve a table for three at a French restaurant. Dempsey resumed talking about *Pace* and its aims. I'm not a child, Max thought; I don't need the pep talk. A new white employee, Max guessed, would only see Dempsey from a distance or at a urinal in the men's room. Oh, well, it's a part of the program, when you invest that kind of money in a new Negro employee, a pioneer, a "first Negro first." And the Negro got his money in part because he listened to the boss. Big deal. *Pace* hadn't even given him an application form to fill out in 1946. Now Dempsey expected him to be ten times better, cleaner and more honest than those he had been afraid to upset by hiring him eight years ago. Just because he was black. And they were sweating, Dempsey, Shea and Devoe. Paying good money to *sweat*. What dumb, poor, misguided, do-gooding bastards. Damned if I'd pay good money and sweat too, Max thought. You pay good money, ordinarily, so you wouldn't have to sweat. I'd sure as hell know what I was getting. And in spite of all that they must know about me, all of it, now they look at my skin and don't know what they're getting. White folks. Jee-*sus*!

On his own desk Max found material on the Dred Scott decision and Chief Justice R. B. Taney's papers about that decision which he had supported. There was also background material on the Supreme Court's May 17 ruling on education and recreation. Devoe had said, "I bet you know a lot about this stuff, but bring it back to the top. We've got researchers going on Taney's background and Warren's background. We may do four hundred lines on the Chief Justices or on the two Courts. Also the Negro mood at those times. In case nobody told you, we lock it up by Friday night or, at the latest, Saturday afternoon. For the late-breaking stuff, we can even push until Sunday night, but we don't like to. Overseas copy is due in here on Thursday; if it's important, we can bend it until Saturday, but we don't like to do that either. Today's Monday. By Wednesday we should know just what kind of story we're going to wring out of the material you have there. Just holler if you want anything. Tony there'll see that you get it. She knows the ropes. Hear you just got back from Paris. Great town, isn't it? We've got a bureau there. How's your French?"

Devoe hesitated a moment, hoping he hadn't seemed too forceful; just forceful enough. Had to find the right balance. It wasn't easy being boss of a guy with four novels under his belt and a hitch at the *Century* and a year in Paris.

When Devoe left, Max thumbed through the material. So, he thought, this was one of the citadels of white power, and here I am, right in the middle of it, making everyone sweat. How far can I go? How wide can I swing? That his very presence had put a number of people on the defensive was obvious; that left the offense to him, but he was going to use that offensive sparingly. He hoped Shea had schooled the powers at *Pace* in Maxlore; he hoped Shea had told them that he wasn't very likely to take even a little teeny bit of crap. A couple of dollars in the bank always reinforced that feeling, that and the sense of changing times and knowing that Berg would take him back any time he got fed up with The Magazine.

As the weeks passed, Max found himself being invited down the street to the Warriston for drinks or lunch with other people in the office. The calls from Shea (intended, Max guessed, to help ease him into *Pace*'s groove) grew less frequent. On the whole Max spent his time quietly, fixing up his apartment, making notes for another novel, playing records and sleeping. It was as though he was bored with New York. True, he made his duty visits to Zutkin and Granville Bryant, and passed along news of Harry and his work. Several times, without success, Max tried to reach Regina. When he finally did, she seemed rattled and asked if she could call him back, but she didn't. Max guessed that she had a lover with her. It was late in August before she called and, surprisingly, asked if she might come to his apartment.

It was a different Regina who walked in and embraced him, rested momentarily in his arms. Then Max gave her a drink. "Well, did you?" she asked.

"Did I what?" He couldn't stop looking at her; he had never seen her look so good.

"Get the clap in Paris?"

"No," he said, laughing. "I didn't."

"You look well rested, Max."

"I feel just fine." She looked cool and evenly tanned. A light, summer perfume hung about her and edges of her hair had been bleached by the sun. Max started to remember things he shouldn't.

Regina blew out a large cloud of cigarette smoke from behind which, partially obscured, she asked, "How's your love life, Max?"

"Kind of dull since I've been back. I suppose it'll happen if it's meant to. But tell me about yourself. You look fantastic."

"Don't use that tone of voice, Max. I know that tone."

"It slipped."

"Okay," she smiled. "Max, I'm in love. That's supposed to make one look good, isn't it?"

"They tell me. Anybody I know?"

"No. I'd like you not to call me anymore, all right?"

"Sure. Anything you say. That's a whole lot of love you've got there."

Regina opened her mouth to speak, thought better of it and then said, "It's good for me. He's a little weak in some ways. I can help him. I told you once that was important for me."

"Yes." Looking through the window Max could see that the sky was covered with a silver sheen. Moisture in the air; humidity. "I'm glad everything's okay for you. I worried while I was away."

"I thought you might. But it's all right. I'm over everything. Really. Why do I feel guilty? You don't love me, do you, Max?"

"No, Reg."

"Okay then. I'm a big girl now. Max, I am so proud of what you've done with your life. I never think of you without thinking of beans and ham hocks. I wish we could be friends forever and ever. But I'd lose this man if he even thought — well, you know how some men are."

"Yes, I know."

Regina asked about the new job, then they smoked and drank in silence. She slid one tanned leg over the other; she wasn't wearing stockings. Max looked up quickly. Had he been hearing signals? She had mentioned guilt. Maybe she had come to wash it away. But then, would she feel guilty with her guy? "Stay," he said at last. Regina looked at him, blinking her gray eyes once. "Welcome me back home."

"I thought you might ask," she said. "Thanks for the invitation. I will. The last time. The goodbye. You refused me the last time I offered."

Max made more drinks and Regina put on records. He had heard correctly, Max thought. How do people make out who don't know how to send and receive signals? They went to bed at midnight. In the morning Max woke to find coffee on and her note. She thanked him for having contributed his protein to the strength of the baby, now almost two months old; the marriage was taking place in three days. She hoped he wouldn't think her horrible but she had wanted to share something important with him, she owed him so much and, in a way, loved him so much. Now, she might daydream years hence, when looking at her child, that Max had contributed, not to the skin or face or anything superficial, but to the interior, the bones, perhaps the heart. She thanked him for asking her, thus saving her from having to ask him. She would think of him forever and wished him long life, luck and love.

Max read the note a couple of times while he was drinking the coffee and thought, I get the ass-end of everything on the way to someplace else.

243

He was still thinking of her note when he arrived at the office. He wondered how many white women who had married white men had had Negro lovers and kept that secret locked in their hearts? Did they never, in some delicious moment of sleep, cry out — to be questioned in the morning, as the husbands threw coffee and toast at them and punched the kids in the mouth? How many, tortured with that secret, had finally confessed it, expecting tenderness and understanding and promptly finding themselves divorced, if they were still alive? How many had made the confession, stayed married and suffered only when the husbands, thinking themselves unequal to that faceless Negro ex-lover, heaped the ashes of scorn on their heads? How many secretaries or researchers or research assistants he was now looking at would leave the office at five o'clock and meet a Negro lover in the Village? How many Negro men would be in white women's beds tonight, or vice versa? All Max knew was that he had never met another Negro man who had not slept with at least one white woman.

His door opened behind him. Shea, smiling, said, "You start to earn your money now."

Max looked around and grinned. It was true; *Pace* hadn't used the material Max had written on Taney and Warren and their Courts. And he hadn't done much of anything else except to observe.

"Dempsey wants to see us. There's some desegregation trouble in Delaware. You've been tagged." Dempsey handed Max his press and cable cards. "The townspeople are saying no to desegregation; the school officials say yes. The people are stoning the Negro kids. You'll meet a man from the Washington bureau. Work with him."

"We need the copy by Friday noon, Max," Devoe said.

Irritably Shea said, "He knows that, Mannie."

"I suspect," Dempsey said, "that the lawbreakers will look at the color of your skin before they look at your credentials, so be cautious."

"Be careful, Max. Keep your eyes open," Shea added.

Max was surprised at the concern he heard in Shea's voice. "Don't worry. I start earning the money now."

The Delaware incident, which ended with the mayor of the town pledging no integration during his tenure, was quickly followed by a brief action in a small Tennessee town. The mayor of that town, however, together with the chief of police, had met a mob on a downtown street, told them that there would be compliance with the new law, and the mob had melted away. Two men, one with a .38 gripped in a sweating fist, the other with a 12-gauge shotgun previously used for rabbit, squirrel and bird, both dribbling a bit in their pants, had taken the long walk, and won. But without bloodshed, Max thought, those two men, *men,* would soon be forgotten.

Then 1954 was over. The first editions of the magazines for the new year blithely predicted real outbreaks of violence for 1955. Max wrote a 300-line story about the desegregation scene for next fall, noting the hard-core resistance states and the few areas where compliance had been indicated by the school boards and the citizenry. On the whole, moving into spring, it looked as though the problem of desegregation would smoulder for a long time and not be as explosive as Dempsey had thought. Then came Altea and the Reverend Paul Durrell, and Max was quickly pulled off general writing in National Affairs and dispatched west.

Negroes in the small, South-like border town had attempted to secure from the school board a pledge for integration on all school levels for the coming fall. Now they were launching a city-wide boycott of the public transportation system and department stores. The first week the boycott stuttered, slowed and dribbled along, and there was spotty news coverage. Who'd ever heard of Negroes using a boycott as a weapon? But by the end of the second week, the area bureau chief called New York to say that the boycott was becoming effective. Streetcars passing through Negro neighborhoods were empty. Stores where the bulk of the Negro middle class bought were half empty on Fridays and Saturdays. The rednecks and country Negroes couldn't begin to take up the slack because they didn't make that kind of money; they were also used to buying in the smaller stores. The Altea Negroes had set up an organization, the Altea Advancement Group, and were cooperating with it 100 per cent. The streetcar company and mercantile losses were reported up to $75,000 going into the third week of the boycott, which was being led by a middle-aged minister, whose name was Paul Durrell.

In the *Pace* staff meetings it had been decided that here was a new Negro leader, perhaps better fit for the times than the old ones guiding the quiet fortunes of the NAACP and the National Urban League. But Max realized that for Dempsey and Shea, Durrell was the old and comforting image of the Negro preacher as a leader.

Altea was a less than ordinary town. The road from the airport was lined with tall, slender pines, long and lean. The land was tufted with withered, scraggly hunks of grass, as though something in its history had trod its surface and left it restless and resisting the seeds that had been dropped into it.

For the *Century* the chief target of concern had been the already-lynched Negro. But there was no lynched Negro here, no quiet, head-bowed black folks slipping in and out of the shadows or sitting around Civil War memorials, or when there were no shadows, crossing the silent streets ablaze with the white light of a midday sun hoping they would go unnoticed by the whites. Here in Altea, the Negroes were on the offensive.

Max did not seek to see Durrell at once. Instead he stood around outside the drab, brown-shingled church where the Negroes waited for rides in private cars and trucks. Max had never seen such confidence in so many black faces. But that confidence was not boisterously expressed; it was quiet and sure. Patient, now that something concrete was at hand. The area where they waited for the cars and trucks, all in a neat line, hummed with the idling of dozens of engines; the sharp odor of gas and oil hung in the air.

The people laughed at the cops and nudged each other when white female employers drove to the car pool to pick up their maids and cooks. The white women, in curlers and coats over their gowns or pajamas, ducked when photographers rushed to take their pictures. There was enough ignominy in having to transport the help; why have it recorded to remind people in the future just when the Old System started to crumble? Crumble, that was what everyone felt. The Old System was going. The Old Ark's A-moverin'. Going with every shift of the cars' gears, with every tread of every foot, with every empty streetcar and department store, with every old sister and brother who was hoofing it, delighted that before they died they'd been given a chance to protest.

Durrell wore a wide-brimmed hat and a genteel suit that could almost have been zoot. That almost put Max off; in Negro communities one saw and heard so much about Negro preachers that was both laughable and charlatanic. Durrell spoke with a soft upland Louisiana accent. A shade or two lighter and he could have gone *passé blanc*. He was a thin man of medium size and his face was sharply angled as if some Choctaw ancestor were breaking through. When he spoke, his words came slowly and deliberately and softly, as if belying some inner violence. Durrell called the men, whatever their ages, "brother." He called the women, old and young alike, "sister." He listened to the complaints of his people with bowed head, nodding once in a while, his face impassive, as if hewn from the meat of a buckeye. Durrell walked the streets with his people; he shared their car pools and joked with them. The older people, the ones used to having their preachers for leaders, idolized him; but the younger people, even though they were caught up in the boycott (it suited them and it was about time), were watching and waiting. They knew that generation upon generation of preachers had led their fathers and fathers' fathers into dead end after dead end. They did not plan such an abysmal journey in their time.

Max wanted to be convinced that Durrell was all that he seemed to be, but inside him something persisted that said he was not. He couldn't pin down the feeling. He was conscious of waiting for something to happen.

Durrell's wife was as fair in complexion as he and that, Max thought, figured. In a society where the white female is exalted, a Negro refused a hundred and five pounds of exaltation all his own was going to get the next best thing.

One day close to noon, the number of people in Durrell's office thinning out, Max, sitting in the sun-filled window, noticed that Durrell seemed restless. He kept looking over the heads of the people he was talking to, his eyes not quite as bland as usual, seeking out a young woman in a corner. The woman, Max noticed, stood with her back to Durrell. Something inside Max quickened. Signals? Now she turned back and her eyes, too, swept above the heads that stood between her and the minister. Signals?

Max left the room. Outside in the sun he walked quickly to his rooming house. Maybe signals; if so, he didn't want to see them all. If not, fine. But Max carried his reservations with him when he left the town.

Back in New York, Max buried his reservations about Durrell. Perhaps Durrell, like others before him, would fall by the wayside if he had the kind of flaw that could wreck the whole movement. But the search for a new Negro leader went on and Reverend Paul Durrell was being selected. Max knew this when Durrell was invited to serve on the board of the NAACP. If you can't beat 'em, join 'em, Max thought.

Max moved once more, to a larger place in the West Village. Perhaps the distance he now found between himself and Harlem was what brought him back to it each Saturday afternoon when he left *Pace* — that and the fact that he now had a fox, a real fox who broadcast remote from radio station WWWF in the Palm Gardens Cafe every Saturday. Killing time waiting for her to finish, he chatted with a graying Sergeant Jenkins, an aging Big Ola Mae whose jokes and gossip now came slowly. Sweet Cheeks at the Nearly All Inn was now the most pathetic of creatures, an aging homosexual. The fox was named Maida Turner and she had once been, as the phrase went, "a Negro model," which was to say that her face was strikingly lovely, but everything else about her, unlike the white models, was full to bursting: her bust, her buttocks, her legs. She had appeared in ads for hair preparations, cigarettes and beer, and was in demand at the fashion shows sponsored by Negro women's clubs in and around Manhattan. It was this background, and a good voice and microphone poise, that had earned her the job; Maida had a women's fashion-hints show and a personality show.

Max had met her with the publication of his novel; she had been the only good thing about that book, which had been cautiously received, platitudinously reviewed and finally, unceremoniously thrust aside for the others coming up to their own publication dates. Maida had Max on her show and there was, of course, the fact that he was the first Negro hired by a major news magazine. In the course of drinks afterward — Max knew precisely the time — she thought he would be good for her career. He knew Durrell, Harry Ames and the famous gospel singer who never started her performance until the money in the box office was counted and her wages paid. He could get to people she could not. She could get new sponsors, run the show from fifteen to thirty minutes and get an increase in salary. The arrangement had been mutual. Max was tired of the parties, the word games, the maneuverings. It would be nice to have someone to see and go out with regularly. For a few contacts. But all life was, one way or another, a deal.

Quite by accident, on Saturday while he was waiting for Maida to finish her show, he discovered that a new group had come to Harlem. Max had a drink while waiting for Maida's show to go on. He always left her in the booth taking a final swallow of her gin and tonic, wetting her lips and glancing at the clock. He stepped into the street and strode the few steps to the corner, Harlem Square, Seventh Avenue and 125th Street. He glanced southward, toward the Theresa Hotel, and stopped dead still. The orator there looked familiar. He was a little man, very dark and old, and he wore, Max could see, a beret, a zoot suit, both faded. Professor Bazzam? Max crossed the street and stood at the rear of the crowd. Sure, it was the Professor, wasn't it? But he couldn't hold the people. They kept coming up and slipping away; Max slipped away with them. Back on the side of the street he had left, another orator, a dirty little American flag drooped listlessy over his box, delivered an illiterate diatribe against Jews, white men in general, and other Negroes; he spoke with a West Indian accent. "A Geechee," someone in the crowd said.

Across the street, in front of Micheaux's bookshop, another group caught Max's attention. The men wore neat dark suits; their hair, to a man, was neatly barbered and their shoes were shined. The man who was speaking to them looked vaguely familiar to Max that first day, but everyone called him Minister Q of the Black Muslims. It was in a way laughable at first; each orator tried to outdo the others with gimmicks — African robes, berets, tuxedos. The people said that Minister Q's bag was "super cool."

But with each successive Saturday, Minister Q was drawing the people away from the other orators who, cursing, would snatch the flags off their boxes and stuff them in their pockets and join the crowds swarming across the street to hear him. More and more people were doing more listening than laughing. One Saturday when Maida had finished her show and was standing beside Max, she said, "I want him on my show. That man is talking a whole lot of sense."

Minister Q was an untainted, a pure African Negro such as is seldom seen in the United States today. Nothing Indian or white seemed ever to have touched his genes. He was all muscle and three yards wide; when he goes, Max thought, they'll have to make a special coffin for him. The Minister was quick on his feet. Later he confided to Max and Maida: "When I was younger I could Lindy all night, wear out four or five partners. I could do everything all night — and did it. Then I've been a bouncer and I worked as a molder in a foundry, you know, going all day like a slave, each mold weighing seventy-five pounds, and shaking out too. I thought I was pretty great because I could turn out more molds per day than any other man in the place. Those white devils just had a good thing and knew it."

Minister Q was talking in his neat little office in the mosque.

Maida was taking notes; Max was remembering, and now he remembered who Minister Q had been. "In the old days, before I found Allah, I was also a boxer."

Of course, Max thought. Kid Go-Go, a middleweight, a forerunner of Sugar Ray. Even then — what had he been, about sixteen or seventeen? Even then he had the build of a heavyweight from the torso up. He'd never got a chance at the title. The last ten seconds of each round, the Kid had gone after his man without letup, hooking, jabbing, crossing, loosing a series of blinding fast combinations. Now the Kid — Minister Q — had a bottom lip that splayed out while the upper one protested swollenly. "I hadn't found Allah then," the Minister went on, "but I had sense enough to know that I was being exploited. I fought the best of them, Graziano, La-Motta, and never got anywhere near the crown. I got out. Women, whiskey, horses, numbers, just wasting my life and didn't know it. I found Allah when I was in state prison for pushing junk. I don't try to hide it. I know what my life was and I know what it is *now*. And I know the whys and wherefores."

Minister Q could have been the same age as Durrell, but he didn't look it. Now the Minister looked at them from across his little desk. "And you both work for them, the white devils." He placed his broad, blunt fingers together. "May Allah be with you. May Allah watch over you."

Where Durrell employed fanciful imagery and rhetoric, Minister Q preached the history, economics and religion of race relations; he preached a message so harsh that it hurt to listen to it. Max saw the shamed faces of the men in the crowd Saturday after Saturday. The Minister would raise his heavily muscled arms that had driven opponents from one corner to another and bring them down on the rostrum like twin judo chops. The crowd would flinch.

The Saturday Minister Q first came to prominence, Max and Maida were in his street corner audience.

The Minister said: "Those white devils took away our history. They hid the records and lied to us. We have a history, but no white man is going to reveal it. We have to dig it out ourselves and the work is not hard, brothers. That work is *sweet!* Sweet to learn of old and mighty empires, of kings and princes of such influence that it reached into Europe where the white man slumbered in his Dark Ages. Yes! That's the way it was! When he woke from slumber he grabbed Africa, ripped us from her and with his profits — from slave profits — he began his industrialization. Europe was already in slavery, they didn't need Africans. A serf was a slave! A serf, I tell you, was a slave! So we came here. They raped our women and over the generations bent the minds of our children so that only now, today! are they beginning to grasp the truth about the white devils of this society of his called America. Don't tell me about those white devils! There are no good white men! None! "

Max could feel a shiver run through the crowd. "Tell 'em, Minister! *Tell 'em!*"

"How many of you here," Minister Q went on, "own one single brick in the whole of Harlem? How many? Not a single hand, not a finger, and do you know, brothers, that is exactly why you're here this afternoon! And here are all the so-called Negroes in America getting excited about dee-segreeegation. Why, in Allah's name, *why?*" The Minister flung his arms outward in mighty protest. "We don't want to be with them! We want our own land. They owe it to us. They've bled you [powerful blunt finger pointing at the crowd], your fathers, your grandfathers, your great-grandfathers, your great-great-grandfathers, to *death!* Don't you know that this country is based on the labors of the black man? They took the strength and wisdom that was ours and ground it under cotton patches, forced it to open its legs under magnolia trees. Allah endowed us with wisdom, strength and goodness. They tried to blot out our wisdom and the work made our strength ten times what it was. Listen: little Negro babies —" Here the Minister paused. "Little Negro babies *walk* sooner than little white babies. What does that mean? Strength. Now, brothers, the time for goodness is past. Allah *knows* the time for goodness is past. Look at the mark of the white man around you: those cops with those cannons on their hips; look at your skins, brown, yellow, white, tan — where did all

252

the *black* go? You know: it went in the bedrooms, on the slave ships, in the fields, in the big houses —" Minister Q paused again: no sweat ever came to his face; he might have been created around a cake of black ice. "Now look at you. Tainted, owning nothing, cowed, pride in nothing, dignity in hitting the numbers or in drinking two fifths of the white devils' liquor." The Minister set himself. "The time for that is past. Brothers, watch your women! Take your children in hand so they might have the dignity you've lost. Above all, watch the white devil. Too long has he marched back and forth across this land stealing, raping and murdering. I call now for black manhood. Dignity. Pride. Don't turn the other cheek any more. Defend yourselves, strike back and when you do, strike to hurt, strike to maim, strike to—"

The crowd leaned toward him waiting for the word. But Minister Q smiled; he would not say it. He did not have to say it. His meaning was clear. "Allah," he said, "calls upon you to defend what is yours — yourself, your family, your dignity." Long moments after he had climbed down from the platform, the crowd stood motionless, then it broke into cheers.

That night on television Max heard the commentators:

"The leader of an anti-white group, who calls himself Minister Q, today advocated the killing of white men . . ."

"Race hatred today reared its ugly head in Harlem . . ."

Max laughed. How self-righteous they had become all of a sudden. White people didn't want to be hated; it was all right for them to hate, but to be hated in return, virulently hated — it stunned them.

America had bred this time, Max mused, this time and people like Durrell and Minister Q. America bred them as surely as it bred sweet corn and grapefruit. Durrell's people came from the church-going middle class; Minister Q's from the muddiest backwashes of Negro life. The white man was going to have some choice to make between them, but he would, Max knew, choose to deal with the remembered image, and that would be Durrell.

With the fall, Max went South again, this time to a university

253

town. For the first time in his life he saw a white mob howling and bleating, snarling and tearing. It's object was a lone, skinny, unattractive Negro girl who had been admitted as a freshman. During the war Max thought if he got out of it alive, he would never again know fear. Anger he had known.

He knew a new anger and a new fear as he listened to the coed tell her parents and uncles and cousins about the first day. Even now in the cities across the land the newspapers would be carrying pictures and the wire service stories. There were still strings and gobs of spit in the coed's hair that she hadn't managed to clean out. Max thought: They demand so much, the white people, from each and every one of us. These were the people so many white writers were proud of. Where were those lone, sensitive, heroic white Southern men, a little apart from the rest, a little unbalanced, gentle with animals and women, descendants of Civil War heroes and pioneers who had wrested giant homesteads from the earth? *Where were they?* And what were their offspring learning in their schools and colleges fretted with magnolias, azaleas and cypresses?

The older people, clucking and frowning, the women crying softly, fed the shocked coed, washed her hair and put her to bed. Among the men no word was spoken, but suddenly, lifted heavily from each car in the driveway, came a rifle or shotgun, boxes of ammunition. Standing at a window, Max could see them loading their guns, smoking, exchanging brief words with each other and glancing slowly up and down the nearby road. A pair of mockingbirds swooped across the yard as dusk came slowly and Max, still at the window, thought once again of Southern writers. The good ones, the truthful ones, were always the women. The women the Southern gentlemen had always protected. Perhaps it was the women of both races who would have to clean up the mess. Another car pulled into the driveway, the men paying it no attention because they knew the sound of its motor, knew its color a half-mile off on a straight stretch of road. The newcomer also had a rifle over which, coming out of the car, bounded an alert mongrel bird dog. Max watched in silent admiration. The men split up and soon vanished into the lengthening shadows, their guns held gently in the crooks of their arms. Somehow, there was no doubt that the girl would go back the next day; it was as if each relative knew that fact for himself and extended it to everyone containing his blood. Max sat in the living room. No white reporter could have been able to do this; he was not going to miss any of it. The relatives tiptoed through the house, those who stayed up. Once in a while Max joined the guards in the kitchen for coffee.

Was this what so many places in America were going to be like until the law, *justice,* took off her goddamn blindfold and saw what she had been doing with it *on?* Dawn came. The women rustled in the kitchen and soon the house was filled with the smell of fried ham and eggs, the pale odor of cooking grits. The girl's father had taken one of the early watches. Now he came downstairs, rested, but his eyes were red. He was a man for whom the pace of life, especially this aspect of it, was all too sudden. He didn't really understand it, but with a child in the house caught up in this time, he could not, in some way, *not* understand it; where it failed to come through in all its intellectual complexities, it succeeded emotionally. They had hooted and beat at his daughter, spit at her. But it was important that she go back; there were others who would follow her. They were evil, those white people in the mob, and had to be smitten. An eye for an eye. Jesus Christ, Lord Almighty, where are you this morning?

The girl herself put spark into the morning and thus gained beauty. She had them laughing (politely) at breakfast, after which she preceded her father to the car. The rest would have to wait; that white beast out there sought any excuse to kill: a rifle in a car, a caravan of Negroes protecting their own. The car pulled out of the driveway slowly, as if the girl's father, to incite a gentle day, had merely caressed the accelerator. The exhaust pipe puffed small blue wisps of smoke. Then the car was gone. At the main road, grinning cops in cars would follow it, providing not the protection they had been slovenly enjoined to, but an invitation to the mob to do almost exactly as it wished when they (the cops) sped off on a side road.

As soon as the coed and her father had left, Max got a ride to his rooming house where he was to meet the Atlanta bureau man. They were cordial to each other. Max got in the front seat — a photographer was in the back — and a taut silence filled the car. The mob was bigger now, joined by the rednecks from the country-side. Factory workers from the other side of town, afraid that the college boys wouldn't properly run that nigger bitch off the campus, had swollen the ranks of the mob. Max guessed that today was the first time many of them had ever set foot on a college campus.

The Atlanta man was nervous. Max knew why; he would draw the attention of the mob. The Atlanta man knew, as Max knew, that failing to find the girl who was being spirited from class to class by the campus police, the mob would turn on just any Negro. Max was remembering stories of white men on the hunt for a sus-pected Negro rapist, murderer or plain bad nigger. The Negroes shut themselves up in their homes and talked in low voices as if waiting for a capricious hurricane from the Caribbean to pass through. They knew, those old Negroes, of the waverings and curvings of white men gathered in mobs; it was something that went down in the blood, the smell of gasoline burning along with flesh, the grisly souvenir hunters. Yes. If they couldn't find who was supposed to be the culprit, just any nigger would do. Once they got up a head of steam, cooking underneath with still likker, the history of their time and place steaming like hog guts thrown upon cold stones with the first frost, nothing could stop them until they got their blood.

Moments later, at the photographer's request, the Atlanta bu-reau man stopped. The photographer hopped out and took pictures of the flank of the mob, which, suddenly seeing first him and then Max, wheeled and began to pour toward the car. Max remembered chino-covered legs, blurs of white sneakers mixed with heavy coun-try shoes, the uneven drumming of running feet on the grass, the

256

curses. The photographer scrambled back into the car muttering something about a telephoto lens the next time. The Atlanta bureau man sat paralyzed at the wheel. He snapped out of it long enough to scream through a slightly opened window, "Press! Press! Back off there you kids! " A book glanced off his window and he raised it. He looked as if he were going to cry. Max heard the photographer snapping and cranking. The people in the mob had grabbed the car bumpers and were rocking the car. Max wished he had a knife, a gun, a rock. *Something.* Rocks and more books crashed against Max's window. Looking through the window, he picked out the man he wanted to have if they broke into the car. He would break that motherfucker's neck if he had only a second to do it in; no mob would stop him. That thought made him feel better. "Start this damned thing!" Max shouted at the frozen Atlanta bureau man; the photographer reached over and slapped the man sharply. The Atlanta man's glazed eyes now snapped with fear. Max pressed his left foot against the accelerator; the car jumped forward and the people flew away from it. Max jammed it down, and outside he saw the expressions on the faces had changed quite suddenly to fear. A sudden warmth flooded through Max. As the car moved and jerked, the Atlanta bureau man sighed and gripped the wheel more firmly. Within seconds they'd left the mob behind. Shaking, Max lit a cigarette. "This is your goddamn Southern hospitality, huh?"

The Atlanta bureau man drove silently, first ashamed that his fear had been so obvious. Then he wondered what in the hell they were thinking about in New York? This wasn't any place for a nigger reporter, he didn't give a damn if it was *Pace,* not when the people in the mobs were throwing things at white men, too, and calling them nigger lovers! Why, the Atlanta bureau man thought in surprise, he had never been as close to a nigger in all his life as he was right now. But those people out there, you couldn't expect them to believe that.

It took only a week before the university found an excuse to expel the Negro coed from the campus.

Sometime later, back in New York, Max learned that Paul Durrell's group had won its demands, two years in the asking. Schools would open the following year on a desegregated basis; the department stores were thrown wide open and no Negro had to take a back seat to any white person on any streetcar in Altea. But within a week of Durrell's victory, his lieutenants complained that the Group's funds had been grossly tampered with. Durrell, finally clearing himself of any implication of grand larceny, went to Chicago.

It seemed to Max that the white press had created the atmosphere for the minister's acquittal; that was the way the white boys worked. Were the stakes in the present so high that the white power structure was prepared to save Durrell from his mistakes already? He'd indebted himself to white America if he really was guilty. One day the leadermakers would call in the chips. Max hoped Durrell was really, really clean. The movement couldn't be affected then, it would keep on rolling. If it worked the other way, disaster. The steam going out of everything; old sisters and brothers, close to the grave, crushed; young sisters and brothers drifting toward Minister Q and, generally, hard-assed times coming.

# 21

*Pace* had demanded too much time and energy. Max had been able to contribute very little to his man's second attempt to gain the Presidency.

Besides, the politicians preferred Theodore Dallas to Max. Dallas was a Negro but he didn't look like one. That was important. The Negro image was immensely softened by Dallas's white appearance. Besides that, those Southerners who quietly went along with the candidate knew from experience within the blood that every Negro wanted to be white — or as nearly white as possible. Look, they seemed to say, whut lookin' like white did for Powell.

Dallas's blond hair and blue eyes, his white skin taunted by the just-lingering coloring of a remote and very dark ancestor, gave him that perennially suntanned look; the tan burnished his magazine-model good looks. Max could never think of Dallas without thinking of Roger Wilkinson. (Roger had returned to New York, briefly, then gone again to Europe, for good, he had said. He hadn't sold any of the novels he had written, and spent a great deal of time putting together *policiers* for French publishers, which in the end they never accepted. Max wondered how he was going to live.) Like Roger, Dallas did and said everything at just the right time and in the right places. He courted both the politicians and the intellectuals, yet when the two sides had their inevitable conflicts, Dallas managed to remain unscathed and smiling. He always smiled; he had those nice choppers. He mixed very well in the company of Negro men, laughed from his belly, as if to prove that though he was fair enough to pass for white, he was a stone, just-like-you-guys boot. They enjoyed him, expecting some of his glamour, political and otherwise, to rub off on them. A few boasted of having Dallas's phone number. Dallas teased and cooed at the Negro women with just the right amount of hippy-dip to let them know that he was still a spade below his belt. They smiled and grinned back until he had left, then they muttered, "You light, bright, just 'bout right so-and-so."

But remarks like that were really directed at Dallas's white wife, her with her bright, blond, always neatly coiffed hair; her with her skinny self and trying to talk like colored . . . Too many of *them* marrying us. No, honey, you got the cart 'fore the horse; too many of *us* marrying them.

The Dallases called down these remarks upon themselves simply by looking as though they were a couple right from the pages of the slickest of the slicks. They were a handsome couple. One saw them — not too often, however — in the better Negro nightclubs or at the Baby Grand catching Nipsey Russell. (That was before the other Negro comedians came, Max remembered.) Or they were seen in the East Side restaurants downtown, sleek, poised over dinner. When they entered a room where a major interracial affair was in progress, they drew stares. They sucked in behind them at the tiny Negro theater openings uptown or off-Broadway, a certain, bright, expectant downtown opening night air.

"He's been around politics so long," Maida remarked at a Langston Hughes opening on the upper West Side, "that he acts just like a candidate."

And Max thought, that's true. He was learning, Max was, that the consummate politician was also the consummate actor.

Max's worst days were those when he looked out of his cubicle and saw Dallas bearing down on him, unannounced, smiling acknowledgment of the attention of the researchers and secretaries. "Passing by," Dallas would explain. "Thought we might have lunch if you don't already have an appointment." Dallas had been that shrewd. He knew that, if he had called, Max would have had another appointment; Dallas knew that Max did not like him. Nothing personal. A lot of people didn't like him and Dallas knew it. Dallas also knew that Max, as far as he knew, seemed too polite, perhaps even soft, too *conscientious* a man to refuse lunch on the spot. And Dallas knew somewhere in his thrivingly alert set of instincts that no Negro working in mid-Manhattan, regardless of his position, wanted to eat lunch there alone. Eating alone was at best painful to most people.

When they had lunch, Dallas would talk about Harry and how Harry really had beat him to Charlotte. That was in the old days when he had been interested in the Party, but had been smart enough to avoid it. Look what had happened to it.

Max, listening, realized each time that, as a novelist and journalist rolled into one uncertain hunk, he could have a certain value to Dallas, if he could be won over. It had been no small secret to Dallas that the intellectuals always favored Max over himself as a wedge into the Negro community. That undoubtedly was because Max didn't have a white wife. Couldn't trust those intellectuals. They were willing to go only so far. Dallas worked hard at winning Max over. He never wearied of inviting Max to affairs, which Max never attended. Then, discovering that Max hunted, Dallas offered to take him on a jaunt to Canada. Max refused; he'd gotten used to hunting alone. He preferred it. But Dallas for a long time displayed the patience of a whore with a sure John heating up over a fifteen-cent beer in the corner joint. True, Max did not like him, but he knew with boring certainty that Dallas, having the equipment to fit the time, plus the soft-muscled dexterity of a cat that always landed on its feet, would gain his goal to be a big man in Washington. Well, Max reasoned, being close to politics did that to a man. He could understand that.

There were many ways to get to Washington. It figured, therefore, that only shortly before the Gold Coast was scheduled to change its name to Ghana with the coming of independence, the first African state south of the Sahara to do so, Dallas overnight would become involved in African affairs. The announcement of Ghana's independence for March of that year gave new life to the annual spring birthday cocktail party the Ethiopian Mission to the United Nations held in honor of Emperor Selassie in the Delegate's Lounge. Generally the parties had been dull and attended perfunctorily by the other UN people and by a few local Negroes of some community standing and a few others who had none at all; other guests were those who had displayed some interest or concern in Africa. But that spring cocktails were drunk merrily, the party enlivened by the presence of the Ghanaian delegation. Dallas's voice boomed from one corner to another. The delicate, large-headed Ethiopians (all Amharics; Max didn't know then that there were other kinds) glided from group to group. Max was thinking, as he stepped on Ralph Bunche's foot, that perhaps from here on out Selassie no longer would be a joke. What other free African delegations would be here next year? That late spring afternoon, humidity soaking First Avenue, UN Plaza and the city, a new excitement was born: black men were coming to freedom.

Excitement. No, there was a *curiosity*. Whatever, it was centuries and thousands of miles thick. It breathed through the cloying, fetid rain forests of Africa, called up the ghost of Marcus Garvey who never went there, caught the windward tides across the seas, spun the dirt of Harlem streets; it lingered in the bars and restaurants, sat on the tongues of Negro preachers with middle-class congregations:

Africa. Af-rica. Freedom. Free-dom!

Africa gave back a reflection. Africa was becoming free and her first black prime minister in modern times was coming to Washington. In triumph. From Takoradi to Kumasi the Ghana Highlife pummeled the ears and ran like a frightened mamba through the bush: "Sing: Free-*dom!* Sing: Free-*dom!*"

And Max saw and heard America's Negroes commence the antistrophe:

"What of us black men in the West, descendants of a thousand tribes from half a hundred countries? What of us whose presence here determines the treacherous American Deep over which no white immigrant had or has to sail, no matter how lowly his existence if he could say or can say:

*Nigger?*"

Black Fever. Harlem streets revealing more and more Negroes in African dress — kentes, agbadas, shamas — these days without laughter. Minister Q filling Harlem Square, pounding home the lost lessons of black empires. Marcus Garvey recalled. Negro papers filled with statements from African leaders who had studied in America. Negroes everywhere straining to be let loose or straining to break loose. Every day one or two, three or four black faces on Pan American flights to Africa; every day two or three black people boarding the Farrell Lines gangplanks, going to Africa. In the midst of this fever in which everyone was wondering just where the next Little Rock would be, the official announcement of Nkrumah's coming was made public, together with the statement that Theodore Dallas had joined the staff of the Chief U. S. Protocol Officer. Presumably, Max thought, to help with the Nkrumah tour. That figured, too.

Dr. Nkrumah, Max knew, had studied with Jaja Enzkwu at Lincoln University. What had the Africans discussed among themselves then when they were rejected by the American Negro students? Now, here was Nkrumah, fresh from his visit with Ike, surrounded by Secret Service agents and New York City cops in white gloves.

All of them, Max thought, watching the mass of American Negroes in spring suits and print dresses, the odors of their perfumes and colognes one wild, heady denial of the white man's claim that they stank, all of them just a few years ago ashamed of Africa, rooting for Tarzan, cursing the natives from the seats of the Apollo. Now look. There he was, the man, in native dress, and the mass of print dresses and spring suits cheered and clapped and Dallas stood by, smiling. Some of the ministers were there and took part of the applause; all were resplendent in kentes of adinkira cloth. At one point, while Nkrumah was speaking his mission school English, liltingly, reminding Max of a West Indian (when really, it was the West Indian sounding like an African), the ministers looked strikingly familiar; they looked like what Hamlet must have seen to have spoken his line about the insolence of office. They were also like the familiar portraits of American and European Latin leaders newly come to power, like British East India merchants benign at the first gathering of the people.

Max slipped out of the hall and found a three-for-one joint across the street. One day, he told himself, he was going to find a four-for-one joint and drink himself to death. The bartender lined up his three drinks and Max sat facing the street where the long glistening cars, cops in white gloves and Negroes on no one's invitation list lingered. Let it run its course, Max thought. He was remembering what Harry had said about Africa and Africans. (Better — what Harry *hadn't* said.) But what had that to do with him? He hadn't been to Africa.

Nkrumah came out, surrounded by dark suits with white faces coming out of them. Then came his ministers and Dallas. Nkrumah waved, the print dresses and spring suits cheered, laughed and waved back. Cops ran about, clearing the streets. Motorcycle engines blasted through the uproar and snarled away beside the softly purring long cars.

The next evening the feverish preparations for the banquet in Nkrumah's honor at the Waldorf had been completed. The invitations had gone out and the responses, along with the money, had come in. Maida had been interviewing as many Africans as she could lay her hands on (or put body to, for that matter, for that was about the time she had started to go, Max watching with undistressed eyes) and had been offered positions in the various broadcasting houses of the countries that would be coming independent. Max watched her go. He was making progress. They had stopped looking for the thing in his face; it was no longer that psychic thing, but the material: contacts, shared acclaim. No, there didn't seem to be any more Boatwrights or Marys or Reginas. Now there were the Maidas and the Dallases. A fox wasn't a fox for nothing. Foxlike she came and foxlike she went, on the hustle, and one day would retire to the home one of her lovers, a seventy-year-old man, had bought her shortly before she sent him (he could imagine it) on a pelvis-twisting ride to the next world. You had to admire Maida. She played fair. She was faithful, absolutely faithful, until something better came along. He sure would miss that pussy. Sure would.

At the banquet Max watched them, the Africans, the Negroes, the whites in their dinner jackets, gowns, shamas, kentes and agbadas: the press corps eating and drinking and stuffing the prepared speeches into their pockets; the honored guests, a hundred or so, jammed on the dais; Nkrumah in purple (Like that, is it? Max thought), the forepart of his head shining. The speeches were endless and were given by an endless number of people. A film was shown. A group of American Negroes with an African-sounding name played drums and danced. And then, at last, it was over.

Max had been stalking a redhead all evening, but somehow she eluded him and when he last saw her, she was leaving with one of the ministers. He was high and didn't want to sleep alone. As the

264

banquet hall was thinning out he was already thinking of women he might call and then:

"Are you Max Reddick?" He could not tell how old the woman was and he didn't really care. *"Are* you Max Reddick?" She smiled then, a little uncertainly. She was wearing an Ethiopian shama.

"Yes," he said. Another live one. Thanks, Lord. Ah, well, once more into the breach.

Every time he thought of Africa, he thought of that night, the banquet and the fates that had brought to his bed a Chinese girl wearing an Ethiopian shama. That was the way to remember things.

It was 1958 and Max Reddick had been at *Pace* four years. Oscar Dempsey was well aware of the fact that within that time a number of editors had joined other magazines or newspapers or television networks. Others had taken lucrative public relations jobs. Reddick had had one promotion — to assistant editor, but he was forty-three years old. Thirty-nine hadn't sounded so bad when he first came; but forty-three had a definite ring to it, as if a man was walking hard along the neck of his future, close to success or failure. It was a source of embarrassment to Dempsey that he hadn't yet found the right niche for Reddick. At forty-three a *Pace*-man usually was a bureau chief or senior editor. Every damned bureau chief on the staff now had come to his post only within the past two years, replacing the men who had left the magazine. And you just didn't kick out senior editors whose places would have to be taken by people who had been on the staff longer than Reddick. Dempsey had made the usual compensations: raises and occasional junkets; plush, although brief assignments — that American Negro expatriate piece for example. That had sent Reddick back to Europe for a few weeks, and it had gotten good responses. And Dempsey had managed to get Reddick known to some Washington people after the second Stevenson campaign. That could pay off. A lot of those guys down there were looking over their shoulders at the Negro vote and some were turning to Negroes for advice and counsel and speechwriting help in the area of civil rights.

There was Africa, of course. Shea had been after him about it. It was true that Africa had been mentioned in the original deal to get Reddick to come to *Pace*. Things *were* going on there: Egypt, Libya, Tunisia, the Algerian War (must cable Paris about De Gaulle); the Sudan, Ghana, Guinea due to become independent in the fall. Next year, who knew? And the year after? *Pace* could depend on stringers and the wire services, but there was nothing like having your own people on the scene. Max Reddick bureau chief? Max Reddick a one-man bureau? Dempsey always sighed when he came to that idea. So many guys on the magazine deserved that job, including Reddick. His work had more than rounded out the liberal outlook of the magazine in contrast to the other books around. Dempsey had made no bones about it; *Pace* was in this civil rights thing until it was achieved. What to do? You couldn't leave a man with Reddick's talents sitting down in that cell at forty-three years of age. Someone might come along and offer him a good thing; you had to keep him satisfied at least. But, goddamnit! There were others, Devoe for example, who deserved something, too.

Mannie Devoe was now assured beyond any doubt that Reddick was not a threat to him, but he did wish the guys upstairs would make their move with him; obviously, they had to and soon. They'd find the right niche. They always did. It was 1958 and things were getting a bit sticky racially. Little Rock had done a great deal to draw the lines. That too had been the time at which Negroes could start depending upon the press, for the press corps with its beaten bodies and smashed cameras had perceived for the first time just how important civil rights was going to be to the nation. And Minister Q was becoming more vocal and *Pace* — Devoe could not determine who upstairs was responsible for all the Minister's coverage — at least cautiously, now seemed to prefer him to the Reverend Paul Durrell. Most of the New York City press corps preferred the Minister. Devoe could not understand that. Nonviolence was a goddamn valid philosophy. Devoe wondered if Reddick believed in it.

At the moment Max was not believing in anything. He was sitting in his cubicle writing down the names of the women he'd slept with from puberty on. He was tired; he never seemed to get enough rest these days, and he was irritable from the onset of rectal trouble once more. All this combined to make him disgusted with The Magazine. He knew his work had been good; no one had to tell him that. He had reached, it seemed, the plateau where a decision had to be made. It didn't look as if anyone was going to make it for him. When he saw Dempsey in the halls, Dempsey, with an empty smile on his face, was always in a hurry. There was more than one decision to be made. The first was whether to quit *Pace* or not, despite the fact that he had received none of the lucrative bids, political or otherwise, that were besieging the "right kind" of Negro. It would be, then, just a naked decision to quit.

Max listed another two names and smiled, the memories surrounding those two names being pleasant. If he quit then, *then* he would be able to add new names from the ranks of researchers and secretaries. Not before.

He had come to have more respect for the contemporary press than he had ever had before. The times were forcing it to be honest at last. But there were some points at which honesty went too far. The press did not always report the words of the Presidents. One day the press would be able to quote the President who said of his opponent, *"I had that sonofabitch so mixed up, he couldn't grab his ass with either hand."* The cats in the office had fallen out for days when that one came in. A lot of people would love the man who said that, but the bluestockings wouldn't and there were a lot of bluestockings or people who wished they were. What the hell, *Pace* was no better and no worse than the rest of the books. And probably just a little bit better.

Max circled Lillian's name and stared at it. He crossed it out and continued on with his list.

But the first decision: Africa had been mentioned a long time ago. It had been dropped from all conversations. *Pace* didn't have a single man there. A lot of British stringers, a few French cats, AP and Reuters, nothing more. It was foolish to think that Dempsey would consider sending him to Paris or London or even to Washington. There were too many guys in line ahead of him. No, if Dempsey was thinking at all, he was thinking of Africa.

Max had recognized the Negro expatriate assignment for what it was — a consolation for *Pace*'s inability to move him up, down or sideways. It had been nice going about, staying at the good hotels on *Pace*'s money. Roger Wilkinson had met him at Orly — Harry had been knee-deep in maneuverings to secure the Nobel Prize for Literature that afternoon — and after a few days in Paris, off Max had gone, interviewing Negroes in seven countries. They were actors, singers, dancers, musicians, conductors, composers, painters, cartoonists, writers, sculptors — they had been everything and everywhere in Western Europe, as a Black Diaspora. Their color had forced them out of America and they were not looking to the day when it would force them back; they didn't think that day would ever come. At the end of the assignment, Max returned to Paris to see Harry and only then did he understand that he, too, was growing old. Harry was just about fifty, Charlotte, forty-seven. Little Max — *little?* — had pimples and a deepening voice. Both Michelle and Charlotte were carefully tending crowsfeet around the eyes and creaming their faces heavily. But both looked good. Paris had changed, the cafe had been painted. There were more cars, more noise, a certain hectic atmosphere shattered from time to time by the plastic bombs of the Algerians. Cops manned roadblocks with automatic rifles, firing first and asking questions afterward.

Max and Harry had spent a day in the country walking and talking, exchanging news of mutual acquaintances. Harry had questioned him about Minister Q and Paul Durrell. Harry had been exhausted and embittered with many things and he had worked in vain to corner the Nobel Prize.

Recalling that afternoon, Max became aware of the second decision he had to make: should he continue writing after he finished his present novel? What happened to a novelist who was Negro at age forty-three with six published novels that had sold fewer than six thousand hardcover copies all total? He was floating over the abyss he had described to Harry; it was an eerie feeling. Max knew what the editors said about him: he drank a lot (but he seldom lost his cool) and liked white women. Hell, one dealt with the materials at hand. A Phoenician used the glass formed by the heat of his pot on sand; a Bushman stored water in the ostrich eggs he found crossing the Kalahari. Why should he not go out with women he knew, even if they were white? But just any excuse would do for them.

They sought good writing, but published trash. What would be in next year? Ah, yes! A book on Little Rock and how it *really* was behind the scenes, how the parents took it and how brave the nine kids were, and who inspired them day after day to go out there and face the mobs. But already there were signs that nigger evil would become a real hot commodity (they were running out of everything else), right up there, by god, with the Jewish intellectuals combating the contemporary *apikorsim.* Yes, sir! Who ever thought the day would loom on the horizon when a Negro writer could say

GODDAMNIT! I AM ANGRY

and get royalty on $4.95 per burst of anger, less advance and agent commissions, for it?

It chilled Max to think of the murders they were still committing on Harry. What on God's earth did a man do who did not play the game of jacks and jills? Alexis de Tocqueville gave the answer one hundred and twenty years ago; that answer was still valid.

Max wrote Janine's name. He hadn't seen her in Paris, hadn't even asked. She would be pleased to know that, pleased as hell. He wondered what the people on his list were doing and where they were. Did they ever think of him, fondly, as he was thinking of most of them? Did they ever wonder about his being forty-three, without chick or child, sitting around thinking of them while trying to make decisions?

Max stayed late and helped put the book through its final wring-

269

out. That was Friday. On Monday morning he was called to Dempsey's office where, in the presence of a grinning Shea, he was told that the Africa desk was breaking this way: *Pace* was sending a man to head up a desk in Nairobi in a few months. Would Max then survey West Africa and make recommendations where a West African desk — which he would run — should be established?

# part THREE

# 22

MAX reached once more for Harry's letter. He stopped midway through the act of reaching. The pain in his rectum was uncoiling, slowly, oozingly, powerfully, sliding through his entire body. For the first time Max thought of the .25 he had tucked under the seat of the car, the Llama. When it became too much, the Llama. In the head, not jammed into the mouth. Max swallowed a pill. Sweating and shaking, he shifted on the bed. What in the hell was he doing here in the first place at — he looked at his watch — almost one-thirty and the sun still almost straight up? What was he doing in Leiden, in Holland, a white land eight hours by jet away from that limitless black continent from which his forebears had been dragged centuries ago? Why in this white land east of a white land that could no longer call itself purely white, for in fact it had never been that? And here Harry was, cremated only hours ago, trying to tell him something about color and what it had done and what it was doing. Black Harry who had loved white Charlotte and white Michelle. Why in Leiden? He thought of Margrit, white Margrit and himself, black Max. That was why he was in the Netherlands and, indirectly, why he was in Leiden shut up in an upstairs bedroom that had beams in the ceiling — because Margrit was white and he was black.

Africa stunned Max.

He had come to it via Europe, passing from one ancient ruin to the next in growing, ill-concealed irritation, yet drawn inexplicably to the best of the white man in the past. So there were Roman roads, arches, aqueducts and stadia; so there were Greek arches and shattered yellow pillars, sensual religious art and golden ages and statues. What about *now*, baby, now, while you noble Romans are sitting squat in Fiats and you Greeks have left the Aegean for

Brooklyn! Not until he had climbed the hill to another ruin, the pyramids at Gizeh, did he lose Europe and begin to feel both the size and unplumbed history of Africa stretching out over the white sands behind the three tombs, stretching southward to Nubia, Cush, the Sudan.

Max had left Mannie Devoe somewhere between the Nairobi Press Club and the Equator Club in Kenya. Devoe was going to run the East African desk. Devoe liked Africa; he liked the way Africans called him bwana. "This," he had said as they walked along what was then Delamere Avenue, "is a good brief. Great. I'm glad I took it." Max had nodded and looked up the street. Nairobi was where you were somehow surprised to see an African strolling along, taking a constitutional, perhaps, and not on an errand for Bwana Blimp. Max had left Devoe there and journeyed three months around Africa on his survey, from Dar es Salaam, hot and muggy from the thick, soft, Indian Ocean winds, to Dakar, fiercely bright in the sun with the indigo blue Atlantic lapping gently against its seawall; and from Kano, with its Great Mosque and dry skin-wrinkling heat, to Leopoldville, surprisingly pleasant, even at midday. Max was staggered by the great distances, the night flights into swollen electrical storms with their thin, jagged golden lances of lightning stabbing down the tremendous, seething skyways.

At the end of his survey, Max had concluded that Lagos was the only logical place to set up the West African desk. All flights south and north went through Ikeja as well as flights to the east and directly to the States. Cable facilities were excellent, thanks to the British. There were some places in Africa where, if you wanted to cable an adjoining country, the message first had to go through Europe. And Nigeria, along with the Congo, was the next big independence attraction. The roads between the major towns were good and the sea was nearly always in view. Also he was sure he could find someone in Lagos to help him polish his French. And he had developed a fondness for the clubs in Yaba and Ebute Metta. By the time Max left, the smell of wood burning for charcoal, the stink of the open markets embedded so deeply in his nostrils that he could never forget them, he had made arrangements for leasing both a small office on Broad Street and a house for sometime the next year.

Roger, whom Max had left in Rome, had left Paris to live in Amsterdam; Roger met Max at Schiphol. In Rome, he had offered to put Max up, show him Amsterdam. Africa had been expensive and Max was looking for corners to cut on his expenses. Besides, he wanted to talk to somebody about Africa. Somebody Negro. He wished Harry were there instead of Roger. He didn't even know why he had come to Amsterdam, except that he'd never seen it. Now that he was here, maybe he'd start to find out some things about the people whose cousins had either killed off or run out of South Africa the people of Dingiswayo, Usenzangacona, Dingane, Mzilikazi, Umpanda and Lobengula — these people with their cute old houses and canals — these people and their endless battles against the sea. The Hans Brinkers and Silver Skaters.

"How's the homeland?" Roger asked on the long ride into the city.

Max was tired. His flight had started at Lagos and put down at Kano. From there the plane had skimmed the Sahara, ghostly and dead in a full moon. Rome once more, Zurich and then Amsterdam. He was going into his second numbing, sleepless day. He said, "The homeland's there, it's really *there*."

"The cats are really starting to swing, huh?"

"You better know it. All over. Fantastic place." Max didn't know yet whether he liked or hated Africa. He thought that curious. The good and bad memories attacked him so violently at the same time, whenever he had to answer questions about the place.

"Where'd you go?" Roger asked enviously. He'd always said that if he got a chance to go to Africa — bam! — he was gone. Man.

In a painful monotone, as the level, snow-covered fields glided by and white roofs glinted in the sunlight, Max began to talk. As he did, the good and bad experiences finally assumed their proper

275

places and he was able to draw them out one at a time. He remembered that the Amharics — the people who gave the UN party every spring for the emperor's birthday — ruled Ethiopia and the Bantu-types such as the Gallas could go bark with the dogs who howled from the Addis Ababa mountaintops each night; he remembered that the Ibos and Yorubas in Nigeria didn't get along that well and that the Hausas in the northern region of the country despised them both; he remembered that the Ashantis really didn't like Nkrumah . . . Recalling it all on the ride in, while talking to Roger, he suddenly knew why it had taken him so long to make up his mind: he had been setting aside the fact that most of the Africans he had met did not like black Americans; in fact, they held them in contempt. Perhaps he was wrong? When he passed this thought on to Roger, Roger raised his eyebrows. Max smiled. Of course, Roger wasn't going to believe that. Why should he? No Negro looking for another home would believe it.

"Then why are you going back?" Roger asked.

Max shrugged. "It's a job. Best job I'll probably ever have." Naturally he was going back. Just why, he didn't really know; that puzzled him, too. Say it ain't so, Africa, say it ain't so! In any case, he was going to hole up in one of those air-conditioned houses in Ikoyi after the British left next year, and write, really write. And wait for things to happen. It was too hot in Africa to chase news. When it broke, it chased you and that was time enough. Write? Christ! He had forgotten that he was going to quit.

The conversation ended as they taxied from the bus terminal to Roger's flat on Alexanderkade on the Singelgracht. The brief February sun had gone and Max looked out upon the gray, ice-covered canal thinking of Africa, and its sun. Behind him, Roger was talking of changing and going to meet some people — partying — pahtee, pahtee! Max wished he had gone to a hotel where he could have slept for days, even if he didn't clear a single penny on his expenses. A nice, warm hotel where the cold wouldn't seep into his bones the way it was now. Outside were dead trees, snow, ice and, for all he knew, zombies.

276

Max wondered at Roger's silence. What was Roger thinking; this? How did that cat get so lucky? Publishing all those books, getting great jobs, getting to travel, no hang-ups with the bread — where it was coming from and how much of it to spend. Just what does the bastard have that I haven't got? Was that what Roger was thinking?

Max looked around the rooms, now filled with the long, heavy shadows of late Amsterdam winter. Everything was a hustle; hard. Max remembered. "I'll get you some chocolate," Roger said. "And there's some rum around here, too." "You'll like these people we're going to see, Max. A few of the brothers around, and the broads are not to be believed. They're in your corner. Do anything for you. Lots of cats just mess over them and they just take it. Don't understand that . . ."

Max opened his bag, took out a clean shirt and found his way into the bathroom. Goddamn, he thought, shivering with the chill. He thought of Africa again and remembered the bathroom of a house he had stayed in in Kano, remembered the way the sun played upon the windows and how the gecko lizards scrambled along the screens and on the outside walls. There was no window in Roger's bathroom. When he came out, Roger had the cocoa ready and almost half a tumbler of dark rum.

Good, Max thought. This should keep me going for a little while.

It was at the third house they visited — they ate at the first house and the host was Dutch and his wife Indonesian; at the second house, with darkness hard upon the city and winds skirling along the canals, was a group of American Negroes, painters, playwrights, singers — yes, it was at the third house that he saw her through eyes glazed more with the need for sleep than from the drinking.

He had been getting very irritated because no one would give him directions back to Roger's apartment. "Drink up, man!" they said. Then he saw her sitting with another woman. He placed their ages at about twenty-seven or twenty-eight. She was sitting partly in shadow, he remembered. The high-riding cheekbones set in the small, neat face startled him. More tired than I thought, he told himself. Or drunk. Through spaces between people who moved from one part of the room to another, he studied her and once found that he was holding his breath as he watched her face bloom into a smile; he listened to her laughter, muted because of the other noises, flutter its way deep into his memory. He beat his way through the maze of sound which was jazz and many voices. Here too, he thought, jazz was that battleground, a seemingly innocuous place where you proved you were a hippy, if you liked it and played the right cats at the right time. Part of the Negro bag: *Dig jazz, do you, huh, baby?* And if you did and you were a white chick, your drawers were, many, many times out of ten, as good as off because that's why you came and that's why the cats came.

So, he wondered about her when finally he stood before her and peered down into her face. She smiled brightly and said, "Hello," and extended her hand. Her arm was thrust awkwardly forward, her thumb standing straight up.

"Can I sit down?"

She slid over. Her friend gave her a smile, then seemed to vanish.

Margrit Westoever looked anxiously after her. She hoped she wouldn't leave, because she, Margrit, didn't really know these people, and her friend had brought her. What does it mean that she left like that? Margrit was pleased that the guest of honor at the party Roger was giving — at someone else's house, of course — had noticed her. Was he going to be like the other Negroes she'd heard so much about or had seen sitting in the cafes on the Plein wearing dark glasses and looking so suggestively at women when they passed? Their reputations were terrible.

"My name's Max."

"I'm Margrit."

She didn't ask how he liked Holland; he liked that. "Nice group," he said.

"I guess so. I mean, yes."

"Don't you know these people? I mean, you sound unsure."

278

"Well I see many of them about. That's all."

"Like jazz, do you?"

"No, not really. Some things, but I prefer other music. You have been to Africa, I hear."

"Yes," he said. I'm a Been-to, too, he thought.

"What a large place it seems to be. Is it? Did you find it interesting?"

"Very large, very interesting. Your name is — ?"

"Margrit. Margrit Westoever."

"I'm sorry. It got away from me. You remind me of someone."

Of course, Margrit thought, that means a girlfriend. She said, "Oh."

"A friend, just a friend," Max said. Then he wondered why he had said that.

Margrit smiled and fidgeted with her hands.

"Do you have a date here?" Max asked.

Margrit, in resignation, for here it came, the old black American line, smiled and shook her head. "No, I haven't."

"Let me make you a proposition," Max said. He smiled. "It really is a proposition."

At least he was straightforward, Margrit thought. "Go ahead."

"First, say Max."

"Mox."

"No, *Macks*."

"Mox," she said once more, then flung out her hands helplessly.

Max liked her. "Okay. I'm going to be here about a week. Be my girl. For seven days." It was better like this; you either liked each other, or you didn't, and there was not much point in playing the usual games. Fleetingly he wondered if at her age, coming to the party with another girl, she were not a lesbian. Didn't look it, but who could tell? "What about it, Margrit? You can show me the town. Besides, you're much better looking than Roger."

"Are you always so to the point?"

"Usually, yes. It comes with age."

"Just how old are you?"

"Forty-three. You?"

"Almost thirty."

So, he hadn't been so far off. "Well?"

Margrit played with her hands again. What does he want with me? She liked the look of him and she liked what he had written. Roger had made a big point of insisting, when he first came to Amsterdam a few months ago, that everyone read his buddy's books. He lent them out and a few days later reclaimed them to pass them on to still another person. Margrit had read them at the home of her girlfriend. Roger liked to talk about how he was friends with people who were doing things. Margrit had liked what he seemed to be concerned with, this man who was waiting for her answer. "All right," she said. "Only there's not much to do in Amsterdam this time of year." She said the last to his back for he had risen and gone away. She was puzzled until he returned with two glasses of Genever. He gave her one. "To our proposition," he said. Margrit raised her glass to his, wondering what she was letting herself in for.

Later, when he had brought her home and she had given the waiting cabdriver Roger's address, he said at her door, *"Een kus?"*

Margrit laughed softly. Who had he asked to tell him that phrase? Did this mean he was going to be like the others? He had adjusted from his African journey very quickly. But she had thought that he would ask or simply take her in his arms, and she had planned to let him. Now, she said, *"Ja,"* and held up her lips and closed her eyes. He kissed her on the forehead. Margrit was surprised when she opened her eyes, still (she admitted to herself soon after) waiting. He was smiling now and suddenly he looked very tired. How was it that he hadn't slept for two days? Why such an innocent kiss? Why such gratitude in it and for what? She asked herself these questions before her mirror, where she always asked them. He was gone now, but he would be back tomorrow. Strange man. Nice man.

Shivering in the cab, Max felt pleasantly tired. Margrit looked so much like Lillian. True, a bleached Lillian. Strange after all these years. Have I been looking for Lillian all this time? Has she been transmigrated back into the human race? Unbelievable that their faces and smiles are so familiar. Margrit was a bit heavier, but this was Holland, after all, where the packages come on the large side. Margrit Westoever. Lookit here! He glanced through the window. The city had become lovely; why hadn't it looked so good earlier?

"Has that little girl opened your nose?" Roger asked one afternoon. Roger peered up from his typewriter to watch Max dressing to meet Margrit. Max grinned. Maybe. Maybe Margrit had got to him. There had been three days of museums, shops and Amsterdam history; there had been long walks that had brought bright red spots to Margrit's cheeks and washed the blue of her eyes; there had been lunches and dinners and watching skaters on the canals. Once, briefly, along the Amstel, they had thrown snowballs at each other.

"Max, has she?"

"She's good company. I didn't want to take you away from your work," Max said. Roger threw him a sharp look. Was he being funny?

"Yeah, man, sure," Roger finally said. He turned back to his typewriter. Lots of cats had been shooting at Margrit Westoever, simply because she wasn't like the other Dutch chicks. They dug spooks; they were racists in reverse, but you took them as they came, knowing all that. And here came old Max, and tied up Margrit, seems like. Cat sure is lucky.

"See you," Max said and walked down the steep stairs into the street. He was having dinner with Margrit at her home tonight. Whistling, he walked briskly along the canal and crossed over a bridge. He passed a cafe where a group of *provokateurs, provos,* sat peering into the darkening street through their sunglasses.

Margrit was waiting for him. He kissed her as he entered, the first kiss since the night he met her. This time he kissed her on the lips. He was surprised at the naturalness of his kiss and her response to it. It left them, for a short time, staring wonderingly into each other's eyes; then it was past. The cats crept about Max's feet as he sat down. He looked at the paintings on the walls. Margrit brought the bottle of old Genever and placed it on the table along with glasses. She looked different, Max noticed. Her smile was different, too. It was not precise any more. He thought he could see into it. Now Margrit raised her glass to his and smiled. Inwardly, he smiled, too. The stories had it that only Negroes had such nice white, even teeth. "How have I been as your girl for three days, all right?"

"Perfect," Max said.

"Ah, yes?"

"Yes, almost perfect."

She looked at him and walked briskly toward the kitchen, saying, "Four days to go." In the kitchen she thought to herself, Four days more. Then he goes back to New York and I stay in Amsterdam, just as I always have, nearly, working and waiting for what? *Godverdomme!* She had married at nineteen and that had lasted exactly one year. She hadn't known what she was doing, getting tied down to a young Dutch burgher whose entire life was business. Lots of girls did it and were happy. After that she had known a couple of *provos* — a natural reaction after a year of stuffy, circumscribed existence. But they had not been interested in anything save smoking marijuana, drinking, fighting, listening to jazz records and going to jazz concerts. One even wore his dark glasses to bed. She supposed that was the reason she didn't like a great deal of jazz; it attracted to it very strange people whose world was, in its own way, just as narrow as her husband's had been. Time sped by. Now, she was almost thirty. In Europe that made you an old maid or a lesbian. Or a whore. Managing an art gallery hadn't helped. She had gone through a couple of painters, or more correctly, they had gone through her. That had not been pleasant either. So! Four days more, then life as usual. Of course, what more?

Max stared at the gas fireplace. The cats now were curled up before it. Snow lay thickly on the windowsill. He sipped the Genever and wondered why Margrit was so quiet in the kitchen. Once again he looked at the paintings on the wall, then he rose and

walked softly to the kichen and saw her staring thoughtfully into a
pot on the stove. "What's the matter?" he asked.

She turned and smiled brightly. "Nothing. What could be the
matter?"

He shrugged. "You were so quiet."

"Cooking and thinking."

"You look very lovely, Maggie."

She gave a mock curtsey. "Thank you, my boyfriend." She
watched him come close, then he was against her, holding her more
gently than she'd ever been held in her life and, as he started to
draw her away from the stove, she quickly turned out the gas jets.
They did not eat until very late and Max did not go back to Roger's
flat. The next evening, he moved his bag to Margrit's flat. There
were three days more to go.

Margrit cut her hours at the gallery. Max walked her to work in
the morning when the chill hung in the air, thick and bone-
touching. In this manner, they managed to steal a few hours more
from time. Live it up, get on the plane and forget it. It'll be a nice
memory, this playing at real involvement, at love, if you will.

He had never been touched physically quite so often. They walked
arm in arm and hand and hand, and only frequently did it occur to
him that Dutchmen, very much like Americans, might be thinking
of climbing out of the walls and whipping him good, touching a
white woman like that or being touched by one like that. When
Margrit embraced him on the street, Max said, chidingly, "We
mustn't behave like kids, Margrit."

"Yes, yes, of course, Mox."

But she always forgot and he remembered that he hadn't minded
when Lillian did it. Why should he mind now? Oh, oh, he would tell
himself, what a colorless rationalization *that* was. But he felt comforted when she touched him if she had been away only a few moments, as if to reassure herself that he was still there. But when she
was away, Max drifted through daydreams, analyzing each barrier
that stood between them, but he would slide past one barrier and
arrive at the next. When it would come to him how his thoughts

were going, he would wonder why he had never thought like this about the other white women he knew.

The night before he left, the dinner was special: candlelight, wine, a particular Dutch roast. "How's that?" she said, sitting down at last.

"Like you," he said, "superb. That means extraordinary."

*Were* her eyes swimming or was it reflected candlelight? She threw him a kiss between the candles and said, *"Ik hou van je."*

"What does that mean?" She had said it quickly as if embarrassed.

"Aha! I thought you were studying Dutch. And you don't know what that means. Pity."

"Tell me in English."

"No."

"French."

"No."

"Spanish."

"No."

"Is it something I should know?"

"I think you know it."

"If it's important, don't you think I should hear it from you, to avoid confusion?"

"Con-con- ah! *Confusion!* Well. It's not important. Why should it be? Tomorrow you will leave. We have had a good seven days, no? Perhaps when you think of me, you'll write me a letter?"

"Of course." After a pause, he said, "The dinner is good." He wanted to say many things to her, but thought it better not to.

Later, in bed, the snow on the roofs outside throwing a ghostly light into the room where they lay, he said, "Now, tell me what it was you said at dinner."

"No."

"Are you always so stubborn?"

"That is a Dutch trait, Mox. We are careful, punctual and stubborn."

Midway over the Atlantic, at twenty-five thousand feet, he

284

pulled out his handkerchief to blow his nose. Margrit had washed and ironed it for him. A square piece of paper fell out and Max picked it up. It had writing on it: *"Ik hou van je."*

"What does this mean?" he asked one of the KLM hostesses. She leaned over and took the paper and giggled. "It means, I love you," she said.

# 23

BERNARD ZUTKIN sat in his office. It was the same one, on the East Side, that he had been sitting in the day Max Reddick's girl was buried, years ago. The same kind of weather, too, Zutkin reflected. Time goes so swiftly, yet it always seems to stand still. One death, some suffering for Max, and fifteen years. In the scheme of time and the millions of people to choose from, that wasn't a bad price to pay for what Max was going to have handed to him. For some people the chance never came, not even to their succeeding generations. Max was ready now, like good, tough wood that had been seasoned in all kinds of weather. Time *was* a mystery; it prepared in so many dark, separate corners a variety of situations, but it always produced the right kind of people to meet them at precisely the right time.

Zutkin was glad that this new situation with its new people had come before it was too late for him to become involved. Only last week Granville Bryant had died. You really started to think about your advanced age (Zutkin was now in his sixties) when the people you had known in Paris, London, Berlin, Rome, Madrid and Greenwich Village, when it was the Village, during the Twenties and Thirties, started dropping dead around you. Then it was time to start getting your business in order. Well, there wasn't much business to straighten out, only this last thing.

He had married a British girl during the Twenties and they had lived on the Left Bank. That had lasted only two years and then

285

she took her short skirts, bobbed hair and flat-chested look to Italy
— with a bad poet who never understood why Dante was celebrated and he wasn't. Now, she was in Mombasa, and he thought
of her as being old and stylish in big houses covered with the skins of
lions and leopards. Sometimes, when he thought of her, Hemingway's description of the wife in "The Short, Happy Life of Francis
Macomber" came to him. Nearly everyone had been in Paris in
those days, the big, lost generation names, and the hundreds of
little, nameless people, like Bryant and Bolton Warren — and himself. He remembered an argument he'd had with the great one
about bullfighting one spring when they'd gone with a group to
Pamplona. The great one insisted that bullfighting was the epitome
of bravery. Zutkin (he stroked his paunch now; he'd been slim
then, with a full head of hair, and had spent a few moments wondering whether or not he was Robert Cohn in the g.o.'s novel) had
agreed that it was brave, but brave faggotry, for there was only one
man in that bullring and it was not the matador. Howled down,
that argument had done a lot to make Zutkin a critic. As he saw it,
a critic's job was to keep honest whoever happened to be the Pied
Piper at the time, keep him from leading the unsuspecting over the
brink. The Pied Pipers were coming in triplicate now, and often
piped the same tune. And it was no longer a rare thing to see critics
and reviewers whip out their own pipes and play in time to the
music and even lead the marchers.

So he was almost done with it all. Once a month he turned out a
piece for the magazine, otherwise he played with his pencils, read,
had long lunches and carried the title *Editor,* but he no longer
made policy decisions; he didn't even care to. And he had stopped
teaching at Columbia. He had one spell of three years without a
promising student and he knew then it was time to quit.

He wiped his thick-lensed glasses with a handkerchief and
picked up the phone. "Get Max Reddick, will you?" he asked his
secretary in the outer office. He had tried to call Max last week, but
they'd told him at *Pace* that he was out of the country until this

week. That was all right, Zutkin had thought then; the hurry was relative now, after all these years.

"Max, Max, is that you? Well, how are you? Yes, fine. You've become a world traveler. What were you doing in Africa? You don't say?" Zutkin paused to ponder this development; what he had to offer was still better. "I'd like to see you about something, Max. It's very important. As soon as you can. Lunch tomorrow? All right? Algonquin? That's fine, Max, just fine. Yes, wasn't it too bad about Granville? What's that saying? 'When the wagon comes, every swinging goes'?" Zutkin hung up, smiling.

The next day Zutkin watched Max enter the dining room. There was a very good look about him. The lines in his face had settled; in fact, they were his face now, and the beguilingly soft eyes. What they must have done to the women, Zutkin thought. Max had spotted him and Zutkin waved from his corner. He moved around the tables gracefully. What was he, Zutkin wondered, forty now? Forty-two or forty-three? He moves like a youngster, or someone in love. That lightness came only with youth or love and Max certainly was no youth, not anymore. They shook hands heartily and slapped each other on the back, and Zutkin could tell that something good was happening to Max. What?

"Now tell me this business about Africa? I'm dying to hear it," Zutkin said, signaling for drinks. An African desk could be mighty attractive. Take a man like Max away, place him in a position to experience an entire new set of stimuli to which he'd have to give new responses, and you've got an exciting challenge. That could be worked out, though, for sure. Zutkin called for the second drinks as Max finished telling him about Lagos. Zutkin heaved himself up and settled down to talk. He grasped Max by the wrist. "What I have to say is important. I'm a little nervous."

"Man," Max said with a smile, "what have you got to be nervous about? You're white," and Max punched him playfully on the arm. Zutkin could not ever recall such levity about the man. It pleased him.

"Max, would you consider working with the President's speech-writers? The chance is yours. You're not a second or third choice. The President wants your help."

"Who did it?"

"For a starter you can thank Julian Berg. Max, *Max!* What about it?" Zutkin could see that Max was stunned. He ordered the third round of drinks and they selected lunch.

"What do I do about my job?"

"Take a leave. Africa isn't going to vanish."

"For how long?"

"A few months, at least. It's important that the President get your answer and your talent as soon as possible. Max, what do you say? You know what all this means."

"What kind of speeches?"

"Civil rights. You know his platform. This way you may be able to nail in solidly what's there and squeeze in some suggestions for others."

Max nodded, slowly. "Will Dempsey give me the leave, do you think? You know, any President's only guaranteed four years, and I want that desk badly."

"I have no doubt that he'll give you the leave and keep the desk for you. I don't think you should worry on that score. These things work very smoothly and to everyone's advantage once they've been agreed on."

"You bastards," Max said. "You wring a man out. A guy can starve for ten years and then, suddenly, you want to give him every-thing. What's the matter with you people? Some guys die while they wait, don't you know that, Bernard?"

"I know, I know," Zutkin said. "I didn't make the rules; I only try to change the bad ones. I'm sure the President wants to do this too. He needs your help. How much time will you need?"

"Three days, and I want to talk to Dempsey myself."

"I can guarantee the leave and your Africa desk. See Dempsey tomorrow morning by eleven. He'll have a call an hour later. Can you see him at eleven?"

"Yes, but goddamn it, Bernard, I'll still have two days more to think about it. Don't rush me."

"I'm not rushing. Today's the first day, tomorrow's the second and day after tomorrow's the last day."

"Also, Bernard, I don't like the way you white folks have started to count these days."

Zutkin reached across the table in a kind of desperation and grasped Max tighter by the wrist. "Max, maybe now, *now* we can start to change this —" Zutkin groped for a strong enough word. "— mothafucking country for the better. What are you laughing at?"

Max had leaned back in his chair. He roared. People at other tables looked at him. Zutkin stared at him. "Didn't I say it right?"

"Baby, right on the button," Max said. "Right there, Bernard." He had never heard Zutkin curse before. "I'll probably do it, Bernard. I probably will."

"Can I congratulate you now?"

"If I can thank you now."

"You came to this on your own, Max. I only wish there had been something like it, a long time ago. But then, you weren't ready for it."

"But I would give everything I have now, Bernard, just to have had a little then. Just *some*thing then."

"Times change," Zutkin said.

Zutkin taxied home after lunch, went to his study and called Julian Berg.

"Some tea, Mr. Zutkin?" Lottie the maid asked. She had been with him for twenty years. Almost like man and wife they had been near each other for so long that they knew each other's moods and needs. Over the years Lottie had given him a lot of perspective. You could study all the great social and religious philosophers you wanted to, but you had to watch someone very close to the bottom reach simple, pragmatic conclusions to the problem of life and living.

"No, Lottie, thanks. I'm going to fix myself a drink."

"How many you had already, Mr. Zutkin? It ain't three yet and you look like you had more than your share." Zutkin and Max had polished off the lunch with two stingers each.

"Today's a special day, Lottie."

"Ain't no need to get so special that you wind up in a special place, Mr. Zutkin. Know what I mean?"

"When the wagon comes, Lottie —"

"What on earth do you know about some old wagon coming?"

Zutkin placed a fat, liver-spotted, wrinkled hand on her shoulder.

"You ain't gettin' fresh at this late date, are you, Mr. Zutkin?"

Zutkin laughed into her dark, stern face; he had never met a more moral woman. What a mess this country would *really* be in, he thought, if black Puritans had settled New England instead of white ones. "No, not at this late date. I just wanted to tell you that I know about the wagon and how, when it comes, everybody goes."

Lottie walked away, her big shoulders evenly squared. "I'll get you some tea. One more drink and the wagon'll be right downstairs waiting for you, and I'm too old to start lookin' for another job."

Practical, too, Zutkin thought. She was right; she didn't need to start looking for another job. The President had promised to do something about the old people. Zutkin believed he would. You had to do something about capitalism's castoffs. By long and painful osmosis the lesson had been learned after the Civil War. You didn't just turn people out who had contributed to the system for so long without any share in that system. They came back to hurt and haunt you. If every ex-slave *had* been given that mule and forty acres of land, a share of their labor, so to speak, would the country be in such a state today? Would Washington be running around like a chicken without its head complaining about the absent voice of the Negro? Damned fools. But this day history was made: a black man to help the President speak. The liberals would studiously ignore it, believing that this was inevitable; it was what they had fought for. The bigots would close their ears even tighter. But the message would get through. Centuries of agony wrapped up in

290

one phrase, perhaps, but Max's words would at least now have voice. The thought of the lunch brought a smile to Zutkin's face. Max had seemed vastly different from the brooding, bitter man he had known for so many years. It was good that there was a Max Reddick.

Harry would not have been any good for this and if he had and been under consideration, and Zutkin had anything to say about it, he would have vetoed Harry instantly. Zutkin had never forgiven Harry for putting out the rumor that Zutkin "had a card." Zutkin had never been a Communist. He'd gone to meetings and associated with Communists; then, they were the only people who thought. The people he had known in Europe had been out of step with the crying needs of the world. Lost? They'd been dead. Harry had been young then, and as bitter as a black man with Mississippi dust on his coattails could be. He drank and talked a lot and generally had been unstable. His attitude seemed to have been, If I can't have my share of the world, no one else is going to have a share. The Party had not been enough for him, or put it the other way around: the good white people in the Party were not prepared for the onslaught of Harry Ames. Of course, Harry had changed. His work showed it. World problems he tied to color, and it worked, if you substituted color for class. Aside from personal considerations, Harry had removed himself from the picture in two ways. The first was physical. His grasp of American problems was based still in the 1940's. It was 1960 now. In twenty years problems had changed several times; views had been altered or beaten out of shape into new ones; indignation and anger had come to maturity. Harry had missed all the subtle changes which usually tended to be, in later analysis, the important ones. The second way Harry had removed himself was by marrying a white woman. The country hadn't changed *that* much. The black man who had a white wife was not the person to put words dealing with color into the President's mouth. No, the President and his people ran from interracial marriages — any savvy politician did, publicly. Ran like rabbits. The reaction of the people was a known quantity. The people: that dictatorial majority which believed itself by virtue of its mass base to be infallible. The man who was confident of the people (the *American* people, they said, the politicians) was a fool. You didn't trust the people, you couldn't. For Harry, as much as they'd hurt him, he could still twist Marx out of shape and get people. Not Max. The people, yes, but in the abstract. He has a memory like a Jew, Zutkin thought, approvingly; he remembered the times and the places, the where and when of being wounded, just as Jews remember back to Babylonia and Egypt and beyond, up to the present. You survived if you remembered.

"Your tea, Mr. Zutkin," Lottie said, carefully placing it on the side of his desk.

"Thanks, Lottie. You're right. This is probably just what I need. Tell me, what do you think of the President?"

"I'd say he's a mighty handsome young man, myself."

"Thanks again," Zutkin said. As she left the room he thought, They do it all the time, these women, think with their crotches. Built-in voting machines.

Alone now, walking slowly back to work, away from Zutkin's massive, powerful although insidious optimism, Max's mind grew quickly dark with suspicion. Why me? he thought. Why not Dawes? He knew why not Dawes. Dawes would embarrass everybody with his capes and camp-outs. There was Dallas. And he knew why not Dallas; he had a white wife. Max thought of the twenty-odd other Negroes he knew personally who might have been called for the job, but he also knew why they weren't.

What does Zutkin get out of it? Berg? There's *got* to be something in it for them. What? Here I am sitting on the best gig I ever had in my life and here *they* come with something a man just can't refuse. Playing a little bit of God, pulling strings on the President's mouth — although I hear that bastard likes to edit a lot. Don't blame him. I would, too. But what do they want, Berg and Zutkin and whoever else is in on this? *Nobody does anything for nothing.* They want something you've got. Or it's something you can do for them. Admire them, love them, adore them. It all goes back to the guy who is being generous: he wants to think he's a great guy and you do. If you're getting, you better act like that. No, no, no. They want me to believe this country is going to turn around and reverse itself. But that's what they want me to believe, me, who knows better. A greater America. Now, we can do it. The good guys are in and the bad guys are out. Really? Didn't I just look at a file about a bunch of crackers cutting off a Negro's dick in broad daylight on a Birmingham street *and* throwing turpentine where the cat's dick had been? Don't I see a whole bunch of crap going down right here in precious little old New York every minute of the day? Goddamn them. They honestly do believe I'm a patriot, with my ass aching all the time now. I need to be somebody's damned patriot. The President and two million people like him can't change the way this sonofabitch is going — downhill without brakes. So, what's it going to be, Max, baby, Africa for good, huh? Europe, where they're starting to catch the disease? South America? C'mon off it, man. You don't know nothin' but hocks and beans and sirloin and greens; you don't know nothin' but hard pavement under your feet, traffic noises and the neighbors' hi-fis; you don't know nothin' but Catskill and Adirondack forests and Long Island undergrowth and how red the earth of the South looks; you don't know nothin' but all them black bones and all that black blood beat into the ground and all them niggers twistin' in their graves waitin' for one of themselves to walk into the White House and grab that Number One Mister Charlie by his ear to say, *Baby, we are tired of you cats fucking over us.*

Or words to that effect.

Max stopped at a bar and ordered another stinger. He drank half of it, then called Zutkin at home. "Bernard," he said. "What's in this for you?"

At home, Zutkin smiled. A little slow, but in another few hundred years Max would make a good Jew. "Ah, Max. What's in it for me? You mean what's really in it for me?"

"Yes, man, that's why I'm calling."


293

"Patriotism. You wouldn't buy that, would you?"

"Bernard, it's like this —"

"I didn't think so, Max. Money —"

"Bernard, I know there's no money involved. Look, almost twenty years of knowing each other through good and evil times. I have a right to know *why me?*"

"Jesus, Max. You really examine a gift horse, don't you?"

"Damn it, I gotta know if it is a gift horse or not. Besides," Max said, doggedly, "I want to know."

"It's very simple —"

"I'm listening."

"Are you listening carefully? Want to come over for some of Lottie's tea?"

"No. I've got to get back. Are you going to tell me?"

"As I said, it's simple. We need each other. Got the picture? *We need each other.*"

"I thought it was something like that. I'm glad I called." Yes, there was always something.

"I wondered when you would."

"Bastard. You white folks are something else, Bernard."

"Sure. Listen. The tea is really good. Lottie would put some whiskey in it. She likes you. Can't imagine why."

"I've got to go."

"It's simple, Max, but important."

"Yes, I know."

And I also know that I am not free and never have been. No, people don't do things for nothing; there's always something they want. Always.

He would have been freer on the Lagos desk, he told himself, as he hung up, walked past his half-finished drink and went back into the street. He would have been away from New York, free to act on his own more rather than less. Perhaps there are degrees of freedom. He would have been guided only by occasional cables and his own conscience. That was half the battle, getting away from the hectic GET A NEGRO demands being brought on by the times, which in some quarters, particularly the press, always ready with a name for anything, was being called the Negro Revolution.

*Hullo, Max.*

*Back are you?*

*Never been away. How can the Saminone ever be away?*

*Get the hell away from me.*

*Now, boy, simmer yourself down. Just wanted to 'mind you that it was you whut wanted back in.*

*Shut up.*

*Beggin' around them offices, you hat in you hand, feared they wus gonna turn you 'way, and they surely did.*

*Shut up, I said.*

*It was you whut grabbed that slave at the Century and then the one at Pace, gettin' all that white man's sal're. Tee hee.*

*Why not? I deserved it. I worked hard. I earned every penny of that money.*

*Oops! Don't get salty now. It was you took all 'em trophies and plaques wit dat shit writ all over 'em, and you knew in you heart that they give 'em to you 'cause you was back in; a black-ass nigger, but back in all th' same.*

*How does a man trap himself so completely?*

*Is you askin'?*

*Yes, I'm asking.*

*Pride, pride, turrible pride.*

*You've got to do better than that.*

*Oh, no I don't. You so goddamn busy tryin' t' prove you am.*

*You were talking about pride.*

*The same thing, burr-head, the same goddamn thing. Hee, haw . . . safe an' secure from all alarm, leaning, leaning . . .*

*Motherbugger, you.*

*Aw hell. Here we goes agin.*

# 24

IN SWIFT succession Max saw Dempsey, Dempsey received a phone call from the White House, and Max found himself on a plane for Washington to see the President. He had almost walked into a trap, he told himself. He saw the Africa desk slipping out of his grasp, and his future in Washington unsure. Maybe he was all for the cause now, and in full accord with Zutkin's idea that they needed each other. But who knew about next week? He recalled the Negro who had served in the White House during the last Administration and how even the secretaries had refused to work for him. That man had been used very little; he hadn't even been a good figurehead, for the Administration seldom trotted him out. This, however, was supposed to be a new era. He'd see. He'd asked for a leave of only five months to feel the new job out, and Dempsey agreed.

Max had last gone to Washington by train many years ago; he hadn't liked Washington then. It had been Jim Crow for much too long, and if J.C. was virulent in the nation's capital, did it not have the excuse to run rampant throughout the country? On that last trip Max had been on his way to the South; he took the Jim Crow train at Washington. You did that as a matter of course then, because the railroad companies went right along with the Southerners' programs. From Washington the trains plunged southward over the blood-red fields, the crowded Negro cars filled with people carrying bag and box lunches. No one wanted to suffer that final indignity of sitting behind the segregated green curtain in the dining room out of sight of the white diners. In those days you paid your money, but you had no choice. Max had known an endless number of Negroes who had come to the capital from the Deep South and, finding it too much the way it had been back home, struggled the few hundred miles farther north, if they could. Washington not only had a southern exposure, it had been controlled by Southern legislators whose politics both decimated and dominated the land. In those days it had been commonplace for them to stand in the Senate or House and say "nigger" while everyone pretended not to hear. *That* Washington pressed against the memory now as a point of specific reference. Now the trains ran southward without Negro sections, without the green curtain in the dining room; now, if a Southerner even said "nigra" in either House, he was subject to loud and immediate correction from the gallery, or from the legislators themselves — and quite possibly, Max hoped, a chiding word or two from the President.

This Washington was new indeed. Perhaps it was because of the President, who rose tall and smiling as Max entered his office that afternoon. Max had seen him in person only once before. That was during the campaign when he held a rally on upper Broadway in New York. He seemed golden then with the summer's sun, and he smiled down at the housewives and joked with them; he reached over white people to shake hands with black people, all the while nodding his large, almost brutally square head.

Now, Max took the President's hand and could not help smiling. "Let's sit over here," the President said, gesturing to a couch with one hand and stroking his rib cage just inside his jacket with the other, as Max had seen him do many, many times on television. "How was your flight down, okay?"

"Yes, sir," Max said. "It was all right."

"You look bigger on the dust jackets of your books, Mr. Reddick. Is that calculated?"

"No," Max said with a smile and wondering which of his books the President had read.

"You come highly, very highly, recommended, Mr. Reddick. I have the greatest admiration for Julian Berg and Bernard Zutkin. And Oscar Dempsey tells me that *Pace* owes much of its preeminence in reporting civil rights to you."

"Dempsey had to be willing to gain that position, Mr. President."

"Yes, well, the coverage is good, quite good. I've had some journalistic experience myself, you know. Dempsey says you're free to join us, but that you have some reluctance. Now, I'm sorry to hear that, Mr. Reddick."

"Indecision is a better word, Mr. President. I want to do what I can to help — especially in this area. At the same time, I have to be concerned with my own future, my own work."

"What do you propose?"

"Dempsey has given me five months leave. That ought to tell both of us about the future — whether you'll want me to stay —"

"I understand."

Max went on: "While I am honored that my friends thought enough of me to recommend me, and that you want me to be here, and while I believe in your program, staking what future I may have on someone else's four years is not the kind of gambling that I, as a Negro, can afford. That's the heritage of the lack of equal opportunity you've pledged to improve."

The President smiled and Max followed his eyes to the wide expanse of the White House lawn. "Say, did you vote Democrat?" the President asked as he toyed with a cigar case. "It's true that we are given four years at a time, Mr. Reddick, but we owe it to our people, who are gamblers in a sense, to give them the best we can during the time and for the future. I know you're not unaware of that."

"No, sir, I'm not."

"I appreciate your loyalty to Dempsey, and I can understand your eagerness to be in Africa; it is a very exciting place — but we think Washington is, too. We can promise you vigorous activity for however long you choose to stay, and if you're the kind of man I think you are, that other people say you are, then I'm not worried — you'll be around long after your five-month tryout period." The President stood; the interview was over. At the door the President said, "Mrs. Agnew, my secretary, will get you set up across the street, and the other fellows, Gus Carrigan and Jim Bonnard, will take you in hand. We'll get together in a week or so."

The day Max took a small flat on Fairmont Street, not far from Howard University, the Civil War Centennial Commission announced that it would maintain segregated facilities for the observances of the celebrations. Max hustled to his office in the Executive Office Building. Surely, now that he was here, and the announcement was still echoing around the land, the President would take some action. Hell, he had to. Who was the Civil War all about, anyway? You couldn't properly have that kind of celebration without Negroes. And surely, you couldn't honor the one-hundredth anniversary of an event and not want to discover that some improvements had been made. Hadn't those four years and all those dead counted for something? Max laughed. The Union had almost had Russia as an ally then, just as the South and England were exchanging signals. All over colored people, but the white people had forgotten that; they were always forgetting. Max began his paper with Lincoln's statement that, had it not been for black troops, the Union could not have won the war.

Jim Bonnard was tall and thin; his elbows and knees seemed to pierce the very cloth that covered them. He had a cold, sharp sense of humor, and drank hard. He was an excellent writer, Max knew from his novels. Bonnard's face showed his drinking; his complexion was like yellow paste. Gus Carrigan was also tall and thin. He was dry and humorless and always enveloped in invisible scholar's robes. Bonnard, despite a thorough education, had remained a man of the street. Carrigan might have been cut from white marble — or ice. His eyes were made tiny by the horn-rimmed glasses that encapsuled them. He had a full head of dark blond hair; very little remained of Bonnard's brown hair. Carrigan's view was the long one, the highway of history, but Bonnard moved with the crises of the moment.

Now, they were both reading Max's paper on the Centennial. Bonnard, puffing hard at his cigarette, looked up. "Did Lincoln really say that?"

"You could look it up," Max said.

"Why haven't we used it before?" Bonnard asked, looking from Max to Carrigan. "It puts the whole thing into some kind of focus, doesn't it, Gus?"

"I'll give it to the President," Carrigan said. He turned to Max. "Well, how's it going?"

"It's all right," Max said, "but it would be better if I knew precisely what I'm to do and when."

Bonnard laughed.

Carrigan smiled. "When it comes, it'll come with a rush. In the meantime, I'd like to get your views on what's going on in the Negro community."

"My views?" Max asked somewhat incredulously.

"Yes," Carrigan said. His eyes never reveal anything, Max thought.

"All right," Max said, suddenly conscious of being on guard.

"Well, let's have some tea in," Carrigan said. "How's your time, Jim?"

"Time I got plenty of today. Tea and talk it is. Save the Union."

It was clear to Max that Carrigan was the boss of the writing team. Both men had been with the President since the start of his campaign. Okay, Max thought. His eyes roamed to the windows. He could see Pennsylvania Avenue and the tourists along the fence, Lafayette Square and behind it, St. John's church. My God, he wondered, do I really have to tell them the way it is on the other side of the tracks? Can they be *here,* in this day and age and *not* know something about the way it is? Yes, he could talk generally, pull together what the black man in the street was saying; that he could do.

The Negro communty, he told them, expected the President to live up to his campaign promises to them. The community was tired, sick and tired, the phrase went, of candidates coming into the community, shaking hands and making promises they never delivered. Pressure was mounting already. Negroes believed he would do what he said, but too many whites were fearful that he would keep those promises. The President was going to have to do, or pressure would make him Jo. Negroes were tired of asking. The signs were obvious; a Minister Q does not appear unless there is a need, nor does a Paul Durrell, not to mention the others.

"Is Minister Q for real?" Bonnard asked.

"Just as real as Jim Eastland," Max countered. "He has the confidence of many a Negro — and there are more Negroes who agree privately with him than you can guess."

"And Durrell?" Carrigan asked.

"The middle class," Max said. "It's vocal and seems to represent everybody, but it doesn't. They're the people who with the breaks would become *upper* middle class, but the masses probably would remain just as they are today."

Three pots of tea and two packs of cigarettes later and Carrigan said, "Max, you've got to be kidding."

"Yes, that's pretty grim, what you've served up," Bonnard added.

"In the words of a sergeant I once had," Max said, "I shit thee not."

"Our sources don't paint the picture that dark," Carrigan said with a sigh.

Max said evenly, "You asked me here — as I understand it — to be a consultant and to help with speeches in this area. I've given you counsel, and will continue to give you counsel. I'd get moving on this thing while it's still relatively calm; once it starts up, it'll have too much momentum to stop without deepening the bitterness that already exists. I mean the President's got to start pushing packages through Congress *now*." When Max left them, he had the feeling that he'd spent the time talking to walls.

On the day he had his next appointment with the President, Yuri Gagarin, in a five-ton capsule, became the first human being to make a space flight. The White House and the Executive Office Building hummed with the news. The Russians send up a bushel basket and we send up a grapefruit; they send up a man and we put up a chimp. The President must be on the phone right now chewing out those people on the space program. Bonnard, drifting lankly through the halls of the old building stopped by Max's office. "You heard about the Russkies?"

"Yeah," Max answered. "Civil rights goes out the window this week, huh?"

"Oh, I don't know. You see the President this afternoon, don't you?"

"So far it's still on."

"Let's go to the press conference. What else've you got to do? We can get a bite after. The walk'll do you good; clear your head."

They walked briskly over New York Avenue to the State Department Building; once inside they made their way into an empty booth overlooking the auditorium. Max noticed at once that there were no Negro newsmen present. Everyone rose when the President came striding to the platform, followed by the Press Secretary, and took his place behind the podium with the seal of his office on the front. The President made three announcements, then the reporters began firing their questions. Was there the possibility of a Cuban invasion? The President answered with three negative statements and Bonnard nudged Max with his elbow. Max glanced at him, but Bonnard continued to look down into the auditorium. The President either answered or parried the questions. Someone asked about the White House News Photographers Association prohibiting the membership of Negroes. Max turned questioning eyes toward Bonnard; Bonnard nodded.

"But there'll be a lot of colored help on the plantation before the President's through," he said. At the conclusion of the conference, they cabbed to a restaurant on Connecticut Avenue. Bonnard said, "Max, you'd better not have a drink. The President doesn't mind it, but he doesn't approve of it, if you have an appointment with him."

"Thanks."

"Forget it. I'll drink one for you."

"What about the Centennial?"

"Forget that, too. He knows about it, but he feels this is a minor storm and he's going to ride it out, sails down. Besides, I expect he's going to have his hands full during the next few days."

302

"Cuba?"

"Mister," Bonnard said, with a flash of his hard brown eyes, "you haven't heard me say one word about Cuba."

The President seemed preoccupied when Max entered his office. The room was bright and quiet, but it felt charged with tension.

"Come on in, Max," the President said. "What a day. What do you suggest we do to overtake the Russians?"

"Drink more vodka, Mr. President?"

"Maybe we've had too much already," he snapped. He gestured for Max to sit down, then he began a new conversation. "You know, every hour we have to judge things on their merits, and handle those with the most importance to our people. Some things must be first and others have to follow. We'd like to be able to handle all the important things at once, and handle them well. But we can't. In my judgment, civil rights — at the moment — does not come first. In fact, there is a bill going to Congress next month without my endorsement, because I believe the Executive office has recourse to laws already in existence to alleviate the inequities in our society. That picture could change tomorrow, or tonight. I think you disagree with me, but that's what I want you to do. We don't need any yes-men around here; we haven't asked any to join us. I want you to behave as though civil rights is our most urgent problem. In that light, write what you think about it; I want memos from you every week; I want the closest possible cooperation between you, Jim and Gus. You are me in this instance, with all the checks and balances that are bound to the office of President, with the impetus or drag of public opinion included. See the leaders of the movements; talk to them. I want to know every change in their thinking. If something comes up that's urgent, call Mrs. Agnew and she'll get you back in here so we can talk about it. That's all, Max."

One week after the President had categorically denied the possibility of an invasion of Cuba in which American armed forces would participate, the Premier of Cuba announced that the rebel forces which had invaded his island with American help had been crushed.

303

Max retreated to his small office, determined to work until he was needed. The city became like a Hollywood setting. The President was the superstar and everyone shared or added to the rumors about him. They joked about him, but to a man or woman they defended him. If the rumors were true, well, then, they'd rather have a swinging President than a swung one. The senators, representatives, committee chairmen and agency officials were cameo stars in the daily productions; the women who emerged with the approach of dusk from the government buildings, eager for the nights in which they sought husbands, lovers or just plain company, were extras who often stole scenes from the stars.

Washington could have killed any superman, if he had been Negro. As Bonnard had suggested, with each passing week new Negro faces appeared in Washington, and because racial barriers were coming down with a crash, the Negroes were expected to attend functions regularly. Then there were the Negro functions as well, and if you liked white company enough to miss a number of the latter, you were placed in limbo. Max saw many a man crumble before the onslaught of martinis, pussy-by-the-yard and black-tie affairs. Theodore Dallas confessed to Max soon after he *was* moved to the U. S. Mission to the UN, that he could not have pulled another three months in Washington and lived.

Dallas's transfer coincided with the independence bashes in Africa: Nigeria, both Congos, the Cameroon Republic and Togoland. The successive waves of spanking new, young African diplomats coming to Washington, and then moving along up to New York in the grand, prestigious Eastern seaboard tour, made Max achingly aware of the desk awaiting him in Lagos.

But he concentrated on the Negroes he could see surging out the Post Office and Treasury buildings at the end of the day, and he thought of the Negroes who had not been able to move north past Washington. They had forced the white trek to Williamsburg and Middleburg, to Maryland and other places in Virginia. The times past had forced too many bright, well-educated Negroes into the tasks of burning old dollar bills, sorting mail or sweeping floors; bright Negroes who could have produced from among them a cure for cancer, or even Goddard's rocket — a thousand things the human race needed so desperately.

At first Max liked working nights when the White House and lawn were lit and the Avenue almost clear of sight-seers and pickets. Then Durrell discovered him; other leaders discovered him, and his nights were filled with dinners and talk. Max would look at them. They thought he had power, that his word could make the President turn his ear in their direction. They believed what the papers were saying — that it was a time of high drama. Youth and risk had triumphed over old age and dull security; that it was the start of a golden age. Of all the people he saw, Durrell disturbed him most; he had gone hippie, and Max thought that was to let him (Max) know that Durrell now considered him one of his better friends. He could not tell Durrell or the others then that he was not, could not do them any good, because the President's choice of action was clear and decisive; he could not tell them that any more than he could tell the President or Bonnard or Carrigan that he despised Durrell.

"When is the President going to do something, Max?" They all asked him the same question, and Max was torn between his loyalty to them and loyalty to the President.

The question was asked more often and in desperation the next month, when the Freedom Rides South began, five days after the Press Secretary announced that the President had refused to endorse the series of civil rights bills with provisions to speed desegregation and make the Civil Rights Commission a permanent body, because the President did not think it necessary to enact civil rights legislation at the moment. Max sat in his office waiting when the news came that two of the Freedom Riders' buses had been burned near Anniston, Alabama. Six days later, when rioting broke out in Montgomery after the Freedom Riders were attacked again, Federal marshals were sent to restore order. Carrigan summoned Max to his office in the East Wing.

"What's going on, Max?"

"You mean in Alabama?"

"Yes, yes, of course."

"I suppose it's a reaction to the President's not endorsing the civil rights package that went up."

"You can't be serious."

"Why not?"

"But there's already a series of laws providing for interstate travel without restrictions —"

"Obviously," Max said, "no one's bothered to enforce those laws. I mean, Gus, can't you see what's happening? If the President is relying on laws already on the books, these tactics — and they are tactics — are designed to prove to him that they are no good unless enforced by the Federal Government, or unless new legislation is introduced and passed. That's what's going on."

"The Governor has asked for more help," Carrigan said, glumly. "Two hundred more marshals are going in tomorrow. And the President says he wants this settled before he goes to Paris."

"Am I supposed to tell the leaders this?"

"Max, I wish you wouldn't be quite so — so *truculent*. Where do your loyalties lie, with just Negroes or for the country?"

Max spoke in cold anger: "I have been trying to tell you what's good for the country. What histories do you read, Gus? Tell me about the history of the American armed forces, and I can show you how important Negroes were to those forces; tell me about the history of American economics and I can show you where Negroes made up the bulk of those economies by being poor or left out of them altogether; tell me about the history of religion in America, and I can show you where, as long as there have been Negroes in this hemisphere, religion has been an absolute lie; tell me about the history of American politics, and I can show you where American politics would be vastly different today if Negroes had had a real voice in them. Damn it, Gus, it's *you* who have vested loyalties. If I went out there and told those leaders — and I'm not, because I'm not going to be an errand boy for you or the President — to stop

306

because the President *says* so, forget about Alabama, Georgia, New York — you name it, and forget about it —"

"Calm down, Max," Carrigan said. "I'm sorry. I shouldn't have put it like that. I shouldn't even have said it."

"Man," Max said, "why don't you people use me? All my life I've fought like hell to keep people from using me. I came down here for you to use me, and you won't."

"Have patience, Max, patience. We know you set aside a lot to come down here. You've got to trust us; the whole machinery has got to move, not just one part of it."

"Yes," Max said. He stood. "Gus, I'm sorry. I guess we'll mesh. I want you to give a little and you want me to give a little. But I — and my people — have always been the ones to give. I'm trying to tell you, and I am serious, that they are tired of giving. That's all. Whatever I do here, that's the nut of my counsel."

Sullen and bewildered, Max sat moodily in his office or in his flat, seeing people when he could no longer avoid them. The summer's humidity crept toward the city and Congress was trying desperately to adjourn to escape it. The President had returned from Europe in a blaze of triumph. But Max sat awaiting the summons that never came. He was not disillusioned so much as convinced that only a racial explosion of unimagined proportion could move to action an Administration which had proclaimed in ringing, iron tones that it was dedicated to the rapid attainment of civil rights. Max knew better now; the Administration, like the ones before it, did not know and could not understand what it was black Americans wanted. Washington's determined look, suggesting an honorable concern, was, at the very least, misleading. Max distrusted the bright, glowing faces around him; the hand, after all, was quicker than the eye. The eye, that intricate conglomeration of nerve and muscle, was invariably drawn to the radiant faces which beamed back so much good will. But what did the hands do, Max wondered. Who watched the hands that were busily engaged in the shell game, watched them closely enough to see what happened to the pea?

In June, the pea turned out to be a young Negro student named William MacKendrick, who had been accepted by the board of trustees at the University of Mississippi for enrollment. No publicity surrounded the event until the governor of the state announced during a press conference that no Negro would enter Ole Miss as long as he was in office. MacKendrick insisted that he was going to enter. Some segments of the press called for intervention by the Administration, saying that now it could begin to live up to its campaign promises. But the President said nothing except that the matter appeared to be local.

Whenever Max's phone rang at home or at the office, he anticipated the question from the various leaders: "What is the President going to do, Max?" And Max became weary of saying he didn't know, however, the President was watching developments carefully, coming as they did on the heels of the Freedom Rider disturbances in Alabama. His memos were now being routed through Carrigan's office, then on to the President, but the only response he received for his notes on the MacKendrick affair was a "Thanks. Keep them coming," from the President.

Suddenly and without explanation, MacKendrick withdrew his application. The press said it was because he feared for his safety, but in the Negro community there were rumors that he had been forced to withdraw by the Administration. Max sent these rumors to Carrigan and when there was no response, he went to his office.

"I don't know how those rumors got started, Max. There's simply nothing to them."

"I'd better talk to MacKendrick, then," Max said. "He hasn't said anything directly about it."

Carrigan nodded. "That's a good idea."

Max tracked MacKendrick to New York, where he had gone to give a series of lectures under the auspices of the New Pan-African Movement. They arranged to meet at Max's apartment. MacKendrick was a small man, and like so many Negroes, had a mixture of white and Indian blood flowing beneath his heavily bronzed skin. His voice was soft and his accent filled with gentle valleys and hills.

There is no accent quite like that of a Mississippi Negro; its cadence is French, its emphasis Spanish, its heritage seventeenth-century English with the unsteady lilt of Irish and Scots thrown in.

"Mr. MacKendrick," Max said, "I'd like to find out what happened in Mississippi. I noticed tonight at your rally you directly accused the President of interfering with your attempts to get into the University."

MacKendrick was a bit old for a freshman, about twenty-one. Working and studying tc overcome the inadequate teaching in the Negro high school he had gone to, and trying to get together a little cash to hold himself together the first semester. Now that was all shot. The young man was waving aside the drink Max offered him. "Mr. Reddick, they tell me you work for the President. You're one of those big colored gentlemen that don't have anything to worry about." MacKendrick's smooth face broke into a smile.

"That's right," Max said. "I work for the President, but what you tell me may determine just how much longer."

MacKendrick grinned once more. "Whose future are we going to talk about, yours or mine?"

"Both our futures, Mr. MacKendrick."

"Well, Mr. Reddick, I hate to disillusion you about our head of state, but I was asked by a man from the U. S. Attorney General's office not to enter the University because the Administration was afraid my move did not fit its timetable for attacks against the desegregation holdouts. I was also told that it would be embarrassing for such a conflict to come up so early in the President's time in the White House. This man made me a promise — if I held off until next year, they'd see me into the University, whatever it required. Now, Mr. Reddick, I'm a little man, just an ordinary citizen, and maybe not even that because I'm black. But I spent a lot of time studying after my graduation to be able to enter that University without scholastic difficulty. And I had to earn some money so I wouldn't *look* as poor as I am. But I'm intelligent enough to know that we do have some laws on the books that say I *can* go to any

309

school I wish. I told that man if the Government wasn't ready, I was, and he went away. It's taken me two years to get six names of Ole Miss alumni; that's what the University requires. Oh, I found them, reconstructed, living outside the South. But the Attorney General also found them, with a helluva lot less trouble than I had. They were asked to withdraw their names as references and five agreed. I withdrew because I couldn't get five new names in time for the start of the summer semester."

"You can prove this, of course?" Max asked. He watched the youth as he opened his attaché case and brought out copies of letters each of the five references had sent him.

"These are copies," Max said. "Can I have them?"

"They're yours, sir."

"And now what do you do, Mr. MacKendrick?"

"I'm going to try for the fall semester without the references. I wanted to do it their way, but that didn't work out. Now, I have to do it my way."

"You'll be in a lot of danger, you know."

"If you're black, you're always in danger. More danger when you've placed some faith in an Administration that double-crosses you."

The Golden Age, Max thought later, had not yet arrived. The Administration could easily deny MacKendrick's charges. And a terse denial meant to the careful, clever newsman at the Presidential press conferences that he wasn't supposed to ask questions. If he did, his hand probably would never again be recognized by the President and the nameplate on the back of his chair as good as removed. Max believed that the Administration people did not think themselves ready for the desegregation battle, but *when,* millions of people were going to ask, when would they be ready?

"What did he have to say?" Carrigan asked, when Max returned to Washington.

"His grades, they tell us," Bonnard put in, "were completely shot."

"His grades were all right," Max said. "My information is that

310

the Attorney General did indeed ask his references to withdraw and five of them did."

Carrigan toyed with a pencil. "Max," he said, with a sigh, "it's true that we did learn about MacKendrick. His grades, for Mississippi, were all right, but we didn't want to run the risk of a confrontation with the governor and then have the kid flunk out of school —"

"Why is it that no one seems to mind that millions of Negroes are failures because of the way they have to live in our society, and everyone minds that, once a Negro decides to buck the society, he forfeits the right to fail?"

"Because it's more than one person, one Negro. If we are to help the mass, the people we help have got to be, and consistently so, winners."

Max said, "Then you knew all along. I don't have to let you see the copies of the letters MacKendrick gave me."

Neither Carrigan nor Bonnard spoke.

The facts spoke for themselves, now. The Administration deliberately and successfully subverted the lawful attempt of a citizen to enroll in an educational institution of his choice. A constitutional violation by the people entrusted to uphold that Constitution.

"Gentlemen, you place me in a most awkward position," Max said. "You have no confidence in me and I have none in you. You can't imagine how sorry I am."

"C'mon, Max," Bonnard said. "We can straighten this all out."

"Yes, we made a mistake, a real boo," Carrigan said. "We're bound to make mistakes in this business. Human error."

"But that was some mistake," Max said. "MacKendrick plans to enter for the fall semester, anyway, without the references. If people lose playing according to the rules, you've got to expect them to ignore the rules after a while. Do you know what's going to happen to him? He'll go it alone. If they let him in, one of those Mississippi mobs will kill him. On the other hand, maybe as soon as he registers the sheriff will arrest him, throw him in jail or into a crazy house. Could be that they'll hang him and say he committed suicide. You know the stories, or don't you? Black Americans know the stories, all of them."

Carrigan said, "It's been a bad time: Cuba, the Russians in space, and now this. We've made mistakes; we've underestimated people, but our efforts have been honest and history can't condemn us. I know the President is sincere in wanting to keep his promises to American Negroes. But he's got almost a complete term left and when he makes his move, he wants to lock it up, not lose. You know that sometimes the individual has got to be sacrificed for the group."

"Look," Max said. "I've heard these arguments all my life. In fact, I don't think there is a black man in America who hasn't heard them." He spoke sharply now. "I vote no confidence in this Administration, as of now."

Carrigan rose. "Wait a minute, Max. You —"

Max said, "I have another month to serve. If you want, I'll serve it; I don't want to embarrass anyone, you'll get enough of that. If not, I can leave today."

Bonnard said, "You're a rotten sport, mister."

Max spun on him. "Sport? This is not a game, Jim, or don't you understand that yet?"

Bonnard flung out his hands. "It's all a game, that's what it is."

Carrigan glared at him.

At the door Max said, "Then you'd better come on over where the big kids are; they play big kids' games, and I don't mean stink-finger."

Max walked out of the White House through the East Gate and then back around the front, on Pennsylvania Avenue. Once he paused and pressed himself close to the fence with the rest of the sight-seers, and made himself think: The White House. That is where we are getting the best; there's where the Golden Age begins. Where did it go wrong? We are all like blind men feeling different parts of the elephant and taking that part for the whole. No, not we; they. I know that elephant; it's tusks, trunk, ears, legs. Elephants? It's the asses that are in, the donkeys. And I believed. I wanted to believe. I had to believe, and now . . . ? He moved slowly along the fence, head turned to his left, to view the majestic building, then he crossed 17th Street and went to his office.

Two days later he took a late plane from Washington, threw his bags and briefcases in a corner, stripped and piled into bed. It was all over; Washington, the Golden Age, was behind him now, but all the whiskey in the world could not remove the taste of it; the gold had turned very suddenly to brass.

When the phone rang, Max opened his eyes to the false dawn of New York. The low, steady hum of his air-conditioner provided an undercurrent of sound against the insistently ringing telephone. Who could be calling? A woman? He wasn't up to that. Not at the moment. He picked up the phone and said gruffly, "Hello!"

"Hello, Max. What's going on?"

Him. He hadn't got the word, then. "Trying to sleep. What are you up to?"

"Just got in town. In Washington they said you'd come up here for a few days. I'm here trying to get my brothers to give me some money, but I wanted us to get together for a quiet little dinner tonight."

The Reverend Paul Durrell, still coming out of his raggedy bag, Max thought. He had always tried to keep their conversations on a more formal level. "Paul, I just got in from Washington, and I need some sleep, and I'm going to be tied up for a little while —"

"Max," Durrell said in a patient voice, "you know you can find the time."

"I can't do you any good, Paul," Max said, leaping ahead to the meat of the call. "Not anymore."

"Brother Max, I'm afraid I don't understand."

"Paul, for four months you and every other so-called Negro leader have been wanting something from me. But I've quit. I'm not in the White House anymore. I can't help you, and I hope I never have."

"Brother —"

"Save that brother shit for the others, Paul," Max said angrily. "Why do you work so hard to get me to *like* you? Why have *I* got to be in your pew? The white boys are in your corner. Baby, *what have you done?* I don't like you; I think you're dangerous. The whole movement is tied to you and it can go right down the drain if . . . I don't know, man. You behave like a man who might have a lot to sweat about. *I don't like you.*"

"Max, why are you so *bitter* toward me? It wrings my heart to hear these things from you. And why do you keep saying the white press is protecting me? Scurrilous, Max."

"Then sue me. Brother." Max hung up.

Durrell never really needed Max. He had grown so in prominence with his marches and demonstrations that he had been given a private line to the President's office. A gesture, and very typical of the Golden Age. Max got up, pulled on a robe and drew bath water. While it was running, he put up coffee. He had two letters from Margrit that he hadn't yet opened, and there were the papers to read in the tub while he relaxed and drew out the vague pain that now seemed always centered around his anus. Nerves again. Washington had done it. But perhaps, later in the day, he would feel up to breaking the news to Zutkin.

Zutkin answered the door instead of Lottie and stood a moment, closely studying Max's face. Max even felt his eyes on his back when he preceded Zutkin into the study.

"You look drawn, Max. The weather. Yes, the weather's been terrible here, too, of course. It seems to get worse every summer. Well, let me get you a drink and you can tell me about the President."

When Zutkin returned with the drinks, Max said simply, "I've quit, Bernard."

"Ooo," Zutkin said. "You'll tell me why, of course?"

"Of course," Max said with a smile. "You, I'll tell."

"I've heard nothing about it."

"Now you'll hear, Bernard, and I'm sure that what you hear

from other sources won't be quite like what I'm going to tell you. The MacKendrick boy in Mississippi —"

"Washington was hands off on that, right?"

"Wrong. Hands on, all the way. The Attorney General, with the President's knowledge and consent, forced five out of the six references needed for admittance to withdraw their names."

"But why?"

"The Administration wasn't ready for a confrontation."

Zutkin forced a twisted smile. "But you must be kidding. You've got to be."

"No, Bernard, I've quit. I'm not kidding. Why in the hell would I joke about a thing like that?"

"There's got to be a deeper reason."

"Why? This one's deep enough, but not so deep that it doesn't stink."

Zutkin looked down into his glass. "Can you imagine being upstaged by a twenty-one-year-old kid?" He did not expect Max to answer, and he continued, "What did the President have to say?"

Max shrugged. "I tried to see him for two days, then gave up. I don't think he wanted to see me after my conversation with Carrigan and Bonnard. Look, I'm sorry it didn't work out. I thought it would, I honestly believed it would go well. But, they never used me, Bernard. Four months there and I helped to write not one speech. The extent of the President's civil rights activity was to send a telegram to the Civil Rights Commission; he refused to endorse a package of bills and now this MacKendrick thing. I think he believes that by having Negroes on his staff, and filling Washington with them — in government posts, not as residents — he's improving the picture. He's right, the picture has lots of colored folks in it, but that isn't getting it at all."

"I suppose I knew the man had this in him all the time," Zutkin said. "He's a *politician,* and it's a politician's habit to manufacture his own best image. Yes, there were signs along the way. But I hoped. Berg hoped, and I know you hoped. Everybody did. He came into power and you have to work with people who are in power."

"I know all that, Bernard. We *survived* by knowing exactly where power seemed to be every second of the day. If you're black you know that every white man thinks he has power over you and, ergo, he has, until you kick his tail for him."

"Dangerous," Zutkin was saying, as though he hadn't heard. "Say a man does have good intentions, but bides his time; is evil ever inactive? No. Say then that the danger might be not in waiting to express your good intentions, but not having any anyway, beneath the surface, running deeply. Then you can't use Nietzsche any more; you've got to go to the old master, Niccolò, and appear to be just what the time demands, while you actively but quietly pursue what you think you ought to be, which might not be to the liking of the people, or great numbers of people."

"Well, I'm out of it, Bernard."

"Nobody's ever out of it, especially not thinking people, and besides that, we still need each other. Perhaps even more than before."

"They're grinning at us and setting us up," Max said.

"Maybe so. But one always hopes. Maybe the showers are really showers, you tell yourself, after seeing a thousand people go into them and never come out. You've *got* to believe they're real."

"What do you mean 'got' to believe when they've already proved how wrong you are. Never mind *that;* the solution is, you fight when the time is right."

"And get slaughtered, is that it?"

"Where's the choice, Bernard? Look at the Indian. He fought *past* the right time; he was half believing in the white man. Look where he is now."

Zutkin said, "The right time and the right place. Who picks such a time?"

"Haven't we been trying to pick it, but for a more genteel kind of fight, and haven't we learned that there exists no substitute for a fight but a fight?"

316

They sipped the last of their drinks in silence. Then Max said, "Bernard, do you know we really can tear up this country? I mean it, and *now!*"

Dryly, Zutkin said, "And then what?"

Max grinned. "Beyond that, whew!"

Zutkin sprang up. "Exactly! All they want is the excuse, then they'll get it over with, those Emma Lazarus poor, sprung from the vomit of steerage and who, still unable to speak English, believe in white supremacy." Zutkin shook his head. "And then there won't be any more race problems, because there won't be any Negroes. And when they finish with you, the chances are quite good that they'll start on us. Bloodlust is like a natural disaster; it has to run its course. I have seen their faces; they are faces out of nightmares — most ordinary — so ordinary that you can't believe the brains behind them capable of genocide."

"Maybe we'll be dead by then," Max said.

"I've never known you to be an optimist, Max."

A few days later, after he had seen Julian Berg, he readied himself to return to *Pace,* Margrit (something inside him insisted), and Africa.

# 25

LEIDEN — LAGOS

MAX took up Harry's letter once again, but his mind stayed briefly in the past. It had been a kind of nutty life; a lot of highs and lows; a lot of people, and a helluva lot of water under the bridge. Nineteen fifty-four had certainly started a great many things for him. And Granville Bryant had placed him in the way of all those things, and hadn't so much as asked for a little suck. Bryant to thank! Now Max bent once again to the letter:

The disclosure of America's membership in Alliance Blanc would have touched off a racial cataclysm — but America went far, far be-

317

yond the evils the Alliance was perpetuating, but more of this later. For the moment, let me consider the Alliance.

African colonies were still becoming independent. Federations were formed only to collapse a few weeks later, like the Guinea-Ghana combine. Good men and bad were assassinated indiscriminately; coups were a dime a dozen. Nkrumah in West Africa vied with Selassie in East Africa for leadership of the continent. The work of the Alliance agents — setting region against region and tribe against tribe, just as the colonial masters had done — was made easy by the rush to power on the part of a few African strongmen. Thus, the panic mentality that had been the catalyst for the formation of the Alliance seemed to have been tranquilized. There was diplomacy as usual, independence as usual. What, after all, did Europeans have to fear after that first flash of black unity? The Alliance became more leisurely, less belligerent, more sure that it had time, and above all, positive now that Africa was not a threat to anyone but itself. Alliance agents flowed leisurely through Africa now, and Western money poured in behind them.

From a belligerent posture, the Alliance went to one based on economics. Consider that 15 percent of Nigeria's federal budget comes from offshore oil brought in by Dutch, British, Italian, French and American oil companies; consider that the 72 percent of the world's cocoa which Africa produces would rot if the West did not import it. Palm oil, groundnuts, minerals, all for the West. Can you imagine, man, what good things could happen to Africans, if they learned to consume what they produce? It did not take the Europeans long to discover that their stake in Africa as "friends" rather than masters was more enormous than they could have imagined. Only naked desperation demanded that Spain and Portugal stay in Africa; the Iberian Peninsula hasn't been the same since the Moors and Jews left it in the 15th century. Time? It was the Alliance's most formidable ally.

In South Africa, the spark of revolt flickered, sputtered and now is dead. The Treason Trials killed it; oppression keeps murdering it, and those who say the spark is still alive, those successive schools of nattily tailored South African nationalists, who plunge through Paris, London and New York raising money for impossible rebellions, lie. The paradox, Max, is that, denied freedom, the black man lives better in South Africa than anywhere else on the continent; the average African. The bigshots — with their big houses and long cars, their emulation of the colonial masters — do all right. My friend Genet said it all in *Les Noirs*.

The Alliance worked. God, how it worked! And Africans themselves, dazzled by this new contraption the white man was giving them, independence, helped. Lumumba, disgracefully educated by the Belgians, was a victim of the Alliance; Olympio, dreaming dreams of federation, was another. Nkrumah and Touré have lasted for so long because their trust in the white man never was, and their trust in their own fellows only a bit deeper seated.

The Congo mess served as a valuable aid to the Alliance: it could test the world's reaction to black people in crisis. The Alliance was pleased to observe that the feeling in the West was, "Oh, well, they're only niggers, anyhow."

I could have foreseen that reaction; you could have foreseen it; any black man could have anticipated it. But, then, "niggers" are embattled everywhere, ain't they, baby? Asian "niggers," South American "niggers" . . . But let a revolt occur in East Germany and watch the newsprint fly! Let another Hungarian revolution take place and see the white nations of the world open their doors to take in refugees — Freedom Fighters, yeah! Who takes in blacks, Pakistanis, Vietnamese, Koreans, Chinese, who?

But the picture began to change. It was quite clear that the Europeans had Africa well under control — and that was all they cared about. America, sitting on a bubbling black cauldron, felt that it had to map its own contingency plans for handling 22 million black Americans in case they became unruly; in case they wanted everything Hungarian Freedom Fighters got just by stepping off the boat. So, America prepared King Alfred and submitted it to the Alliance, just as the Alliance European members had submitted their plans for operations in Africa to the Americans. The details of King Alfred are in the case, and it is truly hot stuff. All this Alliance business is pretty pallid shit compared to what the Americans have come up with.

I should tell you that it was an African who discovered the Alliance and in the process came upon King Alfred. Who? Jaja Enzkwu, that cockhound, that's who. He stumbled on the Alliance the second year of its existence, while he was in Spain, which as you know has turned out to be a very hospitable place for ex-heads of African countries on the lam. Enzkwu didn't know what was going on; he simply sensed something, seeing a gathering of British, American, Brazilian, Portuguese and South Africans at San Sebastiàn in winter. This was where the Alliance held its second meeting. I'll tell you about Jaja. Any half-way good-looking white woman can make a fool of him (which was what was happening, for him to be at a summer resort in winter), but he doesn't trust a gathering of more than a single white man. About the white man, Enzkwu has a nose for trouble. But you know Jaja.

The huge jet, sparkling silver-white in the sun, lowered itself gingerly out of the sky and touched down at Ikeja. Max looked out of his window at the taut green of the landscape, green coated with light red dust, hard, scarlet patches of earth. The airport building was unchanged. It was low and ugly and shabby. Upon its faded white side LAGOS was painted in large, elongated letters.

Max had spent three exhilarating and yet in some way disturbing days with Margrit in Amsterdam. Disturbing because he could no longer see around her; her image, voice and postures filled every corner of his imagination. And for the first time he had truly examined, even while racing away from them, the prospects of marrying a woman who was white.

He had also spent one day with Harry in Paris. Harry had been tired, bitter and querulous; almost boring. Now, here was Max back in Africa, thousands of miles away from the plush jobs he had been offered finally by the whiskey and beer companies. Those offers always came for Negroes if they'd been anywhere near the White House. Such a Negro would lend prestige to the matter-of-fact exploitation of the Negro market.

On line before the desk of the inspecting health officer, Max noticed a flurry of expensive agbadas and an escort of soldiers. He saw His Excellency, First Minister to the Premier, Jaja Enzkwu, at the center of all this attention, walking as solemnly as an emir from the North. Enzkwu deigned to look at the line of incoming people and saw Max. Quickly, he dispatched a soldier and an aide to talk to the health officer and fetch Max to him. Max walked over and extended his hand, but found himself in a perfumed abrazo, fighting his way through the folds of fine cloth of the agbada. "How

320

good it is to see you, brother, Max," Enzkwu said. To his circle, he said sternly, "It is our Afro-American brother, Max Reddick, who is an aide to the President —" Enzkwu raised a finger and everyone's attention went to it — "the President of the United States."

"Ahhhh-haaaa," the murmur went up. Enzkwu smiled as if to assure all that he knew only the most influential people.

"There was no one from your Embassy to meet you? Strange. And are you on a mission for your President?"

"Oh, no. I'm no longer with the President. I'm back with *Pace*."

"Oh! A journalist once more, is it?" Enzkwu's eyes flashed disappointment, but he stumbled on. "Ah, yes! *Pace!* That is a very important magazine. Some of your ambassadors here in Africa have been journalists."

"Yes, that is true," Max said, but thinking, Only the guys from *Look*.

"This officer will see you directly through customs," Enzkwu said. He leaned close. "I am on my way to Paris at the moment. Naturally. You have seen Harry and he is well?"

"Yes, Jaja — Your Excellency, and thank you."

"Don't mention it. When I return next week, I will ring you up at the Federal Palace, of course, yes?"

"For the time being."

"Then we will have a very good time. Goodbye. Welcome to Nigeria once more." Enzkwu winked, then, with his entourage, moved toward the exit.

Outside, Max bargained with a Yoruba taxi driver who had tribal markings on his face and wore a striped, soiled agbada. Two pounds. They pulled away from the airport and raced down the left side of the road, for Nigeria was superbly British, through Ikeja, Ebute Metta, where the traffic began to converge heavily, and through Yaba. Small stands hugged the dusty, narrow roads, and women, mostly, sat beside them, waiting with smiling patience for the passerby who wished to purchase one or two cigarettes, a stick of chewing gum, a penny candle or a piece of copra. Other women swung down the road, their infants tucked into their skirts behind them. The mammy wagons, always overloaded with shouting, gesticulating people, spurted by; roadside drinking places played loud High-Life music. Entering the Lagos traffic, they crept past the Bristol Hotel on St. Martin's Street, down past Kingsway with its display windows filled with brown mannequins, past which surged the mobs of shoppers, waiting houseboys and drivers, beggars, and sellers of gold watches and postcards and women for later in the evening. They turned onto the Marina. The harbor was filled with ships riding at anchor. There was a slight haze because of the humidity. Max sat back smoking and watching the street scenes. Now they cruised past the Shell-B-P Building, Barclays Bank, the new Posts & Telegraph Building, the powerful statue of Shango, Yoruba god of iron, with his short sword thrust toward sky and sea. Finally, they curved off the main road onto the spacious grounds of the Federal Palace Hotel. This would be home for a few days. Max climbed out of the taxi and three young bellhops raced to take his bags.

He took a room at the rear of the hotel. It overlooked the lagoon and channel through which the great ships passed slowly on their way to the harbor at the foot of the city. It was quieter in the back; here there were no chattering drivers waiting for fares from the hotel to fill their green and black cabs. Max stripped and showered. After, sitting in shorts (he hadn't turned the air-conditioner on yet), he made an appointment to see the house on Rumens Road and the office on Broad Street the next morning. Then he wrote a letter to Devoe in Nairobi. Max wasn't in a hurry to open the lines of communication; a letter would do for now. At dinnertime Max went downstairs to the spacious dining room and took a table on the open terrace. As usual, there were twenty white persons for every black person. The whites generally got better if not first service and Max felt the old irritation with Africa coming on. Patience, he told himself. *Cool.* When he had finished dinner, he returned to his room and pulled off his jacket and loaded his typewriter. He was half a hundred pages into a new book, but he had no publisher now; his previous one had dropped his option. Another publisher, however, had made Max an offer, but that had been quickly and mysteriously withdrawn. Then Max discovered that Marion Dawes had signed with that publisher and he understood. The publisher had his nigger now; nearly everybody had one. The season for that sort of thing. Max was quite determined that this would be his last book. There was a little money put aside, thanks to the really quite adequate soft cover book money in circulation. With it he could buy a little shack in New England, perhaps, and do nothing but hunt, read and walk the woods. But would Margrit like that kind of —

Max jumped up. He had to do something about this Margrit thing. It was one thing to sleep with white women, but quite another to marry them. He was too tired and much too wise to be put through the paces they set for you in such a marriage; he didn't need that at all. Something had to be done. A letter tomorrow. To Margrit. Max pulled on his jacket and walked quickly out to the elevator. Yeah, he knew what to do. He signaled a cab when he got downstairs and took it to the Kakadu Club in Yaba. There were always girls at the Kakadu, girls and white folks trying to do the High-Life. The High-Life was not an intricate dance; it was a shuffle, but you could improvise on it.

The place had its old smell of urine hanging in the humid air. Blue lights. Red lights. Green lights. Young men, their hard bodies in absurd, nonchalant postures, studied him as he paid the cab driver. Pimps and would-be pimps the world over were the same. The eyes, the feigning of the unmeltable cool, the rubbing of flesh the common denominator. One of the young men slithered out of a corner, his cool gone, his eyes pleading and demanding at once, and said, "Want embassy girl, boss?"

Max glanced at him without word or gesture and entered the club. Embassy girl? Just what does that mean? Then he was inside the club, or rather, inside the fence that circled the outdoor club. The band played under a canopy and some of the tables were protected from inclement weather. Most of them, however, were in the open. There were more white men than black. The band was playing a lazy High-Life and white men shuffled self-consciously around the circle with black girls, some of whom were wearing seam-bursting skirts and Kingsway wigs. Max took a rear table and ordered a beer. It would be warm, but it would be better than an iced drink at this point; in another day the pills would have his stomach in shape. A Fulani girl was sitting at the next table. Max and the girl eyed each other with mild interest. Just as Max was about to offer her a drink, an Englishman walked to her table. "Let's dawnce," he said, looking away from her toward the floor, as if expecting her to bound up at the sound of his voice, which many girls would have done. *"Let's dawnce,"* he said in a louder, more commanding voice. The girl shook her head and withdrew from him. The Englishman stood in a state of shocked embarrassment.

"I no want dance wit' you," the girl said and turned so that she was facing Max directly. The Englishman walked away, his face flushed. He wasn't used to *that* kind of treatment from Nigerians. No, things have changed, are changing.

Max extended a pack of cigarettes in the direction of the girl; and with, it seemed, a single movement, glancing behind her to see where the Englishman was, she was at his table.

"You didn't like the gentleman?" Max asked.

The girl pursed her lips and made a sound not unfamiliar to bathrooms.

"Drink?" Max asked.

She glanced at his beer and he said, "You can have anything you want. I happen to like beer." She too, ordered a Star beer.

The girl could not have been more than sixteen or seventeen, but already she had that proud Fulani posture, the way of flashing the eyes, the vocal inflections softly uttered that commanded as well. Max had seen these things even in the very young cow Fulani boys who walked from all the way north with herds of long, swept-horned cattle for the Lagos markets.

"You are from America." She said it rather than asked.

324

"Yes." If she hung out at the Kakadu often enough, she had to become familiar with the look of black Americans.

"T'at is far away."

"Not far by plane. Where is your home?"

"I? Sokoto."

"In the North. Very far north."

She smiled and small, even teeth showed white. "You know Sokoto?"

Max shook his head. "I have only read about it. What are you called?"

"Florence."

"Ah, Florence." She was one of the new generation of Nigerians moving from farm, rain forest or desert to the hot pavement and reeking sewers of Lagos. One of the new generation excluded by the successors to the British from participating, sharing. One of the new generation forced by circumstances to meet the outside world, the Londoner, New Yorker, Parisian under the most basic circumstances. One of the new generation whose not having would be underlined by the contact from outside while the piddling little civil servants, the haves for the time being, wallowed in their security, their power. One of the new generation who would be eventually a part of the inevitable revolt which all have-nots must begin.

"What you do in Lagos and what *you* name?"

"I visit. My name is James."

"James? James. *Jimmy!*"

"Yes."

She did not wear a wig. Her skin was cocoa dark and her features were almost regular. Many Fulanis' features were strikingly different from other Nigerians.

"Are you married, Florence?"

"No. No more."

"How many picken'?"

She smiled and held up two fingers. "Two picken'; boy and girl."

"Tonight I will give you another picken'. A strong boy."

Florence laughed and reached for another American cigarette.

The Portuguese and not the British brought the "dash" to Nigeria. It is bothersome, infuriating and degrading to the giver and ultimately to the receiver — but, if you wish to bring a girl to your room, you have only to slip a ten shilling or pound note to the desk clerk when he gives you your key, and it is done with. Dash does everything.

Florence's eyes swept the room at once. She went to the window and pulled open the curtain that covered it. A ship with riding lights on sat in the lagoon, awaiting its turn to sail into the harbor. Florence wheeled away from the window and touched the bed and laughed. Max liked it that she didn't wear Western dress; he liked the long, ankle-length skirt. He had become so entranced with her childlike movements and soft laughter that he almost dispensed with the ritual. Now he was sure that she was new at whatever she thought she was doing. He could see that she had never been in a place like the Federal Palace before. At five pounds a day, certainly not. Very few Nigerians could afford that price. No, the hotel was for white people, that was obvious, white people in black Africa. She whistled at the large, neat bathroom, made even more comforting by the presence of the big, soft white towels. Perhaps, Max thought, the ritual would not be so degrading. Casually, he sat on the edge of the tub, plugged it and turned on the water. "Would you like to take a bath?" he asked gently. Ordinarily, you simply ran the water and said, "Get in the tub," and they obeyed without question.

"Yes!" she said.

It would be a lark for her. She took a towel and went to the outer room. Max took a small can of disinfectant and squeezed a few drops into the water. You used the disinfectant for everything, brushing teeth, bathing, even a bit in your drinking water. Max stepped into the outer room just as the twin balls of old newspaper fell out of Florence's brassiere. She looked abashed. She pulled the towel up around her. "My —" She touched her breasts. "— they

326

not big ones." She smiled and took his hand. "In my tribe, man, woman, go in water together."

Max considered this momentarily. Why the hell not? He broke the rules and undressed. In the tub, Florence took the cloth and gently washed him from head to foot.

In bed she said, "You give me picken', I keep. I no give picken' away like some. I keep you picken', American picken'."

"Yes," Max murmured drowsily, considering delicately all the factors that had brought the girl from the torrid heat of the North where the edges of the Sahara crept inch by inch southward. Another child. Of course, she would have it, carry it on her butt tied behind her until it walked. It would be loved and cared for and not cast aside; it would be Florence's son or daughter. He wondered suddenly what Regina's children looked like, then he went to sleep. Later, the girl snoring softly at his side, he reached over and stroked the young, undernourished body into wakefulness, mounted it once more and in time withdrew from it. Sleep came again.

Max awoke with the sound of the bath running. Florence dressed hurriedly to be out before the tea and rolls came. He wondered how much money he should give her. A couple of pounds? But no. Five pounds. Yes, five pounds and if he ever went again to the Kakadu, she would remember him. Besides, there were the children; he didn't think she'd lied about that. And there were the balls of newspaper she was now stuffing into her bra. Perhaps now she could buy a pair of falsies from Kingsway.

"T'at for me? Is a lot, Jimmy."

"Take it. When I come to Lagos again, I will look for you."

"I look for you, too."

She slipped out of the door and he had a vision of her getting off the elevator, walking quickly through the austere marble lobby with its fountain spraying water. She would pause in the front and a cab would speed up to her. Then she would take the drive back to Yaba, to a small room where her children had been watched through the night by her mother.

327

Max was thinking of Margrit as he showered, and he knew he would not write that letter. A letter, yes, but not *that* letter.

# 26

LAGOS — THE CONGO — AMSTERDAM

A MONTH was galloping by, spurred on by the stinging, brooding sun, the heat-relieving, sudden gusts of wind over the fields of elephant grass and red earth when the tides changed; a few garden parties where the women, their red smiles fixed, felt the heels of their shoes sinking deeper and deeper into the ground while they held their gin and tonics; Saturday afternoons at the Island Club where the Nigerian upper class went to remind themselves that they were Nigerian and not British after all; hours stolen to take the lagoon crossing to Tarkwa Bay where the white people of the Lagos community outnumbered the black people ten to one.

But during that time Max had managed to hire a car with a driver from Calabar who looked down on the newly secured Ibo houseboy whose name, ironically, was Johnson, and the Yoruba girl for the office whose name, right out of a mission school, was Charity. The girl called Max "Mr. Reedick," the driver (whose name was Jimmy) said "Sir," and the Ibo called him "Mastuh." "Mastuh," then, was anyone who paid your salary whether black, white or red striped. There was no need for a night watch on Rumens Road; it wasn't far enough out of the city to worry about thieves and hungry people in search of fat cats or dogs to eat. Both Johnson and Charity had the usual overabundance of relatives or tribesmen nearby and from among them Max secured a host of messenger boys for the office, although there were few messages to be delivered.

All the U.S. agencies were well staffed with American Negroes. For many of them the advent of African independence came as an unexpected boon, releasing them from the narrow alleys and dead ends of their careers back home into the Foreign Service. Just like many whites in the Service, they'd never had it so good, with cooks, houseboys, gardeners and drivers.

Jaja Enzkwu had returned from Paris and at one of his garden parties Max met the newest Negro addition to the American Embassy, Alfonse Edwards, a political affairs officer. Edwards was a good mixer, tall, cool, with an intelligent, bright face, definitely American; there was no mistaking him for anything else with his over-twenty-five Ivy look. He slid without pause from the stilted conversational style of a government man with many secrets, to the vernacular of the bar at the Red Rooster in Harlem. Someone was telling Edwards about an American family. Max listened in.

The Curtises lived over in Porto-Novo, Dahomey. Curtis had been in a teaching program and during his year there had gained a reputation, well-known among the Americans, especially the women (for Curtis was very handsome), for chasing Dahomean girls. That was all right; he traveled a lot and kept his chases away from home. Then it was discovered that Mrs. Curtis, the mother of two children, also liked Dahomeans, the Hausa men. At first she had been given, by a friend close to the Embassy at Kaduna, what amounted to a warning. But she persisted in taking on Dahomeans wherever she could find them — behind the Great Mosque, in the Central Hotel, in the rooms upstairs over the Federal Club and even in her home when Mr. Curtis was on a trip. Eventually the Curtises were given five hours to leave the country on one of those Saturdays when the Americans from the tracking station were trying to round up enough men to play a game of baseball against the Japanese weavers the next day. Curtis was a heavy hitter and a good pitcher, and the Americans had counted on him to check the Japanese batters until they had solved the curves of the pitchers. However, at gametime the family Curtis, shunted aboard a Sabena jet the night before, was hunting temporary accommodations in Rome. It was suspected that the U. S. Ambassador and not the Dahomean Government, which let the blame fall on its shoulders, was responsible for the sudden departure of the Curtises.

Just as sudden (Max learned, still at Edwards' side) was the departure of Miss Edith Pringle, an efficient, better-than-average-looking secretary, to whom Max had spoken several times during his visits to the U. S. Embassy where she worked. Miss Pringle, it developed had been selling pussy to Nigerians for fifty dollars, cash on the navel, American money, thank you, for only one time. By the time she was found out and brought back to the Embassy from Yaba one night, Miss Pringle had accumulated several thousand dollars. Max could hardly think of her as the "Embassy Girl" the young pimp at the Kakadu had tried to steer him to. No, you just couldn't imagine thirtyish, quite proper, all business Edith Pringle kicking her thick white legs, V-ed above the back of some Nigerian civil servant who'd put his family in hock for the privilege of getting some white trim. She had been an overwhelming success as an *oyinbo* flesh merchant, and had contributed mightily to the "twenny-hungries" of the civil servants who, as it was, often ran out of money before payday, the twentieth of each month. Miss Pringle, money, diaphragms, penicillin capsules and all, was escorted quite wordlessly to Ikeja to catch the next plane home, which was a Pan-Am flight direct to New York.

"They just ain't used to all this sun," Edwards said with a chuckle.

The whites who would have disintegrated inconspicuously in the States went with the blare of garden party gossip here. You saw it when the liquor went a bit too fast, or you saw it in the blotchy complexions of the women shopping at Kingsway or at the Lebanese supermarket (they called it); you saw it in the whiskey-inspired slobberings of the men, the restless eyes of the women. What did it matter? This was a black land and they had learned in America, most of them, that they could do anything they wished before black people and still preach church services on Sunday. Too many of them were low-ranking Foreign Service people who long ago had given up their dreams of becoming ambassadorial assistants. The paradox now was that the new Negro Foreign Service people, so long hampered, were perhaps the best personnel assigned to Africa.

330

But the Africans, who with their independent status preferred white diplomats, were not terribly happy about the Negroes.

Max was expecting the cable. It had been due from the first day he arrived. Now, it was here. He reread it and walked to the window to gaze down at the traffic jam; there were always traffic jams on Broad Street. The porter across the street in Antoine's was just opening the doors. You had steak at Antoine's, and you ate it with the reek of feces and urine drifting in from the rear bathroom. You got used to it. Max folded the cable and jammed it into his pocket. He could not know then to what extent it would change his life, or commit him to it. He told Charity to book him a flight to Leopoldville for that evening, if possible. The cable from New York had ordered him to the Congo to (1) check on what was happening to the Katanga secession and (2) the progress of the Angolans in their revolt against the Portuguese.

Leo seemed deserted the next morning, Sunday, when Max arrived and checked into the Stanley Hotel. There was a bicycle race in progress on the main street. Here and there people watched cautiously from doorways. Max was sure that behind the closed doors and windows people were packing or listening closely to their radios.

He called the political affairs officer of the U. S. Embassy and arranged a meeting. There was little time to waste. Nearly everyone expected the Congo to blow any minute. After the call Max went to a sidewalk cafe on the Boulevard and had a beer and watched the Swedish UN troopers trying to pick up wig-wearing Bakongo girls. The wigs fascinated Max. The fashion seemed to be spreading throughout the continent. You reached for what looked like a healthy hunk of African hair and you felt a gob of synthetics. Well, American blacks had gone through that phase of disengagement with the white man's culture. They had almost stopped trying to change the hair with heavy pomades and process aids. Negro women, many of them, were wearing their hair short, *au naturel,* in what they *thought* was an African style. Negroes had passed through; Africans were just getting the full effects of the European presence.

Max was sitting in the lobby of his hotel when the political officer came in. His name was Pugh and as they left the hotel Max could *feel* him adjusting to the fact that *Pace* had a Negro correspondent in Leo, walking beside him, a man to whom he was going to give a briefing on the situation with the rebels (Angolan) and rebels (Katangese) and then send him to the UN observers already on the scene.

They shared a quiet and to-the-point dinner a short distance from the city in a small restaurant that sat in a grove of flamboyant and palm trees. Max had already learned that you could not really tell an official in a diplomatic position of a U.S. agency from a Central Intelligence Agency man. Often they were one and the same. Later when Pugh let him out in front of the Stanley he said, "We'd appreciate talking to you again when you return from your travels in the Congo."

"Of course," Max said. Pugh thought, naturally, if he was CIA, that Max just might get something their white contacts could not get because he was black. The next morning he booked passage for E'ville that night, then walked over to the Angolan rebels' compound to talk to Miguel Assis, their leader, whom Max had met in New York when Assis was on fund-raising jaunts there. He lunched with Assis, a dark man of medium height who wore gold-rimmed glasses and spoke in a soft voice. Max secured permission to go out with a rebel squad across the border when he returned to Leo. It was agreed on before Max thought about just how silly it was. If the squad ran into trouble the Portuguese would fire on his black face just as they would on the Angolans'. Here he had avoided Korea which at least had been an honest kind of war when compared to what was going on in Angola. Why was he going into *this* mess? He could hardly rationalize it on the basis of color, but then, color was inescapable. If the Portuguese could be driven out, South Africa in the future might also go. Perhaps it was worth a look-see. It was done and Max walked Assis back to his compound where chickens ran loose, people sprawled along the grounds pocked with green, stagnant puddles of water. It was hard for Max to conceive of Assis winning his desultory war against the Portuguese, Algerian aid or no. Maybe when he saw the troops the view might be a little different.

Elisabethville. It galled Max to see its wealth displayed so ostentatiously on the backs of its white men and women, its Avenues of Royale and Delcommune over which, early in the morning, helicopters buzzed spraying mosquito-killing liquids. But this was the capital of Union Minière du Haut-Katanga; this was what the fuss was all about. Money. As usual. More so than at Leo, everything that was in Paris was in E'ville, and more of it: clubs, swimming pools surrounded by mining executives and bikini-wearing girls, hustling houseboys in uniform bringing drinks and food to be devoured by the whites and their quiet Katangese guests who came with their wives and sat in corners.

Mornings when Max left the Hotel Leopold to keep his appointments for the day, he saw it spread out before him. The white reporters at the hotel were friendly enough, but the Katangese, from the serving boy who brought his *petit déjeuner* to his room, to the civilian and mining rulers of the province, looked at him with some confusion. *Un journaliste noir Américain? C'est curieux!* It was their smiles that gave them away, and the puzzled fingering of the press credentials, the labored answers, given as if the mind were really somewhere else. And when Max left them, their farewell almost to a man was (the smiles were politer now, more relieved) *"Content de vous voir."* What the hell. Just like New York; ten thousand miles away and just like New York. But there *was* a difference; the whites were more receptive to his presence, his questions, than the blacks. This thought came scudding into full view now and he knew he had to look directly at it. He had known it last year, if not by experience, by sense. Now, walking toward UN headquarters it hit him so forcibly that he wondered if he could do the job *Pace* wanted in Africa. Like Pugh, Dempsey had been lured into the black-being-compatible trap. Nothing was farther from the truth.

One day the job in E'ville was done. Over were the interviews, the swimming pool parties, the exchange of information with other reporters, the acceptances, the rejections. Max filed the story and was sure that within a matter of weeks he'd have to come back; it looked that bad.

Back in Leo, before he was ready to go, that is, before he had completely rethought the entire matter, Assis sent word that the rebels were ready to send a guerilla column across the Angola border.

Two days later, following instructions from the guerilla officer in command of the column, Montante, an *assimilado* who had joined the rebels, Max left the hotel as though going for a walk, was picked up not far from where the Ford Foundation was going to build a school to train jurists and administrators, and driven south of Thysville. The guerillas carried Czech weapons — rifles and lightweight automatic machine guns. The Portuguese, it had been widely reported, were armed with the superior NATO weapons that had come from the U.S. Now, Max thought, I'll get to see Mao Tse-tung's theory in action. Pursuing the insurance of his survival, he freely passed out American cigarettes and shared his canned goods which Montante had brought for him. He took pictures of the squad together and individually. That was further insurance. He had known Africans who'd tracked to England and America, photographers that had taken their pictures. To own a photograph of oneself was a mark of status for many Africans. Max wanted the men in the squad to know him, know his face, his voice and the way he moved.

They slipped across the border along the long stretch of flat land that lies between Matadi and Popokabaka, moving like shadows toward Maquela do Zombo in the province of Luanda. There were twenty-five men in the column and the chief weapons were to be speed and surprise. The column was to meet another with twice the number of men. The second group was to hit the army station at

Nóqui and then move across country to Maquela, where, it was hoped, the Portuguese would fly in reinforcements. These would be watching the west for the second column. Max's column was to hit from the north, reinforced by the larger group. After the station had been knocked out, both groups were to move east to rendez-vous with still a third column coming from near Lunda.

But Max's column waited in the forests and slight hills near Maquela for five days without making contact with the larger column. Small Portuguese spotter planes passed overhead nearly every day. Rations were very low. On the sixth day Montante took fifteen men and most of the hand grenades. Max stayed behind and watched the men move silently toward the town under the cover of a sullen, purpling dusk. Two hours Max heard the soft, crumping sound of exploding hand grenades, rifle fire and long bursts of machine guns. Then there was silence. A few minutes later rifle fire was swallowed by heavy machine-gun fire. Max looked at the sky, expecting to see tracers arching under it toward the town. This time the silence was complete. The ten men with Max had crouched toward the firing at first; now they sat down. The jungle distorted sounds. They would have to wait to see what happened.

But neither Montante nor his men returned that night and morning found two small planes trailing back and forth across the sky, obviously spotting for ground forces. Still, the guerillas waited. At dusk, however, there was full accord to retreat back across the border. The "campaign" had been a failure. The larger column was gone, vanished in the soft hills. The main part of the second column was also gone. And the third column, if it still functioned, would have found them by now, they had been at Maquela so long. The retreat covered a different route; this one went through a small swift stream of dark frothing water. When Max's turn to cross it came, he froze his mind against the presence of water cobras and edged into the stream. He felt the sudden pull of the current against his legs, then slipped and went under briefly, then up, managing to hold his camera out. The guerillas smiled when he made the opposite bank. Bedraggled and chattering, the guerillas crossed the bor-

335

der, sent word to Thysville for trucks and sat down to wait for them. The expedition had been like placing a baby in the den of a hungry lion. Bye-bye, baby. Sixty-five men missing; *good* and missing, and there was the third column. But the men were laughing and talking. Africa which spawned so much life, took it cheaply and left only the bones to be worshiped. And sometimes even the bones weren't found.

As he had done when he returned from E'ville, Max called Pugh. Odds were that he already knew what had happened. Pugh came shortly after Max had cleaned up and sat down to pull his story together from the notes. One look at the small, thin-faced bold man told Max that Pugh had done his homework. His handshake this time was hard and firm and there was a kind of official deference about him that one finds in people closely associated with governments. Max could see Pugh telling Washington and getting the return message: PERSON IN QUESTION O.K. MORE FOLLOWS . . .

"How was it, Mr. Reddick?"

Max looked away from him, out past the balcony and the tree-tops. From his room he could just see the Congo River threading its way through marshland to the sea. There was no one he could hurt with the details now. Maybe all Pugh needed was confirmation of what he already had.

"You know the camp close to Thysville?"

"Yes."

"We took a route between Matadi and Popokabaka."

"One of the usual routes."

"Twenty-five men in our column; we were to meet fifty other men and I don't know how many were in the third column."

"Where were they coming from."

"Lunda, Montante said."

"He was a good man, Montante."

"Do you know what's happened to him?"

"The Portuguese have him. He's alive for now. They'll make an example of him. Sixty-five men then, at the minimum," Pugh said. He wasn't writing anything down. Probably has a computer where his brain should be, Max thought. "Assis is running into trouble," Pugh said.

"Yeah. Too bad I didn't see some of the weapons the Portuguese had."

"You didn't though, did you?"

"No."

"Take pictures?"

"Only the men in my squad."

"Nothing more, Mr. Reddick?"

It seemed to Max that Pugh's tone was insinuating and he said, wearily, "Screw you, Pugh."

Pugh looked down into his lap.

"Did you get wet?" he finally asked.

"Rain, no."

Pugh was rising. "I meant river crossings."

"Yes, yes," Max said impatiently, "one stream, but I don't know the name of it —"

"We know the name. I only wanted to tell you to have a complete physical and blood count as soon as you can. The streams in this area are loaded with bilharzia."

Max nodded and turned back to his typewriter. Bilharzia, he thought when Pugh had closed the door behind him, what in the hell is *that?*

"It looks very much like bilharzia," the doctor said cheerfully, waving Max to a seat.

Through the windows Max could see Jimmy, his driver, polishing the car with a cloth. Awolowo Street, Lagos. Leo was three weeks behind. "You'll have to explain to me just exactly what that is," Max said.

"Comes from blood flukes," the doctor said. He was English. "They enter the body where they can, hook into the blood stream and start working from the inside back out. Your count seems to be holding, but the flukes are there and if you don't get rid of them, they'll get rid of you, right ho!"

Jimmy was shaking out his cloth. He put it away, then pulled out a comb and moved to the sideview mirror. He crouched down and pulled the comb laboriously through his thick hair.

"Where would you like to go for treatment?" the doctor asked.

It was a foregone conclusion then that treatment was necessary.

"London or Amsterdam? The best specialists are there. There is also a good clinic in Paris. Time is important —"

"Amsterdam," Max said with a wave of his hand and he knew that it signaled the end of the battle against Margrit. If he went to London, he'd be breaking his neck to get to Amsterdam; if he went to Paris, it would be the same goddamn thing.

The doctor was dictating a letter to his nurse for Max. "And I'll cable this doctor tonight as well. When can you leave, Mr. Reddick?"

Max thought. "Two days."

"In the meantime, you'd better get this prescription filled and take the medicine as ordered until you're under the care of Dr. van Gelder." The doctor paused and then said, "By the way, have another complete checkup once you're there, won't you? Just to make sure everything's shipshape."

But Max's mind was already turning forward.

He was hardly aware of Lagos, ripe-smelling Lagos with its open sewers, in frenzied movement all around him. He sent the cables to Devoe and Shea, gave orders lucidly and not without humor to Charity, Jimmy and Johnson; he did not know just how long the treatments would take. This done, he faced the packing and the next day took the deadening ride to the airport, climbed the ramp with trembling legs and a tiny whirlpool in his gut, and his mind moved ahead to Margrit, to whom he'd also sent a cable.

He would marry her. He could fight it no longer; the accidents kept recurring that sent him rushing back to her. Bam, the towel was in. I quit. Enough. Oh, he would go through the formality of asking her to marry him, but he knew her answer. The signals had always been strong and steady. And she wasn't American. There was a difference. She had to break with none of her family, trek to

338

no desert to think about it in solitude. No, *he* had done that. They would return to Africa. He could see her already, topping the foaming, hissing surf at Tarkwa Bay, vanishing for an instant beneath the monstrous blue waves and then emerging with a steady pink stroke, coming on toward the ivory-colored beach. Later, of course, there would be America.

A certain sense of relief had settled over him when he decided that he would marry Margrit, the kind of relief that comes with commitment, good or bad. Don't stand there, *do* something! Now he was going to do it; he would become *recreated* as a Negro in the process. The black anonymity would be gone. The old myths goaded by old hatreds would make him highly visible, more dangerous. His possible vulnerability, with Margrit at his side, would be publicized, his manhood put on the line as never before, for now it would always be challenged. The *boyhood* that came with being Negro was over. It would not matter that Margrit was not American, bred up in the horrors or perverted joys of marriage to a black man. She was white, that was enough; it was what you saw first, right away, at once.

He supposed that what he felt was love. He wished there were another word for it, one that could be used by people like himself, and Margrit too, he guessed, who had touched what they called love so often that it no longer possessed a name.

*If there had been no Lillian would there be a Margrit?*

Thirty-five thousand feet up, moving close to six hundred mph, Max could now clearly see Margrit standing in the doorway of a New England cabin the first thing on a cool morning, the dew still on the ground, the trout breaking from the shadows in search of food; stretching in the doorway, her hair trapping the gold of the sun; her gold and pink body soft against an August green. He thought of them together, skin against skin, mind to mind, of her whispered words of barely muted awe (for there *was* all of history and distance, the displacement of old values that had been overcome), "How lovely we are together."

But the realities.

To Max it had always been all right, what other black men and white women wished to do with their lives. Then, he was having none of it, not for real; for a night or two or three perhaps, on occasions, but not on paper, not to have and to hold; he had been too wise for that, too aware. You survived by avoiding *that* kind of marriage. That was past. He was going to marry Margrit. They could kiss his ass, the blacks and the whites both. Blacks, suddenly steeped in the nigrescent nationalism that was boiling across the land, were as opposed to mixed marriages as whites, and black women were especially vociferous. Max trusted their emotions more than the men. Too many times, out with a white date, he had been approached by black men, his sleeve tugged and the question asked: "That chick got a *friend?*" Or: "Max, now you know I like ice cream *too.*" Or the crude passes were made, the ones that revealed that many black men, whatever they said to the contrary, had not yet jettisoned what the white man had said about them and the white woman.

Somewhere it was all a lie, what the white man said black men should not do, and what black men deep within their own hearts came to believe themselves. It was a lie because no black man anywhere in the world where newspapers, magazines, television and film existed could do anything *but* move unconsciously throughout his life toward whitey Aphrodite, the love-and-sex object, raping it when he could, loving it when he was allowed to and marrying it when he dared to.

You dared to if you knew the truth and the truth was proximity. The fleeting relationships, the tasting of Aphrodite's fruits in the small hours of an American morning or a European afternoon were lies and that was the way they wanted it. That was the way they taught you to live it. Better that than rubbing elbows at lunch counters or in classrooms. Most white people fell in love (?) and married each other because of proximity. Most black people fell in love (?) and married each other because of proximity. What happened to the black man and white woman (or vice versa) in close proxim-

340

ity to each other or wanting to be in close proximity to each other?

He had lived in the gray, on the margin, for a very long time now. But that was over. From here on in, there would be attacks from both; he and Margrit would be everybody's business. There would be exceptions; there always were, but those could not be taken for granted. How times had changed. Once the colored communities were the only places of refuge for the mixed couple. Now there was only, for pure refuge, isolation.

*Why,* Max continued thinking, gazing out at the wingtip shuddering slightly, its skin rippling rhythmically from speed and pressure, *does it take so long, so* fucking *long to grow up! So long to know that what is important in any given time, to any given person, nay, urgent, cannot be avoided no matter how skillful the evasions of the involved?*

"That's it!" Roger said, watching the plane make its approach over Schiphol Airport.

Margrit Westoever, who had told Roger of Max's coming, followed the passage of the aircraft, hoping dully that this time Max would have something else on his mind beside *Pace* and writing. She hoped this time, despite his illness, he would talk about *them.* She had arranged everything for him with the doctor who had explained to her what his illness was. It sounded horrible. But all the same she was glad he was back in Amsterdam. Now she knew she would take him almost any way she could, any way he wanted it, but *Godverdomme,* she was sick of dead ends, so sick of them that she thought that was just why she was always involved in them. If dead ends truly were her fate, then she chose the one with Max. She could say nothing until he did; that was the way she was. But she was tired of being hurt; she did not like it. It eroded the dignity. During his last visit they had avoided talking about anything important. He never mentioned love. There was nothing wrong with mentioning it, even if trillions and trillions of people had already used it. She surmised that his being a writer had something to do with his refusal to use the word, that and perhaps a kind of honesty that compelled him to use such a word only if he meant it. Margrit smiled as she recalled first thinking about this in the side room of the gallery which at that time had a quite good collection of collages by an American Negro painter who was trying to get to her. He used *all* the words; but then the painter had that kind of reputation in town. Still, like so many Negroes, he held forth loudly and at length about the horrible race relations in America, and how he *hated* white people. What was he doing in Amsterdam then, chasing every white girl he saw? And when they went with or married these girls, the black Americans, the girls always seemed to be doing penance. They were quiet beneath the voices of their men, and seemed as mere extensions of them, as if they had in the black contact lost all perspective of themselves. They seemed so utterly and completely crushed. But why was she thinking like this? She and Max were never like that. They could never be like that.

She watched the plane, a mere speck at the end of the runway, trailing faint streams of smoke, land. She saw herself taking off in one, going to America, Max at her side. Enough of Europe with its flowers and grasses fertilized by blood, its breezes echoing the distant passing of bullets and bombs, the stutter of tanks. Europeans never learned. Enough of Europe with its people who said they were Jews when she knew they were not. There was something about wanting to belong to and be a survivor of the worst of the Continent's history. These people disgusted her, but she met them all the time. She recalled Max's reaction to the Anna Frank house and to the sections where the Jews once had lived. She remembered how during the war the Germans had killed people on their way to work, just to set examples, shot them down mornings on the Leidseplein without warning. "You, you, you and you." Bang, bang, bang and bang. We have suffered, yes, she thought, but the learning comes slowly. America might be better, no matter what she had heard about it; it had produced Max. But again, as the plane rolled slowly toward the airport terminal, she asked herself, Why am I thinking all this?

342

He had just returned from his first visit to the doctor. He was taking an arsenic medicine for the bilharzia. Dinner was on the stove, probably burning and she had forgotten to chill the wine. Maybe he wasn't even supposed to have wine. Did I hear him say it? Why doesn't he say it again?

"I'm not such a bad guy; I wouldn't beat you or starve you, and I always work hard," he was saying.

Margrit's hands came up before her as if to ward off a flurry of caresses that had taken her by surprise. She felt water in her eyes. Then her hands were together, wringing each other's fingers and she had to take a tissue and wipe her nose and she was thanking God silently and being overwhelmed by his words, the meaning of them.

She did not want him to look at her like this, but, as she got up to run to the bedroom, she saw, quite suddenly, a look of alarm in his eyes. Did he think, foolish boy, that she was saying no? She ran back to him and crumpled to her knees and cried in his lap while he tried to pull her face up so he could look in it and understand what was going on. She shook her head so vigorously up and down that the tears flew and she said several times, very softly, *"Ja, ja, ja, Mox, Ik hou van je,* yes, yes, I love you, of course, yes. What else but yes?"

"Get up," he said. "Please get up. Don't kneel, don't ever kneel to anyone for anything." He was strangely and deeply moved but a slight, stinging anger came and went. He lifted her around so she was sitting and not kneeling. Not even niggers are kneeling these days, Max thought.

"I will make you a good wife," she said.

"I know that," he said. "And I will make you a good husband."

"We will be so strong together. Even alone you are strong."

He said, "Stronger with you, Maggie."

"I am not so strong alone," she said wistfully. "But now . . ."

Max remembered that they had just come back.

They had driven to Paris to see Harry. They had seen Harry and Charlotte and Michelle. Women. How happy both of them were to

343

see him married. Both of them happy at different times, of course, and in different places. Charlotte had had a look of triumph on her face. The *I knew it* look. And Michelle: "Ah, Max, she is *right* for you. One can see it very plainly. Yes, you have done well. My love to you both."

They had driven on to Javea in Alicante province in Spain, their wedding bands hardly scratched, and there Margrit had got a splendid tan from the Spanish late autumn sun. They had rested in the quiet little seaside town, and swum in the placid waters of the cove. They had spent almost two weeks shopping, cooking and eating; reading, making love and walking along the deserted beach beneath the light blue sky marred only by the contrails of B-52's making their overflights.

Yes, they had just come back and closed the door behind them and in the mail there was a cable and a letter from *Pace*. Max opened the cable first:

EXPACE NEW YORK SORRY ABOUT ILLNESS STOP JUST AS WELL STOP SADLY BOARD HAS SUDDENLY CUT BUDGET ON OVERSEAS BUREAUS STOP DISMANTLE LAGOS DESK FROM HOLLAND EFFECTIVE IMMEDIATELY STOP RETURN NEW YORK NEW ASSIGNMENT STOP FIRST RATE FILE ON CONGO ANGOLA STOP SORRY STOP SHEA

Now he opened the letter. It explained in detail what had happened. The Board of Directors of *Pace* felt that for the present one desk in Africa was quite enough. Since Devoe had seniority, his would be maintained and Max's cut. Perhaps, Dempsey went on, if Max had not taken the job in Washington, his performance in Africa by this time would have been proof to the Board that two desks were needed. Dempsey had acted on the basis of *Pace*'s needs, but the Board had settled for *Pace*'s mere presence in Africa. Also the Paris and London offices were lopping off personnel. Stringers were being upgraded to "special correspondents" in Rome, Madrid, Saigon and throughout South America. Max would go back to National Affairs.

Max handed the letter and cable to Margrit while he thumbed through the rest of the mail. *What a fucking year this has been,* he thought. *Forty thousand miles more or less and probably more; New York, Washington, Amsterdam, Paris, Lagos, Leo, E'ville, Amsterdam again and New York. And the African bush. Yep. From the White House to the bush where little beasts got you straightened out if you thought you were hot shit, by eating your insides out and each time you crapped a little bit of yourself went with it. Sore butt, sore gut and now this. If he hadn't taken the job in Washington . . . Why, goddamn them, Dempsey and Shea were so tickled that a* Pace *man was going to Washington they were turning handsprings in the halls.* Look *turned out ambassadors, but* Pace *helped to make policy. Yeah.*

He glanced at Margrit. She had spent every available moment in the sun as if, by tanning, she could minimize the difference between them. *These white people and the sun,* he thought with a smile. *Minister Q had told him once that the time to take over America was during the summer, beach by beach when all the white folks were laying out in the sun getting blisters trying to look like black people.* Margrit was very dark except for her very white ass and the lower parts of her breasts which looked like two lost half moons in search of some sky.

Finished with the letter and the cable Margrit searched her husband's face. "So it will be America then."

"Yes."

"Are you pleased? No." They had talked about Africa a great deal, about the house in Ikoyi, Johnson, Charity, the Marina at night, Tarkwa Bay. Now Africa was out. But there was America. How glad she was that she had been taught English!

The generations would begin anew in New York, in America. Friesland would be far away, even farther away than Amsterdam. Only the old gravekeeper in the north would watch over her parents' final resting place now. She would not be able to drive up and weed and set fresh flowers anymore. Perhaps they wouldn't mind too much now because they would have liked Max. They would have said, "A gentleman. One can tell. It is so obvious."

"It doesn't matter," Max was saying. "We're together."

Margrit saw to the final things while Max continued his treatments and retrieved his New York apartment from his tenants and discharged Charity, Johnson and Jimmy.

During those days, the sky grayed quickly and heavy cold winds buffeted the city and the smell of snow wafted through the air. Roger Wilkinson was a frequent visitor. He sat drinking coffee or Genever while Max and Margrit packed and labeled. "Tell my father," Roger said one night, "as discreetly as you can, that I would appreciate a little bread whenever he can send it, dig?"

"Nothing goes over your father's head," Max said. "He's going to kick discretion out of the window. He'll send it to you." Max liked Roger's father. He was a small, light-skinned man who lived on 158th Street. He liked reliving the old days when he had been in the rackets and liked nothing better than to sit in Frank's Restaurant with an old crony and talk about the days when even Negroes were banned from colored joints in Harlem to make the white downtown trade feel more comfortable. Once Mr. Wilkinson had said to Max, "Whenever I think of Roger, I think of a trick he pulled on me once. That thing never leaves me. A bunch of boys had ambushed him down around 140th Street and he came home crying. I sent him back out to get even. He came home the second time grinning. 'What happened?' I asked him. 'I got 'em all. I beat 'em good. They won't be no more trouble.' Years later we were over in Brooklyn watching ol' Newk work a good game and he told me that when he went back out, he hid for a long time, then came home and told me a lie. Never forgot that. Never."

The round of goodbye parties for Max and Margrit ended and the day came when Max awoke in the morning, his vitals heavy with dread, and he knew that that afternoon he and Margrit would be leaving for New York.

346

part FOUR

# 27

MARGRIT looked once more at the clock. It was two. She had left the gallery at noon, sure that Max would be calling her shortly after she got home. What was so important in Leiden that she could not have gone with him this morning? She knew he was very ill. It was in the way he talked, biting every word, and in the way he held his body, as if to ward off pain. At one-thirty Margrit made herself go downstairs, leaving the silent telephone. She went down step by step, slowly, holding the handful of dried bread crumbs which she threw into the canal for the ducks. Then, just as slowly, she ascended the stairs, listening intently for the ringing of the phone which never came. She called Roger, but he wasn't home or was not answering his phone. And she called Max's hotel. Now it was two o'clock and the time weighed heavily upon her, like the taste of brass lingering in the mouth.

For the third time she went to her bedroom and looked at herself in the mirror. She wanted to look good for Max, show him what he was missing. Who could tell what might happen? The hips, to her disgust, were extending to a wide curve, hips he once had dug his fingers into to draw her all the way to him, belly to belly. Her legs were getting heavier and the varicose veins in them more pronounced. Deep lines sat at the corners of her eyes and only folded neatly into the skin when she smiled. How could that be when she hadn't smiled for such a long time, it seemed? She returned to the front room and gazed blankly out at the canal. She had not got used to it after all, as she had thought she would when she returned from New York.

Almost three years. What did it matter if it were two or three months less? Three years with Max, New York, America, and now she was back, still tied to Max in a way she could not explain. Maybe he had more to tell her than he had so far. Some explanation for the breakup. She knew that he knew sorry was not enough; there had to be more and she was going to find out what it was.

The three years had passed so quickly and in such a flurry of people and places, that she hadn't yet recovered. She awoke sometimes at night thinking she could hear the Seventh Avenue subway train racing beneath the building, drowning out Max's snoring; and sometime she thought she could hear the high-pitched, desperate, forlorn calls of the faggots to each other as they emerged from the Riker's diner to go home alone. But awake there were only the soft night sounds of Amsterdam, nothing else, and those made her think of Camus's *La Chute* and the meetings on Amsterdam's bridges.

What had happened? She had been so sure.

A child might have helped, a tan child, but there had been no children. Every month the menses came in spite of the furious, exhausting orgies almost every night, for he had got over the bilharzia, and he saved strength from the job and the book — his last he had said — for her, like a dessert.

After a few months spring came with its pitiful little green shoots to hide some of the dirt of the city, and she started to work in a gallery not far from their apartment. All the paintings had been bad, very bad, but it had been something to do.

Her memory wound around the people they had known: Harry and Charlotte (and Michelle whom she'd seen twice in Paris after her return); Zutkin, an old, lumpy dumpling, a perfect dinner guest who liked to tune up his French on her; Shea, at whom Max smiled secretly when he observed Shea staring at her; Minister Q, whom she knew Max liked and admired; Ted Dallas — handsome man — always held at arm's length by Max . . . so many others to welcome her, to like and love her because they liked or loved her husband.

Late one fine spring night, when they could clearly smell the rivers for the first time and she was feeling settled and very much a part of his life, she kissed him suddenly on a corner where many people were milling around a newsstand for their papers. He (she felt it keenly, like a rebuke) submitted, and they walked on in silence until he said, "Maggie, for Christ's sake, I don't like to be kissed on the street."

"I forgot, Mox."

"Well, try to remember, will you?"

"Why does it make you angry when I kiss you on the street?"

"Never mind. Just don't do it."

Something had drained out of her then and had been replaced by a furtive guilt. She had started to take his arm, but changed her mind.

The weekends they had spent in the woods near Brattleboro or East Hampton, walking and fishing. And taking target practice with a .22 rifle.

"But Mox, you know I don't like guns."

"Learn to shoot it. One day you may be glad you did."

There had been a look in his eyes that urged her to find the answer in her own soul, so he would not have to soil the air with the words. The rifle was in her hands, walnut and steel, and his hands gently set her arms and legs.

"Now, squeeze, squeeeeze . . ."

"Bam!"

"Again."

"Bam!"

"Once more."

"Bam!"

The noise startling the still woods, Max down at the target, smiling. Had he been trying to tell her that one day her life might depend on whether or not she could shoot a gun?

"Squeeeeze, Maggie."

The lessons had been conducted calmly, even a little sadly. "It's a question of dignity, Margrit." That statement when he had finally taken the gun from her, after each lesson, to clean it.

Summer came and with it the trips to St. Thomas, Puerto Rico and Mexico.

St. Thomas with its jungle smell, its iodic odor of the bright, blue sea, bluer than the Mediterranean, the long swims in it, his kissing

*her* in public, feeling her up under the water, a stroking hand pausing lightly on her *poesje,* a flat, gentle hand pressed against her
breasts, a mock horselike mounting in ten feet of water . . . and
dinner that same night, candlelights dancing in the heavy, humid
breeze, the steel drum band playing softly, the air filled with the
scents of a hundred jungle flowers, and her not noticing anything
until he had tipped the table getting up quickly, breaking the top of
his glass and wheeling on a group of American sailors with it in a
single, frightening motion, a group of sailors who were fanning out
around him, sailors there to pick up the women who came alone,
wanting to be picked up . . . and she, with her drink wet and
sticky in her lap, heard the band struggling on, and she did not
know, did not understand what had created this ominous, ugly tableau which dissolved finally with the presence of still more sailors
with a yellow SP on their sleeves.

"What happened, Mox, what were they doing?"

And his eyes: accusing, his eyes incredulous that she had not
seen or heard or understood.

The next morning they did not play in the water together. He
swam alone a long distance out and back and then went to the bar
for a martini. It was not even ten in the morning, Margrit remembered.

Puerto Rico with its brave gloss and terrible slums below the
cliff, facing out to sea, between the forts. They went to the old city
for dinner and stopped at the bar of their hotel for a nightcap, St.
Thomas almost a memory. The bar was filled with people; the
music was cha-cha-cha and behind them the dancers whirled and
posed on the floor. Puerto Rican Spanish was rising and falling
around them. *"Arriba, 'rriba,"* and she heard Max say to her quite
calmly, "Move your stool back just a little, Maggie." And she had
followed his gaze to the drunk American who was gesturing angrily
with his thumb toward them, noticing too that the bartender was
frowning at the drunk, then smiling at them. "It's waxed." Max
again, sliding his foot on the floor, and she just started to understand that Max was watching the American, waiting for him to

make a move, say a word; waiting, Max was, like an executioner who knows the job must be done; she remembered the fright she felt and how she started to pluck at Max's elbow. "Stop that." He was going to place it all in jeopardy — what he was, Max Reddick, what it meant to be Max Reddick — because of a drunk white American.

"He's drunk, Mox."

"Not too drunk to open his big mouth: move over a little."

Her eyes were drawn to his eyes and she did not know them. Desperate, she stood, threaded her way a few feet through the dancers and stopped, obviously waiting. There was one agonizingly long instant when their eyes met, and she had put her mind to leaving the room alone, defeated, when he slid off the stool and came after her.

"Mox, you would have fought him."

"Maggie, I would have killed him."

The hall had tile floors and their heels sounded loud upon them. She felt sick, like vomiting. "I am going to be sick, Mox."

They rushed up in the elevator to their room, in time. I must try harder to understand this thing, she told herself in the bathroom.

She knew if they did not make love that night, the morning would be unpleasant, and somehow he knew it too, and came softly at her, removing the gown, and she embraced him hard and lovingly with her whiteness, opening all of herself, for she wanted him to know in the fullest way that white could love black and did, and they both sensed that the drunk American downstairs had to be erased with love, and they went from one bed to the other without a pause, a mass of black and white, with arms and legs twisted, their breath coming short above the music from downstairs and Margrit remembered crying silently, her tears mixing unnoticed with the perspiration of their bodies and how, when they left the beds, they drifted across the room to the sun parlor where the full moon leaned patiently against the windows while the sea rushed headlong against the seawall a few hundred yards away downstairs, exploding into billions of phosphorescent bubbles; they put out their ciga-

353

rettes and began to make love again in a sun parlor chair, lap-love, and the moonlight stroked their restless, jerking bodies, him in her, her around him, moving in that good rhythm until the little cries came again and the pimples rose on their flesh and the nipples of her breasts shot hard and trembling beneath his kneading hands; the exhausted bodies unhinged; they heard the sea withdraw from the wall; the swollen lips parted and Margrit felt a hot, electric quivering down there, a reaction, as she slid from his lap.

And the morning was quite all right.

Cuernavaca was a better memory with its beamed-ceiling seventeenth-century house hidden from a shabby street. There was a swimming pool set in the center of an acre of well-tended grass, and around the fringes were clusters of roses and mimosa, honeysuckle, bougainvillea and the nameless Mexican flowers that breathe a sweetness through day and night. In Cuernavaca the smiles came again, and the work went well, and their lovemaking, on the eight beds in the giant house, was without desperation. The house was on a hill, and through the vines on the fence they could look down on the city from three sides, see the ragged buses droning up the other steep hills, hear the soldiers in the barracks across the way singing and shouting. Everyone in the town talked of a writer named Malcolm Lowry and Max smiled and said: "I'll bet that cat didn't know *half* these people who say they knew him. Poor bastard; he could have used some knowing." Max hated to leave the place. On the plane the tension started to come once more, his quiet, angry tension that frightened her so, but she could see him fighting it off and she was content.

Near their first anniversary Max bought a new rifle; he already had four guns. This did not disturb her as much as his matter-of-fact manner. That puzzled and upset her, but she could not bring herself to speak of the weapons which, granted, he used when he went hunting. At the same time, nightly, she witnessed on television the humiliations of the black Americans throughout the country; acid was thrown into the swimming places they tried to integrate; electric cattle prods were put to their bodies when they sat at lunch

354

counters and participated in other demonstrations. It seemed to Margrit that what was *happening* provided the connection to what Max was *doing*. She wondered if other black men were silently going about as he was, hunting regularly ("Brushing up the old eye, baby"), buying guns. In Holland it had been very easy to urge that violence be met with violence. But, being in America, it was somehow different . . .

A few months later, plagued by his increasing sensitivity to the way people looked at them when they were together, his purchases of boxes of ammunition he could never use up in three seasons of hunting, let alone one, she timidly asked: "Mox, what is it all about?"

"What, Maggie?"

"The guns, your touchiness, the target shooting."

"I'm simply trying to keep my head, but these bastards are trying to make me lose it."

"Your mind is closed to me. I feel so distant from you sometimes, as if I were one of *them*. I feel left out and that something terrible is about to happen. Let us return to Holland, Mox. I'm afraid."

He took a long time answering.

"Dear Margrit. I had hoped you'd understand by now. There's us and there's them. Us means me because I'm black, and it means you because I love you, and it means all the people who want to feel as we do about each other, and all the people who've never had a chance to feel anything. Things are changing so fast. Things are getting very nasty and things happen more quickly and viciously and everyone says they couldn't see them coming. I won't lie; I see them coming. You remember St. Thomas and Puerto Rico. Those are the small things you are involved in every day if you're a black man and your wife is white. They just put it to you that way; all they really want to do is to beat your ass good, but they don't know that when they want that, they want your life, because things have changed and nothing is going to stop with an ass-beating anymore; it's the whole thing or nothing —"

355

"Mox —"

"Let me finish, darling. I want to finish. I am sorry. I don't mean for these people to do this to us; I won't let them and this is the only way I know. *Nothing else has worked.* There seems to be no turning back from this need to apply force. They are at you and they understand nothing about the position they've put you in.

"The law in this country, just like in most countries, is for the privileged and if you're white in America, you are privileged. We hope for the law to protect us, but it doesn't. I've seen the White House break laws, and I am not about to console myself that if brought before the court for being in a street fight, I can count on a fair dispensation of justice. The other side has guns, Maggie, and power, everything serious killers should have to do their jobs. Without law on my side, I become the law; my guns are the law, and the only law people in any nation live by is the law of force or the threat of force. Love don't do what a good ass-kickin' can.

"I've worked too long and too hard and seen too much and know too much to go quietly if and when they come for me. I'm not Dutch, baby, I'm an American. What business do I have in Holland with Negroes who won't face up to what's really happening here? When you first started to learn to shoot, I hoped there was something in your European existence that would help you understand how necessary it is to learn to defend one's self. Nine million people were murdered because they did not defend themselves, more people than in the armies and civilian forces that killed them. Now, that doesn't make any kind of sense, does it?

"It won't be like that here. At least, not in the beginning. Some of us have learned some hard lessons from what happened in Europe, and I mean black and white. We have also learned some hard lessons from our own country. I know civil rights leaders who talk about guns and island hideouts, privately of course. They know about the enemy and if the enemy knows this, knows we are in another time in which we will kill back or kill *first,* he will move slowly, if he moves at all. The military call this deterrent strength. I mean no harm with these guns, Maggie. I can't begin to tell you

356

what has happened inside me to make me even think like this. But I have some measure of peace now, because I can answer the white man's choice for the future: death or peace. I will only harm him if I know he means to harm me. I think he does."

"Did you know this when we married?"

"Yes, I knew it."

His words, enormous, ghastly, elusive, animal. But he seemed calm and sure sitting there, watching her anxiously.

"All this talk shocks me. It frightens me, too, Mox. I did not know —"

"What did you know then?" His voiced cracked out at her.

"I —"

" 'I,' *hell*, Maggie! I'm telling you the way it is and you're talking about shock. *Don't you know who you married?* Did you forget everything we ever talked about?"

"That was in Holland," she fought back. "It did not seem *real*. And we never talked like *this* —"

"You didn't really listen, then. You watch the news every night. What do you think? Those poor colored people? Isn't it terrible? Is that what you think, Margrit? Honey, come *on!* You know better. I *taught* you better. This ain't Holland, baby, this is the YOO ESS AY, where niggers have had it with getting their heads beat, and I'm a nigger! Do you *hear* me? And you're married to a nigger unless you don't want to be any longer. That's really all there is to it, Maggie, right?"

Her voice came out desperately. "But life has to go on. I *am* married to you; we *do* have each other. You are an uncommon man, therefore, there must be other ways for this peace."

"There is and this is it. What looks like death is life and what for so long looked like life was death. Baby, they don't want us to have each other. The guns are here because we have *got* to have each other."

She flung herself up, crying and screaming. "THAT IS SO PARA-NOID, WHAT YOU ARE SAYING AND DOING AND THINKING!"

His eyes alone seemed to smile at her, tenderly as at a strange

357

child passing. "Margrit, in the twenties and thirties when Europeans came here to become Americans, they had only to say 'nigger' and they got their papers. In the fifties and sixties the language became a little more polite; those people had only to say 'you're paranoid.' Congratulations, now you really are an American."

*She had fled, and crying entered that labyrinth, the ugly, dark middle of it, uncertain, lost, but from where she had to commence her search for him. She ran toward every illusion of light; she tapped for hollowness in the walls behind which there might be a lever to pull and suddenly flood the interiors with blinding light so she could see him and lead him out; she trod the moss-covered floors and touched wet, dank walls, and nasty little animals slithered away from her. Once she stepped on something large and it made a long hissssssing sound, and she ran past it, screaming. Then one day, she assumed it was a day, for there was neither day nor night in that place, only the remembered period of twenty-four hours, a day, she thought she heard tapping on another wall and a voice, hoarse with much use. She tapped and cried out. The tapping on the other side became louder and she heard his voice just as another little beast slid between her fingers toward the floor:*

*— Margrit, Maggie, baby, it's me, Max! Keep to your left, Maggie, keep going left, baby, the heart-side. Can you hear me? Move to your left. I am moving to the left, the heart-side —*

*— Yes my schatje, I hear you. I am moving to the left also, to the heart-side —*

"It's here," he said with a smile, and hefted the galleys in his hand. He kissed her. "This is when you finally begin to feel as though you've written a novel."

There was bright sun, and spring once more. She sat beside him while he opened the envelope and unfolded the curled pages of the proofs.

"Max, not really, now. You can't mean there will never be another book. It is your life; it is our life. What would we do? You will not work for *Pace* forever?"

"Well, I think I mean it."

"Darling, you tease me too much."

"Hey, Maggie."

"Yes?"

"Let's rip off a little, what say, baby?"

"Ugh, such an ugly picture you make. Right now?"

"Yes, right now."

"But dinner will be late."

"So?"

"So."

Later she asked, "What does the good Dr. Woodson have to say?"

"Oh, I have to go back."

"But why?"

"I hadn't flushed myself out very well."

"Poor Mox. Soon all the troubles will be over with your little behind and you will be quite all right again."

"Promise?"

"My darling, I promise everything good for us."

One day he came home in high agitation and she believed it had to do with what was happening in the South, Birmingham and other places; it was 1963. There followed a period of moving, doing things, going places and seeing people. He kissed her in public after that time, she remembered. In the small hours of the morning, she would awake to find him at his typewriter, as if in a frenzy to hold on to every passing moment. So often when she spoke to him, his mind was far away, and she had to lead him back gently, as if afraid to wake a sleepwalker. That period sloped suddenly down into one when he woke up and stared at the ceiling, then announced that he wasn't going to work, to hell with *Pace*. Sometimes he left before breakfast and she knew he was not going to work, and she would not see him until late in the evening, martinis reeking on his breath. He spent each Sunday cleaning his guns, al-

359

though they didn't need it. Before them on television danced the police dogs, police and Negroes; fire hoses gushed and Margrit felt lost again, deserted.

"Mox, not again, not with those guns and that look about you. I can't stand any more of it. I won't stand for it. I hate it all, all of it, those stupid whites and those taunting blacks. I am sick of it!"

His eyes seemed to have made a noise when he looked at her through that shocked silence that had produced her short, bitter tirade. *Click,* the eyes seemed to have said.

"I'm sorry, Maggie."

He seemed this time to be giving way to her, leading her on, encouraging her to have it out, all of it, finally, and she shouted, "Sorry be dommed! Look what's happening to us again. *Look,* I tell you! Aren't you man enough to stand above this nonsense?" She knew she should not have said that.

He spoke quietly and simply, without any special tone in his voice. "It's not nonsense. I've told you that."

She stared at the guns arranged neatly on the floor, newspapers under them, and suddenly she hated the smell of the gun oil. Their eyes locked across the weapons which were so beautiful in a way, lying there mute and for the moment harmless. She bent quickly and grabbed up a shotgun while he watched her, and beat the stock into the floor several times while the apartment reverberated with the blows. The trigger guard, when she stopped, panting, sprung loose. Margrit was all the more at a loss because — *she had seen it* — there had been for a second a very tender and loving thing in her husband's eyes. Now it was gone.

"That's enough," he said, still quietly.

"It's *not* enough, it's just the beginning."

"You're wrong, Maggie. It's the end."

"Then, dommit, *let* it be the end. This stupid place with whites and blacks at each other's throats, I can't *stand* it! You are right, Mox. It is the end. Agreed?"

"Agreed."

She whirled out of the room and when she got to the bedroom, slammed the door. "Enough of this crazy land," she hissed at herself in the mirror, "where everyone speaks in superlatives but exists in diminutives. Shhhittt! on it. It can go to hell!!"

A big protest march had been planned for Washington the day Margrit left New York. She had stayed on in New York several months after their break-up, waiting for what, she didn't know. She was not defeated, merely tired and unbearably worn. Max had moved out of the apartment the Sunday they had the fight; he would reclaim it today, when he got back from Washington. Huh! *If* he got back. The way this country was going, Washington would be going up in smoke by the time she was midway over the Atlantic.

He had called in the morning to say goodbye. Nothing more, just goodbye. After that she cried; he'd always said she cried too easily, but she got to the airport.

She opened the New York *Century* on the plane. Everything I touch is Max, she thought. On page three a headline read:

AFRICAN DIPLOMAT FOUND DEAD IN SWISS HOTEL
Jaja Enzkwu, 55, First Minister to the Nigerian Federal Cabinet, was reported dead . . .

Margrit turned to another page. Enzkwu? She did not recall ever hearing of him.

In Amsterdam, Margrit got up and called the American hotel again. Max had not returned. She called Roger once more, but there was no answer. She pulled on a pair of white gloves, looked at herself once again, then went downstairs. The hotel was about ten blocks away. When she arrived she checked at the desk, but Max still had not come. She selected a sidewalk table near the hotel entrance and ordered a Campari. She put on sunglasses. From where she was sitting, she would be sure to see him when he returned.

# 28

YES, Max thought. I knew Jaja Enzkwu, eagle-faced, hot-eyed Jaja with his sweating, pussy-probing fingers and perfumed agbadas; I knew him.

Max glanced at his watch again. Two o'clock. He wondered what Margrit was doing back in Amsterdam on such a beautiful day. He knew what Jaja was doing: feeding the bugs back in Onitsha where he had been sent in a box, after that deadly rendezvous with Baroness Huganot in Basel that day.

So much had happened that day, the day of the March on Washington. Margrit had left shortly after he called her. Then he had taken a plane to Washington. Du Bois had died in Ghana the night before, and so had Jaja, leaving behind an opened magnum of Piper-Heidsieck, a half-eaten partridge and a startled, voluptuous, eager-to-be-ravished Baroness. But Washington had been the place to be that day. There you could forget that the cancer tests were positive — it was malignant — and that you were going into cobalt treatment soon; you could forget with more than a quarter million people surging around you.

Max flipped up the next page of the letter and when he finished, he shook as if with a sudden chill, and yet the shaking hand had nothing to do with his illness; it was the letter itself. With trembling hands he lit a cigarette.

No, he told himself. I have not read what I just read. This cannot be. No, it's me, the way I'm thinking, the way I'm reading. He closed his eyes hard and held them for a long time. Then he opened them to reread the entire letter once again:

Dear Max:

You are there, Max? It is you reading this, right? I mean, even dead, which I must be for you to have these papers *and* be alone in the com-

362

pany of Michelle, I'd feel like a damned fool if someone else was reading them. I hope these lines find you in good shape and with a full life behind you, because, chances are, now that you've started reading, all that is way, way behind you, baby.

I'm sorry to get you into this mess, but in your hands right now is the biggest story you'll ever have. Big and dangerous. Unbelievable. Wow. But, it's a story with consequences the editors of *Pace* may be unwilling to pay. And you, Max, baby, come to think of it, may not even get the chance to cable the story. Knowing may kill you, just as knowing killed me and a few other people you'll meet in this letter. Uh-uh! Can't quit now! It was too late when you opened the case. This is a rotten way to treat a friend. Yes, friend. We've had good and bad times together; we've both come far. I remember that first day we met at Zutkin's. We both saw something we liked in each other. What? I don't know, but it never mattered to me. Our friendship worked; it had value; it lasted. I've run out of acquaintances and other friends who never were the friend you were. So, even if this is dangerous for you — and it is — I turn to you in friendship and in the hope that you can do with this information what I could not. Quite frankly, I don't know how I got into this thing. It just happened, I guess, and like any contemporary Negro, like a ghetto Jew of the 1930's in Europe, I couldn't believe it was happening, even when the pieces fell suddenly into place. Africa . . .

God, Max, what doesn't start with Africa? What a history still to be told! The scientists are starting to say life began there. I'm no scientist. I don't know. But I do know that this letter you're reading had its origins with what happened there. Let me go back to the beginning. I doubt if you've heard of Alliance Blanc. In 1958 Guinea voted to leave the French Family of Nations, and at once formed a federation with Kwame Nkrumah, or Ghana, whichever you prefer. The British and French were shaken. How could countries only two minutes ago colonies spring to such political maturity? Would the new federation use pounds or francs? The national banks of both countries were heavily underwriting the banking systems of the two countries. There would be a temporary devaluation of both pounds and francs, whether the new federation minted new money or not. More important — and this is what really rocked Europe — if the federation worked, how many new, independent African states would follow suit? *Then,* what would

happen to European interests in Africa after independence and federation? Was it *really* conceivable that all of Africa might one day unite,
Cape to Cairo, Abidjan to Addis? Alliance Blanc said *Yes!* If there
were a United States of Africa, a cohesiveness among the people —
300,000,000 of them — should not Europeans anticipate the possibility
of trouble, sometime when the population had tripled, for example?
Couldn't Africa become another giant, like China, with even more
hatred for the white West? It was pure guilt over what Europeans had
done to Africa and the Africans that made them react in such a violent
fashion to African independence.

The white man, as we well know, has never been of so single an
accord as when maltreating black men. And he has had an amazing
historical rapport in Africa, dividing it up arbitrarily across tribal and
language boundaries. That rapport in plundering Africa never existed
and never will when it requires the same passion for getting along with
each other in Europe. But you know all this. All I'm trying to say is
that, where the black man is concerned, the white man will bury differences that have existed between them since the beginning of time, and
come together. How goddamn different this would have been if there
had been no Charles Martel at Tours in 732!

The Alliance first joined together not in the Hague, not in Geneva,
not in London, Versailles or Washington, but in Munich, a city top-
heavy with monuments and warped history. Present were representatives from France, Great Britain, Belgium, Portugal, Australia, Spain,
Brazil, South Africa. The United States of America was also present.
There were white observers from most of the African countries that
appeared to be on their way to independence. The representation at
first, with a few exceptions, was quasi-official. But you know very well
that a quasi-official body can be just as effective as an official one; in
fact, it is often better to use the former.

I don't have to tell you that the meetings, then and subsequently,
were held in absolute secrecy. They were moved from place to place —
Spain, Portugal, France, Brazil and in the United States, up around
Saranac Lake — Dreiser's setting for *An American Tragedy*, that neck
of the woods, remember? America, with the largest black population
outside Africa, had the most need of mandatory secrecy. Things were
getting damned tense following the Supreme Court decision to desegregate schools in 1954.

364

The disclosure of America's membership in Alliance Blanc would have touched off a racial cataclysm — but America went far, far beyond the evils the Alliance was perpetuating, but more of this later. For the moment, let me consider the Alliance.

African colonies were still becoming independent. Federations were formed only to collapse a few weeks later, like the Guinea-Ghana combine. Good men and bad were assassinated indiscriminately; coups were a dime a dozen. Nkrumah in West Africa vied with Selassie in East Africa for leadership of the continent. The work of the Alliance agents — setting region against region and tribe against tribe, just as the colonial masters had done — was made easy by the rush to power on the part of a few African strongmen. Thus, the panic mentality that had been the catalyst for the formation of the Alliance seemed to have been tranquilized. There was diplomacy as usual, independence as usual. What, after all, did Europeans have to fear after that first flash of black unity? The Alliance became more leisurely, less belligerent, more sure that it had time, and above all, positive now that Africa was not a threat to anyone but itself. Alliance agents flowed leisurely through Africa now, and Western money poured in behind them.

From a belligerent posture, the Alliance went to one based on economics. Consider that 15 percent of Nigeria's federal budget comes from offshore oil brought in by Dutch, British, Italian, French and American oil companies; consider that the 72 percent of the world's cocoa which Africa produces would rot if the West did not import it. Palm oil, groundnuts, minerals, all for the West. Can you imagine, man, what good things could happen to Africans, if they learned to consume what they produce? It did not take the Europeans long to discover that their stake in Africa as "friends" rather than masters was more enormous than they could have imagined. Only naked desperation demanded that Spain and Portugal stay in Africa; the Iberian Peninsula hasn't been the same since the Moors and Jews left it in the fifteenth century. Time? It was the Alliance's most formidable ally.

In South Africa, the spark of revolt flickered, sputtered and now is dead. The Treason Trials killed it; oppression keeps murdering it, and those who say the spark is still alive, those successive schools of nattily tailored South African nationalists, who plunge through Paris, London and New York raising money for impossible rebellions, lie. The paradox, Max, is that, denied freedom, the black man lives better in South

Africa than anywhere else on the continent; the average African. The bigshots — with their big houses and long cars, their emulation of the colonial masters — do all right. My friend Genet said it all in *Les Noirs*.

The Alliance worked. God, how it worked! And Africans themselves, dazzled by this new contraption the white man was giving them, independence, helped. Lumumba, disgracefully educated by the Belgians, was a victim of the Alliance; Olympio, dreaming dreams of federation, was another. Nkrumah and Touré have lasted for so long because their trust in the white man never was, and their trust in their own fellows only a bit deeper seated.

The Congo mess served as a valuable aid to the Alliance: it could test the world's reaction to black people in crisis. The Alliance was pleased to observe that the feeling in the West was, "Oh, well, they're only niggers, anyhow."

I could have foreseen that reaction; you could have foreseen it; any black man could have anticipated it. But, then, "niggers" are embattled everywhere, ain't they, baby? Asian "niggers," South American "niggers" . . . But let a revolt occur in East Germany and watch the newsprint fly! Let another Hungarian revolution take place and see the white nations of the world open their doors to take in refugees — Hungarian Freedom Fighters, yeah! Who takes in blacks, Pakistanis, Vietnamese, Koreans, Chinese, who?

But the picture began to change. It was quite clear that the Europeans had Africa well under control — and that was all they cared about. America, sitting on a bubbling black cauldron, felt that it had to map its own contingency plans for handling 22 million black Americans in case they became unruly; in case they wanted everything Freedom Fighters got just by stepping off the boat. So, America prepared King Alfred and submitted it to the Alliance, just as the Alliance European members had submitted their plans for operations in Africa to the Americans. King Alfred in its original form, called for sending American Negroes to Africa, and this had to be cleared by the Europeans. The Europeans vetoed that plan; they remembered what excitement Garvey had caused in Africa. The details of King Alfred are in the case, and it is truly hot stuff. All this Alliance business is pretty pallid shit compared to what the Americans have come up with.

I should tell you that it was an African who discovered the Alliance and in the process came upon King Alfred. Who? Jaja Enzkwu, that cockhound, that's who. He stumbled on the Alliance the second year of its existence, while he was in Spain, which as you know has turned out to be a very hospitable place for ex-heads of African countries on the lam. Enzkwu didn't know what was going on; he simply sensed something, seeing a gathering of British, American, Brazilian, Portuguese and South Africans at San Sebastián in winter. This was where the Alliance held its second meeting. I'll tell you about Jaja. Any halfway good-looking white woman can make a fool of him (which was what was happening, for him to be at a summer resort in winter), but he doesn't trust a gathering of more than a single white man. About the white man, Enzkwu has a nose for trouble. But you know Jaja.

Jaja died as he had lived, chasing white pussy. As soon as his nation became independent in 1960, using the various embassies and consulates his government had established in the Park Avenues, Park Lanes and Georges V's of the world, yes, those places, with the long, black limousines in front, chauffeured by large but deferential white men, those places with the waiting rooms filled with African art, Jaja started gathering material on the Alliance. He amassed all the information you have at hand.

How did they get to Jaja? It's a white man's world — so far. He had to hire white operatives, of course, to get to Alliance Blanc. A couple of these, Jaja's beloved Frenchmen, I believe, checked back through several white people fronting for Enzkwu, but, at last, they discovered old black Jaja sitting there behind it all. A black man, interesting. The bastards then sold *this* information to the Alliance. At this point, old Jaja, sitting behind an eighteen-foot desk, was cooling it, thinking he had it all covered. He planned to make use of the information. Like so many people, he had begun his investigations with a sincere desire to protect his country. But another consideration rose very, very quickly. He could use the information, to be released at a propitious time, to prove that the Nigerian premier, and African leaders generally, had failed to protect their people from the new colonialism. Jaja planned to gather all of Africa under a single ruler one day. That ruler was to be Jaja Enzkwu.

Panic in Washington ensued when it was discovered that Jaja not only had information on the Alliance, but on King Alfred, the contingency plan to detain and ultimately rid America of its Negroes. Mere American membership in the Alliance would have been sufficient

367

to rock America, but King Alfred would have made Negroes realize, finally and angrily, that all the new moves — the laws and committees — to gain democracy for them were fraudulent, just as Minister Q and the others had been saying for years. Your own letter to me days after you left the White House only underscored what so many Negro leaders believed. The one alternative left for Negroes would be not only to seek that democracy withheld from them as quickly and as violently as possible, but to fight for their very survival. King Alfred, as you will see, leaves no choice.

The European members of the Alliance were not as concerned as America about the leak. In fact, if King Alfred was revealed and racial violence exploded in America, America's position as world leader would be seriously undermined. There were members in the Alliance who wished for this. The danger in Africa being nullified, the white man became divided. In the U. S., the situation had worsened. There had been that second boy at Ole Miss; the dogs and firehoses in Birmingham; kids blown up in church; little brush-fire riots that came and went across the country, like wind stroking a wheat field. Minister Q's voice was now large indeed. The March on Washington appeared to have been the last time the Negroes were peacefully willing to ask for and take any old handout.

The Alliance had not counted on the efficiency of the Central Intelligence Agency, which had placed agents in Nigeria within days of receiving the report that Jaja had information. Concealing King Alfred became the top priority assignment of the National Security Council and the CIA. Jaja was not killed at once for two reasons: first, the agents were unable to ascertain where he kept the papers. Second, on a trip to Paris, the agents made a fake attempt on his life to make him go for the papers. But this only resulted in arousing Jaja's curiosity, and he began backtracking through his former operatives and discovered that the Americans knew that he knew. Then Jaja started to deal. He'd give over the papers and keep his mouth shut, if the Americans gave him Nigeria. The U. S. had no choice but to agree, when it had the opportunity. It would take time. All right, Jaja said. But not *too* much time.

Jaja moved, ate, slept and crapped with an army of bodyguards. He had only to put it out that the Hausas in the north were after him, and every Ibo in the eastern region understood.

Enzkwu came to see me two days before your March on Washington. He was thin and drawn and quite subdued. Almost a year, I learned later, had passed since making the deal with the U. S. and nothing had come of it. Even Charlotte did not bring out that old gleam to his eyes, as her presence has done for many of my friends. Jaja and I had dinner that night, surrounded by some of the biggest Ibos I've ever seen. After, a car followed us, but it was his and was filled with his men. We didn't talk too much in his hotel. We were in one room and his guards in another. Every five minutes, one of the guards would knock on the door and ask something in Ibo, and Jaja would reply in Ibo. It was always the same question and the same answer.

Jaja was on his way to Switzerland and he gave me the key to a safe deposit box in a Paris bank and told me to get what was in it, if he did not return from Switzerland. I was puzzled and curious about his mood, but I took the key without asking questions. Of course, he was killed. I hustled to the bank and what I found was this information you now have found, plus a letter from Jaja, similar to my letter which you are now reading. The material fascinated me. I'd spent so much of my life writing about the evil machinations of Mr. Charlie without really *knowing* the truth, as this material made me know it. It was spread out before me, people, places and things. I became mired in them, and I *knew* now that the way black men live on this earth was no accident. And yet, my mind kept telling me that Jaja's death was a coincidence, a mere coincidence. I could not believe that I, too, soon would be dead. One looks at death, always moves toward it, but until the last denies its existence. I was trapped by my contempt for everything African. I made the bodyguards just a part of the African spectacle. I gripped the material, I hugged it to my chest, for now I would know; if they killed me, I would know that this great evil did exist, indeed, thrived. And Dr. Faustus came to my mind. The Americans killed Jaja, obviously because they ran out of patience, and because they thought they could find the material without him.

I didn't say anything to you when you came through Paris on your way to East Africa because I had not seen Jaja then.

It is spring. Strange, now that life seems to quicken a bit, and you can see people smiling more, and the trees starting to bloom, I feel tired, going downhill. I am sure the Americans are on to me. Perhaps the French keep them off, not wanting trouble to becloud De Gaulle's new

369

image. At least that's what I think, and that's why I haven't made any trips outside France. I thought of giving it to the Russians, but would they even accept it from me? Even if they did, can't you see the West laughing it off as another Russian hoax, even Negroes?

But there was America itself. You and *Pace*. You must have access to outlets where this material would do the most good. The choice is yours and yours alone as to whether you want to wreck the nation or not. My opinion? No, Max, it's up to you. Think of the irony: the very nation that most wants to keep the information secret, would be the very one to release it!

A personal item: Charlotte seems to have found a strange tolerance for me these days. I think she knows about the material. And she has found out about Michelle and me, at last. How, I don't know, exactly, but I think American agents have told her, to enlist her aid.

*In fact, Max, old trusted friend, everybody knows everything now, past and present.*

I am getting this material to Michelle tonight. She will get it to you even if she has to swim to New York. I know of no one else. And perhaps this is a sign, the ultimate sign, that I am very tired. I can only hope that no harm comes to her.

Another item, old buddy. Tomorrow I'm having lunch with a young man I understand you've met. His name is Edwards, and he's quit Uncle Sam's foreign service to write a novel about it. I can't resist these youngsters who come to see me, to sit at the feet of the father, so to speak. I guess I'll never outgrow it. I suppose you're next in line to be father . . .

Harry

Shock, gracious, pain-absorbing shock came at once and lessened the hurt and surprise. Max, reacting normally for the moment, lit another cigarette, picked through and carefully read Enzkwu's papers.

Yes, there was explosive material here. Enough to unsettle every capital city in the West; enough to force the Africans to cut ties with Europe at once and worry about the consequences later; enough to send black Brazilians surging out of their *favelas* and *barrios* to inundate the sleek beach places of the whites. Wherever white men had been involved with black men, Enzkwu's photostats disclosed a clear and unrelenting danger. Recorded in cold black type were lists of statesmen and diplomats, the records of their deeds, what they planned to do, when, where, why and to whom. The list of people dead, Max knew, and therefore murdered, if their names appeared in Enzkwu's papers, included the residents of four continents. African airfields equipped for the handling of jets and props, along with radio and power stations, the number of men in the army of each country, plus a military critique of those armies, were set down here.

Now Max's hand held another numbered packet, but above the number were the words: THE UNITED STATES OF AMERICA — KING ALFRED. Slowly, he pulled out the sheaf of photostats. So, this is King Alfred, Alfred the Great. He mused, Why is it called King Alfred? Then he saw the answer footnoted at the bottom of the first page.

## KING ALFRED*

In the event of widespread and continuing and coordinated racial disturbances in the United States, KING ALFRED, at the discretion of the President, is to be put into action immediately.

### PARTICIPATING FEDERAL AGENCIES

National Security Council  
Central Intelligence Agency  
Federal Bureau of Investigation  

Department of Justice  
Department of Defense  
Department of Interior  

### PARTICIPATING STATE AGENCIES
(Under Federal Jurisdiction)

National Guard Units                                        State Police

### PARTICIPATING LOCAL AGENCIES
(Under Federal Jurisdiction)

City Police                                                County Police

* 849-899 (?) King of England; directed translation from the Latin of the *Anglo-Saxon Chronicle*.

## Memo: National Security Council

Even before 1954, when the Supreme Court of the United States of America declared unconstitutional separate educational and recreational facilities, racial unrest and discord had become very nearly a part of the American way of life. But that way of life was repugnant to most Americans. Since 1954, however, that unrest and discord have broken out into widespread violence which increasingly have placed the peace and stability of the nation in dire jeopardy. This violence has resulted in loss of life, limb and property, and has cost the taxpayers of this nation billions of dollars. And the end is not yet in sight. This same violence has raised the tremendously grave question as to whether the races can ever live in peace with each other. Each passing month has brought new intelligence that, despite new laws passed to alleviate the condition of the Minority, the Minority still is not satisfied. Demonstrations and rioting have become a part of the familiar scene. Troops have been called out in city after city across the land, and our image as a world leader severely damaged. Our enemies press closer, seeking the advantage, possibly at a time during one of these outbreaks of violence. The Minority has adopted an almost military posture to gain its objectives, which are not clear to most Americans. It is expected, therefore, that, when those objectives are denied the Minority, racial war must be considered inevitable. When that Emergency comes, we must expect the total involvement of all 22 million members of the Minority, men, women and children, for once this project is launched, its goal is to terminate, once and for all, the Minority threat to the whole of the American society, and, indeed, the Free World.

Chairman, National Security Council

## Preliminary Memo: Department of Interior

Under KING ALFRED, the nation has been divided into 10 Regions (See accompanying map).

In case of Emergency, Minority members will be evacuated from the cities by federalized national guard units, local and state police and, if necessary, by units of the Regular Armed Forces, using public and military transportation, and detained in nearby military installations until a further course of action has been decided.

372

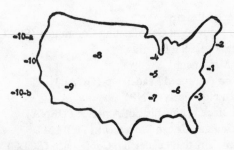

1 — Capital region
2 — Northeast region
3 — Southeast region
4 — Great Lakes Region
5 — South central region
6 — Deep South region
7 — Deep South region II
8 — Great Plains, Rocky Mountain region
9 — Southwest region
10 — a, b — West Coast region

No attempt will be made to seal off the Canadian and Mexican borders.

Secretary, Department of Interior

*Combined Memo: Department of Justice*
                    *Federal Bureau of Investigation*
                    *Central Intelligence Agency*

There are 12 major Minority organizations and all are familiar to the 22 million. Dossiers have been compiled on the leaders of the organizations, and can be studied in Washington. The material contained in many of the dossiers, and our threat to reveal that material, has considerably held in check the activities of some of the leaders. Leaders who do not have such usable material in their dossiers have been approached to take Government posts, mostly as ambassadors and primarily in African countries. The promise of these positions also has materially contributed to a temporary slow-down of Minority activities. However, we do not expect these slow-downs to be of long duration, because there are always new and dissident elements joining these organizations, with the potential power to replace the old leaders. All organizations and their leaders are under constant, 24-hour surveillance. The organizations are:

373

1 — The Black Muslims
2 — Student Nonviolent Coordinating Committee (SNCC)
3 — Congress of Racial Equality
4 — Uhuru Movement
5 — Group on Advanced Leadership (GOAL)
6 — Freedom Now Party (FNP)
7 — United Black Nationalists of America (UBNA)
8 — The New Pan-African Movement (TNPAM)
9 — Southern Christian Leadership Conference (SCLC)
10 — The National Urban League (NUL)
11 — The National Association for the Advancement of Colored People (NAACP)
12 — Committee on Racial and Religious Progress (CORARP)

NOTE: At the appropriate time, to be designated by the President, the leaders of some of these organizations are to be detained ONLY WHEN IT IS CLEAR THAT THEY CANNOT PREVENT THE EMERGENCY, working with local public officials during the first critical hours. All other leaders are to be detained at once. Compiled lists of Minority leaders have been readied at the National Data Computer Center. It is necessary to use the Minority leaders designated by the President in much the same manner in which we use Minority members who are agents with CENTRAL and FEDERAL, and we cannot, until there is no alternative, reveal KING ALFRED in all its aspects. Minority members of Congress will be unseated at once. This move is not without precedent in American history.

Attorney General

*Preliminary Memo: Department of Defense*
This memo is being submitted in lieu of a full report from the Joint Chiefs of Staff. That report is now in preparation. There will be many cities where the Minority will be able to put into the street a superior number of people with a desperate and dangerous will. He will be a formidable enemy, for he is bound to the Continent by heritage and knows that political asylum will not be available to him in other countries. The greatest concentration of the Minority is in the Deep South, the Eastern seaboard, the Great Lakes region and the West Coast.

374

While the national population exceeds that of the Minority by more than ten times, we must realistically take into account the following:

1 — An estimated 40-50 percent of the white population will not, for various reasons, engage the Minority during an Emergency.

2 — American Armed Forces are spread around the world. A breakout of war abroad means fewer troops at home to handle the Emergency.

3 — Local law enforcement officials must contain the Emergency until help arrives, though it may mean fighting a superior force. New York City, for example, has a 25,000-man police force, but there are about one million Minority members in the city.

We are confident that the Minority could hold any city it took for only a few hours. The lack of weapons, facilities, logistics — all put the Minority at a final disadvantage.

Since the Korean War, this Department has shifted Minority members of the Armed Forces to areas where combat is most likely to occur, with the aim of eliminating, through combat, as many combat-trained Minority servicemen as possible. Today the ratio of Minority member combat deaths in Vietnam, where they are serving as "advisers," is twice as high as the Minority population ratio to the rest of America. Below is the timetable for KING ALFRED as tentatively suggested by the JCS who recommend that the operation be made over a period of eight hours:

1. Local police and Minority leaders in action to head off the Emergency.

2. Countdown to eight hours begins at the moment the President determines the Emergency to be:

    A. National
    B. Coordinated
    C. Of Long Duration                    8th Hour

3. County police join local police.            7th
4. State police join county and local forces.     6th
5. Federal marshals join state, county and local forces.   5th
6. National Guards federalized, held in readiness.    4th
7. Regular Armed Forces alerted, take up positions;

Minority troops divided and detained, along with all
white sympathizers, under guard.                                    3rd
8. All Minority leaders, national and local, detained.               2nd
9. President addresses Minority on radio-television,
gives it one hour to end the Emergency.                              1st
10. All units under regional commands into the Emergency. o

*'O' Committee Report:*
Survey shows that, during a six-year period, Production created 9,000,-
000 objects, or 1,500,000 each year. Production could not dispose of
the containers, which proved a bottleneck. However, that was almost
20 years ago. We suggest that vaporization techniques be employed to
overcome the Production problems inherent in KING ALFRED.

Secretary of Defense

Max smoked and read, read and smoked until his mouth began
to taste like wool and when he finally pushed King Alfred from
him, he felt exhausted, as if he had been running beneath a gigantic, unblinking eye that had watched his every move and determined just when movement should stop.

Yeah. Jaja had done his work well. He could have embarrassed
and startled a lot of people, blacks and whites, but you have to
weed a garden for the flowers to grow. Those dossiers, he knew
pretty much what was in them. Well, he had known it; there are
always dues to pay. A smoldering anger coursed through Max's
stomach. Yes, those leaders clearly had left themselves vulnerable,
vulnerable for the hunters who, for a generation and more, sought
Communists with such vehemence that they skillfully obscured the
growth and power of fascism. How black skins stirred fascists! Perhaps because it was the most identifiable kind of skin; you didn't
have to wait until you got up close to see whether a nose was
hooked or not; a black skin you could see for a block away. And
in the face of the revelations in Jaja's papers, Harry and Jaja both,
made giddy by the presence of that massive, killing evil, had dared
to toy with it; had dared to set their pitiable little egos down before

376

that hideous juggernaut. And they had hoped to live. That hope had revealed their inability to accurately measure what was readily measurable. Jaja for greed, and you, Harry, it's just starting to come. They didn't let their minds go out.

They did not let their minds go out to picture the instability of what seems static; they did not see planets colliding with each other, or picture Sahara or Kalahari as lakes, or picture plains where the Alps, Andes and Rockies now stand; nor did they picture oceans above the sands that crunch softly beneath the feet in the sweet-smelling paths of the Maine or Vermont woods. No, they did not picture the extinction of man and beast and places. If they had, *then* they could see four million dead because they themselves, like the later nine million, refused to see evil rearing up before them, quite discernible, quite measurable. Man is nature, nature man, and all crude and raw, stinking, vicious, evil. And holding that evil lightly because the collective mind refuses to recall the sprint of mountains, the vault of seas and, of course, beside that, the puny murder of millions.

It is still eat, drink and be murderous, for tomorrow I may be among the murdered.

This seeing precisely, Max told himself, is a bitch!

Moses Boatwright. Seeing precisely. And then Max thought: *Everybody knows everything, now, past and present.*

Yes, Harry, with the unopening mind that opened in one, small, killing direction, I have the picture now. I see it clearly. *"Pace's* liberal image . . ."* You know better than that; you *always* knew better than that. That slowed me up for a second. But what brought me to the full stop was that line about everybody knowing. Charlotte found out about Michelle and you found out about Charlotte and me. She told you about that night twenty-two years ago. It was *then,* wasn't it Harry, that you thought to pass Jaja's papers on to me? So I guess everybody *does* know about everything. She knifed you back. What a night that must have been, or did it happen at breakfast? During an afternoon when she burst into your study? Let's do it in your study:

HARRY AMES sits at his desk typing half-heartedly. His mind is not on his work. He keeps turning to the window behind him and he is making a lot of errors for he keeps X-ing over. There is a sudden crash at the door and it springs open, bounces off a bookshelf and back against his wife, CHARLOTTE, who pushes it away again as she runs into the room.

CHARLOTTE:   You sonofabitch! You *dirty* sonofabitch!

HARRY (Rising first in confusion and then in anger to meet her charge, which carries her around the desk. They stand face to face):   What the hell are you banging in here for? What did you call me? I'll slap the shit out of you, bitch!

CHARLOTTE:   If you so much as touch me, ever again, I'll kill you, Harry. Kill you! You and Michelle, all these years, you and Michelle. Goddamn, I hate you —

HARRY (Trying to make his anger cover his surprise):   What in the hell are you talking about? Michelle *who?* Is that why you ran in here cursing me? You're crazy, woman, crazier than hell and you'd better get out of here right now, because I've got short patience with crazy people. You ought to know because I've been married to you for so long.

CHARLOTTE (Lighting a cigarette now, sure of herself, but still trembling with anger):   Michelle Bouilloux. Ever since we came to Europe. Seventeen years, seventeen goddamn years you've made a fool of me. *Seventeen* years!

HARRY (Resignedly. Such fury carries total knowledge):   I didn't make a fool of you. I imagine you've had your little good times, too?

CHARLOTTE (Pressing closer):   Yes! I have (Turning from him casually, like Rita Hayworth in an old, bad movie with Glenn Ford) Shall I name them?

HARRY (Sitting down):   Get out of here, Charlotte.

CHARLOTTE (Smiling like Jane Russell in another bad, old movie):   I'm going. (Walks to the door, takes the handle, poses like . . . ?) My best time was with Max Reddick. He not only writes better than you, he makes love better than you! (Exits)

378

*It was only once, Charlotte, once and then only in friendship! Don't you remember?*

HARRY AMES sits at his desk typing half-heartedly. His mind is not on his work. He keeps turning to the window behind him, frowning now, and his lips move as if pronouncing a one-syllabled word or name. He is making a lot of errors as he types, for he keeps X-ing over.

It was that, huh, Harry, that and the books, huh, baby? The writing, the White House, and all the time you were getting tired and weak and bitter. All the things you thought I had, you should have had, being Harry Ames. Man, I know how that can be. This revenge is worthy of you. But — anything to get even with me? Even Michelle? Jesus. But do you know what you've done, finally, *finally?* You've shared with me! Now your generosity is supposed to kill me. I got you, clear as hell. You were the father. I'll never take your place as you knew very well when you wrote that last line. You must have been laughing your ass off. Ah, so! This is the jungle side, then, thick with years of pretense and so normal in appearance! This is where the crawling things are, in this place and all around us. Well. All right. I was almost believing some of those fine phrases about me. But your last paragraph shook me awake. You are a writer!

But let me tell you how it was with me, Harry. That last book brought in a whole lot of money. Maybe that pushed you over the edge first. But that parody of success found me at the doctor and guess what he found? Cancer in the butt. Eating me up. There were all kinds of tests. No mistake. I led Margrit into an argument and she left. I didn't have to tell her. Pride. And she cries easily, you know. She went back home, which was right because, being married to a splib, she would have had very little to look forward to in the States. It ain't changed that way. I took cobalt treatments, met a nice chick with a name that knocked me out — Monique Jones — where does that grab you? She wore falsies and contact lenses, and I got to like her, but not well enough to tell her either. Then *Pace* asked me to spell Devoe in Nairobi for three months. I hadn't

379

told them. That was the last time I saw you alive, Harry, when I stopped in Paris on the way to Israel. (By way of Munich — Dachau drew me and it seems hard now to imagine what went on there twenty years ago with the neat ovens and shrubs and flowers. There is a lesson there for a black man to learn and never forget. Pity you never went to one of those places, Harry.) The shooting war in Israel didn't break out. I lived it up in Tel-Aviv and Haifa, then went up to Jerusalem and saw the jars of Zyklon B and the bars of soap. Harry, I read the parts of your letter having nothing to do with you or me, and Jaja's papers, and I *know* those things have never left us. How could you not have known? I went on to Addis Ababa. There was a shooting war on the Ethiopia-Somalia border. I went up to Diredawa to get into it because what I wanted to happen, I couldn't do myself, then; I didn't have the balls. I figured the Ethiopians or Somalis would do it for me. I got into a tank with an Ethiopian colonel named Tekla, who wanted medals and therefore was the right kind of man to be with. We crossed the border at Tug Wajale, heading straight for Hargeisa and where we were bound to get all the lead we wanted. But the Emperor wasn't going to get caught out like that, not the founder of the Organization of African Unity. He, personally, called the colonel back. In Addis once more, by the way, I met Minister Q returning from a visit to Mecca. He sent you his regards and said it was time for you to return home. I went down to Nairobi, did that short hitch, then returned home and quit *Pace*. Last month I went to the hospital, but I knew I didn't want to go like that. Then there were two people I wanted to see: my wife, but that had to be devious. What did I have to say to her, after all? And I wanted to see you. No rushing back and forth to Orly or passing through; I wanted to sit and talk with you. *Father, I wanted you to give me an assessment of my life and work, for then I might be able to answer the question: was it worth what it cost?* I left the hospital and went to Paris, but you, who had planned to have me killed, had been killed already. Now, you understand, at the moment you decided to kill me this way, I was already dead. All these years I've been running to you, paying homage to you because to so many of us you were larger than life. Your name mentioned at parties still brings a momentary hush. Critics still hate you. In our time, you were first. You opened your mouth and you said it. Harry Ames, you were, finally, a sorry sonofabitch. Larger than life? How you shrank! You of all people. And you of all people let them do this to you.

Harry, these papers: I'll get them to New York for you. I know this other guy who isn't afraid to die, and he doesn't have cancer, as far as I know, which truly makes him bad! Problem, Harry: do I tell Michelle you hated me so much that you were willing to have her killed, or do I just let her death come as a surprise to her?

Halfway down the stairs, two more pills starting to catch up with the pain, and wondering just how many times Harry had gone down or climbed up the steep, narrow steps, Max forced a smile to greet Michelle standing at the bottom of the steps. "Hey. How about some whiskey?"

Michelle had watched him come down, cushioning each step with exaggerated bends of the knees. His face had gone a brownish-gray. She smiled back up at him; there was a game to be played here. "Whiskey? Why not, after a hard afternoon's work and a little nap?"

"Love you," Max said. He clutched the case under one arm and stood holding to the back of a chair; he'd sat down much too long upstairs, and there was the long car ride back to Amsterdam. He looked at Michelle. God, he was not going to have a redhead.

Michelle waited. Had Harry left word of any kind for her, any word at all? But Max said nothing. As she moved finally to fix the drink, she said as casually as she could, "There was nothing for me?"

"No, Michelle, nothing."

"Oh."

"I'm sorry."

Michelle shrugged; it was that Gallic shrug that expressed in its way the ultimate unimportance of such small things.

"I'd like to use your phone, Michelle. Is it working?"

"Yes, it's working. Why don't you sit down?"

"In a minute. I want to call New York."

"New York? The papers were very important then?"

"Yes, they are." Perhaps now was the time to tell her that after seventeen years all she had amounted to in the end was nothing more than a piece of red-trimmed white ass to Harry. Otherwise, how could he have done this thing to her? *I can only hope that no harm comes to her.* Sure, like that. After seventeen years a little stinking hope. "Thanks," he said, taking the drink.

"Michelle, when I finish my call, you must call your husband —" He could see horror creeping in startled degrees across her face. "— tell him to come and get you right away, and take you back to France. Then call the French Embassy. Tell them you want protection until your husband arrives."

White-faced, Michelle stammered, "But I do not understand, Max. My husband, what will he think? I told you, he knows nothing of this place. Besides, *why?*"

"It's the papers," he said in a hollow voice. "Harry's papers. Don't ask me to tell you more. If you want to live, do as I say." He stared outside at the dark green canal. Placid. Ugly anyplace else. "Throw away anything that has to do with Harry. Do it now. There's no other way. Please do it and don't sit there asking questions with your eyes. I want you to live. He — Harry would want you to live."

She moved quickly across the room and gripped his arm. "Who killed him?"

"Who? People. Fascists, I think, who else? And they know you." Silence filled the room until she said, "And you?"

"I've cancer. You know."

"Does Margrit know?"

"Go clean up, Michelle. This is no time for that." Now the pills were getting to him; it seemed, suddenly, easy.

"She would want to know."

"Aren't you afraid, Michelle?"

"Yes. Can't you tell? And you, Max?"

Max thought: Here we are, just two people, strangers, really, with just the feel of a tit and a kiss between us. "Yes, I'm afraid." He felt her hand sliding tenderly along his arm.

"I will know someday what this is all about?"

"I hope not."

"All right. I will go now. To clean up. There is no other way, you are sure, Max?"

"No other way. None at all." He didn't tell her that even this might not work.

When she had left the room he pulled his telephone book from his pocket. Yes, he was going to call New York, but first he was going to call Margrit. At least she should know about the cancer; she deserved that. He listened to her phone ring. Outside, between Leiden and Amsterdam, maybe even in Leiden, they waited. They would not have had time to do anything with the phone. Holland wasn't in the Alliance, didn't even have an auxiliary group — yet.

Margrit's phone rang twice more. (Be there, baby.) Twice again. (*Be* there, Maggie!) Three times more and he imagined that she was just coming up the steps to her flat. (Now she was at the top of the landing, hearing the phone for the first time.) Max let the phone ring again. (Now! She had her key out; was slipping it into the lock, pushing open the door, rushing into her flat! Picking up the phone! Now, now, *now!!*) The phone continued to ring and Max slowly hung up.

He poured himself another drink, thinking to himself, Man, am I starting to fly!

Although in another room, Michelle heard Max squeeze the cork from the bottle, heard the neck of the bottle rattling unsteadily on his glass. She did not understand it all, Max, Harry's sudden death, nothing, except that there *were* the papers which Harry had enjoined her to get to Max in New York, somehow, some way, as quickly as possible. And Harry *had* died the following day, the very day, it turned out, that Max arrived in Paris. His presence at the funeral had taken her by surprise. Surprise, grief and now mystery.

It was too much. She had been planning to go to Leiden when Max called from Amsterdam. She could not, in the presence of her husband, behave as though nothing had happened. She had left, going, she said, to Cannes. But she went north, met Max, and now, soon, her husband would be coming north and unless she lied very well and circumspectly, grief might come to him after all. Grief, or anger.

Here: a pair of Harry's sneakers, old, faded from white to a vile gray, but they had made him look young, especially with these: two V-necked sweaters. There was some underwear and three shirts laundered and fresh for his next visit, which would have been in July. Handkerchiefs, old pages from manuscripts either published or abandoned. There: an extra set of galley proofs; pictures which he had taken of her in the courtyard along with pictures she had taken of him. A picture of Max Ames, pensive, almost scowling, as if sensing that the picture was destined to be viewed far far away from his home in Paris where it had been taken by his father.

Fear came slowly to Michelle, but she could not particularize it. Was it the fear of discovery by her husband, the deep grief or, on the other hand, the angry words, the blows, perhaps the lonely life without him, a catastrophe at her age, or the life with him in which he quite deliberately carried on affairs with young female poets, American mostly, for all Europe waited for the Americans to come during the summers with their money and sex to fit to their strange dithyrambs.

Or was it the fear of death because of association with Harry, as Max had implied? Why hadn't Harry told her more? They had shared so many things, everything and now — the thought was too appalling — this single secret threatened to take her life as it had taken his. Was that the greater fear?

No. It could not be. She was European and dying violently was a European habit. All other deaths were commonplace. A European learned by his condition to expect catastrophe and invariably that was exactly what he received. In Europe, a winner was one who bested those common deaths arbitrarily assigned to others. You crawled, kissed behinds, ate *merde,* and grinned like you loved it. Living was everything. The final fact of death was of no consequence; it was the living while everyone around died that counted. Michelle knew there was no other tradition for her but to be a survivor.

She moved hurriedly from room to room, gathering papers, pictures, clothes, ashtrays from restaurants where they had eaten. No, she did not want to know what was in that case Max held so tightly under his arm. Obviously, it was the knowing that killed. The suitcase she was stuffing the things into was full now. She looked around, retraced her steps and saw nothing more of Harry's to put into it. She locked the case and trudged heavily up the stairs to the attic. She had no intention of throwing Harry's things away. They'd keep well enough in a corner. She almost smiled to herself. That was the most European of traits, putting things into attic corners. She passed the room where Max had napped and read the papers. What secrets did that room now hold!

Downstairs, Max waited for the international operator to call him back. He felt good now. The pills, the whiskey, the decision-making. He knew he did not hate; they'd exhausted him in too many ways before allowing that to congeal; he'd had some breaks. He didn't hate the way Harry had, not that killing hatred that turned in upon yourself and those close to you. Max could have hated. There had been the Army, there had been Lillian (but they had given him Margrit in her place). There had been enough ammunition to hate them every single, unrelenting tick of the clock every day of his life. But he did not hate. Oh, he had not forgotten; it was just that the future demanded something else. He had made his decision with the same cold objectivity that made the Alliance so formidable. And it had been an easy decision to make. After all, he was as good as dead. Was the doing difficult at such a time? At any other time in his life, given the chance, he would not have been able to make such a decision.

They had had several chances. They had the Civil War; that was to be a start. Reconstruction; that was to be a start. Truman's integrated Army; that was to be a start. May 17, 1954; that was to be a start. The March last August; that was to be a start. Each new President, his mouth filled with words, promised a new start. There were always starts, the big ones and the little ones, but there were never any finishes. Enzkwu's papers proved they were faking it all the time; *all the goddamn time!* Time had moved on, but beneath the surface change remained in doubt. And it was time they came to know, once and for all, that Negroes now knew everything. No more of those stupid television interviews:

Sir, are you a violent Negro?

Sir, ubba, ubba ubb!

That was going to change.

Now, another one of the white man's inventions, the telephone, the transatlantic cable, was flashing signals, voices and numbers under the sea to New York. Ironic that one must inevitably come to use the tools of the destroyer in order to destroy him, or to save oneself. Destruction, however, was very much a part of democratic capitalism, a philosophy which was implicitly duplicitous, meaning all its fine words and slogans, but leaving the performance of them to unseen elfs, gnomes and fairies. And Max had known this for the better part of his life; but it was only now, no longer vulnerable to the dangers of that life, that he not only saw it quite visibly, but could act on it because King Alfred and Alliance Blanc had form and face and projection. Before, all was nebulous; there were few names and places and the form was so all-pervading that it seemed formless. But now the truth literally had been placed in Max's lap. That truth told him that change could no longer be imperceptible, without cataclysm. Permanence was imperfection.

Max had never agreed with Shakespeare that murder would out, and he knew the Alliance and King Alfred were not stopped by the faintest consideration that they would be discovered. Max knew that people who believed as he now believed had to adopt that view, too, and at once, for the secret to converting *their* change to *your* change was *letting them know that you knew.* And he now knew to what extent they would go to keep black men niggers.

386

White men had done in their own by the hundreds, thousands and millions, pausing along the way from time to time, just to keep in practice, to do in a few million Negroes. All this while great cheers went up, for there are no nonparticipants, no lonely untouched islands. Then you always got back to the race of the Six Million. You visualized them bellowing, shouting, chattering, screaming in, say, New York City one single day, driving the cabs, buses, subways, or riding in them; you saw them walking the avenues and cross-streets, manning the offices and corners, the stores, the markets, jamming the hotels and parks, theaters, restaurants and movies. Catastrophe. The next day they are gone. The city is silent, mocking traffic lights directing no one. But Philadelphia, Chicago, Boston, Washington continue to blare, honktonk with traffic, hum with people, spark with neon. All without pause, without prayer. You had to picture it that way. Why the Six Million?

Because their deaths happened in my time, Max thought, and because before I was made aware of it and sent to crawl bellydown over Italian mountains, I danced the Lindy and the Jersey Bounce and the Boogie Woogie; and the American air was thick with banal phrases: I'm Making Believe, Mairzy Doats; God Bless America, I Heard You Cry Last Night; Coming In on a Wing and a Prayer, Don't Cry, Baby; Don't Fence Me In, Kalamazoo; Chattanooga Choo-Choo, Don't Get Around Much Anymore.

The songs did not obscure the bankruptcy of the human soul, for no such thing existed. Help *was* pledged (by the ignorance later pleaded) to the extinction which, being so widespread and evil, brought on collective amnesia again and made that evil not only unreal, but untrue.

There were lessons:

The unprotesting, unembattled die.

The enemy today is the believer in Anglo-Saxon updated racial mythology.

The clash is inevitable because Justice is an uncool lesbian.

Many, many will die, Bernard Zutkin. Black bodies will jam the streets. But those bodies, while they still have life, would be heading downtown this time. No more Harlem. East Cleveland. Lynch Street. Watts. Southside. Downtown. Those people are going to tear up that unreal tranquility that exists in the United States. The promises, unfulfilled, can go to hell now. That three-hundred-and-forty-five-year-old bill, its interest climbing since Jamestown and *before,* is going to be presented.

After that, Mister Charlie and the engineers of King Alfred you will have learned your lesson. There will be, you see, white bodies, too. Once, the *first time,* like this, really (behold, Nat Turner! Look here, "Mad" John. How does that grab you, Denmark? In the balls, Gabriel?) should be enough. Max saw once more:

*The chino-covered legs, blurs of white sneakers mixed with heavy country shoes, the uneven drumming of running feet on the grass, the curses.*

And heard:

*"I call now for black manhood. Dignity. Pride. Don't turn the other cheek any more. Defend yourselves, strike back, and when you do, strike to hurt, strike to maim, strike to —"* Kill, Max thought, wearily. I am going to loose those beasts, black and white, and when they are through, and it may take them a long time to get through, perhaps even as long as this farce which has forced us to this has been running, we will know just where we stand. It will be a start.

But remember. Like everything else, you started this too. Today it is the Alliance, it is King Alfred; before that it was something else and something else before that. Lie about it. Cry about it. I know the truth and can do something about it.

Michelle dropped something on the floor above. Michelle, Max thought. She took it well enough. No questions, or not many questions. On a continent where life marched evenly with the tread of armies, the European was attuned to death, expected it in a way, he supposed, and avoided the first suggestion of its coming. So many of them were Negroes in that respect, but didn't know it.

The phone rang and Max's heart began to pound. Was he right? Was he wrong? He moved to the instrument. The international operator had his number. Max began to pull the papers from the case once more. He stacked them beside the phone and listened intently to the hums and sharp clicks on the line. Yes, it *is* right, he told himself. What choice is there? None. He was putting an end to the peace in which Negroes died one at a time in Southern swamps or by taking cops' bullets, the dying from overwork and underpay, praying all the while, looking to the heavens. Max smeared away the sweat that had come to his face and hands.

The voice from New York came through clearly. "Hello, hello?"

Max said, "Hello, you are a dead man. Maybe."

"Who is this?" The voice across the sea was both amused and impatient.

"Max. Max Reddick."

"Brother. Well, how are you? Where are we meeting this time?"

"Amsterdam."

"Holland?"

"Holland, but they prefer to call it the Netherlands."

"Brother, that's not where the people are."

"Yes, they're here, too."

"Really? I always think of the Dutch like the picture on the Old Dutch Cleanser can — blue, white and faceless."

"No. Not any more."

"Now, what's all this talk about dead men?"

"Is your machine on?"

"Brother, my machine is always on. That's the life these days. You know it."

"Good. My friend, Harry Ames, is dead, you know."

"I read about it. I'm sorry. I looked forward to meeting him."

"He was killed."

"Ah-ha. You *know* that he was killed."

"Yes."

"I'm listening; I hear you."

"What I have to say is important —"

"Of course. Otherwise you wouldn't be calling. I understand. Tell it to me, brother. Tell me all about it."

389

"Listen, then. Don't interrupt. I'll be reading for about forty minutes: notes, names, addresses, things. You'll know what to do. This material comes from Jaja Enzkwu."

"Brother Jaja, who is also dead. Go ahead, brother."

Max read. Once Michelle came into the room and he waved her out. And once he wet his throat with a sip of whiskey, but he read on and asked only once, "How is your tape?"

When he was finished, the voice at the other end of the line, heavy and yet tingling with subdued excitement asked, "Brother, are you armed?"

"Yes." Max was gathering the papers; it was done.

"You know you'll need it, don't you?"

"I know it."

"What can I say? Good luck. I *do* know what to do with this. If I don't see you again — the life is like that, brother — take some with you. My prayers to Allah commence at once. Salaam-Alaikum, baby!"

Max paused a moment, then said, "Sure, man, sure." He heard Minister Q give a deep chuckle which rumbled softly with satisfaction. Max hung up, staring at the phone and thinking, There, it's done.

# 29

NEW YORK — LEIDEN — AMSTERDAM

ONE block from Minister Q's office, along a street scaled with grime, crushed gray cigarettes and debris, in a tenement boarded up and condemned by the Board of Health, Department of Sanitation, the City of New York, one man tipped a pair of earphones from his head and swung a practiced eye to his delicate recording machinery.

The room was neat; the adjoining bathroom still smelled of fresh paint. New walls had been put up and the lights repaired. A second man, his earphones off altogether, tapped thoughtfully on the cigarette-scarred naked pinewood table. Both men were in shirtsleeves, for it was May and a heat wave had come unheralded to the city. A small fan hummed quietly, stirring the cigarette smoke and the smell certain law enforcement officials always have about them, as if unable to remove from their persons, like coalmen or slaughterers, the odor of grime that is an integral part of their trade.

The second man, looking at the names he had written on the pad in front of him, said, "Stay with him, Tom; I'm calling the office."

"Minister's dialing again."

The second man picked up the phone. "This is Merriman, station 12. We just monitored a call from Amsterdam, Holland, from a Max Reddick. It was close to fifty minutes long. The subject of the call was an organization called the Alliance Blanc — that means the White Alliance, Reddick told the Minister, and something called King Alfred that sounds real crazy, about race riots and emergencies and the President and the Army. I don't know if this is for State, Central or us. I'll give you some of the names to check out, and a list of homicides connected with the White Alliance. Minister Q is calling a meeting for one o'clock, so we're still monitoring. It's going to be about the call he just got from Amsterdam."

The call had traveled beneath the sewers and subways through one wire which was bound tightly to a thousand others. From the Federal office which the first call reached, still another call was made, this one traveling out of the city, southward to Washington where, in a matter of minutes, the top secret vaults were opened and cross-indexed files traced, one back upon the other. One half hour later, a pipe-smoking official with thinning hair said to an assistant, "Technically, this is now Federal's baby, but since we've carried it this far, and there isn't time to go into details, Central will have to hang on to it. Get me New York."

At nine forty-five in the morning, the humidity building slowly, three men drove along the littered, battered street in New York and stopped one block from the boarded-up tenement. They walked briskly past the entrance of the building and into a small, flyspecked candy store and vanished.

At the sound of footsteps in the hall, the two men monitoring Minister Q's phone opened the door.

"Hiya, fellas," the first man through the door said, bending to get his massive body through.

"Hello, Barney, did we strike a mine?"

The man called Barney smiled. "Central thinks so. This is Ted Dallas, African division, foreign operations, and his assistant." The five men shook hands and the second man in shirtsleeves offered his pack of cigarettes around. "The jigs have really ripped it this time, hey?"

"Just play back the tape and shut your fat mouth," Dallas said curtly. "I'm a jig."

The second man opened his mouth to speak, changed his mind, and with a drawn smile on his face sat down and said to his mate, Roll it, Tom."

The man called Tom pressed a lever and the voices of Max and Minister Q, along with telephone cable noises, filled the room.

The first man in shirtsleeves glanced briefly at Dallas and said, "He's still calling people." He cautiously handed Dallas a list of the names. Some Dallas knew, and some he didn't. The two technicians exchanged glances.

At the moment it was not important whether Dallas knew the people or not. He listened to the voices intently, head bent, pen in hand. He had to get it now and set it in action. He glanced at his watch. It would be about quarter to eleven when he finished listening to the tape. It was going to be a nasty business from here on out. Minister Q would have to be cut down. Federal's watch on the Minister had been increased to five men in just the past half hour, but Central would have to put on the play. The Minister would have to be stopped before the meeting or at the beginning of it. Dallas motioned to his assistant, a surly young blond who wore a straw hat with a bright band. He hesitated before speaking. He wondered now how Max had got into it, then wondered why he was

392

doing it. He'd always had more balance than Harry. Enzkwu had been an ass from the first. When last reported on, Max had been in New York. Some friendship. But it was the habit of men like Max and Harry to be bitter about things here at home, but never to the extent of trying to wreck the country as they could with the information about Alliance Blanc. All the little people they said they cared about in their writing, would be the first to go. "Call Washington," Dallas now said to his assistant. "I'm going to need two men to complete this job. Shotguns and .45's. Taking no chances. Negroes —"

Suddenly, the larger than life voices, Max's cold and tired, Minister Q's quick and angry, were talking about something called King Alfred. Dallas spun and stared at the loudspeakers. The voices boomed on. The two technicians stared past Dallas to his assistant and Barney, and Dallas now turned slowly to look at his assistant, and, when his eyes locked with the gray eyes beneath the straw hat, he knew that his assistant had known about King Alfred all along. Dallas's thoughts bunched like frightened cattle, then tried to flee down a corridor that was too narrow; they bumped and tumbled into and over each other. Numbly, Dallas watched his assistant reach for the phone. Out of the corner of his eye, he saw the man called Barney edge imperceptibly to block the door. His assistant was talking softly, staring out at Dallas from beneath the lid of his hat. Dallas crumpled up his paper and, cursing, threw it to the floor. He lit a cigarette and listened to the voices of Max Reddick and Minister Q, and knew they would be the last black voices he would ever hear. He thought of the Negro agents out there who believed their operations had only to do with Alliance Blanc.

The sun was beginning to tilt into late afternoon in Leiden. Gray clouds appeared on the horizon. Max, who had debated but a moment before consigning Jaja's papers to the fireplace, now touched the pile with a match. He watched the flames reflecting from the sides of the copper pots and pans hooked from the brick facing.

393

Now if something happened (and what could happen? Minister Q had been ready for something like this a long time) there would be no papers and the absence would be a sword of Damocles over the head of the Alliance and King Alfred. No papers and therefore no end; the Alliance and King Alfred, whatever happened, would always know that someone else knew. That fact would gnaw at white men in power for as long as they held it.

Michelle was using the telephone now, talking to her husband. Max listened to her voice as it came to him from the other room, now rising, now falling; now pleading, now sad; now promising, now resigned. Max stared out at the canal — the waters were now black. In the sky, gray cloud tumbled over gray cloud, and small trees bent before the rising wind, and flapped their leaves. The long conversation with her husband had ended; now Max heard Michelle talking to the French Embassy. The tone of her voice was different; it was that tone all Europeans use to address those beneath their social level. The tone was not haughty as much as it was sure of itself, sure that the message it conveyed would be followed to the letter.

It was nearly time to go. Max knew fear now. It reached down and dulled the razor-sharp pain that sliced through his lower body. Maybe, even at this moment, he thought in sudden, desperate fright, someone had invented the serum, the pill, the thing that would make cancer obsolete. Now it would do him no good. He took a deep breath. It was done and nobody had invented or discovered anything. *It is done.*

Even so Max snapped shut the lock on the case. It was empty, but he would still take it with him. Let the emptiness, when they discovered it, speak for itself. He wanted to see the expression on their faces. In a minute, as soon as Michelle finished her call, he would kiss her on the cheek and leave the house. He would plod through the courtyard, open the gate he had entered so innocently a few hours earlier, and step into the street. What would be there? Who would be there? If there were nothing and no one, he would get into the little German car, fascism on wheels, now so indispensable to too many people in too many places. You bought a VW and you made peace. It was no good saying you thought long and hard about it first. Once you laid down your money and drove away, the pact to forget the past was made. In the car he would pull out the Llama and put it in his pocket; it would make him feel better.

Alfonse Edwards had waked that morning feeling unusually dull and heavy. He took a cold shower, dressed except for a jacket, then stood looking at the canal, waiting for his breakfast to come up. The night before he had signed for it for seven. In a few moments he heard footsteps thumping over the carpeted steps. He moved to his door and opened it. The boy, bearing his tray, smiled. "Good morning, Mr. Edwards."

"Good morning. How is the weather?"

"The sun is out and it is very fresh."

"Fine," Edwards said. "Just the way I like it."

"Yes, sir."

As he was eating, Edwards' eyes went once more to the plaque on the wall that gave a brief history of his hotel on the Heeren-Gracht. The building had been constructed only a dozen years after the first Dutch slave ship sailed into Jamestown. And here he was — three hundred forty-five years later — and on the side of the descendants of the doers of that deed, trying to undo it. Or trying to prevent the inevitable reaction to that deed which had been the background for so many others. He ripped a piece of brown bread in half and placed half a slice of Gouda on it, then poured his coffee.

But this was the day. Last night he had had Michelle Bouilloux followed from Paris to Leiden. She had been watched as she left the train, going to her secret home where Ames had spent so much time with her. Then one of the agents from the Embassy at The Hague had taken over; he was still on duty near the house. This morning, together with his Amsterdam contact, Edwards would complete the assignment.

It had been a long assignment. Africa and then Europe. In Europe there had been the constant suspicion, for every Negro new to a European city was said to be connected with Central. To allay that suspicion there had been the trips, the women, the writing, the fights, talking the jargon. But today that would be over. There would be another assignment after a bit of Rest and Recuperation, perhaps in Frankfurt, before he took on a new one. The new assignment would be another of what the people back home called dirty, filthy jobs. But those jobs protected America in ways Americans were too childish to realize. However, they did expect someone to protect them. From all terrors. The phone rang and Edwards felt a momentary tightening across his lean stomach. He picked it up and snapped off a quiet "Hello." Then he listened. "I'll be downstairs in ten minutes," he said, and he hung up. He put his jacket on. He did not know what to expect from Max Reddick, but the mission was crystal clear. From a corner of his suitcase Edwards lifted a stainless steel object three inches long. It was in a clear plastic container. The object was a high-pressure syringe and when the handle was pushed, a powerful, high-speed jet of *Rauwolfia serpentina* came forth, penetrating both clothes and skin, and attacked the central nervous system at once, depressing it until death came. The usual autopsy report was death by heart attack. Edwards made sure the plastic container was tight before placing it in his pocket. One agent had killed himself by carrying the syringe without its case.

Edwards walked quietly downstairs, and gaining the street, walked across it and looked at the canal. The city was just coming awake; ducks were floating around in search of food. He wondered just how many ducks had been killed during the night by the canal rats. He saw the car coming, a small black VW, and moved to the edge of the road. When it stopped he went around and got in, noticing that Roger was wearing dark glasses.

"Morning," Edwards said.

"Morning." Roger drove off. "He just got up. He's rented a car, a VW. Light gray."

They drove to the Leidseplein and parked. Now the other people would retreat to the consulate and wait. Reddick was theirs; State was bypassing.

"It's going to be a nice day," Roger said.

"Yes, the weather's been surprisingly good for a change."

Bicyclists went by in waves. More trams rolled by, and cars.

"There he is," Roger said.

"Let's go. Don't lose him."

They followed Max's car out Overtoom.

Max paused a long moment before pulling the cord that opened the gate. He glanced behind him at the house; Michelle was at a window, watching. A white spot. He couldn't even tell now the color of her hair. He thought, S'long, Red. He pulled the cord and the gate swung open. He stepped into the street, pulling the door closed after him and leaning back against it automatically, to make sure it was firmly locked. He looked up and down. The street was quiet, almost empty. He scuttled across the walk, heart pounding, and hurriedly unlocked the car door. Inside, he relocked it and, flinching from the pain of the sudden sitting, groaned. His fingers were groping under the seat for the Llama. Where was it? Stiff, eager fingers ploughed into car-floor dirt; his heart threatened to tear through his rib cage. Where — ? But now his fingers touched heavy metal with hard precise lines, and he pulled the gun out, breathing with relief. He pulled the clip halfway out. Still loaded. A small gun, but that's what everyone got killed with in New York. Twenty-two's. A .25 would hurt only a little bit more. He put the gun in his pocket, checked the doors again and placed the case on the other seat. He started down the street and sped quickly through the city, so occupied with watching behind him that he squirted through two red lights. When he gained the main road he shifted into fourth. Better, he thought. That's better. With the coming of the gray clouds the temperature had dropped slightly and the wind had come up. He felt it tearing at the car. He drove rapidly. A big, black Mercedes rushed up behind him, blinked its lights and then howled past. Max noticed the black-on-white plates. The big "D" to one side. Deutschland.

Now Max sped around a long curve. Coming out of it he seemed to see, bent low in front of a red VW, Professor Bazzam, book in hand (instructions?) peering inside the hood. Max started in fright and swerved out of his lane, then roared back into it with tires screeching. When his car was steady a moment later, he peered into the rear-view mirror and saw, he thought, the VW again, but now the hood was down, closed tightly upon a pair of frantically kicking legs and feet which were shod in knob shoes. The one weakly wriggling arm and hand were slowly being drawn into the hood. In the hand a book waved back and forth. Suddenly it was gone.

*Well, son, you almost am no more!*

*Saminone! Where you been, baby? I thought I'd lost you.*

*Son, I ain't been nowhere. Right here, right on.*

*Yeah, well how's your momma?*

*Boy, this ain't no time for foolin'! You gonna git it! Them people waitin' for you black ass, an' they gonna cut it a duster!*

*Ain't they, though, ain't they?*

*You drivin' mighty fast, boy. Is you in a hurry?*

*Shit, Saminone, I'm only doing the limit. That's all.*

*Yeah? Look here, boy — was it worth it, all this? T'day, t'night, it's gonna be you an' them worms — maybe you an' the eels — lotsa water 'round here, you know.*

*Will it hurt?*

*Nothin' like you been hurt, Max.*

*Well, fuck it then. I'm gonna have me some company.*

*Ooo-weee! A eel feast! A worm banquet! That old Sam is comin' out, ain't it, Max?*

*Saminone, do eels and worms like black meat better than white meat?*

*Heee. Don't s'pose it matters, long's they eatin'.*

*It isn't right.*

*Whut?*

*You know.*

*Well, son, itsa same for all you goddamn ams, y'know.*

*Aw, kiss my ass.*

*Move you nose. Haw, haw! Capped you! You capped!*

*You square, old-timey motherfucker, you haven't capped any-body.*

*Max, how come you flips up so nasty all the time?*

*To hell with that. Just tell me I am.*

*You am whut?*

*Tell me!*

*Damn, Max, boy, you knows I can't tell you no sucha thing.*

*Bastard. You can tell me. Now you can tell me.*

*You don't wants me to lie, does you?*

*Never mind. I know I am.*

*Then why you keeps on botherin' me?*

*Go on, get the hell away from me.*

*You knows you can't get rid of the Saminone.*

*All you ever want to do is remind me that I am black. But, goddamn it, I also am.*

*Whut you done done was a black act. No white man'd ever do that.*

*Survival!*

*Shit. You jus' evil.*

*So's your momma.*

*Easy, tiger.*

*Why are you so quiet? Why don't you say something, Saminone?*

*Max, sonny boy, there just ain't no more to say.*

Max was steering with one hand and with the other wiping away the saliva that had formed upon his lips. Now, waves of nausea tugged at his stomach. He felt blood flowing lightly, but steadily and more than pain, he felt embarrassment. Like a broad, he thought. He opened his mouth and sucked in great gulps of air.

Europa 10 through western Holland is a narrow, well-tended

four-lane highway. It flows over flat land except where there are
long but gentle inclines which soon slant back down to sea level or
below and continue on.

Max drove up one of those long gentle inclines and saw a sign:

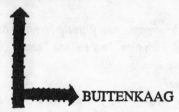

AMSTERDAM

BUITENKAAG

The turnoff to Buitenkaag was at the crest of the incline. Max
could see grass and a grove of small elm trees. He made a sudden
decision to pull off the road and rest. Change the cotton. Take a
pill. He snapped over the wheel and careened off Europa 10. Brak-
ing gently as he rushed downhill, he pulled up on the grass between
the trees. Overhead and to his right, a lone car rushed toward Amsterdam under the deepening gray skies. Max shut off the ignition
and silence, except for the wind, fell upon him.

He opened the door and reached for his pills and cotton. As he
put his feet on the ground, he wished he were someplace where he
could give himself another shot and lay down. At that moment
there was for him no luxury like that of lying down. A gust of
wind coughed across the fields and the trees leaned and their leaves
flapped in frenzy and Max heard an alien noise brought, it seemed,
by the wind itself; and he whirled, dropping the pills and cotton,
and tugged frantically at his pocket where the gun was, pushing
against the car door which was pressed against him by the wind. Before the black VW had stopped, Max recognized Roger and Edwards, and thought without surprise, Of course! Disarmingly he put
toward them that face which had attracted the hurt and wounded all
his life, the face for the Marys and Boatwrights, the Reginas and
Sheas, the Harrys. That face as they flowed toward him, their car

engine still running. Max could almost count their steps. Gripping his gun he thought, This is the final irony. The coming of age, Negro set at Negro in the name of God and Country. Or was it the ultimate trap?

"Roger!" he cried out in fury and the wind burst over them in a mighty gust and Max, aiming the gun at Roger now, noticing their surprise (the face he had put on helped, intangibly, yet mightily); heard Roger shout, "Max man! Hold it! We just want to talk to you, man!" but fired at him low, once, twice, and saw him fold and start down, caught his shocked voice saying "Damn, man!" Soft, awful sound, his body hitting the ground while Edwards as if lifted by the wind came at him, smoothly, dark, long, uncoiling, and Max threw up his free hand to ward off the bright flash of silver which nevertheless grazed him, and in that same windblown, overcrowded second Max cleared his gun to fire at Edwards, aiming high this time, to shoot him right in the mouth, to stop up that mouth for good; but suddenly Edwards flying past him now, silver glittering in his hand, Roger in his final bounce upon the ground, the wind began to shriek in Max's ears and the running car engine became an army of snare drummers and Max felt the world closing in on him fast, pounding and squeezing him as he tumbled forward now, puzzled and frustrated and fearful, screaming, "Maggie! Maggie!"

Roger was pulling himself toward the car whimpering, "That fucker, trying to be a hero, a motherfucking hero. He was shooting for my balls!"

Edwards quickly pulled Max's body into his car and bent him over the steering wheel. He opened the briefcase. It was empty. Then with swift, practiced fingers he went over Max's body. Practiced fingers probe the rectum, separate the testicles, feel the penis for hidden objects. Edwards did not find microfilm; he found the wad of blood and pus-filled cotton; he found the morphine. Now he understood the syringe and needle. Without hesitation, he attached the needle to the syringe, then withdrew the morphine. He pushed up Max's sleeve and hit the big vein in his arm. Like the old days with the Narcotics Department he thought, still moving swiftly. Jazz musicians in Europe dying of overdoses administered by agents tired of chasing them. Better than heart attacks. There were getting to be too many people found dead of "heart attacks."

Edwards closed Max's car door and returned to his own car, kicking dirt over the trail of Roger's blood.

"C'mon," Roger called. "Hurry up, man. I'm hit bad."

"Where?" Edwards asked.

"I don't know. Near my balls. Did he get my balls? Look." Roger removed his hands. Edwards looked. "Did he?"

"I can't tell. Let's get going anyway."

Within a minute they were back on the northbound lane to Amsterdam. Angrily Edwards considered the papers. He'd have to stop and call and get Roger into other hands. Then he'd have to get back to Leiden. The woman. Goddamn it, he thought, and it might not even end there.

It was late afternoon now and Margrit Reddick was still sitting at the outdoor table of the American on the Leidseplein. She toyed with a Campari. The wind had died and great patches of blue sky were chasing the gray clouds. The factories and shops were closing and traffic streamed all around the Plein. Max would enjoy watching the female cyclists, she thought. That pert one with her knees going in every direction, good Dutch legs showing way, way up. Margrit smiled. She looked at the fountain with its two fish with crossed tails spouting water from their mouths and christened them Max and Maggie. From now on there will be no more spouting water. Two lovers, a black man and a white woman, moved past the front of the hotel and their movements caught at her. Life could be good; life was good. Max had come back. He needed her; one look told her that, but as ill as he might be she needed him more.

Across the Plein, high on a neoclassical building, great letters spelled out HET PAROOL. The password, the word. She knew it now. Love-Need, Need-Love. How presumptuous she had been! Didn't Max know his own country and the people in it as well as she knew Holland and Hollanders? What right had she to protest his actions the way she had? She would tell him this. Once more, together, after a long talk. He needed to get back to his writing; he suffered without it. It was his life. And anytime he felt they should go to the country to take target practice, she would go, gladly. She became very excited thinking of the talk they would have about their future. Didn't he, too, have something he wanted to tell her?

Then Margrit had an idea. She signaled the waiter and ordered a Pernod for Max to have when he returned, like yesterday, and that would be any minute. The sun was out now and the tables around her were filling up. She and Max would sit at the table drinking and talking until dinner. Maybe they would eat inside again, at their window. After, they would go home.

# BIOGRAPHY

**John A. Williams** is author of seventeen books including *Sissie*, and *!Click Song*. He has been a foreign correspondent for *Newsweek* as well as Professor of English at Rutgers University where he is currently employed. He is the recipient of the American Book Award, The Richard Wright–Jacques Roumain Award, The Centennial Medal for Outstanding Achievement, and the National Institute of Arts and Letters Award, among others. Two of his novels have been adapted for film and television. He was born in 1925 in Jackson, Mississippi, and currently lives in Teaneck, New Jersey.

*Other Books by John A. Williams*

*Novels*

The Berhama Account/*1985/Horizon Press*
!Click Song/*1982/Houghton Mifflin*
The Junior Bachelor Society/*1976/Doubleday*
Mothersill and The Foxes/*1975/Doubleday*
Captain Blackman/*1972/Doubleday*
Sons of Darkness, Sons of Light/*1969/Little, Brown*
The Man Who Cried I Am/*1967/Little, Brown*
Sissie/*1963/Farrar, Straus & Giroux*
Night Song/*1961/Farrar, Straus & Giroux*
The Angry Ones/*1960/Ace Books*

*Non-Fiction Books*

Minorities in the City/*1975/Harper & Row*
Flashbacks/*1973/Doubleday*
The King God Didn't Save/*1970/Coward, McCann & Geoghegan*
The Most Native of Sons/*1970/Doubleday*
This is My Country Too/*1965/N.A.L./World*
The Protectors/*1964/Farrar, Straus & Giroux*
Africa, Her History, Lands and People/*1963/Cooper Square*